PENGUIN BOOKS

The Last Goodbye

The Last Goodbye

TIM WEAVER

PENGUIN BOOKS

PENGUIN BOOKS

UK | USA | Canada | Ireland | Australia
India | New Zealand | South Africa

Penguin Books is part of the Penguin Random House group of companies
whose addresses can be found at global.penguinrandomhouse.com.

First published by Penguin Michael Joseph 2023
Published in Penguin Books 2024

001

Typeset by Jouve (UK), Milton Keynes
Printed and bound in Great Britain by Clays Ltd, Elcograf S.p.A.

The authorized representative in the EEA is Penguin Random House Ireland,
Morrison Chambers, 32 Nassau Street, Dublin D02 YH68

A CIP catalogue record for this book is available from the British Library

ISBN: 978–1–405–95296–5

www.greenpenguin.co.uk

*This book is dedicated to
three amazing editors . . .*

*Stefanie Bierwerth
Emad Akhtar
and Maxine Hitchcock*

Day 2
Wednesday, 7 December

When the video starts, there's no queue outside the ghost house.

It's early evening; only just opening time.

It's still an hour and a half before they vanish.

It doesn't take long for guests to start arriving. A couple of minutes in, two teenage girls walk-run through the snaking barriers to the front of the line and, when they see they're the first on the ride, start to talk excitedly. A staff member, poised just inside the darkness of the entrance, comes out. He's dressed to match the Himalayan theme of the ride: dark trousers, a battered snow jacket, woollen gloves, rope tucked into his belt, and a headtorch. He says something to the girls and they smile again – and then, a moment later, they disappear into the dark.

More people follow.

The queue builds.

After a while, the same two girls emerge from the exit, laughing. One of them mimics the scream she must have made on the ride. The camera is about fifty feet away – far enough back that it can take in the entrance on the left, exit on the right, and a middle section, which, with the placement of its windows and its broken door, has been deliberately constructed to resemble a face.

Slowly, over the next thirty minutes, the people who go in one side file back out the other. On average, the ride takes just under four minutes from beginning to end.

At 5.51 p.m., Tom Brenner and his nine-year-old son Leo join the queue. Tom is tall and wiry, well over six foot, and has a black baseball cap on. His son comes up to the crook of his elbow and is wearing a bright yellow backpack and a pair of white Nikes, the red tick visible on them, even from a distance. Afterwards, park staff find a selfie of them on Tom's mobile phone screen. They share the same eyes and nose.

It takes them twenty-six minutes to get to the front of the queue. Preceding them are a group of four guys in their twenties: they've spent almost the entire time laughing. Behind the Brenners is a mother and her twin daughters.

As they've been queueing, Tom and Leo have been chatting almost constantly. It seems to come easily to them. A couple of times, Leo says something that makes Tom laugh and, on one occasion, Tom ruffles Leo's hair. Leo spends quite a lot of his time in the queue pointing at things off camera – other rides, other sights at the fun fair. When they get to the final part of the queue – where the line runs along the front of the ghost house – the two of them start gesturing to the middle section of the structure: the slanted windows that look so much like eyes; the punctures in the edifice which imitate the shape of flared nostrils; then the big, open doorway that looks like a mouth, broken at the sides to give it more of an oval shape.

The group of four guys disappear inside the entrance further down and, when they do, the same member of staff beckons Tom and Leo towards him and says something to Tom. Tom smiles and looks at his son, and then speaks to Leo, but it's impossible to make out what he says.

Finally, the Brenners enter the ghost house.

The four men exit three minutes and fifty-six seconds later. One of them does an exaggerated double-take as he tells a story and they all erupt into laughter. The clock in the corner of the footage ticks over for another thirty seconds.

At this point, Tom and Leo should be exiting.

But the clock keeps running.

Another thirty-two seconds pass and then the mother and her twins exit. One of the twins is crying. The mother tries to comfort them as they move out of shot.

Another half-minute and the people who'd been standing behind the mother and the twins come out of the ride. Then the ones behind them, then the ones behind them. It's like a conveyor belt of people, one after the next, heading in and then coming out.

Except two people *haven't* come out.

Another ten minutes pass.

It's around this time that Tom's mobile phone is discovered on the floor inside the ride because, less than thirty seconds later, one of the staff members emerges from the exit, holding the phone in his hand. It's dark inside the ghost house but we find out afterwards that the staff member was alerted to the phone because it was ringing, the screen blinking on and off.

Tom's wife, Sadie, was calling.

She's on a spa break with her sister in Bath.

The mobile phone isn't the only thing the staff member finds, though. He also finds the backpack that Leo was wearing, seven feet from the mobile phone. It's lying on the floor, in one of the ghost house corridors, and it's not until the member of staff brings it back outside, into the light – and then shows it to the guy working the entrance, who recognizes it as Leo's – that the camera reveals what's happened to the bag.

It looks like it's been slashed by something.

There are two cameras inside the ride: one is about a minute in; the second one is right at the end, prior to the exit. Tom and Leo are recorded passing the first camera.

But they never reach the second.

It's the space in between cameras where Tom's phone and Leo's backpack are found. In that same space there are no public entrances, and no ways out of the ride.

It's impossible to explain what happened or where the Brenners have gone.

They've simply ceased to exist.

Like the ghost house has swallowed them whole.

Day 1

Tuesday, 6 December

PART ONE
The First Disappearance

I

Rebekah's hotel was two minutes' walk from Embankment station, so I got a District Line train in from Kew and spent the half-hour journey going over notes I'd made after our last call. In truth, there wasn't much to read back: she recalled so little about the person that she'd asked me to find, and it had been so long since they'd disappeared.

Normally, families knew the missing person intimately.

But not this time.

Here, I was already chasing a shadow.

It was cold inside the carriage, colder in the station, and pretty much sub-zero at street level, the wind absolutely biting even under the roof of Embankment Place. I pulled up the collar of my coat and tightened my scarf as I crossed Northumberland Avenue but neither made any real difference: a week into December, winter was fully embedded, frost on the rooftops, tarmac glassed with ice, and it was the kind of cold that cut deep as a knife. As I approached the hotel, I briefly wondered how Rebekah was coping with this weather – and then, almost as quickly, realized she'd be coping just fine. She'd come from a place every bit as cold as this and had dealt with the kind of trauma most people would go their whole life without experiencing. Rebekah Murphy wasn't going to be fazed by a little cold.

A wall of warm air hit me as I entered the hotel foyer, lights blinking in an elaborate Christmas tree off to my right. A fire had been lit, flames dancing in the neck of the chimney. We'd agreed 10 a.m. but I was a little early, so I found a chair as close to the fire as I could get and spent a while going through calls, texts and emails.

A few minutes later, Rebekah emerged from the elevators.

'David,' she said, as she approached.

She was in her early forties, dark-haired, green-eyed, her right temple marked by a scar that I knew – from what she'd told me already – was a remnant from an assault on her the previous year. I stood, shaking her hand. She had a quiet, unassuming confidence, a calmness I'd already noted on our videocalls. All of it, I imagined, had been cultivated in the emergency rooms and operating theatres of the hospitals she worked in back in New York, where she was an orthopaedic surgeon.

There was a man in his seventies standing behind her.

'This is Frank,' Rebekah said.

I shook hands with him too and wondered who he was. She hadn't mentioned that she was going to be bringing anyone else – she'd left her two girls back in the US with her ex-husband – and I knew her father had died a few years ago. But whoever Frank was, he knew me because he smiled and said, 'Pleasure. Big fan of your work.'

He had a New York accent, unlike Rebekah: despite living in the US since she was eighteen, she still spoke like a Brit, even if some of her words and phrasing had become heavily Americanized. As if sensing my confusion, she said, 'I didn't mean to throw you. Frank coming with me was kind of a last-minute decision.'

And then it clicked: this must be Frank Travis.

I'd read about him in the stories that had helped fill in background on Rebekah. After the assault on her the previous year, Travis had been the NYPD cop that had worked her case. Even without her having to say anything else, I could see the tight bond they'd forged in the time since.

'Frank used to be a cop,' she confirmed. 'This is, uh . . . This is a big step for me, flying all the way out here. I just needed some moral support.'

I nodded. 'I understand.'

And I genuinely did: I totally got her desire to have him here – someone she trusted, who made her feel safe – because she didn't really know me at all and what she was asking me to do – the digging into her life, the questions I'd have to ask about the people that circled it – was something pretty far from safe. I'd met her in New

York earlier in the year while I was there on holiday, a chance meeting in Bryant Park, and we'd got talking, and I'd ended up telling her what I did – and then she'd asked me for a card. But it had taken her two months to even phone me.

Another five to pluck up the courage to get on a plane.

'I just want answers,' she said, even as the doubt lingered in her voice. She glanced at Travis and, again, I glimpsed the connection they had: familial, gentle, protective. 'I just need to know why my mother disappeared. I need to know why I didn't hear a thing from her for almost forty years.'

The three of us looked at each other.

'And I need to know why she suddenly started writing to me.'

2

We headed across Jubilee Bridge to a café tucked away in a narrow residential street north of Waterloo and found a table in the corner. While we waited to order, we talked about Rebekah's girls, her life in New York, and then her life before that, here in England, where she'd gone to school. Eventually, she got out a picture of her mother and handed it to me. It was the physical version of a photograph that she'd messaged to me a few days earlier: her mother was sitting on the front step of Rebekah's childhood home in Cambridge. She'd been pretty: fair-skinned, brown-eyed, her auburn hair a series of tight curls. 'I didn't know if you'd need the original,' Rebekah said softly, her tone neutral.

I thanked her and then got out my notebook and a pen and started going back over some of the more peripheral stuff we'd already covered in our videocalls. Mostly, it was so that I had everything clear in my head but also so that I could hear Rebekah talking, reacting, the fractional movements in her face. I'd been able to see and hear her on Zoom calls, but it was never the same as sitting across a table from someone.

'Just to confirm a few details,' I said. 'Your mum's name was Fiona?'

'Yes.'

'Fiona Murphy – or did she keep her maiden name?'

'She was Murphy, but her maiden name was Camberwell.'

'She was thirty when she disappeared, so she'd be around sixty-seven now?'

'I think so, yes.'

'That means she was born in 1955.' I checked it all off against the information that Rebekah had previously given me. 'It might help narrow a background search if you knew what month she was born in?'

'I think it was March.'

'But you're not certain?'

'I'm sure Dad said it was March, but . . .'

She faded out. *I can't be sure.*

'Your dad's name was Henry, correct?'

'Yes.'

I underlined his name. 'And your mum vanished when you were three?'

'Yes.'

'Do you remember anything at all of that day?'

'Virtually nothing,' she replied, a pained expression on her face. 'Most of what I remember is based on what my dad told me: Boxing Day morning 1985, he was in the kitchen preparing lunch and me and my brothers were upstairs playing with our Christmas presents. Next thing we know, she's gone. Dad didn't hear her leave; didn't hear the door open. Nothing. He went into the station that night and filed a missing person's report. Not that it got us anywhere.'

'She was never found?'

'No.'

'And she never got in touch?'

'It depends what you mean by "got in touch".'

'You're talking about the cards she sent you?'

'Yes,' Rebekah said. 'Condolence cards. My youngest brother, Mike, was killed in a car accident four years ago. A year after that, my dad died. He had cancer. He'd been battling it on and off for years. And my older brother Johnny . . . he's gone too.' A flicker in her face. This one seemed to hurt her most; she'd obviously been close to Johnny. 'Every time, she sent a card.'

'Did you bring the cards with you?'

She reached into her pocket, taking out three envelopes. I slid the cards out of the envelopes: they were condolence cards, all very similar designs – intertwined roses, their wriggling stems creating the word *Sorry* – and inside they were all plain. Nothing printed. Handwritten in each was basically the same message: in Mike's, sent four years ago, and addressed to Rebekah's father: *I was sorry to hear about Mike*; in Henry's, mailed thirteen months later, and addressed to both Rebekah and Johnny: *I was sorry to hear about your dad*; and in Johnny's, posted eight months ago, at the end of April, and addressed to Rebekah alone: *I was sorry to hear the news about John*. It was definitely the same person who wrote all three: every *a* had the same distinctive tail on it; the *h* and *e* in *hear* were very close together and the *h* looked more like an *l* if you glanced at it quickly.

I looked up and saw Rebekah staring at the cards, eyes shimmering, like a ripple on a pond. 'That's it. These are the only times I've heard from her in thirty-seven years.'

I looked at the envelopes, the airmail stamps on them. They'd definitely been sent from the UK. That suggested Fiona was alive and living here as recently as April. But it was going to be impossible to find out from *where* in the country she'd posted them: the envelope didn't have any sort of postmark, let alone a location of a sorting office.

There was nothing on the cards themselves to help me either. Usually on the back of greeting cards there would be small print: information about the company that had made them, or a copyright message. But it was just blank. That meant they were untraceable, which could have been unintentional.

Or very deliberate.

'What did you think when Mike's card first turned up?'

Rebekah frowned. 'What do you mean?'

'I mean, Mike was – what? – eighteen months old when your mum walked out on you all? You don't hear anything from her for thirty-four years and then suddenly she sends her condolences when he dies.' I looked at Mike's card. 'You, your dad, Johnny – you must all have been shocked when it arrived?'

'We were totally floored.'

'Had you assumed she was dead?'

'I don't know *what* I thought exactly. I mean, it was obviously something the four of us talked about a lot, all the way back to when we were kids. Where did she go? Where was she now? Did she have a new family? All the questions you can imagine, we asked them all. But wherever she was – dead or alive – the biggest part for us was why she left in the first place.'

'What did your dad say she was like before she disappeared?'

'He said she was fine.' She paused, mouth flattening. 'I mean, I'm separated – about to be divorced – so I've seen it from the inside. In every marriage, there are things that don't work as they should. You have arguments, and you have things that annoy you, and maybe you even begin to realize that this person you've committed your life to isn't the right one for you. It happens. So Dad admitted they had things like that – but, basically, they were fine. Even if they weren't, though, she had three kids. Johnny was five, I was three, Mike was still in nappies. Why leave *us*?'

She stopped for a second time, glancing at Travis. He smiled at her, winked: *You're doing fine*, he was saying to her.

Rebekah faced me again: 'I've got this hollow inside of me. It's been there ever since I was old enough to process – properly – that she was gone and she wasn't coming back. It shouldn't matter after almost forty years, especially now that I have my own kids, these two beautiful girls that I love with every fibre of my being – but it does. It still matters. In fact, as time goes on, I'm starting to think it matters even *more* now that I have the girls because I can't *ever* imagine leaving them like my mother left me.'

A few moments later, Rebekah excused herself and weaved her way across the café to the bathroom. As Travis watched her go, he said, 'It's been tough on her.'

'Yeah, I can see that.'

'Not just the stuff with her mom. Everything. It's why it's taken her so long to fly out here. It's not that she's been uncertain about wanting to find out what went on with Fiona; she's just uncertain about whether she can take any more heartache.'

'I get it.'

Travis nodded. 'I expect you do.' He eyed me and the subtext was obvious: he'd read up about me, he'd done a background for Rebekah, perhaps to reassure her, and in that research he'd found all the heartache written into my cases – and into my life.

After Rebekah returned, I looped the conversation back around again: 'How come you've never tried looking for your mum before?'

'I don't know,' Rebekah responded, and then ground to a halt. 'Maybe, for a time, I didn't *want* to know, just in case knowing was worse than being completely in the dark. But I didn't have a clue where to start. That was probably the biggest thing. I lived in New York, those cards were coming from England; I had a job, kids, a marriage that was failing. I didn't have the headspace.' She stopped, toying with the last of her food. 'Actually, that's not true. I always had the headspace. She was always there, somewhere. I've been angry with her since I was a kid, but as I got older, the anger became easier to control, and I could force myself not to think about her. If I was feeling really low, I'd convince myself that she died shortly after she left, and that explained it all: the total lack of contact, the total indifference she showed to walking out on me and my brothers. So when that card for Mike arrived, it screwed everything up again because the anger came back. I'd finally reached a point where I could go a day without thinking about how *betrayed* she made me feel. Then, suddenly, *boom*, the first card arrives and she's back in my head.'

'You said you never tried to look for her yourself, but did your dad ever try?' I checked my notes from our previous conversations. 'He worked as a cop, didn't he?'

'Yeah, after he left the military. I think he tried for a while. Like I say, he went into the station and reported her missing. And when that went nowhere, he said he tried looking for her himself.'

'But he didn't get anywhere?'

She shook her head. In truth, there was no way to be sure how hard Henry Murphy had looked, *if* he'd looked at all, just as there was no way of telling if he'd heard from Fiona *before* the condolence card for Mike turned up thirty-four years after she left them. Similarly, there was no way to know if Henry kept details back from the kids about the reasons why Fiona had walked out of the door in the first place. Whatever knowledge Henry Murphy may or may not have been carrying with him was now buried six feet under the earth in a cemetery three and a half thousand miles away.

'You said you were born in Cambridge?'

'Yes. Me and both my brothers.'

'Your dad was stationed with the US Air Force there?'

'Right. Well, RAF Lakenheath.'

'Was Fiona from Cambridge too?'

'Dad said Peterborough originally and then she moved to Cambridge.'

This had been a reccurring theme as I'd got to know Rebekah over Zoom: her memories of her mother were almost entirely built on what her father had told her.

We talked for a while longer but, eventually, I felt we'd gone as far as we could. We discussed next steps, but in truth I didn't have much of an idea myself: this was so different to the kind of missing persons' cases I normally took on. With those, the missing person had usually been gone months, sometimes years, but they'd left behind some trace of themselves: a life, however small, I could get inside.

Fiona had nothing.

I had nothing.

She really was a shadow.

And yet I'd wanted to take the case after the very first Zoom call I'd had with Rebekah because there were things that had immediately snared me. The question of why Fiona walked out on her young family and never returned was one, perhaps *the* most obvious thing to explore. Yet it was the condolence cards that bothered me most. The huge, thirty-four-year time gap between her leaving and Mike's card arriving was bizarre, an incongruous detail I couldn't let go of and couldn't stop thinking about. Three and a half decades of total silence, with absolutely no clue about where she was, and then, all of a sudden, the family were hearing from her. The fact that Rebekah had then received similar cards for both her father and older brother meant, at the very least, that – wherever she was – Fiona was keeping a peripheral eye on the Murphys.

So why not get in touch with them properly?

Why not pick up the phone or write an email?

I didn't know for certain yet, didn't know if maybe she *had* and Henry had just never told Rebekah. But if I was to assume Henry was as confused and surprised as Rebekah at the sudden correspondence, then I had to zero in on what Fiona's motivation was.

Except Fiona was just a series of questions.

And there was one I couldn't stop asking myself.

How did we even know it was her who sent the cards?

3

A snarl of wind stirred me from my thoughts as I entered Victoria Embankment Gardens. Just behind me was Scotland Yard, the famous sign out front in the middle of yet another revolution. I could see Ewan Tasker almost straightaway: he was dressed in a black, knee-length coat and red scarf, but it was his silver-grey hair that stood out. He was sitting on a bench, head down, fingers working a mobile phone.

'You busy Snapchatting?' I said as I got to him.

'TikTok. Get with the times, Raker.'

We both smiled, shook hands, and embraced. It was a couple of months since I'd seen Task but he looked exactly the same. He was nearing his mid-seventies but you never would have guessed. He was tall and broad, strong and fit – except for a dodgy right knee. I suspected most of it came from the fact that he was still working part-time as a consultant at the Met. The work kept him focused, his brain sharp.

'How you doing?' he asked me.

'Yeah, pretty good, old man.' I looked around the park and drew my coat even tighter to my body. 'Have you got time to go somewhere a bit warmer?'

'I'd love to, but this is the only fifteen minutes I've got all day.'

'In that case, I appreciate you coming out like this.'

'Your sunny disposition makes it all worth it.' He smiled at me again and then reached into his pocket. 'As always, you didn't get this from me.' Pinched between his thumb and forefinger was a small, plain USB stick. 'Everything should be on there.'

I took the flash drive from him.

'It's pretty thin,' he said. 'Fiona Murphy – née Camberwell – basically ceased to exist in 1985. I can't find any trace of her anywhere else, in any of the systems we use. Her driving licence ran out in 1988 and was never renewed. Her passport ran out in 1990, same story. The only reason she's still on the system is because her husband filed a missing person's report the evening of her disappearance.'

'Is there any chatter in the report about Henry?'

'You mean was he ever a suspect?'

'Husbands are usually the first port of call in something like this.'

Tasker shrugged. 'I don't think so. I mean, they looked at him, but from what I skim-read, they considered him a straight arrow; a good cop, a solid family man.'

'And Fiona? Any evidence she changed her name?'

'No,' Task said. 'Well, not officially.'

Her driving licence and passport had been allowed to lapse, so she could have started using a different name, literally as soon as she walked out the door. There was no law against that. Where it got complicated was if she wanted to apply for another driving licence or passport: *then* she'd have to apply for an enrolled deed poll, which meant putting her new name on public record in order to access things like foreign travel. If she hadn't done that, and Tasker had found no evidence of it, it meant there were a number of possibilities. One was that she'd died some time during the period between her leaving her family, and her driving licence and passport expiring – and if that were true, someone else, for whatever reason, *did* mail those condolence cards.

The second possibility was that she changed her name, but not officially – an unenrolled change – which wouldn't have brought her into the orbit of any official government apparatus. But it also would have stopped her from ever legally getting behind the wheel of a car, certainly ever boarding an airplane or ferry out of the UK.

Or there was a third option: she went the illegal route and absorbed someone else's identity, which would allow her access to things like IDs and passports without ever risking popping up on the radar. The big question mark was whether Fiona would have had the kind of contacts she'd need in order to make that happen.

'What about the MPU?' I asked. The Missing Persons Unit was

the main UK agency for all unidentified people, bodies and remains. 'Did you manage to speak to your guy over there?'

'I forwarded him on the photo you sent me.' It had been the digital version of the picture Rebekah had handed me this morning. 'There's nothing.'

'No remains matching her physical description?'

'He went all the way back to eighty-five for me. There's a few vaguely in the same ballpark in terms of hair colour and age. But he's pretty sure none of them are Fiona Murphy – at least based on the photograph you sent.'

For now, that was good enough for me.

'Thanks again for this,' I said.

'Sorry I can't stay longer.' Tasker looked off towards Scotland Yard and checked his watch. 'I better get back.'

'Yeah, of course.'

'So where are you off to now?'

I pocketed the USB stick.

'I'm going to see what I can find out in Cambridge.'

Daughter

Rebekah | *This Morning*

As Rebekah exited the café that they'd met David Raker in, she wondered where he'd gone first, what his plans were, and whether he had a feel for this case already, an instinctive sense of where the search for Rebekah's mother might end up.

I just hope it ends up somewhere, she thought.

'He's lost someone he loves.'

She turned and looked back at Frank. 'Sorry?'

'Raker. He's lost someone he loves.'

'I know.' Frank had already done a background on David, and David had sat there himself this morning and told them his wife had passed on.

'But it's written in him,' Frank said as the freezing morning air hit them both. 'You can see it's shaped who he is.' For a moment, as she often did, Rebekah caught a glimpse of her father. Frank and her dad weren't physically alike at all, but sometimes in the way they spoke, the similarities were so stark. 'It's important.'

'His wife dying?' Rebekah frowned. 'I'm not sure he'd agree.'

'No, what I mean is, you can see he uses her death.'

'Uses it?'

'He uses the grief as fuel.' Frank glanced around him, taking in the city, its noise, its chaos. 'I've got a feeling he'll find the order in all of this.'

'So you think he's our man?'

'Yes,' Frank said. 'I think he's *exactly* our man.'

4

On the train up to Cambridge, I took out my laptop, plugged in the flash drive that Tasker had given me and pulled everything off on to the desktop. There wasn't much.

The background on Fiona Murphy – née Camberwell – was thin and based almost entirely on details she'd provided for her one and only passport application in 1979. And she didn't seem to have used the passport much, even once she'd got it: a single trip to New York in 1980, just after Rebekah's older brother Johnny was born.

At the time, Fiona's address had been listed as a house in the King's Hedges area of Cambridge, which Rebekah already confirmed had been the home in which she and her brothers had grown up. But under the *former addresses* section of Fiona's passport application, she'd listed a street in a village called Settlebury, just south-west of the city. That, I assumed, was where she'd moved with her family after leaving Peterborough.

Before Rebekah ever landed in the UK, I'd trawled public records here, as well as tapping up a couple of sources, and had put together a picture of Fiona's family. She had no siblings and her mother had died in 1966, shortly before Fiona turned eleven. The death certificate listed cause of death as a heart attack. It was impossible to say what Fiona's relationship with her father had been like, but when he'd died in 1982, it was from a drug overdose, so it wasn't hard to imagine her childhood as somewhat dsyfunctional. I'd been hoping the missing person's report might add some colour to what I already knew, and answers to some of the questions I had.

It didn't.

Other than confirmation that she *had* been born in March 1955, the report filed by Henry Murphy on Boxing Day night in 1985 was basically worthless. Even so, I tabbed through it, stopping on Henry's description of the day in question: *I was making some lunch out of leftovers from Christmas Day, and at approx. 11.30 a.m. realized I hadn't seen Fiona in quite a while. I'd assumed she was upstairs with the children. When I went to check on her, I couldn't find her. The children hadn't seen her and Fiona wasn't anywhere else in the house.*

He noted the front door was unlocked, and they'd always kept it locked when they were home because they lived on a busy street and were worried about the kids wandering out. Henry also said that Fiona had removed her coat from a rack in the downstairs hallway; otherwise he wasn't aware of her taking anything – not clothes, not cash – and her purse and handbag were still at home. He'd looked through the purse and found her ATM cards were there, as was £15 in change.

Tasker had been right in what he'd said to me earlier: in the subsequent investigation – small as it was – the cops considered Henry as a suspect in his wife going missing, but just as quickly dismissed him. He had a good reputation in the short time he was in the Cambridgeshire Constabulary, which he joined after leaving the air force, an exemplary military record, and character witnesses spoke highly of him as a softly spoken family man who adored his kids. To my mind, that wouldn't have been enough to write him off entirely as a person of interest, but the cops at the time had clearly felt differently and, pretty soon, with no other suspects and no evidence, the search for Fiona Murphy dried up.

I used the train's Wi-Fi to go searching in Google for any mention of her. I'd done the search before, a couple of times, but this time I tried to cast the net wider based on some of the information in the missing person's report.

Zero hits.

That could have meant the case never attracted the media attention it needed to sustain momentum at the time, or it could have been that its age and pre-internet status meant whatever had been written about Fiona back then had become lost over time. I could dig around in newspaper archives to find out for sure, but my sense was that it would be a huge time sink for little or no reward. After all, if the police's search for Fiona went nowhere quickly – which it did – they had nothing to feed the media with. With nothing to feed on, newspapers would just move on to the next story.

I closed my laptop and looked out of the window, watching as a patchwork quilt of flat, frozen fields whipped by, and again tried to line up possible explanations for Fiona walking out on her kids.

Postnatal depression?

So little was known about Fiona's background: she could easily have been suffering from an undiagnosed mental health problem – and it could have been there from before she ever met Henry – and perhaps having kids exacerbated her sickness. Or maybe, if she *had* been suffering from postnatal depression, it only kicked in after giving birth to Mike: he was eighteen months when she disappeared, so still very young.

Bad marriage?

That might have been a contributor to Fiona having depression, but if there was no depression, and it was just a failing marriage, why leave your kids behind? Worse, why not get in touch with them afterwards – or, at least not for thirty-four years?

The other thing that kept coming back to me was that it was also *hard* to disappear, and stay hidden, even back then. It was 1985, so a time before mobiles, the internet and CCTV on every street corner, but even if Fiona wasn't dealing with modern technology, she would have had to have coped with the psychological and emotional side of going missing: remembering a new name or an identity; trying to recall every detail of the back story you've invented for yourself; starting again with absolutely nothing – which Fiona, with no money or assets to her name, would have done – and never being able to let other people get too close to you for fear of giving yourself away. The perpetual cycle of secrets and rules ground most people down over time. They slipped. They made mistakes. Somewhere on the radar, they left a blip, however minor. The fact Fiona never did – at least until the cards turned up – was what was sticking with me. It either showed impressive levels of preparation and incredible discipline – or it showed something else.

I wrote down *involuntary disappearance*.

It showed she never planned to go missing at all.

5

It was three miles from the station to the King's Hedges area of Cambridge – where the Murphys had lived – so I decided to walk it, needing to order my thoughts.

I circumvented the city centre, opting for the more direct route north, and, as I crossed the Cam, a brutal gust of wind hit me. I pulled my coat even tighter, put my head down and carried on my march into the suburbs. I'd hardly spent any time in Cambridge, didn't know the city at all, so a part of the reason for making the trip up here was to paint a picture of the places that Rebekah – and, before her, Fiona – had grown up in. I didn't expect to find anything – it was decades since they'd left – but I wanted to be able to visualize the places they'd inhabited.

I entered a maze of flats, terraced houses and garages and followed a footpath along the flank of a park. Soon I found my way to the former home of the Murphys: a yellow-brick, two-storey mid-terrace, half-hidden behind a five-foot wall, on a busy through-road. The area mostly seemed to be council housing, a tight network of small, identical homes, and while it was a little run-down in places, none of that would have mattered to Rebekah.

For the time they were here, she'd told me they'd been happy.

I took a couple of pictures of the house and then did some more circuits of the surrounding area. When I got back to the property, I tried to imagine the day Fiona left, where she might have gone and what she may have been thinking. The nearest train station was three miles away, but there were bus stops all over, including a bus shelter – which could have been here in some form in 1985 – a few yards away. If she'd got on a bus, where had she headed? And if she didn't use public transport, what then? Could she have walked to a prearranged meeting place? Who had she been meeting?

The address in Settlebury – the village Fiona had lived in after her family had moved here from Peterborough, and before she and Henry Murphy had got the house together in Cambridge – was four miles south of the city centre, seven from where I was, so I decided against walking, and waited for an Uber out on the main road.

When I got to the village, it was little more than a single road fringed by quaint red-bricked buildings. A pub in the centre was thatched, its walls covered by a sea of vines, the grass out front stiff and frosted. I used my phone to lead the way to the site of Fiona's former home: it took me out of the heart of the village and into a road with sculpted hedgerows on either side and narrow lanes peeling off at irregular intervals.

Each of the lanes led down to a grouping of cottages.

After a while, I began wondering if the mapped route on my phone had taken me too far because the lanes halted, the hedgerows clotted and the cottages vanished.

But then I reached another property.

It was the last house in the village, and set back from the road just like all the others. By now, the hedgerows were gone, replaced by a bank of opaque firs, thick as concrete. I checked my phone, saw the pin was dropped into the house on the other side of them, and kept going. A loose stone path had been laid along a shallow grass bank, the bank segregating the fir trees from the road. After a minute, the fir trees ceased and I got to the gate of the house that Fiona had grown up in.

Except it wasn't a cottage like all the others in the village.

It was a mansion.

6

The house was Georgian, a mix of light stone and white render, and sat on its own amongst sweeping, manicured grounds. It was beautiful. To the left was a sunroom, extending out from the property, with a grey slate roof, and to the right were a series of tiered, walled gardens descending into a hexagonal seating area.

There was an intercom embedded in a pillar outside the main gates, so I pushed it and waited, trying to gather my thoughts. What did it mean that Fiona had lived here? The size and majesty of this home couldn't have been further from the council house in King's Hedges she'd shared with Henry, Rebekah, Johnny and Mike.

'Yes?'

It sounded like an older man.

There was a small camera above a number pad on the pillar, so I held a business card up in front of it and said, 'Hi, my name's David Raker. I'm a missing persons investigator. I'm not sure if you can help me or not, but I'm looking into the disappearance of a woman called Fiona Murphy, or Camberwell as she was –'

'Fiona?'

I stopped, dropping the business card away from the camera. I looked into the lens. 'Yes,' I said. 'Fiona Murph—'

'Who are you working for?'

'No one. I work for myself.'

'You're not with the police?'

'No.'

'So why are you looking for Fiona?'

'Her daughter has asked me to find her.'

A pause. 'Her daughter?'

'Yes.'

Nothing from the other end of the line this time.

'Hello?'

As I looked at the house, searching for movement in the sunroom or behind any of the windows, I started to wonder if the guy had hung up on me.

But then, with a buzz, the gate began to shift.

I stepped through the gap and followed a gravel driveway down, between more fir trees, to the sweeping front steps of the house. Just as I got to the bottom of them, the front door opened, a huge slab of burnished oak that creaked back slowly on its hinges. A woman appeared. She was in her mid-forties, serious-looking, her hair scraped back into a business-like ponytail, and she was wearing magenta scrubs and holding a blood pressure monitor by the cuff. She looked me up and down – like I'd already done something seriously wrong – then opened the door a little further to reveal a grand staircase and a hallway with polished checkerboard floors.

'He's in the study at the top,' she said. 'I don't know why you're here, but don't get him over-excited.' She held up the monitor. 'Last thing I need is you marching out of here in ten minutes and leaving him with sky-high BP.'

'I'll be on my best behaviour.'

She just nodded.

'I didn't catch your employer's name at the gate?'

She studied me, something flickering in her face. 'Oh,' she said, and then left me hanging for a moment. 'I'm guessing you're some kind of investigator.'

'What would make you think that?'

'Because it's the only reason he'd invite a total stranger into his house.'

'What do you mean?'

She glanced up the stairs behind her.

'I mean, I'm guessing this has something to do with his daughter.'

The Tourist

Tom | *This Morning*

Tom Brenner hurried out of the doors of the hotel in King's Cross.

It was a vast labyrinth of rooms constructed five years earlier in the even vaster shadow of the station. But as Tom headed south, he barely noticed any of it.

At the corner of York Way and Pentonville Road, he crossed the street, darting between oncoming cars, and made a beeline for the payphone outside Five Guys. The glass on the booth was misty with spray paint, messages scrawled over it, and inside the confines of the phone box, the city noise faded. Tom felt like he was hiding.

I wish I could.

I wish I could take Sadie and Leo and just hide.

The scream of a siren filled the air, ripping him from his thoughts, as a police car whipped past. He watched its lights flashing, neon blue illuminating the frozen windows of the street outside – and then it was gone again, and it was just him, here.

This booth. This phone.

This call.

He picked up the handset, so nervous his fingers were vibrating, and dropped a fifty-pence piece into the slot. She'd told him not to use a bank card, only coins. Once he saw the credit on the display, he went to his pocket.

Inside was a napkin.

On the napkin was her number.

He dialled it slowly, each button press like a little stab of pain, because every button inched him closer to the call connecting, to setting this whole thing in motion.

It started to ring.

You're doing the right thing, he said to himself, and then repeated it again out loud: 'You're doing the right thing.' *Sadie will be proud of you. Leo will be proud of* –

'Hello?'

Tom cleared his throat. 'It's me again.'

He heard her moving. She was on her mobile. She'd told him that if anyone went through her records, no one would be able to connect him to the payphone he was using because there was no CCTV close enough to ID him. As he remembered her saying that, he looked out, searching the buildings close by for video. She was right. He couldn't see any cameras at this end of Pentonville Road. The nearest one seemed to be on the train station across the street, and that was facing away from him. It made him wonder how she would know something like that – something so specific.

How many times had she done this before?

How many other people had phoned her from here?

'You still there?' she said, coming back on the line.

'Yes.' Tom swallowed, looking through the graffiti again, to the cars, the people, the swell of the crowds at the train station. 'We should go to the police.'

'I told you last night, eventually we will.'

'We should do it now.'

'We don't know who we can trust in the police.'

'They're the *police*,' Tom said, desperation in his voice.

'Tom,' she replied instantly, using his name to shut down the doubts that were starting to crush every organ in his body. He felt sick; felt like he was about to faint.

He looked at the napkin, at her number.

What have I started?

'Tom,' she repeated. 'Is it him?'

And Tom thought, *It's already too late.*

Even if I wanted to, I can't back out.

'Yes,' he said. 'It's him.'

The flight landed at Heathrow just before 7 a.m.

As the seatbelt lights went off, he stayed where he was, in a window seat midway down the plane, and watched everyone around him start furiously jostling for position. They were all so desperate to get their coats on and their bags down, and yet they must have known what would happen next: they'd stand there waiting for the doors to open, all packed in like sardines.

He stared out of the window, the skies grey over the terminal. A luggage vehicle was winding its way towards them, the driver being pelted by rain. This was exactly the type of weather that worried him: he figured he could put up with it for a few weeks, maybe a few months, but he'd heard that British summers could be like this as well – wet, and relentless, and grim – and he wasn't sure he could handle it. Not that he had much choice now: he either handled it, or he got back on a plane tomorrow and headed home.

And he couldn't go home.

Not ever.

Slowly everything around him faded out – the other passengers, the hum of all their conversations, the low hiss of the air conditioning – and his head was filled with images of the place he'd lived in for so long. He saw himself barbecuing steaks, he and the guys he'd worked with sitting around in a circle, smoking cigarettes and drinking beer. And then he saw something else: a farm, out in the middle of nowhere, a single, long dirt track the only way in and out; he saw the land it occupied, the pale grass that surrounded it, and the way it perpetually seemed to be moving; and then he saw the farmhouse itself in the centre of everything, elevated so it had a view of approaching vehicles. Its walls were a plain white, its exterior so unassuming no one passing on the main road – if they could even see it from that far away – had a clue about what went on inside.

'*What do you tell your children you do?*'

He kept hearing her voice.

'What lies do you tell them when you go home to them at night?'

Around him, people started moving down the aisle.

It yanked him back into the present and, after a moment of disorientation, he saw that the couple who'd sat next to him on the flight were now gone. He shuffled along the vacated seats, got his bag out of the overhead locker, and then followed the other passengers out, into the bridge. The farmhouse still lingered behind his eyes, like an after-image that wouldn't fade.

He picked up his pace, accelerating away from the other passengers. He was thirty-five, strong, fit, and as he walked, his thoughts switched to the next part of this journey: getting past immigration without raising any alarms.

Feeling around in his pocket, he got out his passport and looked at the photo inside, the starkness of his expression. There was no hint about the man who existed below the surface. He looked like the people in the photographs he used to pin to the walls of the farm: blank, unreadable.

They were hiding secrets. So am I.

He headed for the stairs instead of the escalator, and joined the queue for international arrivals. As he waited, he took in the passport booths up front, manned by five men and one woman in matching uniforms, and tried to get a read on each of them. If he could get one over the other because they were more pleasant, or less inquisitive, or more relaxed, he would do his best to – although if he let people keep going ahead of him until he got the official that looked most amenable, it would get him noticed. Getting noticed meant questions.

Questions meant danger.

His heart was beating a little faster now: he was five people from the front, and based on his training, his instincts, on being able to lip-read some of what the officials were saying, he'd decided that the guy in the middle – a plump man in his early forties – was the best. He seemed friendly, but not overly so. Too friendly, and it was often a disguise for someone who liked asking subtle, probing questions. On the other hand, if they were uncommunicative – like one of the other officials here – they were the type who considered this job on a par with working for the secret service. That meant they'd try to sweat you just because they had a small amount of power to wield.

He got to the front of the queue.

At the far end, the woman waved him over. He hadn't been able to see much in her face, which concerned him because he'd spent a good chunk of his life reading people and even the most sober of expressions normally revealed something. As he got to the desk and put down his passport, he said, 'Good morning.' She didn't say anything in return and looked up at him. As he held her eye, her gaze quickly shifted to his passport, and that was when he knew he was going to be fine.

She was introverted, maybe even shy.

Being shy was a weakness.

'What's the purpose of your visit?' she asked, without making eye contact.

'Well, I've never been to London, so . . .'

He left it hanging.

It forced her to look at him.

'I'm just here to enjoy all the tourist stuff.'

'You've never been to London before?' she replied, immediately looking away from him again, back to his passport. She sounded surprised, the inference in her question clear: he'd come from a country that was only two hours' flight away. But he already knew he was dictating the course of this conversation now, not her. He could feel it like a charge in his veins, the same hum in his blood that he used to get at the farm, when he knew he'd won. He'd spent the flight worrying about landing an official that would see through him, someone smart enough to ask questions that could hurt him, and reveal the lies he'd buried.

Instead, he'd got this bitch.

A worthless nobody.

'No,' he said. 'Never had the chance until now.'

Her eyes flicked to him again, and then she reached for a stamp, marked a page in the passport, and slapped it on to the desk.

'Thank you,' he said, picking up his passport.

And then he was through, on the escalator down to the baggage hall, another excited tourist on their way to Big Ben, and Buckingham Palace, and Oxford Street.

Except he wasn't a tourist.

He hadn't come to London to see the sights.

He'd come here to disappear.

7

I moved up the staircase, deeper into the mansion Fiona Murphy had lived in.

The first door at the top was a study, but my attention was drawn more to a series of photographs lining the wall on my left. They were all of the same man. The nurse – who had introduced herself as Mary – said he was the owner of the house as well as the person who'd spoken to me on the intercom. His name was Jonah Carling.

And he'd referred to Fiona as his daughter.

I looked for her in the photographs. They went back years and Carling was in all of them, starting off as a bull of a man in his twenties and thirties until the decline started setting in in his later years. He stopped mounting pictures of himself in his seventies and eighties, except for one where he was leaning on a walking stick, his face liver-spotted, his eyes milky, shaking hands with a former US President at a charity event. The bull of the man was lost forever. In the end, nothing – not even money – could stop time.

I didn't see Fiona in any of the shots, so wasn't entirely clear what relationship this man had with her. Because, whatever he claimed, he definitely wasn't her real father. Fiona's father had died only a couple of months after Rebekah was born, and – as far as I could tell in the background I had put together – Fiona's family tree had few other roots. Her mother and father were both only children, so Carling wasn't an uncle, and you had to go back two generations to find anything in the way of extended family, and elderly as Carling appeared to be, he'd have needed to be thirty years older to be a grandparent.

At the top of the stairs, I paused, taking in the study. It was stately, with floor-to-ceiling bookcases and a hardwood desk with a PC on it. It was on and I could see a window open, with a colour image: the view from the gatepost camera. I knocked once and heard movement. A sluggish shuffle of feet. The tap of a walking stick.

Jonah Carling emerged into view.

He looked even older now than he had in the photo of him with the President. He must have been in his early nineties, a jaundiced pallor to his skin, a narrow wisp of grey hair clinging to his pink scalp like a cloud skimming the apex of a ridge. He was in pyjamas and a pair of slippers.

'Mr Carling?'

'Jonah,' he wheezed, retreating back the way he'd come, inviting me to follow him. When I did, I could see that he had a bed set up in front of a window that looked over the tiered garden. With effort, he climbed back under the sheets. 'She says I have to rest,' he said, his voice hoarse, and leaned his stick against a table with an iPad and some water on it. 'And I don't want to upset her.'

He said it with a smile, showing me a mouth full of yellow teeth, but I imagined it wasn't far from the truth: the nurse didn't strike me as someone to be messed with.

'Please,' he said, and pointed towards a grey bucket chair, sitting amongst a group of others. By the time I'd grabbed it and pulled it back towards him, Carling was fully settled.

'Thank you for seeing me,' I said. 'This is unexpected.'

'You said you find missing people?'

'I do.'

His eyebrows kicked up. 'And you said Fiona had a daughter?'

'Yes. A daughter and two sons.'

'My goodness. With who?'

'With a man called Henry Murphy.'

I could see in his face that the name didn't seem to mean anything to him. In fact, he appeared completely thrown by all of this: Henry, Rebekah, her brothers. He shook his head: 'I had no idea Fiona became a mother.'

'Your nurse referred to Fiona as your "daughter",' I said.

He smiled a little. 'A colloquial term.'

'So can I ask what your relationship was to her?'

'She lived with me for seven years.'

'Here?'

'Yes. Between the ages of eleven and eighteen.'

It was a small echo of Rebekah's life. She'd spent the equivalent seven years on a sports scholarship in a boarding school in London. At the same age, her mother had been in this house, living with a millionaire.

'How did she end up here?' I asked.

He nodded, as if that was exactly the question he would have been posing himself. 'I was kind of a . . .' He paused, rolled his head a little. 'I was friendly with Fiona's mum, Cassandra.' I saw it instantly, like a light had switched on behind the pearls of his eyes: he'd been fond of Fiona's mother – or maybe something that had gone way beyond just 'fond'. 'Cass and I grew up together.'

'And after you grew up?'

His eyes came back to me and he could see I'd already skipped ahead; that he had given himself away. 'We dated for a while, yes,' he said. 'She was the first woman I ever loved. Maybe the only woman.' He looked around the room, and then out of the window, the memories flooding him. I started to get a sense for something: that his involvement in Fiona's life, in bringing her here, may have been some sort of redemptive arc; a way for him to make up for things he hadn't done but should have.

In my work, regret had become easy to recognize.

'I took my eyes off the prize,' he said ruefully, and started to adjust the bedding at his waist, his narrow, emaciated fingers playing with the starched sheets.

'Is that why Cassandra ended up with Fiona's dad and not you?'

'My upbringing,' he said, looking out at the room again, 'it was dirt poor. Mine and Cassandra's families, we lived next door to one another, these two awful, broken houses that were constantly on the verge of collapse. I swore my life was going to be different. Better. And that's why I got into the markets. By the time I was twenty-five, I'd made my first million . . .' And then he stopped, his words ceasing, his fingers halting their movement at the hem of the sheet. 'But

I was so obsessed by making money that, by the time everything snapped back into focus, I'd lost her. She'd been swept off her feet by another man.'

'Fiona's dad.'

'Yes. Alistair. He was a waste of space.' For the first time, a flash of jealousy. 'A drug addict pretty much from the moment Cass first met him. But by the time she started to notice – or, rather, by the time she realized it was going to be a problem – it was too late. She was pregnant with Fiona.'

I looked at my notes.

'Cassandra died when Fiona was ten, didn't she?'

'Yes. A heart attack.'

'So she didn't think about leaving Alistair before that?'

'She thought about it, I'm sure.'

'Why didn't she make the leap?'

The jealousy was long gone now, replaced by a sadness so lucid it was written into every line on his face. 'Cass was a good person: she'd always try to see the best in others, and she always tried to see the best in him. She didn't want to bring Fiona up in a divided family where she was ferried between warring parents.'

'And you? You stayed in touch with Cassandra?'

'During her marriage? Yes. I kept saying to her, come here, bring Fiona. There was no expectation on my part for anything to happen, I just wanted to see them safe and well, and for Fiona to have the opportunities she deserved.' He looked at me, his eyes a little wet: it was hard to tell if it was tears or age, but it seemed unlikely you'd ask the woman you'd always loved to come live with you if you had no wish or compulsion for something to happen. 'But she never did,' he added.

'So what happened after Cassandra died?'

'I started checking in on Fiona. Alistair, he was scratching around for his next fix the whole bloody time. Fiona was only just eleven, basically bringing herself up. I got really mad.'

'And did what?'

'Well, I hired the best, most expensive legal team that money could buy and I took Alistair to court to challenge for custody. And, a few months after I did that, Fiona was living with me.'

'You adopted her?'

'No, nothing as legally formal as that. It's why you probably didn't find me on any background check.' He looked at me, his mind still sharp. I glanced at the PC on his desk and guessed he'd also done a Google search for me after he'd opened the gates out front. For the first time, a thought bobbed to the surface. *People with money have the power to get what they want – and make the things that they don't go away.* I had no reason to suspect Carling of anything – but he'd got exactly what he'd wanted with Fiona, and eventually her real father *had* gone away.

'So would you say it was more like you fostered her?'

He pushed his lips together. 'What you have to remember is that in the sixties, even into the seventies, childcare – or at least the state's responsibility to a child – was still like the Wild West. If you had a little money, like I did, you could grease the wheels and make things happen, so when I got told I wouldn't be able to adopt her – even foster her – because Alistair wanted to fight me on it, I just called in some favours and brought my authority to bear, such as it was. That Alistair fought so hard for me *not* to bring her here says everything about the man he was: he was never there for her as a father, never *cared* about her, except when he thought there was a chance that he might actually lose her. I guess it was his pride, or the small amount of guilt he felt at failing her. But he couldn't stomach anyone else stepping in and doing right by her.'

'Do you think his reaction was more to do with you?'

A twitch of a smile on Carling's face. 'Maybe.'

'Did he know how you felt about Cassandra?'

'Yes,' he said finally. 'He probably did.'

'Did you have an affair with Cassandra?'

'Oh no,' he said. 'Nothing of that sort. Cass never would have gone for anything like that.' He looked at me, the rest of his sentence hanging in the space between us: *Cassandra would never have gone for it – but I would have done it in a heartbeat.*

43

'So, eventually, Fiona came to live here?'

'Yes. The court granted me a guardianship, initially for a year, but then it was extended once, and then twice, and then permanently. I tried to give Fiona the best opportunities life could bring. I sent her to private school, she learnt the piano, we went on trips together, holidays, to the kinds of places I could only ever *dream* of going when I was her age. I had staff here, so she never had to worry about anything: she could just get on with her studies, her life, friends, and make the best of everything.' He stilled, something patently troubling him, colour forming amongst the fine mesh of blood vessels in his cheeks. 'But there was something wrong with Fiona.'

'Wrong how?'

He glanced at me. 'She liked to hurt people.'

8

I stared at Carling, trying to interpret his use of *hurt*.

There were people that hurt others emotionally and psychologically. And there were people that hurt others physically. One wasn't worse than the other. Both were weapons that could mortally wound. But could that really be who Fiona was?

'She was just so angry all the time,' he said quietly.

'That was how she hurt people?'

'Yes.'

'Was she angry at you? At others?'

'I didn't see her much with others.'

'So how did she hurt you?'

He didn't answer, drawing in a long breath.

'Jonah?'

'Do you have a picture of Fiona's children?' he asked.

I considered pushing on, telling him I didn't, but I wanted him engaged and pliable, so I went to the pockets of my coat and got out a small pile of photographs that Rebekah had handed me. I selected one of her and her two brothers – taken when they were all in their twenties – and handed it over.

'Oh,' he said softly, 'goodness. She looks like Fiona.' His eyes moved back and forth between Rebekah, Johnny and Mike. 'This brother too,' he added, and signalled Johnny. 'He has the same nose, the same mouth.' His gaze lingered on the siblings.

'How did Fiona hurt you, Jonah?'

With another long, drawn-out breath, he said, 'The things she would say to me, the way she threw all the opportunities I gave her back in my face. She was like her dad. She had a self-destructive streak a mile wide. It wasn't there for the first three or four years she was here, but once she hit sixteen, seventeen, she began to sabotage every chance I gave her. It was hell. She just became unmanageable.' He handed me back the photograph. 'Her grades started slipping, I'd be getting calls from the school saying she was being disruptive. I was constantly having to turn up there because she'd done some stupid bloody thing: hit someone, or stolen something, or been caught smoking – it just went on like that, this lurid parade of infractions, until she finally got herself suspended. She never sat her A-Levels – even though she would have aced them.'

'She dropped out of school?'

'Yes.'

'To do what?'

'She said she wanted to work.'

'And did she?'

'Hard to say,' he replied, his voice filled with sorrow. 'After that, I didn't see her very much. She'd come back occasionally, usually when she needed money, but she spent a lot of time away, doing who knows what. I saw her for the last time a couple of weeks after her eighteenth birthday. She packed a suitcase . . .'

He faded out. *And then she was gone.*

'I mean, I get it,' he said. 'Her dad was an addict who basically abandoned her from the day she was born, and her mum was gone from her life before she even became a teenager. And I wasn't blood to her, although I'd always treated her and her mum as if they were. I can see all the triggers.' He looked out of the window again; maybe out to the places he and Fiona had occupied during those initial, settled years together. 'I always hoped she'd come back. I'd sit downstairs and watch the gates sometimes, waiting for her to walk up to them – to see me, to wave. But she never did.'

I made a couple of notes, giving myself a second to think. Could it have been that same self-destructive streak that led to her disappearance in 1985? I didn't want to get into the story of how Fiona had gone missing, because it would derail the momentum I had now, but it was impossible not to wonder if that anger, that need to lash out, might have been the reason she suddenly walked out on her family and her kids. Taking out the condolence cards that Fiona – or someone purporting to be her – had sent to Rebekah and her family, I laid them beside Carling.

'Have you ever received a card with a design like this?'

He picked them up, examining them.

'No,' he said eventually. 'No, I don't think so.'

'I don't suppose you have any examples of Fiona's handwriting here?'

He frowned. 'Her handwriting?'

'I'm trying to work out if these cards came from her.'

Carling opened one of the cards and then he understood: 'She wrote this?'

'That's what I'm trying to find out.'

He thought about it for a moment and then started shaking his head. 'No, I don't think I have any examples of her handwriting. I'm sorry.'

I reached across again and took all the cards back.

'Did you ever try getting in touch with her after she left here?'

'Yes, twice. Once when she was twenty-four – so, 1979, I guess – because I just really missed her; kept wondering what she was up to. The truth turned out to be quite mundane. She was sleeping on the floor of a friend's flat in Cambridge, and the guy I hired said she was working as a checkout girl. It was her sixth job in a year.'

I looked at my notes and realized that must have been only a couple of months before Fiona met Henry on a night out in Cambridge. It made me wonder what she'd seen in Henry that had stopped her so suddenly in her tracks. Her behaviour, the self-destruction, appeared to have come to the surface again six years later when she walked out on her family – but Henry Murphy had been enough to alter her path for a while. Maybe, for a time, Fiona had found the kind of stability with Henry she didn't know she was looking for.

'You said you tried looking for her a second time as well?'

'That's right,' Carling said. 'The second time a friend of mine from the Met got in touch with me. I knew him from a charity we were both involved in. He was newly retired. He said he'd been back into the office to see some old friends and had found out that Fiona

47

had been reported missing by her husband. He saw one of her previous addresses was here, and because we knew each other, he called me and offered to look into what was going on.'

'This was December 1985 into January 1986?'

'Gosh.' He thought about it. 'Yes, that sounds about right.'

'And how did your friend get on?'

'I called him a couple of weeks later, just to check in, and he told me he had nothing.'

'What did he mean by "nothing"?'

'I mean, he couldn't find any trace of Fiona anywhere. In fact, he couldn't find anything out about Fiona at all.'

I frowned. 'Apart from basic personal details like she was married and had kids, presumably?'

'No,' Carling said. 'He didn't even have that much.'

It shouldn't have been hard to find evidence of Fiona Camberwell becoming Fiona Murphy, *or* to find evidence of Fiona Murphy having three children. It was right there in the missing person's report that Henry had filed.

'What was the name of your friend?'

'Mark,' Carling said. 'Mark Levin.'

'And how long was he with the Met?'

'Twenty-five years.'

Twenty-five years and he couldn't find anything.

Something didn't feel right.

'I've often thought about looking for her again,' Carling said, and as he exhaled, I could hear the rattle in his chest. 'I've got organ failure. It's slow, but it's happening. Quite a number of times over the last few years she's been in my thoughts and I've wondered whether to pick up the phone to someone, just so I have an answer before I finally go on.' He pushed out a smile: small, sombre. 'But I don't know . . . Maybe it's best not knowing.'

'Why do you say that?'

'When Fiona left like that, it just cut me so deep. I *know* she wasn't mine but, in my looking after her, I felt so connected to her and her mother. So maybe that's why I haven't looked for her again in the years since Mark did. Because, to be honest with you, David, I've come to realize that, deep down, the only thing worse than not knowing where she is and what she's been doing with her life is realising that she's . . .' He stopped, blinked, his eyes moist again. *Dead*. 'Sometimes the truth is worse.'

'Sometimes it is,' I said, although it wasn't much more than words of comfort for an old man at the end of his life, because – in working missing persons – I'd long since come to realize that the truth was infinitely better than not knowing, however frightening it seemed. The truth could be devastating, and terrifying, and forlorn – but it gave you an ending. Not knowing was like a disease you could never shake: it kept growing inside you, a sickness that replicated and flourished, and refused to die out.

'I'd love to meet her children,' Carling said softly.

I just nodded, not wanting to promise anything. Instead, I said: 'Your police friend who looked for Fiona, Mark Levin – I'd like to speak to him if possible.'

Carling grimaced.

'I take it that's not going to happen?'

'Unfortunately not. He died a long time ago.' Carling paused, a mournful silence. 'Actually, he died quite soon after he started looking for Fiona.'

I glanced up from my notebook. 'Really? How soon?'

'Three weeks, a month – something like that.'

'How did he die?'

'It was tragic, actually. He drowned. Slipped into a canal.'

'And – what? – he couldn't get back out again?'

'He was too drunk.'

I studied his expression. 'And that surprised you?'

'Yes,' Carling said. 'Before that, Mark had been sober for twenty years.'

9

On the train back into London, I went over everything Jonah Carling had told me. Fiona's self-destruction, as Carling had put it, wasn't much of a surprise given her tumultuous upbringing: it sounded as if her mother did her best to shield Fiona from her father's addiction, his absence in their lives, but there was only so much she could do. And after she passed on, it was bound to hit Fiona hard: maybe not straight off the bat, as she was only ten at the time, but grief – the clinging, suffocating feeling of losing someone you loved – always landed eventually.

Yet, despite all of that, the information that Carling had given me on Fiona was actually bothering me much less than what he'd told me about his friend, Mark Levin, the former detective at the Met. Levin had started looking for Fiona around the first week of January 1986 – and just three weeks later, he was dead. According to Carling, Levin had left behind no notes or paperwork on the case.

The whole thing felt off.

Even if he'd only been working it for a few weeks, a man with Levin's level of experience should have discovered that Fiona had been married and was a mother inside a few minutes. Instead, he'd told Carling he couldn't find anything on Fiona at all. But it wasn't just the fact that he appeared not to have done even as much as a basic background check. I also didn't like the fact that – twenty years after he'd given up the booze – he'd got so drunk, he ended up drowning in a canal. I didn't like the fact that it happened so soon after he was employed to search for Fiona either. Him taking the case, him suddenly falling off the wagon, him dying – all of it felt relevant.

I waited for a signal to flicker back into life on my phone, watching as the train passed endless farmland, and then went to Google and looked for Levin.

There was nothing.

And then, a second later, my mobile came alive in my hand.

As soon as I saw the caller ID, my heart sank. It was the same number that had been phoning me for the last four and a half months. I knew I could easily let it go to voicemail, even ignore the message entirely – but, eventually, I'd have to call back.

I didn't have a choice.

This was a trap I couldn't escape from.

Healy

This Afternoon

With a low buzz, a door opened at one end of the room.

The Visitor Centre was long and narrow, the floor a dark grey rubber, the walls off-white, long strip lights all the way down. The ceiling was charcoal-coloured and could have been the sky outside: stormy and turbulent, a flinty shelf of cloud.

Running under the strip lights were three rows of plastic chairs, segregated by low white tables. On one side of each table were two blue chairs; on the other was a single red one. In front of the red chairs, on the floor, was a line. It marked the border between those who came here to visit and those who were here permanently.

Security cameras, half-domes fixed between the strip lights, watched as visitors filed in, heading towards the blue chairs. When they were all seated, there was a lull, expectation in the air – excitement too, especially amongst the children who'd come to see their dads – and then a second door opened at the other end.

Most of the prisoners were dressed in their own clothes but a few arrived at the Visitor Centre wearing grey jogging bottoms and a grey sweater, which meant they were new. New prisoners tended to wear the 'uniform' for the first couple of weeks.

Colm Healy was long past that.

He looked around for who'd come to visit and was surprised to see Detective Inspector Martine Parkes waiting, as far down the room as it was possible to get. She was in a black trouser suit and cream roll-neck sweater and was tapping out a rhythm on her leg with her fingers.

Healy sat in the red chair opposite her.

'We must stop meeting like this,' he said.

A smile twitched at the corner of Parkes's mouth. He hadn't known her before this had started, but he'd got to know her pretty well since, and she did this often: paused, gave herself a second to think, even in response to lines like the one Healy had used.

'How you doing, Colm?'

'Couldn't be better. You?'

'Oh, you know.' A beat. 'Surviving.'

'Yeah, it must be tough not being in prison.'

Another hint of a smile. Parkes was blonde, slim, always well dressed – but it was her eyes that Healy was drawn to. There was an intelligence written into them, a vigilance, a fairness – most of the time, at least – that he liked. In another life, he often thought that he and Parkes could have been two sides of the same coin because those were qualities he'd always prided himself on having when *he* was a cop. In another life, but not this one.

In this one, Healy's career as a cop was dust.

'Is this a social call?' Healy asked.

Parkes's fingers stilled now. Healy knew she wouldn't have turned up here to check on his wellbeing, but he also couldn't think why she would come here alone, or why she hadn't scheduled a formal meeting. If her plan was to work him over with more questions, or try and pick apart his story – like she'd been doing ever since he was arrested – she must have known the first thing he'd do is 'no comment' her and ask for his solicitor.

'I thought we could just have a chat,' she said.

'A chat?' It was Healy's turn to smile this time.

'Aren't you getting tired of all of this?'

'All of what?'

'The lies you're telling.'

'What lies are those?'

'You've already been in here four and a half months. Do you really want to go to court and perjure yourself on the stand? You do that, you're looking at *serious* time.'

'It sounds like I might need my solicitor.'

Parkes didn't seem thrown by the comeback. 'I'm not trying to trick you, Colm. I can't bring anything in here with me, as you know, so you can be totally honest.'

'I wasn't worried that you were recording me.'

She opened her hands out in an appeasing gesture. 'No one at the station knows I'm here, genuinely. This is an off-the-record chat.'

'No one at the station knows.' He smirked. 'Right.'

'It's the truth.'

'I'm sure it is.'

She sighed. 'You and your pal Raker are so alike – you know that?'

'I keep telling you, I barely even know him.'

'See, this is what I mean, Colm.' Parkes looked at him like you might look at an unruly child. Healy kept his expression steady, stoic, his eyes on her. 'I really do think it would be a mistake for you to go into court in the new year and spout this sort of shit in front of a jury.'

'What, the truth?'

'We both know it's not the truth. You *know* Raker.'

'No, I don't.'

'Yes, you do. We've got witnesses who saw you two running around together at that place over in east London.' She stopped, letting him fill in the rest: she was referring to a forest called Hark's Hill Woods – or the 'Dead Tracks' as it was nicknamed locally. 'Actually, it's even better than that. We've got people *on record* telling us they saw you running around togeth—'

'We weren't "running around together".'

'But you *were* together in that place.'

'I was trying to find out what had happened to my daughter.' At the mention of Leanne, he paused, swallowed. 'No one gave a shit about her at the Met – the same people who, I assume, are these fabled "witnesses" of yours – so I had to go get the answers myself. Raker was at the Dead Tracks at the same time trying to find that missing girl. We spent an hour together. It was mutually beneficial. The end.'

'Come on, Colm. He "happened to be there"?'

'What, it's a crime to be in the same place as someone else?'

'No, but you lying about this makes us think you might be lying about the even bigger and more serious stuff that you're being accused of.'

Healy just shrugged.

Keep your eyes on her.

Don't give anything away.

Stick to what you and Raker rehearsed.

'I know a couple of people who worked with you,' Parkes said. 'They had some nice things to say about you, Colm. You were a good cop for a while there.'

She was trying to get a rise out of him.

'I don't want to see good people make mistakes.'

'I'm in here,' he said. 'I guess I've made them already.'

'None of your mistakes are irredeemable. Yet.'

'Is that the official line from your superintendent?'

'He doesn't know I'm here. Like I said, this is all off-the-books.'

'Oh, of course.'

He weighted the response with as much sarcasm as possible – yet, in truth, Healy wasn't sure whether to believe her or not. He couldn't pick the lie in her face, couldn't see any deceit in it at all, but at the end of the day, Parkes was a cop chasing a conviction and that was a powerful incentive to bend the truth. When Healy didn't reply, she said, 'I don't want you in that witness box perjuring yourself.'

'You've said that already.'

'But you don't seem to be listening.'

'Why would I perjure myself?'

'Because you're going to stand up there next year and lie to a courtroom about what happened, instead of telling them the truth: eight years ago, you faked your own death, you altered DNA evidence to pull it off – and David Raker helped you do it . . .'

IO

'David, it's Martine Parkes.'

I moved through the ticket gates and out on to the concourse at King's Cross. I'd ignored Parkes's first attempt to get hold of me on the train – but only to give myself a moment to think. I knew she'd try me again, and as the train pulled in, that's exactly what happened.

'I'm right in the middle of something here,' I lied.

'Yeah, well, this won't take long.'

Before all of this, I wouldn't have let her dictate terms. I might even have just hung up on her. But not any more. 'What do you want?' I asked.

But I knew, because she always called about the same thing.

Almost five months ago, I'd been working a case where a couple vanished from inside a crashed, burning car – and, at the end of my search for them, beyond what I thought had been the conclusion, there was a final, devastating sting in the tail.

His name was Colm Healy.

A man whose death I'd helped fake in October 2014, who I'd helped survive off the grid for that entire time under a series of assumed identities, was finally dragged back to life, his unconscious body left outside a police station. Worse, around his neck had hung a handwritten message: *Seven years ago, I faked my own death. And David Raker helped me do it.* It had been the ultimate act of revenge from a killer called the Blackbird, a psychopath who had dug so deep into my life they'd eventually managed to find Healy.

In the time since, it had been a constant firefight: insulating myself meant denying Healy and I knew each other, something we'd practised in private before Healy was revealed. But we hadn't practised enough. Not anywhere near enough. And not ever in response to a situation like this. Now I couldn't even communicate with Healy about how best to deal with it – and adapt – because any contact we had instantly exposed the lie that we didn't really know each other.

'This is important,' Parkes said.

'It's always "important", but then I turn up and all you do is go over the same crap again.' Sometimes it was hard to keep a lid on my frustration, at the constant phone calls, the borderline harassment, the knowledge that always, at the periphery of my life and my work, there was this: the residual worry that one of these days Parkes was going to pick up the phone to me and *really* have something. 'What do you want to talk about?' I asked.

'Colm Healy, obviously.'

I didn't say anything.

'Did you hear what I said, Raker?'

'Yeah. I heard.'

You want to talk about a man I'm pretending not to know.

I'd helped Healy in the first place because I'd recognized his grief, the way the loss of his daughter, Leanne, had such obvious echoes with how I'd felt about my wife, Derryn. When he hit the bottom – fired from the Met, ostracized by his family – and begged for my help, when he told me he wanted to escape the life he'd ruined and couldn't see a future in, I couldn't do anything else but say yes. I always knew there could be consequences because our list of infractions was long: he faked his death by blackmailing a tech at a forensic lab, switching in someone else's DNA to convince the world that Colm Healy was dead; I'd helped organize a succession of fake IDs for him; we'd paid for those, the houses he stayed in, his entire life off the radar, through shell companies I'd set up; and I'd remained completely silent about all of it, even in police interviews.

The Met were going hard at Healy because he was a former cop who'd actively worked against them when he was trying to find his daughter, and who'd been fired in disgrace. But it wasn't just about revenge. After years of negative headlines and very public corruption scandals, the Met needed to show the public that malfeasance and impropriety wouldn't be tolerated, whether it was officers past or present. They had a reputation to repair and putting a cop behind bars was going to help.

Sometimes, though, it felt like they were coming for me every bit as hard as Healy, perhaps even harder. Down the years, they'd seen me as an enemy, a man who took their cold cases, who solved them when they couldn't, who didn't use traditional investigative tools, and who skirted the edges of the law. If they dug deep enough, they'd find out I hadn't just skirted it, although everything I did was for what I felt was the greater good. But the greater good wasn't a legal argument. My intention had never been to undermine the police, but that was how it had played out in their eyes. I didn't court the media – in fact, didn't speak to them at all – but the largely positive headlines about me didn't help. They were the headlines the Met weren't getting but the ones they craved. That was another reason why they were so focused on exposing me as a liar. A spectacular fall from grace sold newspapers and accelerated clicks, and if the Met could instigate mine, if they could show the ways in which I'd broken the rules, they could finally get me off the board and rebuild their reputation in the process.

Parkes had started talking again: '. . . to the station. We need to catch up about some things that have happened over the last few weeks.'

I took a breath, drawing the exasperation out, and then kept my voice even, pleasant. 'I've told you a thousand times, I barely even know Healy. I met him once or twice, and that was years ago. And yet you still keep coming back at me about it, asking me the same questions. And do you know what the worst part is? This whole line of enquiry is predicated on the word of the Blackbird.'

'Like I say, I want to fill you in on a few things.'

'I'm not in London at the moment,' I lied, trying to give myself a moment to think. Every other time Parkes had asked me to drop in at the station, she'd spent an hour going over the interview I did with the Met in the aftermath of Healy being discovered outside the police station. They were trying to catch me in a lie, a point of difference compared to the last time, and the time before that. Once they caught an inconsistency, they could get into it and prise it open. And there they'd find the truth about Healy and me: that we'd seen each other frequently over the last eight years. I trusted myself not to waver, not to give anything of that history away, and so far I hadn't. I knew I could keep to the story that Healy and I had talked about, and practised for emergencies, in the time before he was exposed.

Healy, though, I was less certain of.

He knew the story every bit as well as I did – that we didn't know each other, that we'd barely crossed paths, and whenever we had, it had been brief. That held up as a deception because almost no one had seen us together over the last eight years. I'd hidden him in south Devon, then in North Wales, and in a few backwater places in between. He'd worked on fishing trawlers, cash in hand. The only person he ever interacted with for any length of time was me.

But while I trusted him as an ex-detective, knew he still had all the instincts to dodge and weave police questions – because, once upon a time, he was on the other side of the table *asking* those questions – I worried about where he was answering their questions from. Prison was a pressure valve and the cops were going to crank it.

'I'm here until ten. When are you back in London?'

'Later on,' I said, vaguely.

'Which is when?'

'Look, I'll come to the station, but unless I'm under arrest or under caution, which I'm not, I'm not rushing back. Hard as it is to believe, I do actually have a job.'

This time, I hung up on her.

I paused, crowds washing past me, trying to think about what the fallout would be if I didn't turn up at the station later. Parkes had largely been pretty fair to me. It felt like she was just doing her job. Sometimes I even got the sense that a part of her didn't much like what she'd been tasked with, but that she didn't have a choice: her bosses were sending orders down the line, and she followed them, or she got put in disciplinary. And it was the bosses I worried about, and in particular one of her superiors: a detective superintendent called Aiden Phillips. I'd had a run-in with him a decade back, on the case that Healy and I had worked together on for the first time. Healy had still been a cop then and Phillips had never forgiven him for going against the Met. But Phillips's major problem was with me: on the case, I'd found a killer the Met had failed to and exposed police corruption in the process; corruption – unfortunately for Aiden Phillips – that had been going on right under his nose. So was that what all of this was? Payback? Was Aiden Phillips trying to force a mistake by making Parkes do the same thing to me over and over again?

Or did the two of them genuinely have something new?

As I headed into the Tube, I thought about my next moves. I had no choice but to turn up at the station tonight, because if I didn't, it created conflict, and if I rocked the boat, the cops came at me even harder. What I really needed now was to speak to Healy, restate our stories, our tactics and try to figure out our endgame.

But getting to speak to Healy was impossible.

Unless I did something I didn't want to do.

Something that was going to hurt.

11

For the moment, I put Healy to the back of my mind. I'd have to take care of it, would have to set in motion any plan I came up with before I went into the station tonight, but for now I returned to Fiona and to the death of Mark Levin.

After a few phone calls, I discovered that, at the time he drowned in January 1986, he'd been living in a terraced house off Warwick Avenue, only about ten minutes' walk from where he died. I also found out that his widow, Georgie, still lived there.

I got off the Tube at Paddington and walked the rest of the way, following the approximate route Levin had used that night.

Today was freezing cold, the canalside virtually empty, and I imagined it was even quieter the night Levin went in the water. This area wasn't as developed then, but even if it had been, it was an unfortunate spot to lose your footing: from where I was standing, I couldn't see anyone coming up behind me because of the way the path kinked and narrowed; up ahead, on the other side of a bridge, it arced to the left. Up top, on the bridge itself, there were no sightlines: drivers and passengers in passing cars weren't going to be able to see the water, much less anyone walking the path.

Alarm bells had been ringing from the very second Jonah Carling had told me about how Levin died, and they were definitely ringing now. Being here just solidified my thinking: this was a perfect place to commit a murder and make it look like a suicide, chosen precisely for its location and its obscured lines of sight. It was also the perfect spot for another reason: there was an escape route on this side of the bridge – a set of stone steps that ascended to the road at the top.

Moving on, I passed under the bridge and then across Rembrandt Gardens to Warwick Avenue. I found the address a couple of minutes later. It was in a narrow, mews-like lane, with cream-render terraced houses on both sides. There was no front garden, just paving slabs and a small, attractive pond, with flame-coloured fish gliding beneath the surface. I opened the gate and buzzed the door.

Before long, I saw movement.

A woman in her eighties answered, her hair a cloud of grey, her body slightly bent, as if she was struggling with her back. She kept one hand on the door and didn't open it fully, just took me in with a pair of bright blue eyes that flashed in the low winter sun. 'Mrs Levin? My name's Dav—'

'I'm not buying anything.'

I smiled. 'I don't blame you.'

Her gaze stayed on me. I took out a business card and held it out to her. 'My name's David Raker. I find missing people.'

That usually piqued interest and Georgie Levin wasn't any different: she reached for the card, looked at my name and contact details, then back to me.

'Missing people?' she said.

I nodded.

'What's that got to do with me?'

'I'm looking for a woman called Fiona Murphy.' I paused, waiting to see if the name registered. 'Her maiden name was Camberwell. She vanished in December 1985. I believe your husband looked for her after he retired.'

This time, her face moved; I just wasn't sure if it was because she remembered Fiona or if it was simply that the mention of *December 1985* reminded her of the husband she'd lost soon after.

'Do you recall Mark looking for Fiona Murphy?'

'Maybe.' A brief pause. 'It was a long time ago but I think so, yes.'

I got the sense it was more than *think*.

'Would you have a moment to talk?'

She didn't look like she was keen and I didn't blame her: it was almost dark, and – other than a business card – she had no idea who I was.

'I don't expect you to invite a stranger into your home, so I'm happy to talk somewhere more public,' I said to her. 'Alternatively, you should be able to find stories on Google about me.'

'Stories?'

'Newspaper stories. Just to see that I'm that person on the card there.'

Her mouth formed an O.

Her brain was going, her eyes flicking between me and the business card she had pinched between her fingers. It felt like, if she didn't want to talk to me at all, she would have already said no, but I took a half-step back anyway – creating a physical space between us – in order to give her more breathing room.

'All right,' she said finally.

'I appreciate it. Where would you like to talk?'

'We can talk inside the house but – no offence, son – I don't know you from Adam, so I'm going to ask my neighbour to come in here and just sit with us, okay?'

'That's fine.'

But then her eyes glazed over for a moment.

'Mrs Levin?'

She continued looking at me, holding my gaze before something finally gave way in her face. 'Call me Georgie,' she said softly.

'Georgie. Is everything okay?'

'It's just this woman you're trying to find.'

'Fiona? What about her?'

She shrugged. 'I think she's the reason I'm a widow.'

12

Georgie's neighbour was a bear of a man called Clive. He was in his sixties, about six-three and eighteen stone, and had a sleeve of tattoos on one arm. As Georgie made us all a cup of tea, he told me how him and his wife had lived next door for years and that 'Mrs L' had been like a surrogate grandparent to his four kids.

'Did you ever meet her husband?'

'Mr Levin? Me and the missus only moved in a few months before he died, so only a couple of times. He always seemed sound.' He lowered his voice, glancing towards the kitchen. 'Mrs L talks about him a lot, but she doesn't talk a lot about his death; the way he died. Drowning like that, I mean.'

'What *does* she say?'

Clive glanced into the kitchen again, saw Georgie was adding milk to the teas, and then leaned in: 'Mostly, she says the same thing. He was "distracted".'

'"Distracted"?'

'In the weeks before he died.'

Georgie came back with two cups, put them down on the table between us and then returned to the kitchen to pick up the third and a plate of biscuits. She'd refused my help, Clive's too. I wondered if maybe she didn't get many visitors, because when I looked around the cluttered, old-fashioned living room, I didn't see any pictures of family, just ones of her and Levin.

'Thank you for this,' I said, picking up my tea.

The TV was on mute, a local news presenter screaming soundlessly as she rode the rollercoaster at Seven Peaks, a huge, winter-themed fun fair somewhere up near the M25. Once Georgie sat down, she switched it off and said, 'So how can I help?'

'You said earlier that Fiona Murphy was the reason you're a widow.'

'Yes.'

'Do you mind if I ask what makes you say that?'

'Mark was just different after he took on that work.'

'Different how?'

She took a breath, turning her cup on its saucer. 'He was a good man. Kind, always patient. That was why I married him. He loved his golf, loved his sport. He was a big cricket fan too. He'd always say, "Come and watch the cricket with me," and I'd say, "But I don't even *like* cricket." It was our little joke. I didn't really mind cricket, I just liked the fact that he asked me. He was my hubby – but a lot of the time he was my best friend as well.' She paused, a shimmer of sadness showing through now. 'Before he took on that work, he'd just retired, was doing odds and sods, finishing projects around the house that he'd put off for years. He was happy. It was nice seeing him content like that because he was with the Met a long time and I know there was a lot he didn't tell me. A lot he bottled up. I mean, it's not like you have to *be* a policeman to understand the things they must see. It's all over the news every night.' She gestured to the dormant television. 'In retirement, I liked it that he didn't have any of that to worry about any more. We would sometimes stay in bed all morning, just reading, or we'd go out for lunch, or we'd go for walks. After he left the police force, it was like a part of him that I'd forgotten even existed . . .' A beat. 'It returned to me for a while.'

'So he retired from the Met when?'

'August 1985. I remember because we had the whole of September off and took a three-week trip to Italy. We didn't travel a lot when he was in the police.'

'And then he contacted Jonah Carling about Fiona?'

'Yes. They knew each other through a charity thing.' Carling had already told me the charity had been the Met Police Benevolent Fund. 'That was when he became different. Something changed once he started looking for that woman. It was like night and day.'

'In what ways was he different?'

She frowned, trying to cast her mind back. 'I don't know. Quieter, I suppose. A little restless. Even when he was with the Met, he never really had a problem sleeping at night, but I noticed pretty quickly, after he took on that work, that he was struggling to go off. I have a memory of waking up once and not finding him in bed next to me, and coming downstairs to see where he was. And he was . . .' She stopped. 'He was in here, about where you are now. He was just . . .' Her words fell away again, then she reached to her tea. 'Honestly? It was like he was in some kind of trance.'

'A man with a lot on his mind.'

'Yes,' Georgie said. 'Yes, exactly.'

'Did he ever discuss his search for Fiona?'

'Not really. I asked.'

'But he didn't want to share?'

'Didn't want to, couldn't, shouldn't – I don't know.'

'So you don't remember much other than Fiona's name?'

She shook her head. 'No. Mark had gone back into the office for a New Year's party, I think – his colleagues had invited him, even though he'd just retired – and he said he saw that woman, Fiona, on a missing person's poster in there. One of the previous addresses listed underneath was a house that belonged to Jonah Carling. He knew Carling, so he picked up the phone to him.'

'Okay. And what about Mark's drinking?'

'That's the thing,' she said, 'he *wasn't* drinking.'

'Not until he took the case?'

'No.'

'Was he an alcoholic?'

'He had some problems with the booze when he was younger. First part of our marriage too, I suppose. I don't know if he was an alcoholic, but he was drinking too much. But then he stopped. He'd been dry for twenty years . . .'

'Did you see him drinking straightaway?'

'As soon as he took on Fiona's case? No, absolutely not.'

'Did you see him drinking at all?'

'No.'

'So, he was either drinking in secret – or the first time he got back on the booze was the night he drowned?'

'Yes. And I don't think he was drinking in secret. I would have smelled it on him, seen the evidence of it. I think it's more likely that, for whatever reason, he got back on the drink that night, and then he liked the taste of it again, and he kept on drinking, and . . .' She came to a halt. 'And then he fell into that canal.'

I nodded. 'Is there anyone else you can think of who it might be worth me speaking to? Maybe people Mark worked with at the Met or family he may have talked to?'

'We don't have much in the way of family.'

'No kids?'

'No.' Something flickered in her face and it wasn't difficult to see that, inside her, there lay a deep well of sadness and the explanation for why there were so few family photographs.

'Do you know if he left behind any notebooks or paperwork?' I asked her, realising what a long shot it was: it was a thirty-seven-year-old case her husband had essentially told her nothing about, but I waited her out all the same.

'I'm not sure,' she said eventually.

'I know it's a long time ago.'

'It is, but there may be something upstairs.'

I leaned forward. 'You still have some of Mark's work things?'

'I don't know about that but there's a box in the loft you could look through.'

'Would you mind if I did?'

'No.' She blinked, sniffed, her eyes a little wet. 'If there's something there that can tell me why Mark ended up in a canal, then you can take every last thing I own . . .'

13

The attic was accessed via a hatch and a pull-down ladder. At the top, I could see a light switch and flicked it on and took in what Georgie had stored here: cobwebbed furniture; suitcases; old duvets and sheets.

Six big cardboard boxes.

There didn't seem to be much of interest inside the boxes at first glance: as I went through one, and then the next, all I could see was a reflection of the living room – lots of clutter, ornaments, keepsakes, much of it covered in a fine layer of dust.

But then I got to the final box.

I realized straightaway that this was the one Georgie was referring to. On top were some old golf trophies and, when I took those out, I found a plastic sleeve with photographs inside. Mark Levin stared out at me from the top one: I recognized him from pictures Georgie had of the two of them downstairs. I took them out. In one, he was in an office somewhere at the Met – a board full of pinned photographs and paper behind his head. Other men – presumably other cops – were either side, one of them in the middle of taking a drag on a cigarette. I didn't recognize any of them.

Levin looked to be in his mid-thirties – which probably meant the picture was taken in the seventies, as he'd retired from the Met at the age of forty-four, having done his twenty-five years. I set it aside and went to the next one: he was older here – maybe by a decade – and was with some friends outside a golf club. One of them was the same guy who'd been smoking in the shot taken at the office Christmas party.

Under that were older pictures of Levin in his childhood, with a couple who I guessed were his parents, and then some of him and Georgie in what must have been the initial stages of their relationship: they were late teens, early twenties. These photos were damaged or actually torn in some cases, which was presumably why they hadn't made the cut as part of the picture frames in the living room.

Under the photos were some card files, elastic bands around them.

I took the first one out.

On the front, in black marker pen, it said: *1981–1985*. I snapped off the band and flipped the front open. Inside was a mish-mash of paperwork from cases that Levin seemed to have worked on. The pages were all photocopied, and there were few pictures. Mostly, it was just raw information.

There was something else too.

None of the cases appeared to be complete.

In fact, each case only contained enough paperwork to give a general overview of what had gone on – the major moments, significant beats. What had prompted Levin to make copies? What had he hoped to achieve? Were all of these unsolveds?

Even if they were – and the idea was for him to bring them home and, in the quiet of retirement, start to look at them again – there was no way there was enough material here. Great chunks of each case were missing, so reopening them would be like trying to solve a puzzle without most of the pieces.

I closed the *1981–1985* file and opened another.

The front of this one was marked *1975–1980* and there were only a couple of cases in it, again incomplete. Under that was another, marked *1965–1975*. I opened that, laying it next to the others: a few more cases, except these were thinner, the starkness of the black and white photocopies bringing home the age of the cases, and the differences in complexity – and volume of paperwork – between a modern investigation and one from the sixties. Looking at the dates, then at the information on a few of the pages, it seemed a pretty safe bet that 1965 was when Levin had first made the switch from uniform to a detective in CID. Again, though, if these were all cold cases, and Levin's intention had been to try and solve them in retirement, why not copy every page? And why bring *these* cases home? Over the three decades that Levin had been a cop at the Met, he would have led or been a part of countless other investigations – what was it about these eleven?

I packed everything away again, except for the files and the photograph I'd found of Levin and his colleague from the Met, and took them downstairs.

'Can you tell me who this is?' I asked Georgie.

I showed her the picture of the man who'd appeared with Mark Levin in the office photograph and then again, a decade later, at a golf tournament. It was possible the man might not be around any more, but I figured it was worth a shot.

'Oh,' she said, 'that's Len.'

'Len?'

'Len Graves. He worked with Mark. They were friends.'

'Is Len still around?'

'Last I heard, he was in a retirement home north of the river.' She looked at the files I was holding. 'What are those?'

'They're old cases Mark was involved in.'

'Oh.' She appeared to remember them then. 'Yes, of course.'

'Do you know why he made copies of all of this stuff?'

'No. No, I have no idea.'

'Did you ever see him looking at these files?'

'No,' she repeated. 'I didn't even realize those were there until – what?' She looked at Clive. 'Nine, ten years ago?' He nodded in response. 'Clive was helping me clear out the shed, because we had gales and the roof got ripped off, and we found them buried in there.'

'They were behind some old tools,' Clive added.

'Did Mark spend a lot of time in the shed then?' I asked Georgie.

'He sometimes went out there to think when he was still with the police; just to clear his head. He loved woodwork, so he'd often chip away at something.'

So did that mean that Levin had deliberately hidden the files out

70

there? Or had he taken them to the shed – presumably with the intention of going through them – and forgotten about them? Why would they be hidden behind some tools if that was the case? And why would he bring them home at all if they didn't matter?

There was something else as well: despite all the police files, the golf trophies, the decades-old photos, the clutter, despite all the physical memories of Mark Levin's life for almost four decades that had been consigned to a series of cardboard boxes, one thing was missing.

Anything at all – any note, even a line – about Fiona Murphy.

It was like he'd never searched for her at all.

Devil

Unknown | *February 1985*

After landing at Heathrow, he spent his first week in London living in a dive near the Elephant and Castle. It had once been a huge, probably beautiful Victorian terrace house, but now it was a crumbling hotel, a peeling sign out front announcing it as THE ROCKINGHAM. When he checked in, the manager – a guy in his fifties, pot-bellied and with a cigarette propped between his lips – said, 'You can pay for an hour, or you pay for a month.'

'I'll pay for a week.'

'Suit yourself. Tenner a night.'

He handed seventy pounds over.

'Room 12. Second floor.'

He took the key and his suitcase, saw the elevator was out of service, and headed up the stairs. On the second floor, he walked all the way down to the end, passing a shared bathroom. Ideally, he didn't want to have to share, because when you shared with others, they got to know you: your face, your behaviour and routines.

But he didn't have a choice.

This place had been organized by Larsen and, on the phone, during the snatched conversations he'd been able to make at the payphone seven kilometres east of the farm, Larsen had assured him everything would be fine: 'No one will be looking for you there,' Larsen had said. 'It's the same place I stayed in when I first came out here. No one will notice you arrive, no one will notice you leave. It's a black hole.'

Larsen meant people came to the Rockingham to hide.

Or they came to disappear completely.

*

The room had a leak in the ceiling.

He noticed it on the first night, had seen the brown, concentric circles it had created, but he'd decided against bringing it up with the manager. He didn't want the attention.

On the second day, he went out and bought a bucket and placed it under the leak. Later on, he went to a phone box on New Kent Road and made the call he'd been told to make on the afternoon of his second day in London. He'd been given a number, nothing else, and at an answerphone, he left the message for Larsen – 'I'm in place' – and his room number.

That night, he listened to the soft *tap tap tap* of the leak in the ceiling hitting the metal. He couldn't drop off, but then he hadn't slept well at the farm for months either. He'd just lie awake inside its darkness, worrying and listening. It was why he'd had to get out of the country. Just because they hadn't come for him yet, it didn't mean they wouldn't. On the phone, Larsen told him it was a matter of when, not if, so at the farm he'd got into a routine of lying awake, eyes open, waiting for an attack; of spending all night listening for cars on the dust-blown track that wound up from the main road, or looking for movement in the tangle of grass that encircled the building. But when he did sleep there, when he finally got that snatched hour in the dead of night, at least the farm had been quiet.

That had been the whole point of it.

Here, nothing was quiet. It was just constant noise. He'd never been in a city like this before, where sound was perpetual; ceaseless traffic – car horns, the roar of engines, sirens, people shouting, the squeal of trains.

But he was going to have to get used to it.

This city was his home now.

On the third night, in the early hours of the morning, he finally dropped off.

'What do you tell your children you do?'

He keeps hearing her voice, even in these fleeting moments of sleep. But as her words echo through his head, the rest of the dream fills in, colouring, coming to

73

life, and he realizes he's not in the farmhouse, not in the room watching her scream and cough, blood at her nose, saliva on her lips. He's far away from her, far away from the farm, flat on his belly in the baking heat half a decade before any of that took place.

He's twenty-three.

He's seeing everything through the eyes of his younger self — so he can't see how he looked back then — but he knows. He remembers.

He can feel his youth.

Through the bush, he suddenly sees movement. The enemy. He glances to his left, where Larsen is on his belly too. Larsen gives him a sideways glance and brings a finger to his lips. He tears his gaze away from Larsen, his heart hammering even harder, and looks back to where the enemy is. He can see there's three of them, emerging one behind the other. They're all armed, eyes scanning the horizon.

One of them is just a kid.

He glances at Larsen again and, this time, Larsen makes a signal, a gesture that means 'left-hand side'. When he returns his attention to the enemy soldiers, he can see who is on the left, who it is Larsen has ordered him to take out: it's the kid.

He looks about fifteen.

He's all gangly limbs, a body that hasn't fully developed yet, skin so smooth that sweat just runs in rivers down his face, undisturbed by bumps, or blemishes, or scars. Out in front of him is his Kalashnikov, the end of the barrel tick-tocking from right to left as he walks, like a metronome. One of his arms is clamped hard to the underside, but even that appears awkward: his arms seem too small, too meagre.

This is a man's war.

And this is just a child.

He looks at the kid along the sights, feels the stock in against him, feels his finger on the trigger. He's shot the Vektor many times, firing it into the bush at the enemy. He's killed people before.

But he's never shot a child.

He knows inside the borders of this dream how the next part will go. Larsen will fire first, taking out the soldier in the middle. Bosman, on the other side of him — the third of them — will take out the soldier on the right. Then it's his turn. Three shots, three deaths. In this dream, he can already see it all coming.

He knows how the next minute plays out because it's seared into his memory: by the time the report from their shots has been swallowed by the humidity of the bush, the enemy soldiers will be face down in the dirt, half their heads missing.

A boy will be dead.

A mother will be mourning.

He knows all this — can see it in his dream so lucidly — because he's lived this moment over and over, returned to it, excavated it. He's searched these memories and wondered often if this was the start.

If this was the moment he changed.

If this was the birth of a devil.

PART TWO
The Informant

14

Len Graves, Mark Levin's friend and former colleague, was in a retirement home in Camden, just off Haverstock Hill. I took the Tube to Chalk Farm and found it easily enough – it was two vast, conjoined Victorian houses, with a brand-new extension at the front. They had an open-door policy so, even though it was now after 8 p.m., visitors were allowed at any time until nine.

I asked at the main desk where I might find Graves.

'He's probably in the day room,' one of the staff responded, and pointed along a corridor to her left. I thanked her and followed it down, passing a conservatory, an office, and then a second big space with a roll-down projector screen. Residents were still dotted around everywhere.

In the day room, I asked a woman to point out Graves to me and she gestured to the far corner, where a couple of men – both in their mid-to-late eighties – were talking to each other. 'He's the one in the blue shirt,' she said.

I walked over.

'Len?'

He looked up, so did his friend, and I could see them trying to figure out who I was: I didn't work at the home, I wasn't a friend or a relative that they recognized – so who was I?

'My name's David Raker.' I held out a business card. 'I'm an investigator.' He took it from me without saying anything, fished his glasses out of his top pocket, and as he studied the card, his friend left, telling Graves he'd catch up with him later on.

As I waited, I looked at Graves more closely, seeing the echoes of the younger version of him that had been captured in Mark Levin's photograph. The same vivid green eyes. The same slim physique. He seemed in pretty good shape, looked fit, and still had a dense covering of hair, even if it had got finer with age.

'So you work for yourself?' he asked, looking up at me.

'Yes.'

He gestured to the empty seat beside him.

'And you used to be a cop?'

'No.' I sat down. 'Grab your crucifix: I was a journalist.'

He laughed a little and then his gaze went back to the card. 'That's an unusual route into your type of work. I mean, I knew quite a few journalists in my time and, don't get me wrong, you lot were always the best drinking buddies. But most of you didn't give two hoots about anyone except yourselves. If we dangled even a *hint* of a big story in front of you, you lot were like rabid dogs in a cage.'

'I wasn't that type of journalist.'

'Oh, you were the fabled one with morals.' It sounded good humoured but I got the impression it wasn't a joke. 'Where did you work?'

'I was at *The Times*.'

'Doing what?'

'I was abroad a lot. I spent time in Iraq and Afghanistan. I lived in the States, and then South Africa before that.' I swung my bag around, and took out the cases that Mark Levin had kept in the loft. 'But I'm not here as a journalist. That part of my life is history. I haven't worked on a paper, haven't written a word, for a decade.'

He eyed me and I could see the blueprint of the old techniques he'd used at the Met: holding my gaze, trying to prolong the silence – but, after a while, he either realized it wasn't going to work, or he saw enough in my expression to know that I was genuine, because he said, 'Okay. So how can I help?'

'I'm trying to find a woman called Fiona Murphy.'

I watched for a reaction. Nothing.

'She disappeared on Boxing Day, 1985.' I got out the photograph of Fiona and handed it to him. 'Murphy is her married name. Her maiden name was Camberwell.'

He took it, examining her.

'I don't recognize her,' he said. 'Was she part of a case I was on?'

'Not that I'm aware of.' I took the photograph back from him and then flipped open my notebook. 'Four months after he retired from the Met, a friend of yours tried to find her.'

This time, something sparked. 'Oh,' he said, 'you're talking about Mark Levin? Blimey. He's been gone a few years now.'

'Do you remember him working this case in retirement?'

'I remember him working *a* case in retirement. I hadn't retired then, but the two of us used to play a round of golf a couple of times a week and we'd always have a catch-up – usually at the nineteenth hole.' He paused, smiling. 'I'm pretty sure that was where he told me he'd taken on some private work.' He glanced at the picture of Fiona. 'Fiona Murphy. Actually, that name does ring a bell now.'

'I know I'm asking you to go back a way here, but is there anything you can remember him saying about her case?' I stopped, giving him the chance to reply, but he was just shaking his head. 'The search for Fiona began in the first week of January 1986 and Mark drowned on the twenty-first. I've just spoken to his wife: she says Mark was different during the last weeks of his life.'

Graves nodded, like that tallied with what he knew as well. 'Yeah, I've bumped into Georgie a few times down the years, and she always says that.' He took a breath, his pale fingers a little crooked as he played with my card. 'They were married so she'd know better than me if that was true.'

'You're obviously familiar with how he died?'

'Yes, of course. He drowned in that canal.'

'And he was drunk.'

'Yes,' Graves said, his lips pressed together.

'You mentioned the nineteenth hole earlier . . .'

'That was a joke. I mean, we'd go to the clubhouse after a round of golf, obviously, but Mark was never on the booze. In all the time I knew him – maybe fifteen years – he never touched a drop. We'd both enjoy a pint – but his was always a pint of lime and soda.'

'Did he ever talk to you about his drinking?'

'He'd been sober for twenty years – there was nothing to talk *about*. As I said, I knew him a long time, and I never saw him take a drink.'

'So it surprised you when you heard?'

'That he got hammered the night he died? Absolutely.'

'You didn't see any signs of him being back on the booze before then?'

'Nothing.'

I placed a hand on the files.

'I found these in Georgie's loft,' I said, holding the manila folders out to Graves. 'There's eleven cases there. I haven't had a chance to properly go through them myself yet, but I had a brief skim-read on the train over here and I can't figure out what interested Mark about them.'

He took them and started going through them. 'He photocopied all of these before he left?'

'It looks that way. Any idea why?'

He was still leafing through them, lost in them – but, eventually, he shook his head. I felt a fizz of frustration but mostly I felt concerned that I was being drawn further and further away from the reason I was here in the first place: Fiona Murphy. I'd come to see Len Graves thinking I might be able to construct a bridge between Fiona and Mark Levin after he'd started his search for her. But right now, it felt like I was lost.

'From what I can see, those cases are all unsolved,' I said.

Graves nodded. 'I remember some of these.'

'Do you think that's what interested him about them?'

'It's possible, I suppose. But the only private work he talked to me about taking on in retirement was this Fiona Murphy woman you're . . .'

His voice trailed off.

He'd got to the last of Levin's files.

His gaze was on the disappearance of a woman on Thursday 19 December 1985. I'd noted the fact that she'd gone missing only a week before Fiona had vanished but hadn't been able to see anything else that might connect the two.

I tilted my head, and saw the woman's name and a black and white image of her face. Jennifer Johnson. She was last seen at a nightclub in Soho.

'Len?' I said. 'Have you remembered something?'

'This file,' he replied quietly. 'It's more complete than the others.'

He was right and it was something I'd noticed on the Tube up here: the other ten cases were between three and eighteen pages each. The Jennifer Johnson disappearance ran to twenty-seven.

Now I looked at it again, it might even have been the whole case.

And there was something else I noticed now as well: Levin had had some involvement in all of these investigations, but most he wasn't out front on. With Jennifer Johnson, even though he was retired, he'd been the one who'd filed the original missing persons report.

'Do you remember Jennifer?' I asked Graves.

'I do, yeah.'

'What do you remember about her?'

'Not much. Just that . . .' He paused. 'She used to be a grass.'

'An informant? For the police?'

'Yes.'

'Was she Mark's informant?'

'Yes, she was.'

I glanced at the photocopied pages in his hands, and a moment later he looked across at me. There was something else in his face.

Something he buried for his friend a long time ago.

'What's going on, Len?'

He looked at the other cases. 'I think these might just be noise.'

'Noise?'

'I don't think he was ever really interested in these other investigations.' He held up the Jennifer Johnson file. 'I think he used them as a hiding place for this one.'

'Why would he want to hide Jennifer Johnson?'

For a second, Graves didn't move.

'Len?'

'Because Jennifer wasn't just Mark's informant,' he said. 'She was his lover.'

15

'They were having an affair?'

Graves's eyes were still on the photograph of Jennifer Johnson.

'Not all of this stuff is clear to me now,' he said, and then paused again, and for the first time he suddenly seemed old, greyer, his green eyes dimmed. 'It all came out after Jennifer went missing, so, I guess –' he looked at the file again, '– December 1985. I remember Mark and I went for a round of golf after my shift was over, and I knew straightaway that something was wrong with him. He was normally full of beans – from tee-off to clubhouse – but he was different that day. His game was a mess, I could hardly get a word out of him, and we normally had something to eat when we were done but he just went straight home. I'd known him years by then, and I knew there was zero point in trying to prise the details out of him. With Mark . . . if he wanted to talk, it came out in its own time.'

'So he eventually told you about the affair?'

'A few days later, I picked him up and he just . . .' Graves stopped. 'He just burst into tears, right there in the car. I remember it like it was yesterday. I didn't know what to do to start with. I think I just asked him what was up.'

'And what did he tell you?'

'He said he and this woman had got very close. I don't remember the exact details, but he told me about Jennifer, said he had been seeing a lot of her, that she'd disappeared a week or so before Christmas and he'd been looking for her.'

'So he didn't actually say they were having an affair?'

'He didn't need to. It was obvious.'

'Okay. But I'm guessing Georgie had no idea what Mark was up to?'
Graves looked at me grimly. 'No.'

'Did Mark think Jennifer had come to harm?'

'I think that was the assumption.'

Jennifer disappeared on 19 December 1985, Fiona exactly a week later; both women were similar ages – Fiona had been thirty, Jennifer was twenty-nine the night she was last seen alive.

'You said Jennifer was Mark's informant. What sort of information was she giving him?'

'Obviously, I didn't even know she existed before he told me everything. That's the whole point of informants: the only person who knows that relationship exists is the cop and the grass. Back in the early-to-mid eighties, Mark was doing a lot of work – along with plenty of others at the Met – on trying to bring down this gangster called Jed McNamara. He was this absolute low-life in the East End who thought he was the second coming of the Krays. Drugs, guns, prostitution, murder-for-hire. He was a scumbag. Mark said he first came into contact with Jennifer when the Met raided one of the strip clubs McNamara ran in the West End. It sounded like she'd got in with the wrong people and had ended up as a waitress there, tottering around in heels and a thong delivering drinks to violent, drunken arseholes. Mark identified her as someone who could help the Met and then I guess they started to see more of each other as she was feeding him information.' He faded out, looked at me. 'He told me he managed to get her out of that life.'

'She stopped working for McNamara?'

'McNamara got a bullet in the back of the head the year after she disappeared – the end of 1986 – so his empire crumbled soon after. But, even before that, we were slowly getting our claws into his operation, dismantling it from the inside. Beginning of the eighties, if you threatened to walk away from McNamara and his crew, and especially if you were likely to talk to people like us, you'd be face down in the Thames the next day. But by the time Mark managed to pull Jennifer out of there – so, I don't know, 1983, '84 – McNamara was too busy plugging holes in his business to care. Mark said he got her out and managed to get her a job at some posh club.'

'The Castle, right?'

I gestured to Jennifer's missing person's report. On the front page, where her basic details were listed, it said her last place of employment was a private members' club in Holborn called The Castle. She'd worked in the restaurant. Its website was – presumably deliberately – vague, but said its membership was 'drawn from diverse fields including politics, arts and sport', and that The Castle gave them 'the perfect opportunity to connect with each other and grow their interests'. There were *About*, *Sign In* and *Membership* tabs, as well as photographs of the interior, which showed the restaurant, a rooftop pool and health spa. I couldn't find prices on the website – you had to use the *Membership* tab to contact them – but I found prices on websites *about* The Castle, and on those it said membership started at £4,000 a year.

'How did Mark get her a job there?' I asked.

'Our old chief super used to be a member.'

'So he pulled some strings for Mark?'

'Yeah, but I don't think Mark told anyone the whole story.'

'You mean about Jennifer's past?'

'Exactly. I think she and Mark basically fudged her work history, fudged her references. I mean, not that I care – everyone deserves a second chance – but Mark really went out to bat for her. That day he told me about her, it just kept coming – all this information – and I thought to myself, "You've got it bad for her."'

He looked across at me, lips tight.

'Did you ever go to The Castle yourself?' I asked.

'No. I think it's one of those places where you can only become a member if you're invited by another member, but you automatically get membership when you join as an employee. So Jennifer got a job there, became a member, she was then able to invite Mark, *he* signed up – and then I guess the two of them used the club to meet up in so they could continue their . . .' He stopped. *Affair*. 'Can I ask you something?'

'Of course.'

'What's all this got to do with her?'

He was pointing at the picture of Fiona I still had on my lap. I looked down at her, asking myself the same question. Levin had told Georgie that he saw a poster of Fiona pinned to a wall in the Met when he'd gone in for the New Year's Eve party; at the bottom of it Jonah Carling's mansion had been listed as a previous address. But I was starting to think that might have been a lie on Levin's part. It seemed more likely now that his reason for going to the party might not just have been to catch up with old friends, but to look for leads in the disappearance of Jennifer Johnson. Perhaps that had even been his sole reason for going in. Either way, he must have been digging around for similar cases to Jennifer and found Fiona – and, once he did, he then went to Jonah Carling and offered to kickstart a search for her.

But then what?

If he'd connected the two women, where was the evidence? Where were the notes Levin must have made? Where was *anything* from Fiona's case at all?

'To be honest, I'm still trying to figure that part out,' I said. 'Do you know how long the affair was going on?'

'He met Jennifer in '83 or '84, so a year? Two? After he told me that he'd taken on paid work and was trying to find this Murphy girl, I remember thinking, "I hope Mark doesn't go and get too obsessed with *another* woman."'

'"Obsessed"?'

He stopped, took a crisp white handkerchief from the breast pocket of his shirt, and dabbed at the corners of his mouth. 'I know it probably doesn't seem like it, given everything I've told you, but Mark was a good man. Too good sometimes.'

'Too good in what way?'

'He just got way too emotionally involved. In my years at the Met, I saw a lot of different cops – some good, some bad. Mark was one of the good ones, but he could never turn the tap off. He could never leave his cases at home. And with someone like Jennifer, where it went way *beyond* just working her case, well, that was dangerous.'

'Dangerous in what way?'

'He was burning himself out trying to find the answers. I mean, he wasn't only mourning the loss of a woman he'd obviously really cared about; he wasn't just working her case in his own time, harder and deeper than any crime that landed on our desks during his time at the Met; he was *then* working this other thing – this Fiona Murphy – simultaneously. All of it, all that pressure – Mark was the kind of guy who shouldered it all. He'd end up trying to fix things that sometimes couldn't be fixed.'

'What do you mean?'

'Like with Jennifer's parents. First few weeks after she vanished, he kept going back and forth to see her parents. It wasn't his job to do that, and they had no idea who he was to Jennifer, but it was like he felt he *had* to. The amount of miles he did trying to fix their grief . . . I don't know if it was guilt, or remorse, or just that excessive emotional investment he put into his cases, but he kept doing it – these constant journeys up and down to their house in Peterborough, to assure them –'

'Wait a second, wait a second. Peterborough?'

'Yes.'

'It says on the missing person's report that Jennifer was born in Leicester.'

'Yes, but I think the family moved to Peterborough when she was a baby.'

I felt a charge of electricity.

Fiona and Jennifer had disappeared within a week of one another. They'd both been almost exactly the same age. Both cases were investigated by the same man.

And now something else.

They'd both grown up in the same place.

16

I took the train to Leicester Square.

The whole way I kept thinking about what Len Graves had told me. It seemed almost certain that Fiona Murphy and Jennifer Johnson's disappearances were connected. I didn't have a smoking gun, a cast-iron evidential connection, but there were too many similarities to ignore now – the dates they went missing, their ages, their shared home town. The fact that the same man was looking into both cases was another compelling link. Mark Levin had gone to Jonah Carling, offering to instigate a search for Fiona, which meant he'd found the same connections I had.

And probably others.

But if that was true, why had Levin then conducted such an amateur search for Fiona? Why was there no paper trail, no indication that he'd ever done *anything* in an effort to find her? When Jonah Carling had called him after a couple of weeks to check in, Levin had claimed he'd found no trace of Fiona anywhere. *Literally nothing.* But that must have been a lie because he'd have had to look at Fiona's missing person's report in order to discover the similarities to Jennifer.

So why wouldn't he tell Carling the truth?

I let some ideas play out in my head, and after a while, I kept coming back to the same one: *Levin had found some other connection between the women and had kept it close to his chest. Because it was big. Big enough to put him, and anyone he confided in – like Jonah Carling – in danger. But then someone found out what he knew. The same person who pushed him into that canal. The same person that then went on to steal everything he'd collated on Fiona and Jennifer going missing. The only thing that person missed were the eleven files that Levin had hidden away in his shed.* It was just a theory, but it fit with everything I'd found out up until now.

As soon as I left the Tube station, I called Carling's number.

He sounded a little groggy.

'Is everything okay?' he asked.

'I just have a couple more questions.'

'Of course. Anything.'

'Do you remember a friend Fiona might have had called Jennifer Johnson?'

'Jennifer.' A long pause. 'That doesn't ring any bells, no.'

I felt a little of my fire douse.

'That doesn't mean she *wasn't* a friend of Fiona's,' he added. 'The older she got, the more . . .' He stopped. 'One of the many things we'd argue about was this place.'

'Your house?'

'She didn't like bringing friends here. I think she was embarrassed by its size. Or maybe she was embarrassed by me. I don't know.'

A much longer silence this time, full of pain and regret.

I moved on. 'How old was Fiona when she moved to Cambridge?'

'From Peterborough? Ooh, seven or eight.'

I'd been wondering if Fiona and Jennifer might have been school friends, but Fiona was ten months older than Jennifer and – because she'd been born in March 1955 and Jennifer in January 1956 – they would have been in different school years. So if they'd mixed, had it been outside of school? A club? A local organisation? Or had they lived near to one another and become friendly that way?

I asked Carling if he knew the name of the junior school Fiona had attended when she lived in Peterborough. It was a long shot – he hadn't yet become a part of her life then – but as he'd been keeping in contact with Fiona's mum, Cassandra, it was worth a go.

He told me to give him a second.

I kept walking, picking up my pace. The night was glacial, snow-flakes flittering in the air as I headed down Shaftesbury Avenue.

Carling came back on the line: 'Eastgate Primary.'

'Is that from memory?'

'No, I've got some of her things here.' He sounded wistful again. 'After Cass passed on and Fiona's dad was out of the picture, I took ownership of a lot of the stuff that Cass kept from when Fiona was a kid – you know, drawings, her school photos, that sort of thing. Anyway, on one of the photos of her – she must be about five or six in this picture – it's got the name of the school printed on it.'

'Have you got a home address anywhere there for Fiona?'

'Yes. Raddison Avenue. It's on the back of a school report here.'

I thanked Carling and hung up, stopped and got out my note-book, and wrote down the name of the school and the road Fiona had lived on in Peterborough. Next, I called Ewan Tasker. He was still at Scotland Yard, about to head home. I asked him if he could do a quick search for me.

'Is it going to land me in the shit, Raker?'

He was joking. Well, maybe *half*-joking.

'No,' I said. 'I just need an address.'

'Okay. Hold on.' He went to a computer. 'What's the name?'

'Jennifer Johnson. DOB 3 January 1956.'

The tap of keys and then: 'She's missing.'

'Yeah, since December 1985.'

'And you think her address is still going to be useful?'

'I'm actually looking for previous addresses if there are any.'

'Last known address is here in London: Flat 4A, Signal Lane, N1. That's up in Islington.' That was the one I had, listed in her missing person's report.

'Nothing else?'

'Just the address of her parents.'

'They were in Peterborough, right?'

'Yeah. 102 Fortescue Road.'

It could have been her childhood home. I thanked Tasker, ended the call, went to GoogleMaps on my phone and put in 102 Fortescue Road to see where it took me.

As the pin dropped, I felt a shot of adrenalin.

Eastgate Primary, the junior school that Fiona had attended, was *on* Fortescue Road, Jennifer's house only a stone's throw from the school gates.

And there was something else too.

Raddison Avenue, the road that Fiona had lived on, was a cul-de-sac opposite the school, Fiona's childhood home right on the corner.

The women had basically been neighbours.

17

The red-brick, four-storey building was just off Shaftesbury Avenue.

I pushed the buzzer for the top floor and waited, resetting my thoughts. This visit wasn't about Rebekah, or my search for Fiona.

This was about Healy.

My heart was beating fast. I hadn't been back here in ten years and didn't have a clue as to what kind of reception I was going to get.

But it was too late to back out.

'Yes?'

I leaned into the intercom. 'It's David Raker.'

The door bumped away from its frame. I moved inside, past an unmanned front desk to a set of elevators at the back. Calling the lift, I waited, thinking again about Healy, picturing him alone in a cell at Pentonville, and about the conversation I'd had with Martine Parkes earlier. She'd asked me to drop in at the station before 10 p.m. and it was already well after nine. I'd still be able make it to Parkes tonight but I liked the idea of being late. It was a petty and ultimately insignificant power play, but I'd danced to the Met's tune for nearly five months and I was sick of it. Any victory – however small – I took.

Immediately outside the elevator on the top floor there was a set of double doors with windows that allowed me a glimpse into the open-plan office beyond. The space was small, but there were twenty empty desks and two cube-shaped meeting rooms, the blinds half-drawn at both. A woman was working at a desk right outside one of them, AirPods in. She looked like she was transcribing.

Just then, my phone started buzzing.

Speak of the devil.

It was Parkes.

'I'll be there,' I said, by way of a greeting.

'Don't bother,' she replied.

'What are you talking about?'

'I've just landed a case. I'll give you a call tomorrow.'

She hung up.

As I stared at my phone, I felt a wave of relief. I wasn't going to have to go into the station tonight, which meant I could switch my full attention to this.

I pushed a buzzer next to the doors.

Inside the office, the woman at the desk looked up at me, took her AirPods out and then made her way over.

'You must be Mr Raker,' she said as she opened up.

'David.'

She pointed to one of the cubes. 'Just give her a minute.'

I entered the cube and set my bag down. Suddenly, I felt nervous again. I took out my notebook and pen and laid them on the table. And then I heard voices and footsteps.

A second later, the person I'd come to see appeared in the doorway.

I didn't know what kind of reaction I would get from her but I was relieved to see it was a smile. She still looked so good. She'd cut her hair short, into a stylish bob, was fit and immaculately dressed. She came in, putting down a notebook of her own, and – closer in – I could see there were a few more lines on her face, as there were on mine, time showing itself on both of us. But it didn't detract from her beauty. If anything, at fifty-three, she seemed to have grown into her body even more, a natural colour in her cheeks, her smile still the one that – even if a room was packed, and people were vying for her attention – made it feel like you were all that mattered.

It was hard to believe it was ten years since I'd last seen her.

Or ten years since we'd broken up.

Elizabeth Feeny pulled out a chair and sat down, the two of us still not having said anything, but smiles on both our faces. For a moment more her dark eyes held mine, and then, finally, she said, 'So what sort of trouble are you in this time, Raker?'

Healy

Healy looked around the Visitor Centre.

In the next group of chairs down from him and Parkes, a new prisoner – still wearing his grey jogging bottoms and grey sweater – was leaning forward, elbows on his knees, talking to a girl of about four. It must have been his daughter. The girl was listening intently to what her dad was saying, giggling every so often, and when she did, the sound was so perfect, so unblemished and innocent, it was possible – just for a second – for Healy to believe he was somewhere else; somewhere better. He tried to listen to what the man was telling the girl, but the room was too noisy, so instead he remembered the conversations he'd had with Leanne when she'd been that age. He couldn't remember many, but he remembered some – and every one filled his heart.

'Colm?'

Parkes's voice ripped him from the memory.

'What?' he said, irritated.

'Did you hear what I said? You faked your death, you altered DNA evidence to pull it off, and David Raker helped you do it. Why don't you just tell me the truth?'

'I told you, I don't know the guy.'

'Colm.' She stared at him. 'Come on.'

He stayed silent.

'Faking your death,' Parkes said, 'that's not actually the problem. It's the other stuff you've accumulated along the way. I mean, the reason you haven't seen the light of day since July is because you're a flight risk – and you're a flight risk because, basically, the court can't trust you not to whip out another fake ID and go missing again. But you can change all this, Colm.'

'Yeah?'

'Yeah. And you don't have to perjure yourself.'

'This again? Really?'

'I'm trying to make you understand.'

'What's being a flight risk got to do with perjuring myself?'

'Nothing. I'm simply illustrating how the cards are already stacked against you here.' Parkes paused, searching Healy's face. When he gave her nothing, she said, 'So let me be even clearer: there's two reasons you're still eating shitty prison food four and a half months after we put you in handcuffs. One is a decomposed body we found eight years ago. It wasn't *your* body, because you're sitting here today in this beautiful Visitor Centre, and yet the DNA evidence the lab produced for us says that it was.' She looked at Healy once again and, once again, he didn't say anything, but it was harder to sustain eye contact with her this time. Much as he liked her eyes, much as he saw decency in them, there was an intensity sometimes that made him squirm in his seat.

Casually, he looked out at the room – just so he could break eye contact with her – and said, 'All of this: you've told me it all before.'

'Yeah, well, let me go over it again.'

'Don't bother on my account.'

But she picked up the conversation as if she'd never even stopped: 'We've been to the lab and interviewed everyone there. The Met has been using them for years, without any issues, but that doesn't exclude any of the techs as a potential suspect, which is why we're still there interviewing all their employees past and present. If you colluded with someone there, we're going to find out. *Or* something else happened: you personally managed to tamper with that DNA evidence before it ever arrived at the lab. Am I getting warm here?' Parkes linked her hands, clearly not expecting an answer, and not getting one. 'But let's just say, for the sake of argument, that we *don't* end up getting to the truth, because you and Raker are such smooth operators that the whole DNA switch turns out to be a complete dead end for us . . . Well, we've still got you, Colm, because we went to that house you were renting under an assumed name up there in North Wales – the one you'd been living in for over two years before you were finally outed – and we turned that place inside out, and amongst other things we didn't like, we found a fake passport with your photo in it.'

Healy waited, saying nothing, trying to use the noise of the Visitor Centre to focus on. He didn't want to give Parkes anything – not a movement of the lips, not a shift of the eyes. He didn't even blink. Instead, he thought of Raker, wondering what he was doing right now, what discussions Parkes had had with him, and where she might find inconsistencies between their stories. The two of them had prepared for exactly this moment, war-gamed ways in which this might play out – maybe not in exactly the order it had gone down, but they'd prepared for a day when Healy's death was finally exposed as a lie.

But it was only going to work if they maintained the structural integrity of the lie: the minute one of them made a mistake, the whole thing collapsed. The problem was, he couldn't even talk to Raker about it, hadn't been able to talk to him since way before he was tossed in prison: if they talked from here, the call would be recorded; if Raker came in like Parkes had today, it would be noted. Healy was behind bars, awaiting his court date, because he'd taken the hit for both of them: they'd accepted that might eventually be the case, should the day come, because it was Healy's deceit – his contact at the forensic lab that he'd blackmailed; his death they'd faked – that Raker had helped to cover up. But that didn't lower the stakes for either of them. If they strayed from the story, Raker would soon be in here too.

'Here's how it's going to play out,' Parkes said. 'You probably won't get anything for faking your own death, but you'll maybe get three years for the passport if we can prove it's a repeat offence, which – spoiler alert – we're about to. We thought it was unlikely you went eight years off the grid using a single ID – so we followed the trail back to the sweat shop who made you the last passport you had, and we closed them down, and now we're going through every piece of tech they own. I'd be willing to bet we find you in there somewhere – and maybe Raker too, who I imagine would have contacts dodgy enough to organize those IDs for you.' Parkes paused, contorting her face into a frown. Healy could feel his heart rate increasing. 'So that'll be three years give or take. And then, as I said earlier, we've got the DNA tampering, which – if we prove it – could be another five. Oh, and you'll be up there in that court lying through your teeth about all this, pretending you don't know Raker, so – as I keep telling you – perjury will get thrown into the mix at some point later on down the line when your lies finally fall apart. And perjury? That could be another, I don't know, let's say conservatively five years. So, play your cards right, Colm, and you could be looking at thirteen years in here.' She stared at him. 'How's that sounding?'

Healy stared back at her. His guts were twisting: it was the first time someone from the Met had spelled out the kind of sentence they were going for. For four and a half months, he'd sustained himself with the idea that he could do a year, maybe a year and a half: if he took the hit on forging one fake passport, and was unlucky enough to get some time for faking his own death, his solicitor said he was looking at eighteen months, two years at the most, less the time he'd already served here. But now Parkes had taken an axe to that. There was no way that Healy could ever do thirteen years.

Worse, at some point, other prisoners on the floors of the wing he was in were going to find out that he was an ex-cop. He'd managed to keep it quiet until now – and the guards, who may have read his file, clearly hadn't told anyone either – but he knew it was only a matter of time. And once the secret was out, he'd be spending the next decade of his life looking over his shoulder and waiting for a shank between his ribs.

Panic tremored through him. Then he stopped himself.

She's trying to fuck with your head.

'So, what's it to be, Colm?' Parkes asked.

'This "off-the-books" chat doesn't sound a lot different to our normal chats.'

'I want to help you.'

'It doesn't sound much like you do.'

'I actually think we can help *each other*.'

'Yeah? And how's that?'

'I can get your family in here to see you.'

The words hit Healy like a train.

He felt himself push back in his seat. Almost instantly, he had the same thought again – that she was playing him, trying to screw with his head – but he couldn't stop himself this time: 'What are you talking about?'

'Your two sons. They haven't been in yet, right?'

He swallowed; said nothing.

'Well,' she said, 'I spoke to Liam and Ciaran this week.'

He leaned forward a little. 'You did?'

'Yeah. Your ex-wife Gemma too. They all want to see you, Colm. They want to know why you walked out of their life eight years ago and pretended you were dead.'

'Don't fuck with me, Parkes.'

'I'm not.' She stared at him. 'I'm not.'

'I tried calling my boys.'

'And they didn't answer. I know. They told me.' Parkes grimaced. 'I don't know why that is. You know them better than me, even after all this time. Maybe it's too painful for them. Maybe they're too angry at you. Maybe they just don't know what to say. But I can get them here for you, Colm. I can sit them down and tell them that your life might be a bit of a mess right now, but you're genuinely trying to do the right thing. I think that'll make a big difference to them based on what I've heard: to know you've changed. To hear that you won't let them down this time.'

That last part stung.

But only because it was true.

He'd let them down constantly when he was a part of their lives, over and over again, on repeat. His one great regret now was that he could only ever make it up to two of his children: Leanne was gone, taken from him by a killer neither he nor Raker had been able to

99

stop. At the thought of that, as Leanne's face formed in the darkness of his head, he felt a sudden, overwhelming surge of emotion.

'Are you okay?' Parkes asked softly.

'I'm fine.'

'Did you know Liam's girlfriend is pregnant?'

He glanced at Parkes. 'What?'

'You're going to be a grandfather, Colm.'

The news completely floored him.

'She's two months. The baby's due in July. I don't believe you've even met your daughter-in-law, have you? Liam's girlfriend? Nice kid. They seem happy together.'

Healy looked around.

Two rows down, a mother was cradling a newborn.

'We can get your boys in here. And, personally, based on conversations I've had with my DCI, with the CPS, I think we can get most of your charges dropped too.'

He gave himself a moment. Why was she coming in here now offering to be the bridge between him and his estranged family? Why would anyone be willing to drop his charges? But it didn't take him long to find an answer. *Because it's an exchange. She's going to offer me a deal.*

'I get a lesser sentence if I give you something you need.'

She nodded. 'Exactly.'

'And – what? – all of this goes away?'

'Not all of it – but maybe most of it.'

'Meaning what?'

'Meaning maybe you only do time served.'

That meant he could be days away from getting out. He felt a flutter of excitement. 'Okay, so what do you want from me?'

Parkes came forward in her seat.

'We want you to give us David Raker.'

18

Liz had moved in next door to me a few weeks after Derryn died.

She'd been there as I'd grieved, as good to me in the aftermath, maybe better, than friends I'd known my whole life. And then, after a couple of years, when the ghosts of my grief, and loss, and heartache had stopped returning to me as often, we found ourselves drawn to one another. Our friendship became something more.

I'd never regretted it, even though – in retrospect – I hadn't been ready, and it hadn't been fair on Liz. I'd moved on from Derryn in my head, but not in my heart, and so, over time, the threads that had bound Liz and me together began to fray, and soon after that, the whole thing unravelled. Ours had been a quiet, and in some ways unremarkable, ending, but one that hurt her deeply because it felt like I played her somehow: she thought I'd lied about how damaged I still was, deliberately concealed it from her, but the truth was I didn't realize until a few months in. And, more than that, and perhaps worst of all, in her eyes I'd also lied about my work: I'd played down my obsession with missing people; I'd disguised how perilous my cases could get; and I'd failed to acknowledge that, if we were going to make a life together, it wasn't just me who was at risk when I strayed deep into the shadows.

'How are you doing, Liz?'

'I'm pretty good.' Her eyes lingered on me. 'You look pretty good too, Raker. You need to give me the name of your moisturiser.' She signalled for the woman who worked for her to come in. 'Do you want something to drink?'

'Just a coffee would be good.'

'Two black coffees, please, Iris,' she said to the woman, recalling, even after a decade, how I took it. After Iris was gone, Liz flipped open her notebook. On the front, embossed in gold, was a logo and the name of her firm: FEENY & COMPANY.

'How's Katie doing?' I asked.

Katie was her daughter. Liz's face brightened: 'Oh, she's great. She's working for evil corporate overlords at a bank in Canary Wharf. Well, actually, at the moment she's on maternity leave. She had a baby in August. A little boy.'

'That's amazing, Liz. Granny Feeny, huh?'

'Yeah. We're all really made up. Well, Katie could probably do without all the sleepless nights.' Liz went to the back of her notebook, where there was a sleeve on the inside cover, and took out a photograph of Katie and her baby boy. I told her about Annabel, my own daughter, who I'd never even known about until she was an adult.

Iris returned with the coffees. On Liz's mug, it said, *What's the difference between a solicitor and an angry bull? The solicitor charges more.*

'I really appreciate you seeing me,' I said. 'I know it's last minute.'

'I was surprised to hear from you. And, I admit, intrigued. I thought to myself, "You know what? It's been a long time since I sat alongside David Raker somewhere and listened to him spin a story I know isn't *quite* the truth."'

She smiled, but it was a dig. Not that it wasn't accurate: there had been a few times during our relationship – and before it as well – when Liz had come out to whatever police station I was being held in, and I'd told her enough to help navigate police interviews, but not all of what had gone on. Back then, I kept telling myself that I was doing it to protect her, to protect her career as a solicitor, her daughter, her life. But now I saw it for what it was: I'd never fully allowed myself to trust her.

'I'm after a little legal advice,' I said.

'Of course you are.' She picked up her coffee mug, taking a sip, her eyes still on me. As she put it down again, she picked up her pen, waiting.

'You remember Colm Healy?'

She nodded. 'I do. How's he doing?'

'He's currently in Pentonville.'

She made an *oh* with her mouth. 'What did he do?'

'Faked his own death. Maybe tampered with evidence.'

Liz eyed me. 'Maybe tampered with evidence – or actually did?'

'Are you asking as my solicitor?'

'I'm just asking.'

We held each other's gaze.

'He didn't get bail because they think he's a flight risk.'

'And is he?'

I paused, turning my coffee mug, and then told her about Healy's history: she knew about his sacking from the Met, because that pre-dated our split, but she didn't know anything after that – and obviously knew nothing of his faked death.

'Okay,' she said. 'So he needs representation?'

'He has a solicitor but . . .'

'But what?'

'But I'd rather he had you.'

'I get the sense you're trying to butter me up here, Raker.'

I gave myself longer to think. 'The police have been told by some-one that I helped him.'

'With what? The evidence tampering?'

'Yes. A DNA switch at the lab.'

'And *did* you switch out some DNA?'

'No.'

Her eyes stayed on me. 'But?'

'But I knew what Healy made happen at the lab and didn't say anything to the cops when they questioned me. And I've organized a series of fake passports for him over the past eight years. And through a series of shell companies, I've been the one paying for the places he's been staying in since he faked his death.'

'So not much then?' Liz replied witheringly. 'Do the cops know any of this?'

'No. Well, I don't think so.'

'So you've been lying to them for eight years?'

I looked at her, saying nothing, and she leaned back in her chair, hands behind her head, and let out a long breath. It spoke way more than words about how she felt. *So you're still doing this*, she was saying. *Still spinning stories that aren't quite the truth.* Except this was more than just *not quite the truth.*

'What exactly are you asking me for, Raker?'

'I need to speak to Healy.'

'So go in and speak to him.'

'It's not as simple as that.'

'Well, there's a surprise.'

'We don't really know each other.'

She paused again, eyes narrowed, studying me – and then my meaning seemed to land. She made a sound, halfway between surprise and disappointment.

'You told the cops you don't know him,' she said softly.

'More that I don't know him that well.'

'Shit. Not much has changed in ten years, has it?'

'Look, I know I've got no right to come in here and ask for your help like this. I know I hurt you.' I stopped, watched her, the reaction in her face: the wounds I'd left her with were old and didn't affect her in the same way, but that didn't mean those wounds weren't still there. 'I don't expect any favours. I just . . .' I took a breath. 'The things I've done for Healy, I did for the right reasons. He was hurting badly. He was grieving his girl. He was days away from taking his own life. When I look back now, there are a lot of times when I've wished I'd never stepped in, never helped, just walked away. It would have saved me a lot of money, and a *lot* of anxiety. But I couldn't do that. I couldn't abandon him. It just . . .' I shrugged. 'It isn't who I am. I've made mistakes, but this wasn't one of them.'

Liz was silent.

'I just need to talk to him,' I said. 'You can go in there and set up a call between us and no one at the prison will be able to listen into the conversation because they –'

'I know how legal privilege works, Raker.'

'I know. I know you do.' I held up a hand. 'This is the only way I can speak to him without anyone knowing.'

'So you're not really after representation at all?'

'Yes, I am, because I think he –'

'No,' Liz said, cutting me off. 'What I am to you is a glorified messenger.'

I shook my head. 'That's not it.'

'That *is* it.'

'It's not. Honestly. I want you to help him.'

'So you *do* want me to be his solicitor?'

'I think you'll do a much better job than the guy he's got represent—'

'Don't blow smoke up my arse, Raker.'

This time I said nothing, waiting her out.

'So let's get this straight,' she said finally. 'The Met, who hate you because you aren't a "proper" cop, and who *also* hate you because you've spent your entire career post-journalism solving the cold cases they couldn't, thereby embarrassing them in public and in the media –'

'That's never been my intention.'

'– have now cornered the only person in the world who actually knows the truth about who you are and what you've done. And that truth is that you kept quiet about a DNA switch at a forensic lab, you helped a man fake his own death, and you provided that same man with fake documents for eight years. Oh, and you hid payments to him behind a series of shell companies – shell companies being the legal equivalent of going to the FCA offices and using a megaphone to invite them to look into you. *Plus*, there's all those times you've sat in interviews with the cops and spun some half-truth about what *really* went on in your cases in order to protect . . . I don't know. Victims. Missing people. Whatever you think in your head needs to stay secret. I mean, I get that you think you're doing it for the right reasons, but that sort of thing tends to niggle cops at the Met, which is another reason why I imagine they're very interested in going after your pal, Healy – because he probably knows quite a lot of what you *didn't* say in interviews.' She paused, stared at me. 'How am I doing?'

'Pretty good.'

'Is there anything else I should know?'

'Just one thing. A woman called Martine Parkes is leading all of this. But she's working under the direction of Detective Superintendent Aiden Phillips.'

Liz smirked. 'Phillips. Shit, you really *are* breaking out all the hits tonight. He absolutely hated you.'

'Well, I don't imagine much has changed in ten years.'

'So all of this is just some personal vendetta for him?'

'No. The Met have had three or four years of terrible headlines, so first and foremost it's a chance to rebuild some trust. In their eyes, Healy's a corrupt cop and I'm a fraud operating way out of my depth. Phillips will be selling this to his bosses as an opportunity to show the public the good the police can do.'

'And if you two are the vessel for that, all the better.'

'Exactly.'

Liz tapped her pen against her notebook.

'I'll tell you what I'm going to do. You tell me everything you know – and I mean everything, no corner-cutting – about what's going on here, and exactly what the police might have, if anything, and after that I'll make a decision.'

'You can't unhear this stuff, Liz.'

'I think what you really mean is, you don't want to tell me all the details if I'm not going to take the case.' She stared at me, eyes fixed on mine. 'That's tough shit.'

'I just don't –'

'This is how it is, Raker. I'll take the case if you tell me the truth.'

'I've told you the –'

'No, not the abridged version. We're not back in 2012.'

'What does that mean?' I said, frowning.

'It means, if there's even a *flicker* in your face of the man that lied me to ten years ago, I'm done here. And then Healy goes down. And maybe you go with him . . .'

19

By the time I got home from Liz's office, it was almost 11 p.m.

Waiting on the doormat were more forms to be signed for my upcoming house move, a long, protracted sale that was finally going through after Christmas. I picked up the forms and tossed them on to the kitchen counter, not just because I was too exhausted to deal with them now, but because a part of me didn't want to have to. It was an act of denial: for months, I'd told myself selling up was the right thing to do – that I needed to move on from the place I'd shared with Derryn, where I'd spent her last days nursing her, where the memories of her were written into every piece of furniture, every flower in the garden, every colour on every wall – but the closer the day came, the less certain I became. It felt like a betrayal, as if I were leaving her behind. Forms, phone calls with solicitors, sending money, all of it hurt – and I knew packing up what was left of her things in a month was going to hurt even more.

I got the fire going, showered, changed and made some food, then watched TV, trying to concentrate on something that wasn't Derryn or the house move, the work I'd taken on for Rebekah Murphy – or the disaster I could see unfolding with Healy.

But I couldn't keep the thoughts at bay for long.

I went back over my meeting with Liz. Even though I really, genuinely trusted her, I still felt uncomfortable with having to reveal so much. She'd agreed to speak to Healy for me, had – in theory – agreed to set up the call with him that I needed in order for us to reinforce our barricades against Parkes, and against her boss Phillips. But, despite everything I'd told Liz this evening being legally under lock and key at her offices – all the minor, and sometimes much more significant, ways in which I'd bent the law by helping Healy – it didn't bring me any comfort: a lot of what I'd told her were things that only one other person, Healy, had ever really known about. So much had been interred inside my head for so long that it felt frightening giving voice to it all.

Locking up the house and setting the alarm, I went through to the bedroom, notebook in one hand, the file that Mark Levin had kept on Jennifer Johnson in the other. I was absolutely fried but I wanted to take a closer look at Jennifer's case before I tried to sleep because I knew, if I didn't, I'd just lie awake thinking about it anyway.

I started with the picture of Jennifer that had been paperclipped to the original file and photocopied by Levin. She was dark-haired, dark-eyed, her hair long and pulled to one shoulder in the image. She was seated in the photograph but in her file it said she was approximately five-eight and weighed 10 stone.

I looked at her employment history.

Again, it was vague, listing only her most recent job at The Castle members' club. She had last been in work for a shift on 17 December, two days before she went missing. It said she'd been employed at the club for eighteen months, and had apparently been very happy. I wondered how much of that had been down to the job itself and how much could be attributed to what was going on in the background with her and Levin.

I switched to her last known movements.

Levin had filled it in based on what friends of hers had apparently told him – but it felt more likely most of this was based on what he knew himself of where she was in her last couple of days. He made reference to her home address, which was the flat on Signal Lane, and how one of her friends, Rita Wong, had called her on her landline the day before she went missing. They'd spoken for 'thirty minutes about going to Slinks nightclub in Soho the following evening'. That had presumably come direct from the friend herself. The rest of it, though, felt like Levin skirting around the fact he spent some of the day of Jennifer's disappearance *with* Jennifer: she went to a restaurant 'with a friend' for lunch; they then went to a pub; then the friend saw her back to her flat and 'stayed there' until 6 p.m. After that, the 'friend' left Jennifer's flat and Jennifer got ready to go out to Slinks. Of course, it was possible the 'friend' referred to in the missing person's report wasn't Levin at all, but someone else. It was more likely, though, that it *was* Levin, as everywhere else in the file, whenever it referenced an actual friend or contact of Jennifer's, their full name was used. After that, Jennifer went to the nightclub and was never seen again.

I stared at the pages, wondering if there was any mileage in considering Levin as the person who'd had a hand in Jennifer's disappearance. But based on what Len Graves had said, on how upset Levin had been in the days after the disappearance – and also how driven he appeared to be in finding her – it didn't really feel plausible.

So what are you left with?

I pulled my pad towards me and then wrote out a timeline of what I knew so far. It was something I liked to do because it often cleared a path through the clutter.

1956 – 1963 | Fiona and Jennifer live in Peterborough
1966 – 1974 | Fiona goes to live with Jonah Carling
Summer 1979 | Fiona meets Henry Murphy
End of 1983/Start of 1984 | Mark Levin begins (or may have already begun?) an affair with Jennifer Johnson
19 December 1985 | Jennifer Johnson disappears
26 December 1985 | Fiona Murphy disappears
Start of Jan 1986 | Levin begins the search for Fiona (and is already looking for Jennifer)
22 January 1986 | Levin drowns in a canal

I grabbed my phone off the bedside table and saw that it was now after midnight. Finding Rebekah's mobile number, I texted her and asked if she could give me a call back when she woke up in the morning.

Almost immediately, my phone started ringing.

It was Rebekah.

'I hope I didn't wake you,' I said.

'Oh, no, I'm awake. I had a little nap earlier in the day, so my internal clock is all over the place. I just FaceTimed my girls, actually.' She made a joke-sobbing sound on the line, but being emotional about leaving her daughters behind – and especially after seeing them both – was, I imagined, not far from the truth.

'I was wondering if I could just ask you a couple of quick questions.'

'Sure. Okay.'

'Does the name Jonah Carling mean anything to you?'

'No. Who's he?'

'He's a guy that knew your mum when she was a teenager.'

'No,' she said again. 'No, I haven't heard of him.'

'Okay. What about the name Jennifer Johnson?'

'No. I don't think I know that name either.'

'Did your dad ever talk about your mum's friends – people she grew up with, knew, saw, kept in contact with?'

Eventually, quietly, she said, 'No. I'm really sorry.'

'It's all right,' I replied, because it wasn't her fault. But, again, it brought home to me just how little Rebekah and her brothers must have known about their mother.

It also made it clear that I needed a different angle.

And, in the morning, I knew exactly where to start.

Room 634

Tom | *This Morning*

Tom Brenner finished up the call with the woman, placed the receiver back on the cradle and stood there for a moment inside the phone box. He was struggling to breathe. The fear was so intense, it was like a virus in his chest, squeezing his lungs until it felt like his ribs were on fire and his throat was closing. He tried to calm himself, looked to the Five Guys next to him. People were sitting at window seats, eating burgers, picking fries out of brown paper bags. He watched a row of three teenaged girls, all of them in a half-circle around one of their phones. After a few seconds, they burst into laughter.

He envied them.

He wanted to be in there now, eating at a table like they were, where nothing mattered. Instead, he was here – in the shadow of King's Cross station – terrified about what came next.

What have I started?

Tom closed his eyes.

How did I end up here?

But he knew.

He could trace it all the way back to that night four months ago.

That night had been a Wednesday in late August.

He'd been standing at the sink, washing dishes. It was just after 6 p.m. and he had to be in work by eight. But before the madness of another shift started, he just enjoyed the comforting sounds of the house – of his wife, Sadie, in the living room on the phone to her sister; of his son, Leo, on the floor beside her, joypad in hand, the Xbox controller clicking as he played *Minecraft*.

Tom worked as the night manager at the Regala in King's Cross, a huge hotel on York Way, east of the station. He'd had the last two nights off and had loved it. The summers were always busy, even in the dead of night, and the Regala was such a maze-like sprawl that he rarely got a moment's peace. Most of the night he was on his feet, running from one firefight to the next, so being home – being close to Sadie and Leo, even if he wasn't in the same room as them – was exactly how he liked it.

'Tash says hello,' Sadie said from behind him.

'Is she okay?'

'Yeah, she's fine. It was thirty-nine degrees there today.'

Tash lived in Lanzarote. Sadie pulled a chair out and sat down at the kitchen table and, when Tom was done with the dishes, he came over and kissed her.

'Are you all right?' she asked.

'I'll be forty this year,' he said, putting his hands on her shoulders, his fingers gently working her neck. 'I don't know if I still want to be doing nights when I'm forty-five, or fifty. Rushed off my feet the whole time, knackered in the day because I can't sleep – it's just not fun any more. The thought of going in tonight . . .'

He grimaced.

Sadie took one of his hands in hers. 'I thought you liked the nights because it meant you could be around for school pick-up, for Leo's bedtime.'

'I did,' he said. 'I do. But Leo's going to be ten soon. In a couple of years, he'll be at senior school and won't need dropping off and picking up. Another few years after that there won't be a bedtime – or, at least, not one where I'll be tucking him in.' Tom paused again.

'If you want to find something else, you know I'll support you,' she said, and gave his hand a squeeze. He kissed her again. 'There's tons of hotels in London,' she said. 'Someone, somewhere will have a role with daytime hours.'

'I'd still have to work weekends, though.'

Tom could see that Sadie was searching for the right thing to say. Hotels were all he knew. He'd been working in them since he left university. If he didn't want to work nights, he just had to find a duty manager role somewhere; if he wanted weekends back, that was more complicated.

'You could retrain as a teacher,' she said, smiling.

Tom laughed.

'I don't know what's worse,' he said. 'Teenagers or hotel guests.'

Three hours into his shift, Tom decided it was hotel guests.

It was the summer holidays on both sides of the Atlantic and, even late at night, that meant a constant flow of people. At 10 p.m., he checked in a busload of American tourists, and then a second at 10.30, and then a third just after 11 p.m. who seemed to be entirely populated with Olympic-level moaners. They didn't like the floor their room was on. They didn't like the choice of channels available. There weren't enough pillows or the duvets were too thick. Or they were just irrationally pissed off about the speed of the Wi-Fi in public areas, which, to Tom's mind, was plenty fast enough. By the time the last of them had left for their rooms, he was bristling, and ended taking it out on, and later apologising to, the waiting staff clearing up in the dining area.

At 1 a.m., he made use of a brief lull, and grabbed a chicken sandwich and a strong black coffee from the kitchen. He took both through to the back office. It was quiet, as it always was at this time – all the admin staff worked regular nine-to-five hours – so he used one of the PCs and checked the news headlines.

At 1.30, his phone buzzed.

Someone was complaining about noise on the sixth floor.

He downed his second cup of coffee, grabbed a breath mint, and then headed to the front desk to get the details from the staff member who had taken the complaint. A guest had phoned down from the top floor to say that there was a TV being played loudly in the room adjacent to him. This was bread and butter for Tom. Almost every night he had to deal with noise complaints.

He took the elevator up to the sixth floor and then headed left, down to the end. The further he got, the more he could hear of the TV: it wasn't ridiculously loud but there was a bassline thumping.

He knocked on the door of 634.

When the hotel had first opened five years ago, they'd included a small set of speakers in the rooms, so people could connect their phones or devices, but that had been an absolute disaster. He'd spent his first two years as night manager repeatedly going to rooms and asking guests to turn the music down, so when management had decided to do a refit in year three, all the speakers were removed.

Tom went to his phone and checked for the name of the guest – a Mr Bauer – and then, as quietly as he could, knocked for a second time. 'Mr Bauer, this is the –'

The door opened.

A man in his sixties filled the frame. He was taller than Tom – six-two, maybe more – broad, and in good condition: he was in a dressing gown, the front open, revealing a towel around his waist. His body was dotted with water, his head too, where he'd lost most of his hair and closely shaved what was left at the sides. 'Oh,' he said, looking at Tom apologetically and then at his name badge, 'I'm really sorry. I was just showering off and didn't hear you knocking.'

'Sir, my name's Tom. I'm the night manager here. Unfortunately, we've had a few complaints from guests about the volume of your TV –'

'Shall I turn it down?'

'Yes. Please.'

'Of course. Actually, I'll turn it off completely.'

'Thank you.'

'I really am so sorry.' He immediately walked over to the TV – which Tom could see was tuned to a radio station – grabbed the remote control from the top and switched it off. As he came back, he said, 'There, that should be better. I have a bit of an issue with my hearing . . .' He gestured to his left ear.

'Well, I appreciate it, sir.'

'Sorry again,' the man said.

Tom surreptitiously glanced over the man's shoulder. The chair at the desk had been moved over to the bed: in the mirror on the left-hand side of the room – which reflected back a little of the other half – he could see it. A half-finished bottle of wine had been placed on top as well as two empty wine glasses. The chair was right next to the bed, and although he couldn't see much more, he could see enough: a naked male was secured to one of the bedposts with a pair of handcuffs.

They turned up the music to drown out their sex game, Tom thought, looking at the man who'd answered the door. *You go for it, fella*.

Tom hadn't done this sort of thing in his twenties, so couldn't imagine he'd be tying Sadie to a hotel room bedpost in their sixties. Clearly, though, this was one of the reasons why the man was in such good shape for his age.

'Good evening, sir,' Tom said.

'Evening,' the man said, and pushed the door shut.

Tom remained where he was, listening to the hush of the corridor, thinking again about what he'd seen in the mirror, and as he pictured the bed, the chair with the wine and the glasses on, and the wrist secured to the bedpost with the handcuffs, he realized he'd seen something else there too, but hadn't registered it at the time. It had been on the chair with everything else, partly obscured by the wine bottle.

A roll of duct tape.

Day 2

Wednesday, 7 December

PART THREE
The Castle

20

I arrived at The Castle just before 10 a.m.

It was at the eastern end of Bedford Row – an attractive, quiet street overlooking Gray's Inn Gardens – and was a huge, red-brick Georgian building with five floors of white sash windows. There was nothing external to indicate who the building belonged to – or that there was a private members' club housed inside – but there appeared to be more than enough room for the spa, rooftop swimming pool, restaurant and walled garden I'd seen in pictures on the club's website.

I pushed a buzzer at the front entrance.

'Hello?' A voice on the intercom.

'I've got an appointment with Ian Kirby.'

Kirby was the manager at The Castle. I'd got up early and made some calls to the club, and as soon as I mentioned the word 'investigator', I quickly got passed up the chain. Sometimes you had to play the percentages: calling myself an investigator was the truth; not bothering to correct the assumption that I was a cop, wasn't.

'My name's David Raker,' I added for whoever was listening on the other end of the mic. As I waited, I felt the cold of the morning pressing at me. The sky was stark and cloudless, and had been all night, and now everywhere – every roof, windowsill and doorway I could see – was dusted in a thick sheen of frost. A short, sharp noise returned me to the moment and, as a buzz sounded through the intercom, the door swung gently away from me.

I moved inside to an immaculate foyer, with marble floors, white pillars and a reception desk whose front section was made from what looked like an entire, intact tree trunk. The foyer was decorated as if it were a sitting room in a country estate, with a big, elegant fireplace in one corner, shelves loaded with books and antiques, portraits on the walls, and studded leather chairs. There was a Christmas tree too. A man was sitting behind the front desk, talking into a headset, and along a wall on the opposite side of the foyer were five unmarked doors in a line, with card readers next to them. There were signs above each one: GYM; HEALTH SPA, POOL and ROOFTOP DECK; RESTAURANT, BAR and MEETING ROOMS; WALLED GARDEN; and STAFF ONLY.

'Mr Raker,' the receptionist said and handed me a plastic pass in a clear wallet. 'Please keep this with you at all times. I'll just call Ian.'

A few minutes later, a slim man of around sixty emerged from the staff door, the heels of his tan brogues clacking against the polished marble of the foyer. He was five-ten, dressed in a dark blue suit, with a powder-blue shirt, and had glasses and dark, grey-speckled hair. He held out a hand to me. 'Mr Raker?'

I stood and we shook hands.

'I'm Ian Kirby,' he said. 'Welcome to The Castle.'

Using his keycard, Kirby took me back through the door he'd come out of.

'This is the bit our members don't get to see,' he explained in a soft north-east accent. Some of the doors were open, with people at desks inside, and on the walls next to each door were signs for Administration, Human Resources, PR/Marketing, and Guest Services. At the end was his office, a boxy room full of shelves, filing cabinets and clutter. 'Please, grab a seat,' he said, and moved around to the other side. 'Can I offer you a drink? Tea, coffee, something cold?'

'I'm good, thank you.'

He nodded and sat. 'So you said on the phone you're an investigator?'

I took out a card and handed it to him.

'Missing people,' he said quietly, examining the card and then placing it down on the desk in front of him. 'Who's missing?'

'A former employee of yours.'

'Really? Who?'

'We're going back a few years here.'

'How far?'

'Nineteen eighty-five.'

He eyed me as if waiting for a punchline. 'Oh. You're not joking.'

'Unfortunately not.'

'Well, I'm sorry to throw a spanner in the works, but we don't retain former employee info at all, let alone for people from forty years ago.'

I nodded, expecting as much. In fact, it would have been suspicious if they'd retained four-decade-old records. But my visit had just as much to do with getting inside The Castle and building a picture of the place in which Jennifer Johnson had worked, the place she and Mark Levin had often been together in, and whether any of it could be linked back to the disappearance of Fiona Murphy.

'How long have you been working here?' I asked.

'Since 1994. I started as manager of the health spa.'

'And you've been the overall manager since when?'

'Since 1998. Can I ask the name of the person you're looking for?'

'Fiona Murphy,' I replied, flipping through the pages of my notebook, 'but I'm also interested in a second woman called Jennifer Johnson – she was the employee here I talked about.' I stopped, watching his face for a sign that either of those names meant something. But as he'd only started working at The Castle nine years after Fiona and Jennifer had vanished, all I got back was the expected blank.

'You don't retain employee details,' I said. 'What about membership records?'

This time, a polite smile formed on his face. 'Certainly, we won't have records for members who last attended the club in 1985. And, after a member fails to renew, or leaves, or perhaps passes on, we obviously delete all the information we have on that person. But, even if that weren't the case, I can't share personal details like that with you, Mr Raker. I'm sure you understand. Data protection and all that.'

'Of course. Do you have any employees who've been here a long time?'

'As in, "here in 1985"?'

'Exactly.'

'No,' he said. 'I'm actually the longest-serving employee here.'

'Okay.' I changed tack. 'Can I ask you about the owner?'

'The owner?'

'I did a little reading up before I came here today and it says the club is owned by someone called Samuel Apphis. From what I've been able to find out, I think he took over this place back in the eighties?'

'Yes, that's correct.'

'I couldn't find much about Mr Apphis online.'

'No,' Kirby replied. 'No, Mr Apphis is a very private man.'

'Actually, I didn't find anything at all.'

It wasn't an exaggeration: I'd gone looking for background on the club and, in a couple of articles, I found reference to a businessman called Samuel Apphis buying out the Castle family. The Castles had been the original owners, all the way back to its opening in 1920, and after the club had been passed down through two generations, Will Castle – the grandson of the initial proprietor – had made public his intention to sell, and had sold it to Apphis.

The huge information gap on Apphis bothered me.

He was literally a blank. I couldn't find any history on him, there were no pictures of him; I essentially had no view of him as a person or entrepreneur at all, and what there was amounted to little more than the same, vague, repeated references to him having a number of business interests all over the world. The problem was, I couldn't find out what those business interests were, no matter how deep I dug, and while I couldn't say for certain it was relevant to my search for Fiona, it was an anomaly I didn't like: even intensely private people, as a few articles described him as – and Kirby himself had already echoed – left some sort of footprint. Apphis shunning the limelight was a perfectly legitimate decision, and because The Castle was a private company, he didn't have to front up to shareholders, which also allowed him to stay in the background, beholden to no one. But I also couldn't find a mention of him in relation to any of the other companies he was supposed to have owned. His so-called business interests – on paper at least – didn't seem to exist. Even a silent investor should have been named on company accounts somewhere, and those would have been in the public domain. Whether he avoided publicity or not, or craved his anonymity, he should have made some sort of mark. So that was what niggled me: if Fiona was a shadow, this guy was pitch-black.

'Why the big secret?' I asked.

'Oh, I don't think it's really about him being secretive. He prefers his businesses to do the talking.'

'Which businesses are those?'

For a second, there was something in Kirby's face – there and then gone again – and then he pushed out a smile, and everything suddenly looked false, like he'd pulled on a mask. 'I don't understand how any of this is relevant?'

'I'm just curious, I suppose.'

Kirby opened his hands out. 'As I say, he's a very private man. In all the years I've been here – even in my time as manager – I've only met him a handful of times.'

'So you don't know what other businesses he owns?'

'It's not something he really discusses with me.'

'So it *is* kind of a secret?'

'No, it's not a secret.'

'But he doesn't discuss it with you.'

This time, Kirby didn't say anything.

'Does he discuss *this* business with you?'

'Of course he does. I'm the manager.'

'But you said you've only met him a "handful of times"?'

'In the flesh.'

'So you talk mostly over Zoom? Via email?'

'Really,' he said, 'what's the relevance of this?'

'I'm just trying to get an idea of how things work here.'

'Why, is that going to help you find your missing person?'

'It might.'

But he didn't want to answer. The look he'd given me, his refusal to co-operate on Apphis: both things had set off a low-level alarm. I'd come here not expecting to find much of anything; now I was wondering if I'd glimpsed the edges of a secret.

'Is there anything else?' he asked.

'Would it be possible to get a tour of the club?'

'Are you thinking of joining us?' It was subtle, but it was obviously a putdown. I clearly didn't look like the type of person who would be able to afford the fees here. 'I have a few meetings,' he added, 'so I'm not going to be able to do that. But I could ask if a colleague might be able to step in.'

'That would be great, thank you.'

He got up and headed out. I waited, going back over everything Kirby had said. It didn't amount to much – and it sounded unlikely I was going to get the answers I sought from anyone who was working today.

But there was something going on here.

'Unfortunately, no one is available right now,' Kirby said from behind me, re-entering the room. He stopped at his desk, not sitting down, the inference obvious: we were done. It made me wonder how hard he'd asked around amongst his staff, but it also made me more certain than ever that my instinct was right.

'Okay,' I said, standing, shaking his hand, 'well, I appreciate all your help.'

'Let me show you out.'

As he headed back through the door of the office, I checked my pockets, making sure my notebook was there, and happened to notice something on his desk. I hadn't seen it when I'd entered.

A membership card.

I had a split second to think about what I was doing – a split second to take in the fact that there were actually four cards, and a Post-it note stuck on top, with *Handed into Lost Property* written on it – and then I reached over and slid out the bottom one.

A second later, the card was inside my coat pocket.

21

After leaving The Castle, I walked down to High Holborn, then into Lincoln's Inn Fields, checking over my shoulder the whole time. I didn't expect anyone to be following me, but – after swiping the membership card – I wasn't about to take any chances. Checking around me again, I found a bench enclosed by evergreen trees, wiped the frost from the seat, and removed the card from my coat pocket.

It was black with an embossed logo on it, one I'd seen repeated throughout the décor during my brief visit to the club. In the bottom left was a name, printed in grey.

Nicholas Houser.

Under that was a six-digit number.

I grabbed my laptop out of my bag, and then used my phone as a hotspot. Going to The Castle's website, I clicked on the *Sign In* tab that I'd seen earlier. It took me through to a second page with a login window.

Name.

Membership number.

I put in *Nicholas Houser* as the username and then copied the number off the card before hitting Return. The box stuttered. I closed the gap between first names and last names and made it all one word, then hit Return again. This time, the box disappeared. The screen went completely black for a moment.

I was in.

It loaded up a very basic profile page. There was no financial information on it, no personal information either, other than a small photograph of the guy whose card I'd stolen: he was in his thirties, blond-haired, with a beard. The lack of sensitive data was probably why the security was so minimal. And, really, beyond the login, it was little more than an intranet. On the right were a series of links, but all it accessed were contact names and emails for staff members at the club, including Ian Kirby; a PDF of a membership handbook; a history of The Castle itself; and then another PDF.

This one was more useful.

It was a floorplan.

As I headed back to the Tube, my phone started ringing.

It was Martine Parkes.

'Sorry I had to put you off last night,' she said, 'but I need you to come in to the station now.'

'I'll be in when I can,' I replied.

'Be here in the next hour.'

'That's not going to be possible.'

'Or we come and arrest you and *drag* you in.'

I didn't reply.

'Believe me, David, you're going to want to hear what I have to say.'

Holt

Unknown | *February 1985*

It began with a knock at the door.

It was late in the evening on his fourth day in London, and – aside from going out to get food – he'd spent the entire time at the Rockingham in his room. The leak in the ceiling was still hitting the same bucket, and he was still emptying it out every day. He was eating the same crap from the same supermarket, and failing to concentrate on the same book. He wasn't used to being sedentary. His mind, his body had always had a purpose.

He got up and went to the door, leaving the chain on. Out in the hallway, a man in his early twenties – dressed for winter in a trench coat and woollen hat, and with a bag over his shoulder – stared back at him.

'You gonna open up or not?'

He released the chain and the young man came in.

'I'm Mike,' the man said, putting his bag down on the bed and unzipping it. He didn't take his coat off, didn't even bother removing his hat, just reached into the bag and brought out a camera. He glanced around the room. 'Go over there.'

Mike was pointing to a wall next to the television.

He did as Mike asked, adjusting the shirt he was wearing, tidying his collar. He watched as Mike fiddled with something on the camera and then looked him up and down. 'Just stare into the lens and don't smile.'

The flash went off and then it was done: Mike moved back to his bag, put the camera inside, and said, 'Someone will be back in touch with you in a couple of days.'

Two days later, his sixth at the Rockingham, there was another knock at the door. This time, it was after 11 p.m. and he'd been lying on the bed, listening to trains rumble past. Slowly, he'd been starting to get used to the rhythms of the city – its noises, its routines. He still didn't like it, still hated the cold and the rain, the frenzy of London – but maybe, just maybe, he would settle. The previous night he'd slept for four hours straight, without dreaming once, which was probably the most he'd had in one stretch for six months.

He got up and went to the door.

Another man – like Mike, young, in his twenties – was waiting on the landing. He was pale and had a scattering of stubble, and his dark eyes were moving along the hallway. When they pinged back, he said, 'I'm Gerald. I've got your things.'

He let Gerald in.

From inside his jacket, Gerald took out a brown envelope and looked around the room. 'I'd forgotten what an absolute shithole this place is,' he mumbled. And then Gerald paused, studying him, a hint of a smile playing at the corner of his lips. 'You must have done something really fucked up if you're lying low in this dump . . .'

He gave no response.

'Whatever,' Gerald said, and reached inside the envelope. Out came a British passport. He watched Gerald flicking through it, finding the first page, holding it up for him to see. His photograph looked back, the one that Mike had taken against the wall a couple of days before. 'You're Gary Holt now,' Gerald said.

Gary Holt.

That was the name written on the page opposite his photograph. Gerald tossed the passport over and he caught it, opening the front cover, wanting to see what other new information he had to learn about himself.

Occupation: Manager.

Place of birth: London.

Date of birth: 1 October 1959.

'Manager?' he said to Gerald.

'Yeah, it's nice and generic. Means whatever you want it to mean.'

'This isn't the year I was born.'

'Exactly. Makes it harder to connect the dots.'

'And London? How am I going to explain that?'

'What are you talking about?'

'I don't have an English accent.'

'So you were born here and then moved somewhere else for twenty-six years. Who fucking cares? It's all bullshit, anyway. My advice: take a good look at the information in that passport, learn it, create a back story – and stick to it.'

They stared at each other.

'You got a problem with that, "Holt"?'

Holt. Gary Holt.

Start accepting it, he thought. *Start thinking of yourself as him.*

Finally, Gary Holt said, 'No, I don't have a problem with it.'

'Good.'

Next, Gerald brought out an electronic keycard. It looked like the type they'd started using in hotels a few years back. Or, at least, hotels that weren't complete dives like the Rockingham. He tossed it at Holt.

'What's this?' Holt asked, catching it.

'Look, mate,' Gerald said, 'I'm just a middle man here. I don't even know why I've got half this stuff. I'm a forger, not a bloody postman. I do passports, driver's licences, all that shit.' He paused, dipped into the envelope and pulled out a folded piece of paper. 'Speaking of which . . .' This time, he stepped forward and handed it to Holt. It was a British driver's licence, the paper pink and green. 'I do work for Larsen, Larsen pays me: that's the sum total of what I know about that guy. You both got the same accent, though, I know that much.'

Holt didn't say anything.

'You two escaping from something?'

Still he remained silent.

'Whatever,' Gerald said again. 'Larsen posted that keycard through my door this morning and said to include it with the passport and the driver's licence. Never saw him to talk to, so couldn't tell you the reason why he wanted me to include it.'

Holt glanced from the keycard to Gerald.

He was holding out a crinkled Post-it note now, folded in half. Holt took it and unfolded it. There was a handwritten address in the centre.

'He'll meet you in the changing rooms there at six a.m. tomorrow.'

'Why does he want to meet here?'

'How the hell should I know?' Gerald folded up the envelope he'd brought all the documents in. 'All I know is Larsen paid me extra to give you the keycard and to tell you to meet him in the changing rooms at the address he wrote down. So that's what I've done. After that, I couldn't care less. If you two fancy getting into your birthday suits and soaping each other down in the showers, go for it.'

But Holt wasn't listening any more.

He was looking at the keycard and the address on the Post-it note.

He wondered what The Castle was.

22

When I got to Bethnal Green police station, she made me wait just as I knew she would.

I liked Parkes, not least because she'd mostly been different to a lot of the cops I'd dealt with down the years – less guarded, more willing to share, more willing to judge me on what she saw, not on what she'd heard from others. But sometimes she slipped back into old habits, to techniques that became ingrained in detectives after a while, whether they realized it or not: the elongated silences, the mini power plays, the tiny advantages they believed they were gaining.

Twenty minutes later, she finally came through to the front desk.

'Sorry about the delay, David,' she said, but didn't bother waiting for my reply. Gesturing for me to follow her, she took me through a door, then through a series of others, deep into the bowels of the station. Eventually, we ended up in the same, cramped interview suite as always. Its size and lack of windows made it good for sweating suspects and, even if she insisted I wasn't one, our conversations always had that dynamic: her asking questions, me batting them off; her waiting for a mistake, me trying not to make any.

She offered me something to drink but I told her I was fine, and then she just leaned back in her chair, pad on the table in front of her, and eyed me.

'Rumour is, Colm Healy is changing his solicitor.'

I kept my expression neutral.

Parkes would have found out at some point; I just hadn't expected Liz to move so quickly. She must have set everything in motion first thing this morning – and she must have been most of the way to making it happen if Parkes already had wind of it.

'Did you hear what I said, David?'

'I heard. What's that got to do with me?'

Parkes smiled again. 'Right. Because you two barely know each other.'

'Is this what I came all the way out here for?'

She flipped the front cover on her notepad. 'I wanted to speak to you last night about some other things but this is far more interesting to me.' I suspected the *other things* part was a lie, or an embellishment at least, as I doubted she had much beyond what she normally threw at me. But the fact that she was going to dig into Healy's new solicitor gave me pause. She read from her notes: 'Elizabeth Feeny.'

I feigned surprise. 'That's who he's hired?'

'It seems so.'

'Well, that's a smart move because she's a good lawyer.'

'Why would he choose her?'

'You'd have to ask him.'

'Oh, I will, don't worry. But I did a little hunting around and I can see that Ms Feeny and you have some history together.' She meant professional history because whatever nascent relationship Liz and I had ten years ago had never blossomed into something large enough to be on the radar of Parkes. 'In fact, you know what?' she continued. 'I can see she acted as your solicitor right here in Bethnal Green station around the time you and Healy first teamed up.'

'This again?'

'A lot of people in the Met, they don't believe you've been entirely honest with us down the years. In fact, a lot of cops here think you've very deliberately kept information back from us. And, of course, by extension, because they believe that, they believe you're now doing the same with Colm Healy.'

'Are you one of those cops? Is that what you're saying?'

She didn't respond.

'Your colleagues just don't like me working missing persons cases they failed to solve. And I'm sure they also don't like the fact that, down the years, some of the very worst people I've exposed have been dirty cops.'

'Like Healy.'

In my eyes, Healy was never a dirty cop – or, at least, not the type I was talking about. But I didn't argue the point.

'Like Healy?' she said again.

I just shook my head. 'I'm sick of repeating myself, so why don't you get out your phone and record this part so I don't have to go through it all again?' I held her gaze, knowing she would never put any of this on tape because all of these meetings – and what she hoped to gain from them – were deliberately off-the-record as it gave her more room for manoeuvre. She could ask direct questions, gently toy with me, even accuse me, and it would never come back on her or the Met. I goaded her: 'You don't want to record any of this?'

A twitch of another smile, her eyes lit by the jaundiced glow of the overhead strip lights. This was the dichotomy of Parkes: she was dancing to the tune of her bosses, she sometimes fell back on predictable police tactics like forcing me to wait at the front counter for her, but I got the sense she actually, genuinely respected me – which was more than most of her colleagues did. Either way, the smile signalled that I'd moved a piece on the board by asking her if she wanted to record us, and now she didn't have a move to make in return. This was what it had been like since the start: a strange, unspoken and endlessly repeating game of cat and mouse.

'Can I go?'

'Of course you can go, David,' she said, like it was my decision to turn up here, not hers. I got up, grabbed my coat. 'You have a good trip to Cambridge yesterday?'

Instantly, I froze. 'What?'

'Lovely city. I haven't been for years.'

I held her gaze but, inside, I was squirming.

How did she know where I'd gone?

And what else did she know?

'You *did* go to Cambridge yesterday, right?'

'So – what? – you're following me now?'

'No,' she said, as if it were the most insane thing she'd ever heard. 'No, this isn't North Korea. A colleague just happened to be on the same train and recognized you.'

' "Just happened to be on the same train"?'

'It's true.'

'And I'm assuming it's a colleague who "just happens" to work with you?'

'Actually, no, she doesn't work with us.'

'Then why's she picking up the phone to you?'

'I guess she recognized you and thought we might be interested.'

That sounded like bullshit – but what was the alternative? That they *had* put someone on me? That felt like a big waste of resource in an organisation that had to account for every single penny. It was also edging dangerously close to harassment – or at least a lawyer could argue that point – given the fact I hadn't been charged with anything and continually, willingly returned here to answer the same questions on repeat. Except neither of those things – the waste of resource, the harassment threat – meant they *weren't* following me.

I didn't care about them knowing I'd gone to Cambridge, because everything I did up there had been perfectly legitimate. What worried me was what they may have seen after I'd got back to London. Specifically, I was worried about them knowing I'd gone to see Liz. As I thought of that, I thought of Parkes's opener, her questions about Liz becoming Healy's solicitor, and about how quickly that information had reached her.

'So what's up in Cambridge?' she asked innocently.

'I don't think that's any of your business.'

'Are you working a case?'

'We're done.'

She kept her eyes locked on mine as she slowly got up from the table, knowing that, even if I wanted to leave, I couldn't. I needed her to get me through the security doors and back out into the freezing cold of the day. And I was desperate for that cold now. I could feel heat prickling my skin, my throat tightening.

I followed her out.

At the front counter, she nodded at me but didn't say goodbye, and then I was barrelling towards the exit. The temperature hit me like a wall. I stood there for a long time, breathing it in – and then nerves scattered up my back, tracing the ridge of my spine, as the idea someone had been following me fully landed.

I looked around.

Opposite the public entrance to the station was Museum Gardens, some of its trees stripped for winter, others as full as if it were still the middle of summer. There were people walking its paths, more probably sheltered from view. There were so many hiding places there, it would have been easy for someone to disappear, to watch me.

You're being paranoid.

But it was too late now.

I couldn't shift the feeling.

Because maybe I wasn't being paranoid at all.

23

As soon as I got home, I swapped phones.

I kept a spare in my bedroom, along with a second laptop, and took both out of the cupboard and started charging them. As the phone charged, I texted Liz on it, telling her that my other phone had died. I didn't want to have to get into the reasons why I'd been forced into using a back-up mobile. It would only feed into doubts she already had about me.

A couple of minutes later, she texted back.

> Set some things in motion. Going to call H today and
> try and get in to see him asap but that could take
> 48hrs (or more) to sort.

I thanked her and then told her about Parkes:

> How would the Met know about you/him already?

She texted back a couple of minutes later:

> Probably heard from someone at the prison. I put in a request
> late last night, so the prison would have had my request to
> see him early AM today. Word travels fast. People know
> people.

It didn't really settle my nerves. I was still bothered by the fact that someone had seen me on a train to Cambridge and instantly got on the phone to Parkes. It meant that, internally at the Met, I was being discussed. And it was more than just people casually complaining about me working their unsolveds; now it felt like Parkes and her boss Phillips were actively raising awareness and in pursuit of me, not just trying to catch me out.

I made myself some lunch, thinking of Healy, and then – as I wolfed down a sandwich – glanced out at the driveway.

Someone was at the front gate.

He was in his sixties, wearing a blue parka, a grey suit underneath, and wedged between his arm and body was a leather slipcase. He looked like a salesman. He'd paused at the gate, his free hand on the frame, and was eyeing the house and the driveway that led down to the garage and back garden.

I shifted away from the counter, and as I did he must have registered the movement through the kitchen window because his eyes immediately pinged in my direction. The sun was on that side of the house, shining into the glass, so it was unlikely he'd seen much, but he must have seen enough, because he started making his way up the path, towards the front door.

The doorbell chimed.

I gave myself a second, wondering if I should answer, and then decided against it – if he really was a salesman, I didn't want to waste time listening to him pitching.

He rang the doorbell again, and when he got no response for the second time, something came through the letterbox and dropped on to the mat. It was a business card. Through the frosted glass panel on the door, I watched him turn and head off, his silhouette slowly receding.

I picked up his card.

Ryan Gilligan.

He was with the estate agency I'd sold the house through.

I opened the door and stepped out on to the porch, and as I did, he must have heard me, because he swivelled on his heel. 'Oh, Mr Raker,' he said. 'You *are* home.'

'Can I help you with something?'

'Yes.' He came back. 'I'm Ryan from Bowdens.'

I held up the business card. 'I can see.'

'Yes. Yes, of course.' He stopped short of the porch and looked along the front of the house. 'Such a lovely house, this one,' he said, and then returned his attention to me. He had grey eyes, one of them a little bloodshot, a roadmap of red vessels forking in at his iris. 'You're moving south of the river, right?'

'I am.'

'Kew's nice. You'll like it there.'

'What is it I can help with, Ryan?'

'Oh, of course,' he said, and unzipped the slipcase he had under his arm. 'We just have a couple of forms we need you to sign. Nothing serious. Just dotting the I's.'

I took the paperwork from him.

One was a feedback form, with the Bowdens logo and *Your opinion matters* printed along the top. The other was a checklist of things to remember to do before completion, like passing on warranties and building work certificates, or contacting places like surgeries, banks and utility companies about a change of address. The feedback form just asked for a contact name, not a signature, and the other was a long list of items with boxes to tick next to each one.

I frowned. 'There's nothing to sign here.'

He stepped closer to me, looking at the forms, and I caught the scent of him, a mix of cigarette smoke and aftershave. 'Oh, you're right,' he said. 'That's weird.'

I glanced at him, him at me.

A prolonged beat.

'I must have got confused.' He blinked, like he'd just snapped out of a daydream. 'I'm really sorry. I'm quite new at Bowdens, so still learning the ropes.'

He looked at the forms again.

'I need to get going,' I said to him.

'Of course. Sorry to have wasted your time.'

He took back the forms, returned them to the slipcase and said goodbye as he zipped it up again. I waited as he took off along the path and then headed inside the house, watching from the shadows of the kitchen as he got to the gate. Once he was there, he paused again, looking back at the house, at the windows, at the driveway, at the garden. It was a strange moment, as if he was trying to commit it all to memory.

A second later, he was gone.

I stayed where I was at the kitchen counter, thinking, my finger tapping out a gentle beat on the nearest worktop, and then dug out Gilligan's business card and dialled the direct line printed on it.

'Good afternoon, Bowdens.'

'Hi,' I said, 'I was wondering if I could speak to Ryan.'

'No, I'm afraid not, sir. He popped out about half an hour ago.'

'Do you know where he's gone?'

'He's just visiting a client. He should be back soon.'

'Okay, I'll call later, thanks.'

I ended the call. It tallied up: he'd popped out half an hour ago, he'd gone to see a client, and he must have stayed local in order to be expected back so soon – which made sense, as Bowdens was only a ten-minute walk from me. Maybe I really *was* getting paranoid. Or maybe Parkes floating the idea of someone from the police tracking my movements had rattled me more than I'd expected. That was probably the whole idea of her doing it: sow the seed, stand back, see if I fell apart.

I closed my eyes.

Clear your head. Focus.

When I opened them again, I saw that the laptop had finished charging, the power cable switching from amber to green. I pulled it out but didn't move, my hand on the MacBook, my brain firing as the same doubts clawed their way to the surface.

Something still didn't feel right.

I flipped up the lid on the laptop and went to the browser, putting in the URL for the Bowdens website. The front page had a property search function on it and a 'Top 10 featured houses' under that. There was a horizontal menu bar of options.

Buy. Sell. Rent. Valuation. Contact.

About.

I clicked on the *About* tab and it took me through to a brief biography of the company, and then – under that – a *Meet Our Team* section, with staff photographs.

Ryan Gilligan was five faces down.

I felt a twist in my gut.

It wasn't the same man who'd just come to my house.

24

I opened the door to the estate agency.

Behind the front counter, big enough that it almost went wall to wall, a woman smiled at me. To my left was a waiting area, to my right a bar fridge with soft drinks and bottles of water. The rest of the office extended out behind the counter, four desks on either side, a map of London on the back wall with mini SOLD flags all over it.

'Good afternoon, sir,' the woman said.

'Afternoon.' As soon as I stepped up to the counter, I could see two trays on the right: one was a feedback form with the Bowdens logo and *Your opinion matters* in type along the top; the other was a checklist of things to remember to do before your completion date. They were exactly the same forms that the man claiming to be Ryan Gilligan had handed me at the house.

There were no business cards on the front counter, so in order to get one, he must have actually spoken to the real Gilligan. I was struggling to understand the endgame, though, not just because I didn't have a clue who the guy at my house really was, but because I couldn't figure out why he'd chosen Gilligan. Was it simply because he knew that, if I thought he was from Bowdens, my guard would be down and he could get close to me? I remembered the way the man had eyed my home when he first arrived, then again when he left, as if scoping it out.

Had it been reconnaissance?

And then I had a second thought: could it have had something to do with my visit to The Castle this morning? Had I set something in motion?

'What can I help you with today?' the woman asked.

'Is Ryan around?'

I looked over her shoulder. I'd dealt with someone else for my house move and I didn't see her here today, and didn't know any of the others. There were three men.

'Yes, he is,' the woman said. 'Can I take a name?'

'David Raker.'

I watched her wander off to a desk at the back, where a slick-suited man in his late twenties was at his computer. The woman spoke to him, then he looked back at me, his face a complete blank. He did his best to conceal it, though, breaking out into a smile when we made eye contact – as if we were old friends – before coming over to me.

'Hi,' he said, 'I'm Ryan.'

'David Raker. I'm an investigator.'

In unison, the faces of Gilligan, the woman who'd gone to get him for me, and a Bowdens employee seated at the desk nearest to us all formed into the same expression. Surprise. Curiosity. Mild panic. Again, I was playing the percentages: I would show Gilligan my card once I got him alone, and make it clear I wasn't a cop – but having him believe it was some kind of official visit would get us going faster.

'Could we speak in private?'

I'd seen a door for a meeting room in the far corner.

'Yes,' he said, a little flustered now. 'Yes, of course.'

On the way, I noticed on each of the employees' desks there were small, clear plastic containers with business cards in, which explained how the man who'd come to my house had ended up with Gilligan's. Once we were inside the meeting room, I didn't prolong the misery any longer for him, told him that he wasn't in any trouble and handed him my card.

'I need your help to identify someone,' I said.

'*My* help?'

'A man came to my house this afternoon posing as you.'

His face blanched. 'What?'

'It's nothing to worry about,' I replied quickly, holding up a hand. 'I think you were just the person whose business card he happened to have. I need to try and find out who this guy is. Do you have CCTV instore?'

'We have a camera in there.'

He indicated the main floor.

'Can you access footage onsite?'

'Yes, the equipment's in the back.'

We crossed the office again, to a door on the opposite side. Along a short, bare corridor was a staff room and a video suite. There wasn't much to it: just a desk, a chair, and a Mac.

I woke the monitor from sleep and said, 'Do you mind if I take a look?'

'I, uh . . .' He paused. 'Maybe I should ask my manager.'

I didn't want him to do that because it would just slow everything down. And I realized pretty quickly that it was an option Gilligan didn't particularly want either: when he talked about his boss, something passed his face.

His boss intimidates him.

'Is your manager in today?'

'No, he's on his day off.'

'Do you want to call him at home?'

That looked like the worst possible outcome for Gilligan.

'I'm not sure that, uh . . .' He stopped.

I cranked up the pressure. 'Why don't you give him a call?'

'I, uh . . .' He looked between the monitor, which was now showing a black and white image from the camera installed on the main floor, then back to me. 'I'm not . . .'

'Call him at home. I'll wait.'

'It's fine,' he said, trying to restore some of the confidence to his voice, standing up a little straighter to show me that he was a guy who could make his own decisions. I wondered for a moment if this might be the reason why the man who'd come to my house had zeroed in on Gilligan: he saw that the sharp suit was just a façade. This was someone who could be manipulated easily.

'How many walk-ins have you had today?' I asked, searching the desktop and then the hard drive. I quickly found what I needed: the camera downloaded footage in one-hour chunks, and in a folder on the hard drive was seven days' worth. It looked like video that was older than that automatically deleted, freeing up space.

'Ryan,' I said again, looking over my shoulder at him. He was keeping an eye on the corridor, nervous but obviously trying to conceal it. 'How many walk-ins today?'

'Uh . . .' He paused. 'One, I think.'

'Do you remember when?'

'Around lunchtime.'

It was just after 4 p.m. now, so I didn't have to look hard to find the one-hour downloads from 12–1 and 1–2, but just to be on the safe side, I started with 11–12 first.

Opening the video, I clicked Play and then switched to 2x speed. Gilligan was seated at his desk, on the phone to someone. I upped the speed to 4x. He finished the call, another employee appeared from the staff room, a third came in from outside, and then the three of them talked for a while.

The video ended and I switched to the 12–1 file.

It picked up the second after the last one had finished. The staff only stopped chatting about ten minutes later, and then they returned to what they were doing on their computers. More talking. More phone calls. No one came in.

I closed the video and opened 1–2.

It took three minutes.

At 1.03 p.m., a man entered through the front door. He stopped at the counter and spoke to the same woman I had. From where the camera was positioned, it was hard to get a perfect view of his face.

But I could see enough.

It was him.

25

I leaned in closer to the CCTV video, studying the man who'd come to my house. He must have known he would leave a trail, must have factored in the idea that his lie about being Ryan Gilligan would catch up with him, and quickly. But it didn't seem to matter to him. And I could only really think of one reason why that would be the case – because he was confident I'd never be able find out who he was or why he'd pretended to be an estate agent.

Onscreen, the woman at the counter left him at the front while she went to get someone. As soon as she was gone, the man went to the end, looked in the in-trays and – with a quick check of where the woman was – took a sheet of paper from each. When she returned from Gilligan's desk, the forms were partly hidden behind his legs. The woman didn't seem to notice, mostly because Gilligan had got up from his desk and was coming over to see them both. I kept my eyes on the man, studying him closely, more convinced than ever that the reason he'd come to Bowdens was because he'd found out my house was with them and knew it would be a way to get close to me. I thought of the moments before he'd put Gilligan's business card through my letterbox and had started to walk back down my driveway: I'd shifted inside the house and my movement had registered with him. That was why he'd *then* put Gilligan's card through. He'd known I was home but not answering. He'd used the business card to draw me out.

Like a predator drawing out its prey.

Onscreen, the man shook hands with Gilligan.

'Ryan,' I said, pausing the video.

Gilligan turned at the doorway.

'You remember this guy?'

He edged closer to the Mac. 'Yeah,' he said, leaning in. 'He was the bloke I was telling you about who came in around lunch.'

'Was he selling?'

'Looking to sell, yes.'

'Did he give you his address?'

'I, uh . . .' He stopped.

'Or even the area he lived in.'

Gilligan didn't say anything, searching long enough for an answer for me to realize that it was going to be a *no*. No, the guy hadn't mentioned his address. No, he didn't give an area either. Right now, Gilligan was probably trying to figure out how he'd had a conversation with a potential client and failed to get either of those things out of them. But, to me, it just further confirmed who I was dealing with. Someone who didn't give up information. Someone in control.

Someone dangerous.

'Do you remember anything you talked about?' I asked.

'He was just, uh . . .' Again, Gilligan ground to a halt. He couldn't recall a single important detail about the conversation. And, as I watched it play out onscreen, I saw why: the man was in and out of Bowdens inside four minutes. As Gilligan got up from his desk, pointing to some houses on the wall behind him, the man swiped a business card, pocketed it, and then stood, feigning interest.

I dragged the cursor along the timeline, moving the footage back and forth, trying to get the best angle on the man I could – and when I finally had it, I hit Print.

'Can I message the video file to myself?' I asked Gilligan.

Gilligan looked panicked again, completely thrown by all of this, so I used his temporary confusion and AirDropped the 1–2 p.m. video to my phone.

'Where's the printer?'

Gilligan hadn't taken his eyes off the monitor.

'Ryan, where's the printer?'

'Uh, this way.'

He led me back out to the main floor. In a printer close to the front counter, an image of the man was waiting for me. I picked it up, looked at him again, and then thought about two things: the idea I was being followed by the Met, and the membership card I'd swiped at The Castle.

I had a hard time believing this guy was a cop. Impersonating someone else, if discovered, was a sure-fire route to collapse an entire investigation. The police had to abide by the rules and this broke every rule in the book.

So could this man's sudden appearance be connected to my visit to The Castle instead? The timing certainly fit. Maybe Ian Kirby had got back to his desk and instantly noticed there was a membership card missing. Except, if Kirby actually had any idea I'd taken that card at all, and he'd asked this man to retrieve it from me, why do it in this way? Why pretend to be Ryan Gilligan? It seemed more likely Kirby had no idea I'd taken the keycard – which meant, if this man worked for him, or The Castle, he was looking into me for some other reason.

Maybe because I'd been asking questions about the club's ownership.

Or maybe because I was asking questions about two missing women.

Healy

This Morning

It was the noise that got to him.

Even in the dead of night, there were always sounds from some-where. Most of the time, it was voices, the low hum of conversation from other cells. Occasionally, it would spill over into shouting. A few times, he'd heard screaming, the tell-tale cry of someone in terrible pain. Right now, it was his cellmate's snoring. Healy flipped back the covers and kicked at the bottom of the bunk.

His cellmate stirred, turned over, and went silent.

Healy pulled the blanket up over himself again, rolled on to his side and closed his eyes. The pillow felt flat and lifeless – like lying on a towel – but he tried to ignore it; tried to force himself to drop off. But, slowly, in the dark of his head, the same video began to play: Martine Parkes's visit fourteen hours ago, what she'd said to him about getting his charges reduced – and what he'd have to do in return.

Betray Raker.

Nausea bubbled in his throat.

Betray the one person who has looked out for me over the past eight years. He turned on to his back again, opening his eyes, staring up at the underside of the bunk, and tried to imagine what the cops wanted.

It's pretty obvious, isn't it?

Something they can really nail Raker with.

Raker had broken the law before, but every time he'd done it, Healy had never had a problem with it. Whatever lies Raker had told the cops down the years – and Healy probably didn't know all of them – were always for the greater good. Healy genuinely believed that. If you went into the shadows to confront the kind of monsters

149

the two of them had faced down the years, you weren't coming out again if you only played by the rules. And so even these moments, even *contemplating* betraying him, made Healy feel sick. He loved his boys, desperately wanted to see them. He wanted to explain his choices, and why he had to disappear. He wanted to be a father again, a grandfather for the first time. He craved the normal family life that a man his age should have had. But he didn't want his kids visiting him in prison for the next five, or ten, or thirteen years. He didn't want Liam to bring a baby into this place, to be forced to look at his first grandchild from the other side of a line on the floor that none of them were allowed to cross; to have to sit there as a prisoner, a convict, an embarrassment to his sons. It would be torture. Every part of him wanted to be free, wanted to look his sons in the eye and beg for their forgiveness, and tell them everything would be different now. Yet he couldn't pull the plug on Raker. He couldn't give Martine Parkes what she wanted. The idea was abhorrent.

So you're just going to accept thirteen years in here?

The sound of snoring had started again.

His cellmate was a twenty-one-year-old kid from Essex called Jordan who was in the second year of his sentence. He didn't really tell Healy a lot about what he had done to earn a top bunk in Pentonville for five years and that suited Healy fine because he didn't much want to discuss what *he* was inside for. But Jordan seemed an okay kid. In his time as a cop, Healy had seen a lot of Jordans: wide boys who got too deep into something bad and weren't smart enough to manoeuvre their way back out.

He rolled over again, facing the wall this time. Somewhere behind it, he could hear the gurgle and clunk of the hot-water pipes. As Jordan continued snoring, Healy thought of Raker once more, of what Parkes had said, of the deal she'd been dangling. Healy had made his peace with having to do jail time, but only when he'd thought it would be months. Maybe a year.

Not years, plural.

Not most of the rest of his life.

*

Roll call started at 6.30 a.m.

Healy had only dropped off just before 4 a.m. so, as he listened to the blare of the alarm, it took him longer than usual to rouse himself. Every bone ached, and not just because he'd only slept for two and a half hours. The pillows were shite, the mattress was like cardboard. His back hurt, and his hips hurt, and his neck hurt. He hauled himself up into a seating position.

Jordan swung off the top bunk.

'Morning, boss,' he said.

He always called Healy 'boss'.

Healy watched while the kid pulled on a pair of tracksuit trousers and looked at himself in the tiny, dirt-specked mirror stationed on a wall above a metallic sink. He started to play with his hair. As Healy got to his feet and grabbed his jumper, he caught Jordan eyeing him in the mirror's reflection.

'Something wrong?' Healy asked.

Jordan shook his head. 'No, boss.'

He didn't know Jordan well but he knew him well enough to understand some of his tics, and he could see that something was definitely up.

'Spit it out, Jordan.'

The doors buzzed.

Jordan was pulling on his trainers now. Outside, Healy could see men filing out of their cells and lining up in front of them.

'It's nothing,' the kid said, once his shoes were on.

'If it's nothing, then you won't mind telling me.'

For the first time, Jordan glanced out through the door – and that was when Healy realized he might be in trouble. It was just a feeling, a sixth sense, but he could see something in Jordan's expression that set alarm bells ringing.

'You were a fisherman, right?' Jordan said.

Healy nodded.

'Then why are people in here saying you were a copper?'

26

As soon as I got home, I grabbed my laptop, AirDropped the video across from my phone and opened the file. I'd been over it a few times at Bowdens, but now I went through it more forensically, using the cursor to tab through – slowly, carefully.

In total, he was onscreen for four minutes, eight seconds.

As I watched, I remembered again how he'd looked at me, how he'd looked at my house, assessed it, absorbed all the information that he thought he might need. In the video, he was the same: he didn't move much, except once, just before he left, when he glanced up into the eye of the camera, as if he'd known the entire time exactly where it was located. The movement was so quick – a flick, nothing more – that, when I paused it, trying to get a front-on view of his face, he was blurred.

Shortly after, he got up and headed for the door.

As I watched him go, the same thought occurred to me: he must have known I'd expose his lie about being Ryan Gilligan. Just from the way he sat, behaved, held himself, I could see he was in control – but his lie *lost* him that control.

Onscreen, he pulled open the door to Bowdens. As soon as he was outside, he headed right.

That was when I noticed something new.

I'd missed it on every other watch.

He doesn't actually leave the frame.

I hit Pause. I'd watched it all the way through to this point four times already, and every other time it looked like the man had vanished out of the frame completely, heading right – on foot – down Ealing High Street in the direction of The Broadway.

That wasn't the case.

Outside the estate agent's, right at the very edge of the window, he stopped. It was almost impossible to see him, which is why I'd consistently overlooked it before.

Almost impossible.

But not completely.

At the edge of the window, I could see his hand, down at his side, and a little of his shoulder. It looked like he was waiting for something – or some*one*. I used the cursor keys to inch the video on – frame by frame – slowing it to a crawl.

Twenty-two seconds later, something happened.

A car pulled in to the kerb.

It went most of the way past the window, only its rearside visible. I held on the image of it, trying to identify a make and model. It looked like a Mercedes hatchback.

Red.

Five-door.

The man moved. I could barely see him, because I couldn't see the front of the car. The only reason I knew he'd moved was because – just once – I glimpsed his hand again, the blue sleeve of the coat he was wearing, heading in the direction of the vehicle.

I took a screen dump of the image, opened it and magnified the shot, seeing if there was any way I could get a better view of the registration plate on the car. It was at an angle from me, and zooming in only blurred the detail. But I could make out some of it.

I grabbed a pen.

W??8 ?PL.

I played the rest of the footage but at no time did the man come in to view, and soon the Mercedes had accelerated away. I looked down at the partial plate number.

Three letters. One number.

That still might be enough.

I called Ewan Tasker.

'Three times in two days?' he said by way of a greeting.

'I know,' I said. 'Sorry, Task. This'll be it, I promise.'

'What are you after?'

'I've got a partial plate here.'

I read it out to him and told him the colour, make and model. The plate was either going to be 2008 or 2018 – and, from what I could see, it didn't look like a 2008 model Mercedes.

'Okay,' Tasker said, coming back on the line.

'You found something?'

'Red Mercedes A180. Two thousand and eighteen plate.'

'Who's it registered to?'

A couple of key taps – and then nothing.

'Task?'

I could hear a definite and obvious hesitation on the line.

'Task, who's the car registered to?'

He lowered his voice. 'Us.'

'"Us"? You mean, the Met?'

'Yes,' Tasker said. 'That Mercedes is an unmarked cop car.'

27

The Mercedes belonged to the Met.

Which meant the driver was a cop.

Did that mean I was wrong and the man who'd come here – who'd pretended to be Ryan Gilligan – was a cop too? I thought about Parkes knowing I was on the train to Cambridge. I thought about the residual worry I'd had ever since, that I was being followed, that this wasn't just the Met trying to catch me in a lie – through repetition, through wearing me down – but a concerted, co-ordinated, highly organized effort to put me behind bars. But would an officer really deliberately misidentify themselves?

'Raker, you there?'

Tasker's voice returned me to the moment.

'Yeah, I'm here. Can you find out who signed out the car?'

'Is this going to blow back on me?'

I understood his concerns. With the potential involvement of the Met, this became something uglier, more precarious.

'No,' I said. 'I've never let it happen before and I won't let it happen now.'

He told me he'd call me back and, after he hung up, I flicked through my notebook, going over everything I'd found out over the past two days.

Moving the Christmas tree out of the corner of the room, for the next twenty minutes I used a space on the living-room wall to tape up pictures of everyone involved – so far – in my search for Fiona Murphy. I then grabbed a pad of Post-its from the spare room and started to tack them up too, putting notes, reminders, and small details next to each photo. Finally, with a soft pencil, I drew lines between each picture, where there was an established connection.

Once I was done, I stepped back from the wall.

I felt as certain as I could be that Fiona and Jennifer knew one another. On the pencil line between them, I'd stuck a Post-it with the question *Friends?* written on it. Maybe they weren't best friends, but I refused to believe that they were totally unaware of each other, and in no way linked. And if they *were* friends, that, in turn, opened up possibilities elsewhere: that they were still friends into adulthood, and that Fiona's decision to walk out on her family on Boxing Day 1985 was directly attributable to Jennifer's sudden disappearance a week before; it was distinctly possible that one event informed the other.

From Fiona and Jennifer, I'd drawn a line to Mark Levin.

Again, I allowed the idea I'd been kicking around to emerge: that, while he was alive, Levin had found something big in the disappearances of the two women – big enough for him not to want to risk telling anyone about it, including Jonah Carling, until he got to a stage where he was ready to go public. But his search for answers had painted a target on his back. Someone had killed him in order to silence him and then they'd cleaned up. It would explain why Levin had left nothing on Fiona behind – because all the evidence he'd collated had been destroyed by his killer. I felt a cold finger down my spine as I thought of Georgie Levin and the idea that someone – in the aftermath of her husband's death – might have been inside her house.

On the table, my phone burst into life.

The number on the display was one I didn't recognize but I knew it was almost definitely Tasker calling me back about the red Mercedes. To hide us ever being in touch, he used about five different burners.

'The name of the cop who signed out the car is illegible,' Tasker said. 'It left the station at 10.47 a.m. this morning, but that's about as much as I can tell you. The signature's a mess. The "Print Name in Capitals" box is just a squiggle.'

It was obviously deliberate.

If anyone looked later on, no one would know who had the car.

'I asked,' Tasker went on, 'because I knew *you'd* ask, and, no, there's no CCTV in that part of the building, so there's no video that's going to tell you who it was. The only video you're likely to get is of a red Merc exiting the car park at Central South.'

'Central South? So that's – what? – Walworth?'

'Correct.'

There were thirty-two boroughs in London, and those were divided up into twelve Basic Command Units, or BCUs. Central South covered Southwark and Lambeth, and the main station within the area was at Walworth. If I'd had any thoughts about any of this being the endeavours of Parkes, or the people who worked with her, that seemed unlikely now: she was based in Bethnal Green, at the Central East BCU. The red Mercedes had left from a car park five miles south-west of where Parkes was based, on the other side of the river. But if it wasn't Parkes, it might have been someone else: whoever the cop was who'd been on the same train as me to Cambridge.

'For what it's worth,' Tasker said, 'I've got some names for you.'

'Names?'

'It looks like only about eight detectives ever use that car.'

I didn't recognize any of the people he read out to me, but I wrote them down all the same. He gave me their rank and, where possible, any history he'd found on them. After I was finished, I said, 'I appreciate this, Task.'

I pulled a chair out, dragged my laptop towards me, and started to google the eight detectives Tasker had listed. It was just dead end after dead end.

'I'm going to have to lie low for a while after this,' Tasker said.

'I understand. Like I say, I really appreciate everything you . . .'

I stopped.

'Raker?'

'Just hold the line a sec, Task.'

I'd got to the last of the eight detectives.

DS Letitia Scargill.

I didn't recognize her name; didn't recognize her face either. She looked as if she was in her forties, medium build, and was sharply dressed; in every photograph of her I found online – which wasn't many – she had her hair in intricate, shoulder-length braids with a black headband keeping them out of her face.

It wasn't her name or appearance that had stopped me, though.

It was where she worked.

The Serious Crime Review Group.

The SCRG was a department at the Met that, every two years or so, pulled fifteen to twenty cases out of storage in order to review them. They were basically checking that nothing had been missed the first time around, and to see if there was the opportunity to apply new, modern forensic techniques that hadn't been available at the time the original case was investigated.

'Task, absolutely the last thing, I promise.'

'You better be taking me to The Ritz for this.'

'Can you tell me what cases Letitia Scargill has been looking at?'

'What, you mean what's logged on the system?'

'Yeah, if possible.'

'You'll have to give me a sec,' he replied and then I heard him start to move: the fading in and out of sounds, voices, doors opening and closing. As I waited, I looked at my wall, following the lines from Fiona, to Jennifer, to Levin, to The Castle, to here.

'Got it,' Tasker said.

'What does it say?'

'It looks like she was nosing around in the PNC yesterday.' PNC was the Police National Computer. 'She was looking at two women who went missing in 1985.'

Watcher

Rebekah | *This Afternoon*

Rebekah rubbed at her eyes as she waited for Frank.

The jet lag was starting to bite: it was just getting dark outside, Christmas lights coming to life at the windows of the hotel, but her body was doing its best to convince her that she was still in New York and it was late morning.

Earlier on, she'd led Frank around the city, helping him tick off all the tourist sites he'd never done. And although Frank didn't admit it, just as Rebekah knew he wouldn't, he was worn out, so when they returned to the hotel, Rebekah suggested they go to their rooms for a couple of hours. Unable to drop off herself, she'd come down here, to the empty hotel bar, and grabbed a booth overlooking Regent's Canal.

She ordered a coffee and went to her phone, checking for messages, hoping for something from David Raker. There was nothing. Before long, she was back where she normally ended up: her photos. Pain bloomed under her ribs as she looked at her father and her brothers, and then stopped at her favourite picture of them. They were all laughing. Rebekah wished she could remember about what.

The one after that was a scanned-in shot of her mother.

'What if the reason she left us is just the reason we always thought?' Rebekah had said to Frank earlier as they'd sat and had lunch. 'She never wanted us, never wanted to *be* with us, didn't want to be a mother. How's that going to help me?'

Frank hadn't spoken for a moment, holding his silence like a breath.

And then, quietly, he'd said, 'Even if it *is* that, you need the truth.'

'And what if David can't find the truth?'

'I think he will,' Frank said.

She'd looked at him, waited.

'In my experience, the truth never stays buried forever.'

Rebekah swiped off the photograph of her mother, back to some pictures of her daughters, and then glanced up from her phone.

Someone else was seated in the hotel bar now, their back to her, a laptop open in front of them. Rebekah wasn't sure if it was a man or a woman as they were wearing a hoodie and the hood was up. She returned her attention to her phone, to the pictures of her daughters. But then, in her head, something registered.

She looked up again.

On the person's laptop, a sliver of it visible to the right of their body, it appeared like a video window was open, the laptop's camera showing a reflected image of the person's shoulder and what was behind them.

Rebekah could see herself.

Suddenly, the person in the hoodie snapped the lid closed, picked up the laptop and headed out of the bar.

They were gone inside ten seconds.

Rebekah sat there, looking at the now-empty table, immediately dismissing the question gathering in her head like a storm cloud.

Except it wouldn't quite dislodge.

And so she let it come again.

Had that person just been recording me?

PART FOUR
The Intruder

28

I headed north to Letitia Scargill's house, trying to work out a plan of attack.

Twenty-four hours ago, she was looking at the official missing persons reports for Fiona Murphy and Jennifer Johnson. This morning, she'd fudged the paperwork on a police pool car so no one would know she'd taken the vehicle out. At lunchtime, she'd been the driver for a man who'd lied to me about who he was.

I didn't know if she was going to be home.

All I knew was that I needed answers.

Traffic was slow, snarled up by an accident, but I'd barely been in the car ten minutes when my phone started buzzing.

It was Liz.

'You okay to talk?' she said.

'Yeah. What's up?'

'I spoke to Healy earlier on.'

I pictured the last time I'd seen him: it had been at the house we'd rented for him in North Wales. I remembered the shaved hair, the red beard, the sadness that lingered in the angles of his face.

'How did he sound?' I asked.

'I don't know. I don't really know him any more.'

'Gut reaction, then.'

Liz paused. 'He sounded scared.'

Healy

This Morning

As Healy stared at Jordan, it was hard to keep his expression neutral, hard to suppress the shock and the panic and the fear – but he managed it. Just.

'Who in here reckons I'm a copper?' he said.

Jordan stared back at Healy for a moment, the two of them facing each other inside the narrowness of the cell. They'd shared the same space for the last four and a half months but it had never felt as small as it did now.

'Jordan?' he said again. 'Who told you that?'

'What difference does it make if it isn't true?'

'I just want to know who's spreading rumours about me.'

One of the guards appeared in the doorway. Before Jordan got a chance to reply, the guard looked between them and said, 'What is this, some sort of mothers' meeting?'

'No, boss,' Jordan said, obediently.

'Mr Healy?'

'No, boss,' Healy echoed.

'Then get in line and stop fannying around.'

Jordan headed out and Healy followed, the two men falling into place beside one another for morning roll call. As Healy stood there, watching the guards working the two floors above them, he scanned the faces up there that he could see. No one was looking down at him – no one seemed interested – but that didn't mean anything.

Jordan had heard a rumour about him from somewhere.

Which meant someone in here knew the truth.

And, before long, so would everybody else.

*

164

After roll call, the prisoners dispersed, most of them – like Jordan – returning to their cells to have the breakfast that had been handed out the night before. Healy wanted to confront Jordan again, but he had to go and get his meds first. Under the watchful eye of staff, he queued up and took his antiplatelets, then his blood pressure pills, and, after that, he hurried back to the cell. Jordan wasn't there.

Healy grabbed a pre-packaged croissant and went to the door, looking up to Twos and Threes, which was what the staff and prisoners called the second and third floors. He couldn't see Jordan up there either. Finishing the croissant, he wolfed down a banana, boiled some water and made himself a coffee, then sat on the edge of his bunk, thinking.

'Mr Healy.'

One of the guards, Sanderson, a tubby, fair-haired man in his early fifties, was hovering in the doorway. A piece of paper was in his hands.

'You've got a phone call this afternoon at two-thirty.'

'A phone call?' Healy frowned. 'I think that might be a mistake, boss. I had a visitor yesterday.'

'You don't think I can tell the days of the week apart?'

'No, I didn't mean that. I just meant –'

'Some solicitor wants to speak to you – and someone here must have owed her a favour, because she only put the form in last night and it's already been signed off. You'll be speaking with a . . .' Sanderson looked down at the printout. 'Ms Feeny.'

It took a moment for it to click. '*Elizabeth* Feeny?'

'That's the name I've got here,' Sanderson responded.

Confused, Healy's thoughts started racing.

'Are you going to take the call?'

'Yes, boss,' Healy said.

'Then someone will be back for you later.'

Sanderson exited the doorway and left Healy alone again. From outside his cell, he heard voices, shouting, guards making conversation and giving orders, but it hardly registered as anything more than white noise.

All he could think about was Liz Feeny.

He hadn't seen her in at least ten years. But now she wanted to talk to him. Maybe she was going to ask him to shift representation to her from the solicitor he had now. And there was really only one reason she'd do that.

One reason she'd even know he was in here.

Raker.

A phone was waiting in a consultation room on the other side of the prison.

The guard took Healy in, watched him take a seat, and then exited again. He remained outside, visible through a glass panel in the door.

At exactly two-thirty, the phone started ringing.

Healy picked up. 'Hello?'

'Colm, it's Liz Feeny.'

'How you doing, Liz?'

'Better than you, I'm guessing.'

He glanced at the guard standing outside the door. Even though he knew he wouldn't be able to hear – that this entire conversation was protected under legal privilege – Healy kept his voice deliberately low, leaned into the phone and said, 'What's going on?'

'Straight to the point, as always.'

'Are you going to get me out of this shitehole?'

'If by that you mean "offer you representation", then yes.'

'Did he ask you to call me?'

'I've managed to cobble together some stuff in the few hours I've had. If you want me to go forward with your case, we'll need to set some things into motion so –'

'*Did* he ask you?'

Liz paused for a moment. 'Yes.'

Healy sat back in his chair, thinking.

'I thought you'd be happy about that,' Liz said.

'It's not that. I just really need to get out of here.' His mind was racing, trying to run down all the routes he could take and which one got him out of here quickest.

'Colm?'

'Yeah, I'm listening.'

'Are you all right?'

'I'm fine,' he said. 'It's just this dump.'

'Okay, well, he wants me to arrange a call between you both.'

'To do what?'

'Well, as I understand it, you two don't know each other.' She paused, giving Healy a chance to catch up: *Yes*, she was saying, *Raker has told me*. 'The way he sees it – and I tend to agree with him – is that, in order for you both to continue *not* knowing one another, you need to be singing from the same hymn sheet. You haven't had a face-to-face meeting for almost five months. You need to regroup, restrategize.'

'We can't do a face-to-face.'

'Not physically in prison. But we can do another call.'

He nodded. 'What am I looking at here, Liz?'

'Looking at?'

'The Met say I could get thirteen years.'

'The Met said that?'

'Yes.'

'It's just them trying to put the fear into you.'

'They say they've spoken to the CPS.'

'I'm sure they have.'

'You know the basics of my case, right?'

'I've read it overnight, yes.'

'So what am I looking at?'

'You're not going to be in there for thirteen years, Colm.'

'Eight? Ten?'

Liz took a breath. 'Only if everything goes spectacularly wrong.'

'And if it doesn't?'

'Hard to say.'

'Best guess.'

A beat. Two. 'You might get a year. Maybe less. It depends on a lot of factors, but mainly on a good defence, which I can give you if you decide to let me represen—'

'So, even if it goes well, I'll still be here for another *year*?'

'We can try and persuade the court you're not a flight risk.'

'You mean, try again to get bail? How long will that take?'

'To go before a judge?' She went quiet again. 'Weeks.'

He groaned. *Weeks*. She seemed to think that was fast, but it wasn't. *It wasn't anywhere near fast enough.* And now he couldn't even speak to Liz, because he was scared he'd have to acknowledge the thoughts that were in his head: Parkes, what she'd said when she'd come in the day before, and the promise she made to him.

Time served if he co-operated.

If he went with Liz, he could be in here years.

If he took the Met's deal, he'd be out in days.

29

'What do you mean he sounded scared?' I said.

Liz didn't reply. In the background, I could hear her tapping a pen.

'Liz?'

'Do you know if the Met have been in to see him?'

'Yes, of course they have.'

'No, I mean informally?'

'As opposed to what?'

'As opposed to scheduling an on-the-record meeting.'

'I don't know. Why do you ask?'

'He said the Met told him that he could get thirteen years if everything sticks. That's not how they tend to work. I mean, every copper has a pencil-sketch of what sentence a suspect might get for what charge – but plods don't tend to articulate that in an interview. So I don't know . . .' She stopped. 'Something feels weird.'

I took a moment to think.

'Parkes,' I said.

'What?'

'I bet Martine Parkes has been in to see him.'

'If she's gone in as a member of the public, that's morally grey.'

'I don't think she or Phillips are particularly worried about that. If you speak to Healy again, tell him he needs to begin refusing visits from her.'

'I suspect he knows that already.'

'If he knows it, then what's he still doing talking to her?'

'Because he's not just scared, Raker. He's lonely.'

Liz was right. Even Parkes was company; someone to talk to, some connection to the outside world he'd been ripped from almost five months ago. I understood it, and I felt a wave of sympathy for

Healy, especially as he'd spent so much of the last eight years alone. But Parkes wasn't his friend.

She was a vessel for her boss, who loathed him.

Who loathes both of us.

'*Do* you think he could get thirteen years?'

'No,' Liz replied, instantly, definitively.

'So what could he get?'

'Harder to say.' She paused, seemed to be playing it out in her head. 'They have that fake passport he was found with. From what I've seen so far, it also looks like there's an evidence trail to him via *other* IDs he's used over the past eight years. Or maybe I should say, that you've organized for him.' She gave me a chance to tell her anything else I'd kept back, but I'd told her everything the previous night at her offices. 'They raided the forger in south London you used and found "a clear connection to" Healy. Reading between the lines, that probably means his face and the other IDs he's used since he "died" have been found on a computer somewhere.'

'What about faking his death?'

'Faking a death itself isn't necessarily the problem; it's the fact that he committed a crime once he'd done it. Those forged passports are a crime. Tampering with evidence is a crime.'

'There's no proof he tampered with evidence.'

'It's a safe bet that the cops will keep digging until they get to that DNA switch. If they do, we might be able to argue that it's *not* evidence tampering, but simply a mix-up at the lab depending on what the Met find. We could pretend that it was an accident, or incompetence, or that two sets of DNA were simply labelled wrongly. It's hard to make that call, though, until we see what they've got. But here's the thing: a jury is going to look at what *else* Healy has been keeping secret – multiple false identities, the faked death, the rented houses being paid for through shell companies – and it's going to place him in a suspicious light. We could paint the lab as some clownshop operation – *maybe* – but, to a jury, there's already an established pattern of untrustworthiness.'

'They won't get to the bottom of the DNA switch.'

'Why, because you're such a genius?'

'No,' I said, 'but we covered our tracks.'

'We can talk about this more in the morning, but all that aside . . .' She stopped again. 'I still think there's something going on with him.'

'You said you think he's scared.'

'Yeah. But I think it might be more than that.' Liz was silent for a moment. 'I think he might be wrestling with something.'

30

Letitia Scargill lived in an end of terrace in Wembley.

I parked four doors down from her, on the opposite side of the road, and then switched off the engine. My car was facing away, so my view of her house was via the rear-view and side mirrors, and I'd made sure to back in close to the car behind me so she wouldn't be able to see my plate. I had to assume she already knew it, that she knew my face, my personal information – and maybe plenty else.

Softly, my watch beeped. It was 9 p.m.

The house was dark, completely unlit, and her car wasn't on the driveway, so it seemed likely she wasn't home yet. I didn't know how long it would be before she was or what my plan was going to be when she arrived, but I'd figure it out.

From my pocket, I removed the printout I'd made of the guy who'd posed as Ryan Gilligan and unfolded it. I couldn't see every detail inside the gloom of the car, but I could see enough, and remembered the rest: in his mid-sixties, probably six-two, broad and well built, with thinning hair, shaved at the sides. I closed my eyes for a second, picturing him at my house. Letitia Scargill was forty-one, so would have only been four when Fiona disappeared. But the man – her possible accomplice – was at least twenty years older. He'd have been in his mid-to-late twenties in 1985, which would have made him pretty much the same age as Fiona and Jennifer.

On the drive up from Ealing, I'd bought myself a coffee and now, as I stared at the man, I peeled the lid away and gathered my thoughts. Steam curled off the surface, filling the car with a bitter scent. I took a mouthful, needing the caffeine kick, and the warmth too. The car was starting to cool down fast, the night numbingly cold. I didn't want to run the engine, because it would draw attention to me, so I rationed out the coffee instead, taking deliberately small amounts and savouring the heat of it. It had been a long day already, with a flood of questions – and it was only going to get longer, and there were only going to be more questions. It didn't help that some of those questions would forever go unanswered.

Jennifer Johnson was most likely dead.

Mark Levin definitely was.

Henry Murphy was in a cemetery three and a half thousand miles away, and I had no idea about Fiona. If it hadn't been for the cards that she'd sent to her former husband and her children, decades after walking out on them, I would have believed she was dead too. Except, as I kept reminding myself, maybe she wasn't the one that had sent them.

I leaned over and opened the glovebox.

I removed the cards and took them out of their envelopes. All three had the same handwriting – the same quirks on the same letters – all three had pretty much the same message, and although all three cards were slightly different, they were all clearly designed by the same person or company. But which person and which company? Even if, somehow, I managed to find out where they were made, it wouldn't necessarily help me identify the sender.

But it might help me get closer.

I grabbed my phone from my pocket and, one by one – the flash blinking on and off as I did – I took the best photograph of the front of the cards that I could. I then went to Google and uploaded the first of the photographs, seeing if I could find an image match – either the card itself on sale somewhere on the internet, or a card that was in some way similar. I hadn't bothered to do it the day before because it seemed like such a long shot, but a day on I was willing to give it a chance.

Soon, though, I realized my initial instincts were right.

Ten thousand visually similar results, but none of them were the cards that Rebekah had received. I uploaded the two other pictures, just to be sure, and then spent a while going through the matches to make certain I definitely hadn't missed anything. I hadn't. It was another dead end.

Tapping out a rhythm on the wheel, I laid the cards on the dashboard, looking at the designs under the soft orange glow of the street lights.

And then my attention shifted.

In the rear-view mirror, a pair of headlights emerged at the bottom of the road. I watched as they got closer, the rest of the car forming out of the murk of the night.

Letitia Scargill had arrived home.

31

It was a Toyota that pulled into the driveway. A street light coloured the driver's side door, revealing Scargill at the wheel, and then she came to a stop and killed the headlights.

As she climbed out, I finally got my first proper look at her. She hadn't changed much from the photographs I'd found on the internet: same build, same cut of trouser suit, same hairstyle, the braids dancing on her shoulders and kept back from her face by the same type of headband.

She paused for a moment, door open, lit by the car's interior lamp. She had her phone out now, staring intently at the screen. Eventually, she disappeared along the driveway.

I put the condolence cards away and then waited, finishing my drink, starting to feel cold now. Reaching into the back seat, I grabbed my coat and wriggled into it, flipping up the hood. It had been so long since the heaters were on, breath was starting to form in front of my face.

Twenty minutes passed.

And then, at 9.50, there was movement again.

In my rear-view mirror, Letitia Scargill reappeared, coming back along the driveway towards her car. She stopped: she was at the tail end of the Toyota, mostly concealed by shadows, but not enough for her to be hidden entirely. Her head was down, her arm moving back and forth across her face.

What was she doing?

Finally, she moved again, coming past her car and stopping again at the end of her driveway. That was when I realized: she was wiping her eyes.

She's been crying.

I sank down, into my seat, trying to prevent myself being seen, and watched in the side mirror as she got closer. She had her phone to her ear, and a moment later, she was talking to someone: 'Yeah, I'm on my way.'

She was almost at my car.

'An hour at most,' she said. She was smiling now, but it felt fake, as if she were trying to fool herself into pretending she was happy. 'No, it's fine, I've just had a long day and need to be up early.' She listened for a moment, then chuckled. 'No, I mean it: an hour max. It's all the drinking time you're getting out of me tonight.'

Her tone must have sounded convincing to the friend she was talking to, but on her face there remained obvious signs of distress: wet eyes that reflected back the nearest street light; a flush to her cheeks, clear even at night.

She passed my car.

'Okay, I'll see you at the pub in ten minutes,' she said, and hung up, dropping her mobile phone into her pocket. Slowly, the dark of the night began to swallow her.

I looked at her house again – windows black, doors closed.

She was going to be away for an hour.

I grabbed my lockpicks.

32

A minute later, I had the side door open.

I paused there, taking out a pair of latex gloves, and then pushed at the door and let it swing back on its hinges, waiting just in case she'd set an alarm.

Silence.

I headed inside.

As the door clicked shut, the sounds of the house faded in: I could hear the refrigerator, the tick of a clock. Ahead of me was an archway into the living room; to my left was the hallway. I headed into the hallway, where I found two more doors and a staircase: the first door was for a toilet; the second was for another, taller archway into the living room, just at the front end of the house.

Ideally, I wanted to turn on my phone, to use the flashlight function, but it was too risky. People out on the street might see. Instead, I entered the living room and waited, allowing my eyes to adjust to the dark.

Starting with a bookcase, I moved from there to a sideboard and then a TV cabinet and found nothing of note in any of them. On a dining table at the far end of the room, where the patio doors looked out over a small, two-level garden, there was a laptop charging. It belonged to the Met, a sticker on the front confirming as much. The second I flipped the lid up, a password box appeared. Closing it again, I headed for the stairs, taking them two at a time.

On the landing, I paused: there was a little more light here, the lamps out on the street able to carry across the tops of the trees in Scargill's road and settle inside as an insipid amber. To my left and right were bedrooms; ahead was the bathroom.

I went to the bedroom on the left first.

It was obvious it was the one that Scargill slept in, the spare bedroom on the opposite side of the house little more than a single bed and a wardrobe.

In the corner of her bedroom was a dressing table, and on a shelf in the bay window was a line-up of framed faces. I moved closer: photos of Scargill, with two women of about the same age, the similarities between the three of them suggesting they were sisters; Scargill with her father, with groups of friends. There were no obvious indications in the pictures that she had a partner, but that was exactly the problem: I knew nothing about Scargill – her history, her career, her life.

I took photographs of her family and friends – just so I had a visual record – and then turned my attention to her fitted wardrobes. I went through clothing, just in case she'd left notes in the pockets, business cards, things to help me make a connection to what was going on, but again drew a blank. So far, I couldn't find anything to help me understand what she and the man were doing in the red Mercedes earlier on.

On one side of the mattress, squeezed in between the fitted wardrobe and the frame, was a bedside cabinet with three drawers. I worked from the bottom up: more junk, some old books, charging cables, foreign currency. In the top drawer it was the same, except, sitting on top of the mountain of old, discarded detritus, was an iPad.

I took it out and switched it on.

Immediately it was obvious that the tablet was for personal use. There was nothing remotely connected to her work as a detective.

I went to her Facebook feed, which she didn't seem to use much. Instagram she used even less: she'd posted one photo two years ago of her with her sisters. Her sisters were the same women I'd seen in the photographs. From there, I went to Chrome, seeing what her bookmarks were, but there was nothing of any interest.

Then I went to her *History*.

She'd either not used the browser in two days or the *History* for the past forty-eight hours had been deliberately erased. Before that, she appeared to have used the internet frequently. I tried to imagine why there was a gap. What had she been looking at that she didn't want to leave evidence of? In order to even think that way, she must have been entertaining the idea that, sooner or later, people were going to find this iPad and search it. So was she worried about someone like me breaking into her home and going through her stuff? Or was this more about what the cops might find?

Why would the police – her colleagues – search her home?

I put the iPad back where I'd found it. As I did, some of the junk shifted around inside the drawer, and a folded piece of paper I'd seen a few minutes ago caught my eye again.

It was a letter, the logo now visible at the top.

Something plunged inside me.

It was from The Castle.

33

The letter itself was mundane – just a thank you to Letitia Scargill for renewing her membership for another year – but as I thought about everything else I'd found out so far on this case, I could see the letter for what it was: yet another arrow pointing in the direction of The Castle.

Jennifer Johnson had worked there.

Mark Levin had been a member there.

Now this: someone else who, however peripherally, was orbiting my hunt for Fiona. I hadn't found a direct connection between Fiona and The Castle – yet – but I was increasingly confident that I would.

I grabbed my phone and went to The Castle's website. Tapping on *Sign In*, I put Scargill's name into the username box, then copied her membership number on the renewal letter into the second box. A click later, I was inside the club's intranet again. I knew already I wouldn't find anything revelatory; my goal was simply to find out how long Scargill had been a member.

The answer was four years.

I thought once more about the man pretending to be Ryan Gilligan, about the timing of his arrival – just a few hours after I'd quizzed Ian Kirby about the ownership of the club and the two missing women. And then I wondered again if the man was a cop like Scargill – or something else.

An employee of The Castle.

Someone who solved problems.

Problems like me.

If I was right, if he *did* work for the club, if he'd got to Scargill somehow and was now using her access at the Met – which would explain the database searches for Fiona and Jennifer, and maybe

Scargill leaving home in tears earlier – I just couldn't work out the other, greyer areas in between. Why pretend to be Ryan Gilligan? Why do something that meant putting my focus on him? Why show his face to me at all?

Then, quietly, I heard a noise.

I paused, phone still in my hand, the letter on the floor next to me. Had Scargill got home from the pub early? I listened to the sounds of the house.

Nothing.

Slowly, I put the letter back in the drawer, making sure the iPad and junk underneath were in about the same position I'd found them, and listened again.

Silence.

I stood, pocketing my phone, and padded across the bedroom to the landing. If it was Scargill, she would surely have put the lights on. So could it be someone else? Or had the noise been external? This house was foreign to me: I didn't know its tempo, its pulse, what noises came from where.

After a couple of minutes of watching, waiting, I made my way downstairs, checking over the living room, then the kitchen, then the downstairs toilet.

The house was still empty.

No one seemed to be inside.

I opened the side door.

Pausing, I looked both ways along the driveway, then stepped out into the cool of the night, soft-closing the door behind me. I crouched down, resetting the lock using the picks so Scargill would never know someone had been inside her house.

Just as I was getting back to my car, movement caught my eye.

Someone had entered the street, footsteps echoing, thick clouds of breath gathering above them.

They passed beneath a light, looking in my direction.

A second later, they stopped dead.

34

Letitia Scargill didn't move.

One half of her was painted orange by a nearby street light. The other was still rooted in darkness.

I held up a hand. 'I don't care what you've done.'

She didn't say anything; still didn't move.

'I really don't. I just want to know what's going on.'

There was a change in her face now, almost an acceptance that she'd expected this moment to come – just not as soon as this. She took a step forward, into the light, and said, 'How did you find me?'

She had a soft south London accent.

'I saw your car in some CCTV footage.'

She glanced over her shoulder. It was brief, but there: the look in her face was of someone scared, someone worried about what might be following in her wake. Or *who*. I thought of the man who'd come to my house.

'Have you talked to anyone else?' she asked.

'What would I tell them?'

'Whatever you think's going on.'

'What *is* going on?'

She didn't reply. Instead, she said, 'You haven't talked to the Met?'

'You clearly don't know everything about me, then.' I smiled at her, an attempt to get her to settle. She was smart, so she knew what I was trying to tell her – the cops didn't like me, didn't trust me, were basically my enemy. Why would I tell them anything?

'This whole thing . . .' Her words faded away.

'Is someone blackmailing you?'

It took her a long time to summon up the answer; a long time to open the floodgates to whatever came after this. But finally, quietly, she said, 'Yes.'

'Is it him?' I got out the CCTV image of the man and took a couple of careful steps towards Scargill. The printout wasn't the best, but even in the subdued light of the road, I could see from her face that it *was* him.

'Yes,' she confirmed.

'Who is he?'

She looked over her shoulder a second time.

She's terrified of him.

'If you want to talk,' she said, 'let's talk inside.'

I let her pass me and then followed her across the road, back to her house. As she made her way down the driveway, she reached into her pockets for a set of keys.

But then, outside the door, she paused.

She'd had a moment of clarity: I'd been getting into my car when we'd seen each other. Did that mean I'd come from her house?

If I was going to get her to trust me, I had no choice but to lie.

'I don't break into houses if that's what you're thinking. I was just seeing if you were home.'

She pushed the door handle down, checking to see if the lock was still secure. 'No offence,' she said, and then opened up.

I followed her in, watching as she felt around for a switch on her left under one of the kitchen cabinets. A strip light flickered into life above us.

'Do you want something to drink?' she asked.

'I'm fine.'

I pushed the door shut and she immediately reached past me, sliding her keys back in and securing the lock. Even after the dead-bolt had made an audible click, she tried the door handle three times to make sure it was definitely closed.

She looked at me, didn't say anything.

As I waited in the kitchen, she disappeared through to the hall-way, and I could hear her try the front door. I heard her walking around in the living room, checking the windows were locked, the patio doors, then there was the metallic rattle of runners along poles as every curtain was drawn. I spent another minute alone in the wan half-light of the kitchen as she went upstairs, the same sounds, the same checks up there.

When she returned, she backed up against one of the counters. The kitchen window was just a black square now, nothing of the back garden visible, and, as I faced her, I could see a reflection of myself in it – pale, ghostly.

'Did you mean what you said?' she asked, her voice muted. 'That you don't care what I've done?'

There was something ominous in her choice of words, something that told me it was going to be hard to stay neutral once we started along this road. But I needed to get her talking, so I nodded and said, 'Were you the one that called Parkes about me being on that train?'

'Yes.'

'Then I want to know why you followed me to Cambridge yesterday – and I want to know why you were in the PNC looking into the disappearances of Fiona Murphy and Jennifer Johnson. Those are the things I care about.'

She seemed to realize now that she was cornered.

Talk, don't talk: it was all imperfect.

She turned around, reaching over the sink to the levers for the blinds. She lowered them down, all the way to the tiled sill.

The locks were turned.

The curtains and the blinds were all down.

She was safe, cocooned – for now.

Looking at me, she said, 'You haven't talked to Martine? Her boss?'

Martine. She was on first-name terms with Parkes, so that explained why she felt so comfortable picking up the phone to her and letting her know that I was on that train to Cambridge. The real question was whether she did it for her own reasons, or because the man who'd come to my house had told her to; and if he'd told her to, I needed to know why she was willing to do his bidding like that. I shook my head and said, 'No, I won't be talking to Parkes, Phillips, or anyone else at the Met.'

'So you're just super chill about all this, is that it?'

A little twist of anger in her words, which I guessed had nothing to do with me or the fact that I was now standing inside her house, and everything to do with how she'd ended up in a situation where she was ferrying around a man that frightened her.

'No, I'm not super chill about it.'

'What about if I don't talk to you?'

I held her gaze and said, 'I think it's better if you do.'

It wasn't a threat, but it was close.

I got out my mobile phone. Straightaway, she started shaking her head: 'No. If you record me, I don't talk.'

'Sooner or later, this is coming out.'

'Then I'd rather it was later.'

I put my phone down and got out my notebook instead.

'So where do you want to start?' she said, weakly.

'Why don't we start at the beginning?'

Argus

As instructed, Holt waited for Larsen in the changing rooms at The Castle.

He was tired. He'd barely slept all week, but he hadn't slept at all the previous night. The Rockingham wasn't the kind of hotel that offered a wake-up call, so he spent most of the night rolling over, listening to the sounds of the city, worried about being late.

He hoped Larsen was going to move him soon.

He checked his watch, saw it was ten minutes past six, and then looked out at the changing rooms. They were long and narrow, a bank of lockers on the left, an alcove with some showers on the right, and two doors at the end that he knew were for a steam room and a sauna. At the very end was a set of enclosed spiral stairs: Holt had got here early and taken the stairs up to see where they went. They led to a rooftop swimming pool.

He hadn't had a chance to look around the rest of The Castle, but he thought it was a weird place to meet. It made him wonder why Larsen would choose it. He tried to mine his knowledge of Larsen for an answer, his memories of the man, the person he'd served with, but he came up short. Larsen, like Holt, had run from something back home. Holt didn't know what his former CO had fled from, which put Holt at a disadvantage because Larsen knew *exactly* why Holt had fled – but Larsen had come to London to start again.

Holt had often wondered what it was that Larsen could have done.

How bad it must have been for him to run like he did.

And whether it was worse than what Holt had done.

*

'What do you tell your children you do?'

He just looks at her from behind his desk, rolling a pencil back and forth with his finger. As he listens to her screaming the same question at him again, his attention drifts to the bumps and fissures along the edge of the desk. He can feel them under his elbow. When he moves his arm slightly to the right, he finds another gouge in the wood, and rolls his arm over it, as if by doing so he might remember how it got there. He knew it would be there, because he's used this desk so much, but he can't remember how that gouge was made. It's unusual for the damage to be on his side. Normally it's on the other side.

Their side.

That side of the desk is littered with pockmarks: chips, breaks, splinters; tiny cracks and dents – the desk has been in here two years and it's become as much of a weapon as the gun in the top drawer to his left. As he thinks of that, he remembers a time, a few months back, when he had one of the boys in here with a can of polish.

The kid found a tooth embedded in that side of the desk.

'What do you tell your children you do?'

She's still screaming the same words at him.

He watches her again, waiting for her to tire herself out. She's almost there. The tears have come now as she realizes all of this is futile, that she has one choice and that's to co-operate; the blood is starting to dry and speckle around her pulped nose; and the strings of saliva have stopped falling on to her chest, and her legs, and the floor, because she's getting thirsty from all the screaming and her mouth is dry.

'What do you tell them when you tuck them in at night?'

The fire is definitely going out.

He rolls his elbow over the same gouge.

'Huh? What do you tell them?'

He just stares her down. She can't hold his gaze. Most people can't. It's one of the reasons he's so good at his job. The small things – the small advantages – are what matter when you're trying to destroy an enemy. These people work in fields. They clean, they cook. And even the ones who put in the time to get qualified in something – even when they pick up their second-rate degrees from their Mickey Mouse universities – they aren't fighters. They're administrators, and teachers, and accountants. These people aren't rivals. They aren't killers. They're nothing.

Her head has dropped to her chest and it sounds like she might be crying. He can tell she's trying to hide it from him, trying not to let him hear how he's finally broken her resistance. But he waits her out for so long that – eventually – she looks up and says something else.

He can't quite hear her.

He stops rocking his elbow across the gouge, stops rolling the pencil with his finger, and comes forward in his seat. It creaks under his weight. He's a big man and keeps himself in good shape. That's another advantage he has.

She mutters.

'You got something to say?' he asks her.

Her face is streaked with tears, her cheeks marked with winding routes. It's impossible for her to do anything about it, impossible to wipe them away, because her hands are behind her back, her wrists are bound with rope, and the rope is tied to the legs of the chair she's on. The chair is in the middle of the room, like an island, and it's bolted to the floor.

'You got something to say?' he repeats.

Silence.

He waits.

Finally, quietly, he hears, 'Do you know what you are?'

'No,' he replies. 'What am I?'

She looks up at him, tears welling in her eyes.

'You're the devil.'

Larsen arrived twenty minutes late. Holt hadn't seen him in a year and a half but he'd hardly changed. He was stocky, a five-foot-nine battering ram. People underestimated Larsen because of his height – and that was always how he beat them. Holt had never met a tougher fighter in his life, or anyone smarter. He'd let his hair grow out – it had always been short when they'd worked together – and he'd shaved his beard, but he still had the same tan skin, same fierce blue eyes, the same subtlety to his expression. Within their unit, Larsen had been nicknamed 'Argus'. Holt never really understood why until a lot later on down the line, when, around a barbecue one night, Larsen himself explained: Argus Panoptes was a giant in Greek mythology who had a hundred eyes.

'He sees everything,' Larsen had said.

As Larsen came towards him now, hand out, Holt realized there was another small difference in his former CO: he was dressed for winter. But not the sort of winter they'd got used to in their previous lives; this was a different kind of winter, one that Holt was going to have to adapt to. It was a winter where the cold lingered even after the sun had come up, where the rain fell for days, and the grey was like a pall.

'Have you managed to survive the Rockingham?' Larsen asked.

'It's been fine, sir.'

'I'm sure it hasn't.'

'I appreciate all your help.'

'I wasn't going to leave you hanging,' Larsen said. 'You were always my best soldier. You were always the one I trusted implicitly.'

Even all these years on, even though Holt was thirty, a grown man for whom these things shouldn't have mattered, he felt himself gather, felt his chest swell.

Praise from Larsen was still everything.

'Thank you, sir,' Holt said.

'How was the flight?'

'It was fine.'

'No problems at immigration once you got to Heathrow?'

'No, sir. The passport held up.'

'Good.' Larsen checked his watch. 'I'm sorry I'm late.'

'It's not a problem.'

'It *is* a problem. I hate tardiness.'

Larsen gestured for Holt to follow him. They headed towards the spiral staircase and took the steps up. The rooftop pool was still empty. The water itself was covered, the small cabin-style changing rooms at the other end padlocked shut, and all the loungers were stacked in one corner.

Larsen led Holt around the pool, in the direction of the changing rooms at the far side, and as they walked, Holt looked out through the windows embedded in the high walls surrounding the water. Flashes of London appeared and disappeared.

They stopped next to one of the windows.

'I'm not going to dress it up for you,' Larsen said. 'It takes some getting used to. The weather's shit. It pisses it down for weeks on end, and then the sun finally comes out for a day, and it's still freezing cold. It's an adjustment.' Larsen's eyes were on the window next to him. Holt didn't say anything, because he already understood: it had been bitter ever since he'd got here, and it was maybe even colder today. It didn't help that they were up here on the rooftop.

'And there are other things,' Larsen said, his voice softer. 'Smaller things. I mean, most of these people –' Larsen waved a hand at the city, '– they're soft. It won't take you long to realize that anyone under fifty-five here has never had to fight for anything. They don't know what it is to wage a war like we did. But that's what gives us the advantage here.'

'Yes, sir,' Holt said, not really understanding.

'Have you had a look around?'

'The Castle? Not yet, no.'

'But you've seen a little of it?'

'Yes, sir.'

'What do you think?'

'I don't, uh . . .' Holt was thrown. 'I don't know a lot about these sorts of places, sir. I imagine on the few sunny days Britain gets, it would be nice up here.'

That made Larsen smile again. 'I've just put in an offer for it.'

Holt frowned. 'Sir?'

'This place. The Castle family are getting itchy feet. I've put in an offer.'

'I don't know what to say,' he said, honestly, because he didn't. Why would Larsen want to buy this place? And how the hell could he ever afford it?

'Well,' Larsen corrected himself, 'Samuel Apphis has put an offer in.'

'Apphis, sir?'

'That's my version of Gary Holt.'

His alias.

'You know *why* I want to buy this place?' Larsen asked.

'No, sir.'

'At the moment, because the Castle family can't turn a profit, they've opened the club up for anyone. Anyone can come in off the street, pay at the front desk, and access facilities like this –' he pointed at the swimming pool, '– and we have no clue who they are. But, once this is mine, I'm going to change all that. I'm going back to a members-only model. Because if it's members-only, suddenly you've got names, addresses and phone numbers for every person who passes through the doors. Don't get me wrong, I believe I can make a lot of money from this place, but if we have control over our membership, if that information is at our fingertips the whole time, this building can also become our fortress.'

'You can see where the threat is coming from.'

'*We* can see,' Larsen said, and reached out and took Holt by the shoulder. 'We have enemies at home who want to find us. You came here on a false passport, and now you have a new identity – just like I do – but that doesn't mean we're safe. You and I, we need to remain vigilant. This place can help.'

Holt nodded.

'Once I take over, I want a full list of people we let through those doors. I want backgrounds. I want you to do what you do best and gather every scrap of information you can find on *everyone*. And then once we have that, my friend, this place will become our Argus.'

35

I watched as her fingers felt for the countertop, grabbing it as if it were an anchor. 'You ever heard of The Castle?'

'It's a private members' club in Holborn.'

'Do you know much about it?'

'I had a chat with Ian Kirby this morning. I asked him a few questions, he got a little uncomfortable – and then, a few minutes later, he was showing me the door.'

An expression crossed her face, difficult to read. 'Four years ago, I joined the club. I couldn't really afford it but people at work said it was a great place to network. I started as a cop relatively late, when I was twenty-seven, so it felt like I was always playing catch-up. I did three years as a constable, then took my National Investigators Exam, then went into the trainee detective programme, before I finally got a DC posting when I was thirty-one. After that, I hit a wall. I was ambitious, I felt I was good at what I did, I worked on some big cases, but whenever I applied for a DS role, someone else always got it. *Always*. This went on for . . . I don't know, five, six years. I really liked the people I worked with, but I never used to socialise with them. My old man was an alcoholic, so I rarely drink. That was why, after a shift, I always used to come home instead of going to the pub.'

She stopped, rubbed at an eye. 'Anyway, one day this guy gets promoted over me and he's only been a DC for five minutes, so I went to my DCI and asked him why I kept getting overlooked, and he said, "No one knows anything about you, Letitia – this isn't only about ability, it's about where you fit in, about how you work with other people." I was raging, because I knew what he really meant.'

You don't come to the pub with us.

'And then my DCI told me about The Castle,' she said. 'He said that was where a lot of decision makers at the Met were making connections. "You don't have to go to the gym, or use the pool," he said, "you just need to be seen by the right people." So that was what I did. I spent money I couldn't afford on a club I had no interest in, and started talking to people who'd constantly passed me over for promotions. And it worked. Inside five months, I was suddenly a DS.'

The colour ebbed from her cheeks.

'Except, what you don't realize about that club, what *no one* realizes inside or outside is what's going on below the surface. All the detectives who are members, all these crazy-smart people who are in there all the time propping up the bar, or sitting in the steam room – the majority of them don't even have a clue.'

'About what's going on below the surface?'

'Yes,' she said, and pointed to the printout of the man in the CCTV video. It was still in my hand. I glanced down at it, at his face, and then back up at Scargill. '*He's* what's going on. He's like this shark, this animal that keeps moving. You have no idea he's there until he *wants* you to know, and by the time he wants you to know . . .' She swallowed, her gaze drifting towards the printout in my hands – towards it, but not quite all the way. It was like she didn't even want to have to look at him in a photograph. 'By the time he wants you to know, it's too late.'

'Who is he?'

It was like Scargill hadn't heard me.

'I've seen a lot of shit in my time,' she said. 'You work as long as I have, turning up at all these terrible fucking places, seeing the kinds of things no one should ever see, you tend not to frighten too easily. But, every so often, your axis tilts. You remember that you *do* still get scared. *Really* scared. You remember there are people like him.'

'Who is he?' I repeated.

'I don't know.'

'You don't know his name?'

I could see the doubts written into her face, the worry that she was handing all of this over to me without a fight; a cop revealing her crimes to a total stranger. But then she glanced at me again and it was like her thoughts were inscribed on her: *It's too late.*

I've already been found out.

'Okay,' she said softly. 'Okay.'

It was only one word, but it was loaded with so much. I'd heard the same tone on other cases I'd worked, written in the eyes of people who, like Scargill, had become ensnared in something terrible, something they couldn't escape from. Guilt and fear were the fuel that, in the end, always transported moral people to a moment like this.

The confession.

'Holt,' she said. 'The name I know him by is Gary Holt.'

'The name you know him by?'

'I don't know if Gary Holt is his real name.'

'What makes you think it isn't?'

She reached to one of the cupboards and took out a glass, filling it with water. 'Because I've seen what kind of man he is,' she said, drinking. 'And men like him – men that operate like he does – don't give you anything you can use against them.'

It made sense based on what I'd seen of Holt so far.

'So how did you first meet him?'

She paused, remorse stark in her face. 'I've got two sisters. We were always close growing up. We had to be. We never really knew our mum – she died when I was two – so Dad brought us up.'

I thought about the similarities between her and Rebekah. Except Henry Murphy had meant everything to Rebekah.

It was obvious Scargill's father was very different.

'The way our dad was,' she said, 'it messed us all up. One of my sisters is older than me by eighteen months. She's smart as hell, so driven. It's all career with her. She's the top dog in an advertising agency in LA. She never stops, just works. I guess you don't have to be a psychologist to figure out why.' *Because as soon as she stops, she has to think about their childhood.* 'Me, I bummed around for ages, not really sure what I wanted to be. That was why I joined the police so late.'

And then nothing. Just silence. That was when I knew that, wherever this led, it began with her youngest sibling.

'Delilah,' she said. 'Dee.'

'That's your youngest sister?'

'Yes. Dee's just different. She couldn't escape from all the crap we saw growing up. She started boozing and then, after the booze, it was drugs. I can't even tell you how many times she's been clean. Fifty? Eighty? Maybe more, I don't know. I stopped counting after a while. The longest she's been off the drugs is eight weeks. Celia, my older sister, she basically doesn't have anything to do with Dee anymore. She cut her out of her life. I've thought about it too. I've thought about cutting the rope. I mean, she's been constantly in trouble with the law. At work, whenever it's come up, I've basically had to disown her. I have to pretend we don't talk any more. I stood in front of an SIO once and said, "I don't see her as my sister" – and it was the best performance of my life, because then I came home after and cried my eyes out.'

'What's all of this got to do with Holt?'

'Everything,' she said, a tremor in her voice. 'One time I was at The Castle when I got a call from Dee. I took my phone into one of the meeting rooms – they're just off the bar and restaurant – and Dee's crying. She's in trouble. She says to me, "I sold this guy some of the shit I scored and he's just OD'd on me." I said to her, "What did you give him?" She says, "Heroin." But I can tell that's not the whole truth, so I say, "Heroin mixed with what?" And she says, "Fentanyl."'

A hush settled between us: 30 milligrams of heroin could kill an average-sized adult male; it only took 3 milligrams of fentanyl to do the same.

'I wanted to scream at her. I wanted to say, "What the *fuck* were you thinking?" But I just tried to clear my head. I said to her, "Did you put the drugs in his arm or did he inject it himself?" and, even though I knew it wouldn't make a difference – that she was going to prison whatever, given her record, given the countless time she'd been in trouble – I thought, *Please don't let her have put it into his arm*. If she put it into his arm *for* him, injected that shit into his vein, it would be manslaughter. And then a judge would take one look at her record and he'd pull the trigger. It wouldn't be a few years behind bars . . .' She stopped, her silence filling in the rest.

It would be ten. Or fifteen. Or life.

'And did she?'

'Yes.'

'So what did you tell her to do?'

Except I knew. I could see it all over her face.

'She said they were in an abandoned house in Walthamstow. I asked her if anyone had seen them go in, and she said no. I asked her if there was anyone else in the house, and she said no. I told her to wipe down the syringe, leave it with the body and get the hell out of there. She said she couldn't – she couldn't just leave his body there – and I said, "If you don't, you're going to prison for the rest of your life." I mean, she was my sister. She was a complete screw-up, but she was my sister.'

She faded out again.

'So that's what this Gary Holt guy has over you?'

She nodded.

'How did he find out?'

'All the rooms at The Castle are bugged. That's the only way he could *possibly* know. I was in that room, with the door closed. I was alone the whole time. There was tons of noise coming from the bar, so even if he'd been standing just outside he wouldn't have heard me. That room being bugged – it's the only way.'

'Okay. What happened next?'

'He cornered me in the gym one day. I'd never met him before – not to talk to, anyway – but I'd seen him around The Castle very occasionally.'

' "Very occasionally"?'

'Like, once or twice.'

'What about the owner of the club, Samuel Apphis? Ever seen him?'

'No. Never. People talk about him sometimes – they say he's some kind of a recluse – but I don't know anyone that's ever met him.'

'Okay, so Holt cornered you. When? The next day?'

'No. He waited eight months.'

'What?'

196

'He spent that time finding out absolutely everything he could about me, because when he cornered me, he knew it all: my background, my life, where I lived, my routines, right down to shit like the place I got my morning coffee from. He'd been studying me. He was referencing things I did once a month, or once every quarter. I just stood there, unable to talk, frozen. He has this way of speaking, this way of looking at you, that makes you feel like you're completely exposed . . .' She swallowed.

'He told you he heard you on the phone to your sister?'

'Yes.'

'And he threatened to reveal what you'd done?'

'Yes.'

'Unless you did what?'

She looked at me. Her lip trembled.

'Terrible things,' she said.

36

She took another sip of water, wiped her mouth.

'Most of the time, he just wants access to the police databases. He wants information on people. It's all these small tasks, all this disparate shit, that, on their own, don't look like very much, and I can never marry up. And I've tried looking, believe me. I've tried looking to see what the connections are. But I can never find anything.' She paused, the quiet filled with the hum of the refrigerator. 'I've started to wonder if he might have been in the military.'

'You think this Holt guy was a soldier?'

'It's like intelligence gathering, you know? It's like he's building backgrounds on people. These little pieces of information that I guess he figures he can use.' She glanced at the printout. 'First thing yesterday, he called me. He always phones from a blocked number. He said, "I need you to look at two cold cases for me." I work for the Serious Crime Review Group – cold cases are my thing – so I thought, *at least this time, I'm not going to raise any red flags*. All he wants to know is whether there has been any recent activity on the investigations into these two women. That's it. And so I go in, have a hunt around, and I see both of these women are basically forgotten. No one's as much as looked at the cases since the early nineties.'

'You're talking about Fiona Murphy and Jennifer Johnson?'

'Yes.'

'And you have no idea why he asked you to look at them?'

'No. So I go back to him and tell him there's nothing new on either one, that these are some of the coldest cold cases we've got on the system – but I can tell from his voice that something's still agitating him. That's when he says he needs me to follow you. I said, "What the hell are you talking about? *Following* people? This isn't what we agreed." And he says, "We never *agreed* anything. You work for me, you do exactly what I ask, or your pals at the Met get to hear that phone call with your sister."'

Hear it. He had a recording of the call.

That seemed to confirm Scargill's bugging theory.

'So what did you tell him?'

'That you went to Cambridge. I told him that I followed you up there, saw you go to that council estate, and then you got a taxi somewhere. I couldn't follow you without you seeing me, so I just waited at the station. On the way back, I sat behind you. We're almost in London when he phones me again and says he wants me to call Martine Parkes and tell her you're on a train to Cambridge.' Scargill opened out her hands. *I have no idea why.* 'This is why I think he might have been in the military. He's built this complete history of me and he knows I'm friendly with Martine. He also knows there's something going on between you and her; that she and her boss are looking into you.'

'And so you called her.'

'Yes. Made up some bullshit about hearing she was looking into you. I made it work.' She ground to a halt. 'That's what I've learnt to do for him: just make it work.'

I stopped, gathering my thoughts. 'He was asking you to look into Fiona and Jennifer before I'd even made the connection between them myself.'

'What do you mean?'

'I mean, I didn't even know Jennifer Johnson existed until last night. Rebekah, Fiona's daughter, only landed a few hours before Holt asked you to look at those files. He was way ahead of the curve – minimum half a day, in reality probably more.'

'There's a flag against her name.'

I stiffened. 'What?'

'Rebekah. She has a flag against her name. Neither of the women's cases has been reopened, absolutely nothing new has been added to them in investigative terms since the nineties – but, in Fiona Murphy's case file, where her next of kin are listed, her daughter's name has been flagged.'

'What does that mean – "flagged"?'

'It means if there's an update to Rebekah's entry, it sends out an alert.'

'To who?'

'I don't know. That information isn't listed. But given that the flag is on the PNC, I'd say someone internal at the Met – either another cop, or an indexer.'

'An indexer? You mean someone who works on the database?'

'Yes,' she said. 'This is how Holt works. This is what I'm trying to tell you. He spreads the workload, little jobs dotted around, never giving one individual too much insight into what his endgame is. He'll tell me to look at those two women, or follow you around, but he'll tell someone else to do something different. Plus, there are tons of cops at the Met who are also members of The Castle. It could be anyone.'

'Are Parkes or her boss Phillips members?'

'I don't know about Phillips. I don't know much about him. But Martine definitely isn't. She hates that shit. Networking, old boys' clubs, cliques, kissing arse. She's way too much of a straight arrow. But, like I said earlier, even if she doesn't know anything about Holt, he knows about her.'

I felt a momentary sense of relief. Parkes wasn't a member, which meant she wasn't compromised like Scargill. But Aiden Phillips could be.

'You said this flag goes off when someone updates Rebekah's entry?'

'Yes.'

Something flashed in her face. I studied her, trying to understand what I was seeing. 'Does it send out an alert when she enters the country?'

'Yes.'

Which was how Holt was so ahead of the curve: Rebekah had entered the UK two days ago – the day before our first meeting. As soon as she cleared immigration, her name hit the system. An alert was sent out to whoever had set up the original flag, and then they called Holt to tell him Rebekah was in the country. She was the only one left who might want answers about what happened to Fiona, and if she ever came looking – like now – Holt would know. I thought of how much foresight that required, how much planning, and wondered what else this man had put in place.

'Is Rebekah in danger?'

'I don't know,' Scargill said.

'Has he asked you to do anything similar recently?'

' "Similar"?'

'Database searches, trailing people, that sort of stuff.'

'Before he called me about those two women, I hadn't done anything for him for a couple of months.' She juddered to a stop. 'I know I'm helping him hurt people just by giving him information. I know I'm doing a terrible thing. I *hate* the idea of it. But if I walk away, my sister goes to prison. So do I.'

I thought of Healy then, of the last four and a half months of his life, of all the days he'd spent living exactly the same nightmare that Scargill was trying to prevent.

'Have you ever refused him?'

'All the way back at the start,' she said, 'when he first began blackmailing me, I tried to fight him. I started to watch him, started trying to find out more about him. I thought I could use it as a weapon.' She shook her head, as if that were the most naïve thing she'd ever done in her life. 'That didn't last long. I went to see Dee one day – this was during one of her attempts to get clean – and I turned up at this place she was staying in and he was there.' She blinked, as if – even now – she didn't want the memory in her head. 'He was just sitting there on the bed beside her, pretending to be one of the staff there. He had this big grin on his face, this light, conversational way about him that had completely fooled Dee. And she didn't get fooled easily. But when he looked at me, the message in his face was so clear: *I know you're following me, I know you think you're cleverer than me, but you're not. If you pull this shit again, your sister dies.* So I stopped. That was three years ago.' She slumped. 'I've never done anything like that since.'

I gave her a moment and then pushed again: 'So he hasn't forced you to follow anyone else apart from me; the only database searches he's asked for recently are on Fiona and Jennifer. That just leaves this morning.'

'Yes,' she said softly.

'He asked you to drive him around today?'

'Yes.'

'Why?'

'I've no idea. He doesn't tell me. He never gives a reason.' As she paused, I searched her eyes for a lie – but I couldn't see one. 'Coming to your house like that, it was probably reconnaissance; to meet you in the flesh, size you up.'

'But why pretend to be an estate agent? It was high risk, and – from what you describe – he's not the type of man who takes risks. And he must have known there was a good chance his lie would cave in quickly.'

'I don't know. I've got no idea how he thinks.'

'Or who he is, or even his name.'

'You don't get it.'

I held up a hand. 'I do. I get it. I've only seen a little of him but even from that, I can see enough. But I can't do much if I don't have a clue who he is.'

She glanced at me. 'When I first tried to fight back – you know, just before he went in to see my sister – I watched him one night. It was late. Quiet, no one around. I was hiding out in the park opposite The Castle, waiting for him to leave. Eventually, he comes out – this is the early hours, maybe five in the morning – and pauses outside the doors, checking everywhere. He didn't want anyone to hear him. Then he makes a call.'

'To who?'

'I don't know.'

'Did you hear his conversation?'

'I heard it. Not that it made any difference.'

I frowned. 'Why not?'

'Because he wasn't speaking English.'

37

I looked at Scargill. 'What are you saying? You think he's from somewhere abroad?'

'I don't know.'

'What language was he speaking?'

'It was hard to tell from where I was.'

'Best guess.'

'European,' she said. 'It could have been German.'

'That doesn't mean his name *isn't* Gary Holt.'

'No, it doesn't. But when you go looking for Holt on the system – which I did in those first few weeks; in fact, when you go looking for him basically *anywhere* – it all gets . . . weird.'

'Weird how?'

'He was apparently born here in London on the first of October 1959, but in the – what? – twenty-five years between that date and February 1985, when he started paying National Insurance, there's nothing.'

'What do you mean, "nothing"?'

'I mean, for the first twenty-five years of his life, he's just a blank. I went through every database we have, and every government department, called in favours *everywhere*. The name Gary Holt is just an empty space.'

'So – what? – you think he came here in 1985 on a false passport?'

'Or he came in on his real passport and changed his identity once he got here. Or neither. I don't know. All I know is from the day he was born to the day he started paying taxes in this country in February 1985, it's a complete void.'

But why would he want to hide who he was?

And there was something else too: Holt first appeared on the radar in February 1985, and in December 1985 both Fiona Murphy and Jennifer Johnson disappeared.

That can't be coincidence.

'You said you think he was speaking German?'

'Languages aren't exactly a strong area for me but I'm pretty sure it was German.'

'I don't remember hearing him speaking with an accent earlier. Did he have an accent when he talked to you?'

'No, never.'

'So he could just speak German as a second language?'

'He could. Like I say, I don't know for sure. All I know is the first twenty-five years of his life don't exist.'

I looked at my notebook, at everything I'd written down, then at the black and white image of the man in the footage. In 1985, the Cold War was almost over.

Almost over – but not quite.

Could Holt have been East German? If Scargill was right and he had a military background – and especially if she was correct about him working in intelligence – it was possible he could have been a Stasi agent. But why flee the country? At the time, there were something like 190,000 official and unofficial Stasi employees, and most were just reintegrated back into society after the Wall fell. I read once that seventeen thousand members of the East German secret police ended up in ordinary jobs in the civil service. There was no reason for someone to flee the country.

Unless they'd done something heinous.

Something even the Stasi couldn't stomach.

'Are you really not going to tell anyone?'

Her question brought me back.

'No,' I replied. 'I meant what I said earlier: whatever you tell me tonight, it stays within these walls. But it can't be like this forever. If I track down Holt, if he talks, it's going to be hard for what you did to stay buried. All of this – everything you know – it'll eventually come out. The truth always does.'

She rubbed at her eyes again, smearing a little make-up.

'Aren't you scared of him?' she asked.

'I need to figure out who he is first – and what bothers me the most right now is him coming to my house earlier.'

The change of subject was deliberate, an attempt to keep her focused, because she was starting to wane. It was obvious that she wanted this to be over now; she'd made a confession, and it hadn't made her feel any better.

'You said he's meticulous, he plans, he's always moving forward. So what does he achieve by creating a lie that's so easy to unpick? I knew something was up about two minutes after he arrived at my house.' I paused, trying to get my head straight. 'He would have known there was a high probability of me looking into him, and then finding him on CCTV, and then finding you and your car. Why would he want to expose you to me? If he did that, he lost you as his source and compromised himself in the process. It just makes no sen—'

But I didn't finish my sentence.

I looked at Scargill, her head angled to the side, her skin grey, eyes misted, and then out to the shadows of the kitchen, to the house beyond, its darkness, its silence.

'Shit,' I muttered.

Scargill glanced at me. 'What?'

'He *wanted* all of this.'

'What are you talking about?'

'He wanted me to ID your car.'

And he knew, once I did, I would come here.

My stomach dropped.

I thought of the noise I'd heard when I'd been upstairs before Scargill got home, of how I'd eventually convinced myself that it had been nothing; peripheral sound from outside. And then I pictured how Scargill had moved around the entire house – upstairs and downstairs – when we'd first arrived, checking windows, doors, and locks. She'd done it to secure the place, to make sure no one could get in. And that was exactly what he wanted.

She and I, in the same place, both of us locked in.

Like fish in a barrel.

'He's already inside the house,' I whispered.

Kian

Tom | *This Afternoon*

Tom Brenner arrived in King's Cross to make the call from the same phone box he'd used the day before. It was already dark, another winter's night settling like a shroud on the city. He pulled his coat tighter and looked around him, checking to see if anyone was following him.

'Is everything okay, Daddy?'

Leo.

Despite the fact that he was literally at his side – a tiny nine-year-old hand in Tom's – Tom had almost forgotten his son was there. *This is insane. I should never have involved him in this shit.* 'Yes, mate, everything's fine,' Tom said, projecting an air of calm. He felt irrationally angry: angry he'd been forced to bring his son with him to make this call, angry that he had to make this detour out of King's Cross station again to do it. But he tried not to show Leo.

He just squeezed his son's hand.

'Daddy just has to make a call, okay?'

'Okay, Daddy,' Leo said. The innocence of his son's response – the fact that he accepted Tom's explanation for what they were doing, without question – almost cut Tom in two.

'Once I've made the call, we'll get back on that train and the fun begins.'

Leo beamed. 'Cool!'

Tom looked around again, searching for obvious signs that he was being watched. No one stood out; no eyes were on him. Not that it brought him any comfort: in his head, he was still trapped in a memory, a four-month-old image of the man who answered the door to Room 634, of the naked guy that Tom had seen on the bed behind him in handcuffs. *And the duct tape on the chair next to them.*

He reached the phone box.

'Just wait outside, okay, mate?'

'Okay,' Leo said.

'Daddy has to make a special call from this payphone, so you be a big boy and look after this, all right?' Tom handed Leo his mobile to play with.

Inside, he let the door close, waited until he was partially concealed – like the last time – behind the white graffiti on the glass, and then got out the same napkin as before with the number of the burner phone on it. Dropping a coin into the slot, Tom dialled. As he waited for it to connect, he thought again of that night in August and what he'd seen in Room 634.

And then he thought of the afternoon two days ago when he took Leo to the dentist after school – and how, there, he finally started putting it all together.

The magazines in the dentist's were all old, so Tom leafed through the pile and selected the most recent. It was a copy of *East/West* from October. He'd only read *East/West* a few times before, but he knew they were a huge, international weekly news magazine with a TV channel and a radio station. He'd actually listened to the radio station for a while when it first launched, but had got annoyed with the adverts.

'Daddy?'

He turned to Leo, who was sitting next to him – still in his uniform – his legs gently swinging back and forth, the toes of his school shoes brushing against the thin carpet. Tom knew it wouldn't be long before they weren't brushing the carpet any more, but fully planted on it.

'Yes, mate?' he said, putting an arm around Leo.

'Can we go to Seven Peaks this year?'

Tom's eyes went to his phone, which he'd handed to Leo to play with to offset the boredom of the waiting room. On it, Leo had a YouTube video playing – the sound most of the way down – of a rollercoaster heading into an inversion. The second before the train entered the loop-the-loop, the video paused, freeze-framing the people in the front car: two teenagers and what Tom assumed were their parents in the seats behind, all open-mouthed, their faces a mix of exhilaration and sheer terror.

A graphic flashed: *Are you ready?*

'This is the best bit,' Leo said. 'Watch.'

Another graphic: *No, but seriously, are you READY?*

'Daddy, are you watching?'

'I'm watching, mate, don't worry.'

The rollercoaster whipped into the inversion. The view from the top of the loop was brief but spectacular. Tom could see some of the rest of Seven Peaks: the fake mountain tops, the painted-on snow. Every year, the fun fair descended on to a tract of land up near the M25, staying there for four months. All the videos Leo had been watching were from the previous year. He and his friends at school had, all of a sudden, become obsessed with rollercoasters.

Another graphic appeared onscreen: *Hold on tight!*

The rollercoaster dropped and the screaming erupted again. Leo was smiling, his face lit up. Tom wished he could bottle this, because these were the moments that mattered, the moments that reminded him why he still worked nights at the Regala. Much as he loved Sadie – and he loved her very much; loved it when the three of them were together – his job gave him the chance to be alone with Leo when Sadie was at work, and he realized, when he was an old man, when he was at the end looking back at all that he'd done, these were the memories he would take with him.

'Can we go, Daddy? Can we?'

'You really want to go on that thing?'

'Yeah!' Leo said. 'I really, really do.'

'I know, mate, but those loop-the-loops, that drop . . .' Tom whistled.

'That drop's nothing.'

'It doesn't look like nothing.'

Leo made a face, like he wasn't even remotely scared.

'The thing is, mate, they've probably got height restrictions on the –'

'You've got to be one point four metres tall.'

Tom smiled, looking at his son. 'Oh, is that right?'

'It is. I checked. How tall am I?'

'I reckon you're almost there,' Tom said, giving himself some room for manoeuvre if they got home, grabbed the tape measure, and Leo came up just short.

'Can we go, then?' Leo said, excitedly.

'Yeah, if you're big enough, I'll take you this week when Mummy's away.'

Leo grabbed Tom and hugged him hard.

'You're the best, Daddy!'

Tom felt another huge surge of love for his son.

Leo sat back down again and picked up from where he'd left off.

Tom retrieved the copy of *East/West*. It was mostly long features, none of which he was going to have the time to read now, even if the appointments ran later than they were already. A ten-page article on Russia. A six-page investigation into new sexual assault allegations in Hollywood. Tom absent-mindedly turned more pages and then stopped. A new headline looked out at him:

WHAT HAPPENED TO KIAN BAUER?

It was a double-page spread. The headline on the first page had a photograph of a man in his early forties under it, and then the article was on the right. Tom looked at the man, at the intro under the headline: *East/West journalist has been missing since August.* He studied the journalist's face, his smile. *Do I know him?*

'Daddy?' Leo was showing him the phone again. 'Daddy?'

'Just give me a second, mate,' he said to Leo.

And then – as he looked at the man again – a memory flooded Tom's head, a wave of recollection so fierce it was almost dizzying. He could suddenly remember checking Kian Bauer into the Regala. And, off the back of that, another moment formed, the whole thing playing out like an old home movie: Tom striding along the corridor towards Room 634, knocking on the door and then checking his phone for the name of the guest inside.

Kian Bauer.

Except Bauer wasn't the one who'd answered the door. It had been a man in his sixties. And, at the time, Tom had looked at the man and the towel around his waist – at the second guy on the mattress beyond him; at the pair of handcuffs fastening that man to the bed, at the duct tape – and he'd dismissed it. It had been some sex game. It had been a couple having fun. There had been nothing to see in that room that Tom hadn't seen a million times before as the night manager.

But maybe everything that night had been a lie.

In the cold of the phone box, the line connected. 'Hello?'

'It's me,' Tom said.

'You okay?'

'Not really, no.'

'Everything's going to be fine, Tom,' the woman said, but it was just words and they brought Tom no comfort. He looked out of the phone box again, through the gaps in the graffiti, checking on Leo. His son was still playing on Tom's mobile phone and hadn't questioned Tom's story about having to make the call from a payphone. In that moment, Tom was grateful Leo was only nine.

'Tom?'

'I'm here,' he said, his voice giving way a little.

'This'll all be over soon.'

'Will it?'

'It will,' the woman said. 'I promise.'

'I'm worried about my wife and son.'

'They'll be fine.'

Tom felt himself flush with anger. 'Why can't we just go to the police?'

'Because I told you: we can't trust the police.'

Tom sagged, swallowed. 'It's only been two days but every single day has felt like a week.'

'I know.'

Two days ago, I was in a waiting room at the dentist talking to my son about rollercoasters. I was happy. I was safe. Why did I have to pick up that magazine?

Why did I have to do the right thing?

He thought of Sadie, of Leo.

'Are you sure you don't want to meet tonight?' the woman asked.

'I promised to take my son to Seven Peaks.'

'It can't wait?'

Tom glanced out at Leo. 'I've booked the tickets already and my wife's away for a few days. If I change plans, all it's going to do is create suspicion.'

'Fair enough. I'll see you in the morning then.'

'Yes.'

'Be there at nine. After that, you're home and dry.'

'I hope so.'

'Trust me, Tom. This is almost over.'

Somewhere, a police siren rang out.

'Just don't forget to bring the footage of him,' the woman said.

38

Somewhere above us, a floorboard softly creaked. I looked at Scargill, then up at the ceiling, and put a finger to my lips.

He's been in the house the whole time.

Listening to us.

Finding out everything we know.

I moved to the kitchen door and looked along the hallway. The front door was still secure. The stairs were on the right and there was enough light from the kitchen to see the steps were clear. On the left was a downstairs bathroom, the door pulled shut: he wasn't in there because Scargill had gone in and pulled the blinds closed earlier.

I headed through the archway leading from the kitchen to the lounge. Going to the patio doors, I tried them – still locked – and then looked to the second archway at the other end of the living room. The two archways allowed you to move in a circle through the house: lounge, hallway, kitchen; lounge, hallway, kitchen. At my shoulder, in a low voice, Scargill said, 'But I checked upstairs earlier.'

'Do you have a loft?'

Her face fell away.

He must have already been in the loft when she was checking over the house. And earlier, when I'd been snooping around – when I'd heard movement downstairs – he could have stayed out of sight by using the archways: looped around me, gone up to the loft, hidden inside, waited.

Another creak.

I moved back through to the kitchen and glanced at Scargill, her at me: she was terrified; I was concealing it better, but inside my guts were twisting.

And then the fog cleared, and I realized something. We were

downstairs, he was upstairs: the exit was next to us, literally only a few steps away. We didn't need to get past him to get out of here. We didn't need to stay and fight. We could just run.

I leaned into Scargill again: 'We're going to go out the side door.'

Relief flooded her face.

She immediately went for the door, desperate to get out of here. I put a finger to my lips again, telling her to be quiet, and then watched the hallway as she slowly unlocked the side door. The lock make a soft click, barely even there, but in the silence of the house it was like a gunshot. I held up a hand and told her to pause, waiting for a reaction from upstairs.

Nothing.

I looked at Scargill again; nodded. She gripped the door handle and pushed it down and although the door made no sound as it came away from the frame, I could hear the change in air pressure, could feel the cool air wash in straightaway. On one of the counter-tops closest to me, a pot plant shivered in the breeze, its leaves making a muted rustling sound. Another creak from upstairs. Scargill paused, looked at me.

I gestured for her to go.

She stepped out into the dark, the light from the kitchen creating a slanted rectangle on the concrete of the driveway.

But I didn't move.

Something didn't feel right.

This was too easy.

Scargill frantically waved me towards her: *Are you coming or not?* Grabbing the printout of the man off the table, I pocketed it, slid my notebook back into my trousers, then moved to the side door.

I stepped out on to the driveway.

And then time slowed down.

Above me, at the very periphery of my vision, I saw a window was slightly ajar. It was the only one on this side of the house; it looked like a bathroom window, tall and narrow, the glass patterned and frosted. Through the thin gap between the frame and the window, something was poking out; a tube of some kind.

It took me a second to register all of that.

And less than a second to realize it wasn't a tube.

Pnff. Pnff.

Ahead of me, I saw Scargill stumble as a projectile thumped against her thigh. And then I felt something strike mine. The impact – hard as a bullet – instantly unbalanced me and, as I staggered to the side, as I looked down at myself, trying to understand what had just happened, I saw something embedded at the top of my leg.

It was a tranquillizer dart.

39

I looked down at the dart planted in my thigh like a flag, then glanced at Scargill, already on the floor, desperately trying to get to her feet again. And then I looked up.

The barrel of the rifle slid back inside the bathroom.

The window closed.

He's coming.

'Raker?' Scargill said, her words already slurred, her hands still trying – and failing – to use the side of the house to haul herself up. I grabbed hold of the dart in my thigh and yanked it out – and then something else registered with me.

I wasn't dizzy. I wasn't unsteady.

I felt normal.

It took me a beat, but then I saw it: the dart had hit my front pocket – and inside my front pocket was my notebook. I tossed the dart aside and took out the book: the hard leather cover had been pierced, and so had about the first fifty pages, the sedative exploding inside and soaking the entire middle section. My notes had blurred, run, most of them now lost forever. But the dart hadn't reached my skin.

The drug wasn't in me.

Scargill finally slumped to the ground, half in shadows, her back against the side of the house. The instant she hit the floor, she was out: head flopped forward, arms collapsed at the elbows, both palms facing up at her side.

I retrieved the dart I'd cast aside, pocketed the notebook and hurried past the kitchen door towards the rear of the house. As I did, I looked inside and glimpsed a knife block on the counter across the other side of the room. Did I have time to go in and retrieve one? A second in, a second out. It wouldn't take me long.

A shadow shifted in the hallway.

No. It's too late.

I hurried on, towards the padlocked side gate. In front of it – between the edge of the house and the gate itself – was a space for me to step into and hide. It was dark here, the shadows thick because there were no street lamps this far down and no lights on the back of the property. I grabbed my car keys, and – eyes still on the kitchen door – felt around for the strongest, sharpest key I had. I clenched the key between my first and second fingers, the blade – the ridges, the notches, the tip – poking out, the rest of the keys on the ring contained in my closed fist. In my other fist was the dart, sharp end facing out from the bottom of my hand.

I slowed my breathing, tried to quieten it as much as I could, not wanting to give him any advantage he could use. But I couldn't do the same with my heart. It was thumping so hard my chest had begun to hurt.

Time seemed to crawl, the low murmur of the city – police sirens somewhere, cars out on the North Circular, music from a house nearby – bizarrely out of place. If I'd closed my eyes, it could have been a normal night in London. But there was nothing normal about this night: I was hiding in the dark, a woman was unconscious on her driveway and somewhere inside her house was a predator.

Come on, where are you?

I gripped the key and the dart even tighter.

I know you're in ther—

He stepped into the doorway and paused, his head turned away from me, eyes on Scargill. Backlit by the kitchen, he was almost a silhouette as he came down the steps from the door, on to the driveway. Gravel crunched softly under his feet. A rifle was in his left hand, the barrel facing down, and I could see a little more of him now as he stepped further away from the kitchen: he was the same build as the man who'd come to my house, and he moved the same way. But this time he wasn't in a grey suit.

He was in black, head to toe.

I pushed myself up against the gate, even though I knew he

wouldn't be able to spot me. But it was instinct, a reaction to seeing the man who'd just spent an hour patiently listening to Scargill's confession, and finding out what I knew in return; who'd fired tranquillizer darts into us like a hunter tracking game. And now it was obvious what was next: Scargill had confessed everything, had clearly been struggling with the weight of her secrets for a while, and that made her unpredictable, which was dangerous for him; and I was edging closer to unravelling who he was, what was going on at The Castle, and how it connected back to Fiona Murphy. I wasn't there yet, but he'd read up about me, my history, done all the background he needed, and he knew, if he did nothing, that I'd get there eventually. So he'd laid a trail of breadcrumbs for me to follow in order to get me and Scargill together. And now he was going to wipe us from the map – sedate us, take us somewhere quiet, put us in the ground.

Except only one of us was out cold on the driveway.

He moved forward, passing Scargill without even looking at her, then along the side of her car, vanishing for a moment in the darkness, before reappearing at the gates. He looked both ways, his back still to me. I could see his face in profile for a moment as he turned left and then right.

The bridge of the nose.

His eyes.

He was wearing a military-style balaclava.

He turned and looked down the driveway in my direction. He was too far away for me to see much, but I knew the cogs were turning. Whatever he'd fired into Scargill had put her on the floor in under thirty seconds. Even if I could take more of a hit because I was bigger than her, I wasn't going to last much longer. So if I'd made a run for it – if I'd got as far as the road – I should have been face down in the street.

He started to come back.

I was grasping the key and the dart so tightly now, it felt like they might break in my hands. He vanished into the dark at the side of the car. I glanced at Scargill – tiny clouds of breath gathering at her lips in the cold, dart still in her leg – then back to Holt. He should have reappeared by now. He should have come back out from behind the car.

But he hadn't.

I couldn't hear him any more.

I couldn't see him.

I knew he must have been there, hidden in the murk between the car and the fence that separated Scargill's house from the next one. So what was he doing?

Shit.

He knows exactly where I've hidd –

I didn't even get to finish my thought.

40

He sprang from the darkness, covering the ground between him and me inside a second. I'd barely managed to get the key halfway up, level with my waist, by the time he was on to me, arms reaching into the shadows, his whole body like a battering ram, knee up, rifle reversed so the butt was facing out. It felt like being hit by a truck. We smashed against the gate, old wood panels in the middle disintegrating instantly, and as I fell through the ragged chasm on to a hard brick path, his full weight landed on me.

A knee went into my ribs.

The butt of the rifle cracked against my cheekbone.

Pain, and light, and breath all rushed me at once, a dizzying blitz that totally disabled me. I was stunned. My face was on fire. Before I'd even blinked, he jammed a hand against my throat and started squeezing. It was like a clamp. I reached for oxygen that wasn't there, his fingers tightening, his knee still in the space under my ribs.

Through the balaclava, I saw the same grey eyes as earlier, the same man who'd come to my house, who'd pretended to be Ryan Gilligan, who called himself Gary Holt, and who might have been someone else entirely. And then, as he squeezed even harder on my throat, everything started to fade.

I can't get him off.

He's too strong.

My head was swimming. I couldn't catch my breath. I closed my eyes and – the second I did – the darkness started to take me away.

No, you need to fight.

It's fight or die.

I opened my eyes again, forced everything I had left into my arm, into my hand, and swung the key up, off the floor, like a catapult. It pierced his neck, blood flecking my face. His grip released instantly, his cry muted inside the balaclava, one hand going to his collar, to the space above it where I'd torn a hole. As a surge of air chased up my throat, I jabbed the tranquillizer dart into the nearest piece of him I could find.

His stomach.

He cried out this time and rolled off me, on to the path. I started coughing, trying to move away from him, crawling on my belly towards the patio doors at the back of the house. When I looked back, he was four feet from me and still staring at his stomach, at a space near his hip, where the dart was sticking out of him.

'Letitia?'

A male voice out on the driveway.

'Bloody hell, Letitia, are you all right?'

Holt's gaze pinged to me.

Someone had heard us.

A neighbour.

He pulled the dart out of his stomach and got to his feet. I did the same, using the patio doors for support. I swayed, my head pounding, my face on fire where it had connected with the rifle, and by the time I reset, he was no longer in the back garden.

I heard something out on the driveway – the neighbour saying, 'Hey!', then the sound of an impact, a struggle, of someone hitting the floor. I staggered through the gap in the fence, still unsteady on my feet, just in time to see Holt disappearing at the top of the driveway. On the floor next to Scargill, a man was moaning, holding his face. I noticed something else too: Holt had removed the dart from Scargill on the way past.

I hurried up the driveway as fast as I could, realising my mistake. He'd taken Scargill's dart and now he had the one he'd fired into me too. The evidence was gone. At the top, I looked to my left, in the direction that Holt had taken. I couldn't see him anywhere. There was a whole raft of flats at the end, a three-storey maze of doorways and windows that was easy to vanish in.

'Are you okay?' I asked, going to the neighbour, helping him up.

'What the hell just happened?'

'Letitia had a break-in.'

'Bloody hell. Are you a friend of hers?'

'Yeah,' I said.

Lying felt easier for now.

My head throbbed. My throat hurt. My ribs were bruised.

The neighbour looked at Scargill. 'Is she okay?'

I glanced at her, looked her over again.

Something was different now.

What was different?

'Bloody hell,' the neighbour said again. 'This is scary.'

And then my heart plunged.

'*Fuck,*' I said and dropped to my knees at Scargill's side. 'Call an ambulance.' The neighbour didn't move. 'Call an *ambulance.*' I handed him my phone and turned back to Scargill. Now I could see what was different: there was no breath at her lips.

No mist forming in the cold.

'Letitia?' No response. '*Letitia?*'

Slowly, I lifted her chin up.

Blood sloshed out over her clothes. I heard the neighbour behind me making the 999 call, even though I knew it was already too late. Holt had taken the darts with him to dispose of the evidence, but not before he'd used one of them on the way past.

He hadn't managed to silence me tonight.

But he'd silenced Letitia Scargill.

He'd cut her throat.

Healy

This Afternoon

He spent the first thirty minutes after the call with Liz in his cell.

Jordan didn't come back at all during that time.

And then, at four, the kid finally returned. But Healy didn't get a chance to talk to him. A guard appeared in the doorway and gestured for Healy to exit the cell, and as he and Jordan passed each other, Jordan didn't even look up.

The guard led Healy along Ones, through a series of cream-coloured security gates, and then into a wide corridor that led to the showers. In his short time at the prison, Healy had managed to get a gig cleaning the showers and toilets twice a week, which would have been his idea of a nightmare on the outside but was preferable here to spending twenty-three of every twenty-four hours in an eight-by-twelve room. A mop in a bucket full of soapy water, and then a second bucket full of tatty cleaning products, were waiting for him when he got there.

'I want to see my face in those floors,' the guard said to Healy.

Healy forced a smile. 'Yes, boss.'

The guard watched over him as he mopped the floors, the mop out in front of him, arcing from one side to the other as he worked his way along the shower taps. The whole time, he was thinking about Jordan, about who in here knew what about Healy's history; and if he wasn't thinking about that, he was thinking about Raker, about Liz's call earlier, about what he and Raker could achieve even if Liz *did* set up a second call. Liz had all but admitted Healy might still get a year.

And that was best-case scenario.

Just then, he heard movement behind him.

He didn't take much notice of it to start with, as the staff were rarely still for long, their footsteps constantly echoing through the creaking hallways of the prison.

But then he glanced across his shoulder.

The guard was gone.

In his place were two men.

He recognized both of them from roll call: their cell was up on Twos, the floor above his, but on the opposite side. They faced each other first thing every morning, every lunchtime and every evening before lock-up.

Healy's heart rate increased as one of them, the older of the two, took a step in his direction. He was in his forties, grizzled and scarred, and had a buzz cut. When he tilted his head slightly, rolling his neck until it clicked, the strip lights in the shower block reflected in his scalp. He was short – maybe five-seven – but he was muscular, biceps straining against the circumference of his shirt sleeves, jaw set, lips tight. He had a look in his eyes that Healy had seen over and over during his time with the Met – when you hurt people, it stained you, and it was a stain that never washed out.

The other guy was taller, slimmer, maybe late twenties, and didn't scare Healy as much. He seemed in deference to the guy with the buzz cut.

Buzz Cut edged closer, coming around a row of sinks. Healy side-stepped and tried to see where the guard was. Was he in on this? Or had these two been watching and, as soon as the guard stepped away, moved in? Because the guards trusted Healy, and he'd given them no trouble in the time he'd been inside, they often left him to his own devices in here, checking on him intermittently until he was finished.

'It's Healy, right?' Buzz Cut said.

His face hardly moved when he spoke, his mouth tight. Healy said nothing, just kept an eye on Buzz Cut's movements. He was in front of the sinks now, the width of his shoulders, the back of his head, reflected in a series of bathroom mirrors, his image disappearing into infinity. Healy could see his own reflection too. He looked terrified. He didn't want to look scared, knew that it would be worse for him if he did, because fear was like a scent, and this guy was an animal. But he couldn't help it. 'Look, I don't want any trouble w—'

'A fisherman,' Buzz Cut said. 'Is that what you are?'

Buzz Cut made a sudden, aggressive snorting sound.

It stopped Healy dead.

A pig noise.

'You ain't no fisherman.'

When Buzz Cut got no response, he made another pig noise and, at the door, the younger man broke out into a smile. He was finding it hard to keep his eyes on the corridor beyond the shower block, his attention now almost exclusively on Healy.

'You ain't no fisherman, *pig*.'

And then he made the same snorting sound again – except this time he wasn't trying to mimic a pig. He was gathering phlegm in his throat. A couple of seconds later, he spat it out on to the floor, only a few inches from where Healy was standing.

'You know what happens to pigs in here?'

'Stay away from me.'

'Yeah? And what are you going to do if I don't?' Buzz Cut made a sudden movement forward and then stopped, getting the reaction he wanted: Healy flinched, pushing the mop out in front of him, jabbing it into the space between them. Buzz Cut laughed. 'Look at the fucking state of it, Pat.'

Pat. *Patrick?* That was the tall guy.

Buzz Cut took another step closer to Healy.

They were only a few feet apart now.

'I fucking *hate* cops,' he said, suddenly serious again. 'But do you know what I hate even more?' He slowly looked Healy up and down, like he was the lowest form of life he'd ever seen. 'A cop that don't even have the balls to admit to what he is.'

'Roz,' the younger man said. '*Rossiter*, he's *coming*.'

Rossiter.

Healy filed both names away.

The younger man dropped to the floor and pretended to tie a

shoelace. As he did, Rossiter backed away, his eyes still glued to Healy. The guard was coming back.

'I'm gonna gut you like one of your fish,' Rossiter hissed.

And then the guard appeared.

'Mr Rossiter, Mr Patrick: what are you doing in here?'

'Just on our way back from the kitchen, boss,' Rossiter responded, everything about him different now. 'Jake,' he said, gesturing to Patrick, 'needed to take a leak.'

'And – what? – were you holding his cock for him?'

'No, boss.'

'Then get back to Twos.'

'Yes, boss,' Rossiter said, politely.

But just before he disappeared from view, he glanced at Healy again, his eyes flaring – and a smile wormed across his face so ugly it almost buckled Healy's knees.

It said, *This is only the beginning.*

Sooner or later, we're going to get to you.

You're never leaving this place alive.

Day 3

Thursday, 8 December

PART FIVE
The Journalist

41

By 1 a.m., Letitia Scargill's house was swarming with police.

My clothes had been bagged, my nails scraped, and an initial account of what happened had been given to the first officers at the scene. I kept it simple and close to the truth: I found out Scargill was following me; I came to see her and she'd agreed to speak to me; we entered the house and realized someone was inside, so exited out the side door – and then the intruder attacked me and murdered Scargill.

The killing of a police officer had created an immediate tension, a charge in the atmosphere that was palpable from the second the cops arrived on the scene. I was glad for the neighbour providing me with an alibi. It felt like eyes were still on me, suspicions rife, but at least the neighbour could tell investigators I wasn't the one that cut Scargill's throat.

Even so, forensics worked through the rooms of the house, looking for evidence of a struggle, a crime, anything at all that contradicted my account of us both having been in the kitchen, doing nothing more than having a conversation. Mostly, though, their work was concentrated on the exterior, along the side and into the back garden, which was why they'd kept me away from it and put me in the back of a police car. The only consolation was that the heater was going in the front.

I didn't feel warm for long.

Thirty minutes later, a Volvo pulled up at the edge of the cordon that had been put in place, and two people got out. One was Martine Parkes. Next to her was someone else I recognized, although I hadn't seen Detective Superintendent Aiden Phillips in a very long time.

They made a beeline straight for the car I was in, so had clearly already been briefed on where I was. That probably meant they'd already had my account of what had happened piped through to them as well. Parkes opened my door, not saying anything for a moment, just looking at the clothes the police had given me to change into, and then took a step back and said, 'I think you know DSU Phillips.'

That was an understatement and all three of us knew it. I looked at Phillips and a half-smile twitched at the corner of his mouth. 'How are you, David?' he said.

He was in his late forties, Scottish and softly spoken. His hair had thinned out since the last time we'd spoken, but he was still slim, fit, dressed immaculately. Ten years ago, he'd had a habit of playing with a thin silver band on his ring finger. He'd turned it repeatedly, over and over as he'd interviewed me. I didn't know why I remembered such a small detail in this moment, but what I did know was that he wasn't going to be doing it today: he didn't wear a wedding ring any more – and whatever had happened between him and his partner happened a while ago because there was no imprint on the skin either.

Parkes gestured to the house. 'What a mess.'

'What are you even doing here?'

She frowned. 'What do you mean?'

'I mean, this isn't your borough.'

Parkes glanced at Phillips, but he didn't move, didn't look back at her. He just kept his eyes on me as Parkes said, 'Letitia and I knew each other.'

'I know. That's why she made that call to you.'

They both looked confused.

'About me being on the train to Cambridge.'

Parkes's expression shifted; Phillips remained impassive. Now they knew that I'd found out who had phoned them from the train. Ultimately, it probably made no difference, because I wasn't about to tell them that the real reason I'd ended up here had nothing to do with that call and everything to do with the fact that I'd found out about Scargill's connection to a blackmailer and killer; to a man who I believed knew exactly what had happened to Fiona Murphy, *and* to Jennifer Johnson, thirty-seven years ago. I wasn't giving the Met a single thing until I got the truth about the two women. So this would do for now: let them know that I'd found out that it was Scargill who'd called them and try to put them on the back foot.

'So why *are* you here?' I said to Parkes.

'Why do you think? Word reached us about what had gone on tonight. Given everything else that's going on with you, David, you must understand the reasons why we felt it necessary to come –'

'Okay, so why are *you* here?' I looked at Phillips.

What Letitia Scargill had told me was still fresh in my head: Parkes wasn't a member of The Castle, so I didn't have to worry about her being the glue bringing the two big dangers in my life – Holt and Healy – together. But Scargill hadn't known if Aiden Phillips was a member. It would have surprised me if he'd become compromised, even if he was, because he'd always been so conventional and by-the-book, but I didn't trust him before the search for Fiona had started, and without the certainty of whether or not he was in league with Holt, I trusted him even less now.

'This is a bit below your pay grade, isn't it?' I said.

'A police officer has been killed,' he replied, simply.

'Right.'

'We need to get you back to the station,' Parkes said.

'Get me back to the station to talk about this? Or get me back to the station to go over all the same shit as yesterday morning?'

'Tampering with evidence is a crime. So is forging a passpor—'

'I'm sure your boss is suitably impressed with you already.'

Parkes's cheeks flushed.

I felt a pang of guilt at shutting her down, at belittling her in front of her DSU. But it was out of my mouth before I could stop it, a slow build-up of frustration, tension and pressure finally detonating.

'David,' Phillips said, 'we're going to go to the station, where you'll give the team investigating this case a second statement and answer whatever questions they might have for you. After you've done that, DI Parkes and I will talk to you. And after that, we can all move on.'

'Move on?' I smiled. 'Okay.'

Parkes's embarrassment had passed and now she just looked enraged; Phillips maintained exactly the same stance, his expression unmoved.

'So,' he said, 'shall we get this over and done with?'

42

After I'd finished giving my first formal interview, one set of cops left the room and another came in: Parkes and Phillips. I expected them to be oblique, to dance around their intentions, but instead they admitted straight off the bat that they were looking for connections between what had happened at Scargill's house and the investigation into Healy. Their candour surprised me, and concerned me. At the back of my head I knew it couldn't be good that Phillips was sitting in on this – at his level, nights interviewing suspects were years behind him – but if they were trying to set another trap for me, I couldn't see it.

'So how did you end up at DS Scargill's house?' Phillips asked.

'As I told the other officers, I saw her following me.'

It was a lie, but it was the simplest, hardest-to-dispute lie.

'You mean on the train to Cambridge?'

'Yes.'

'As I understand it, she wasn't following you.'

Except, of course, I knew she was, at the request of the man who'd gone on to take her life, but Scargill had fed a different story to Parkes: on the train, she recognized me and knew Parkes was looking into me. I said, 'Okay, well, if she wasn't following me, she was obviously interested in what I was doing. I wanted to find out why, so I followed *her*, found out she was a cop, got an address and went to find some answers.'

'How did you find out she was a cop?'

I fed him another lie: 'Because I watched her go into a police station.'

'Which one?'

It was a little test to see if I really *had* followed her to the station she worked in – which, of course, I hadn't. But I knew which station Scargill had been based in.

'Walworth,' I said.

After that, I went over all of the same ground: I went to Scargill's home, we talked briefly, but before she could tell me why she was following me, we were surprised by an intruder in the house; the intruder tried to make a run for it, I tackled him, he escaped, and then on the way past her he cut Scargill's throat.

'Any idea why he would want her dead?' Parkes asked.

'No.'

'Why not kill you?'

'I think that was what he was *trying* to do.'

'The plan was to kill both of you?'

I shrugged. 'I don't know.'

I don't know was just an easier response – even though I knew exactly why the man calling himself Gary Holt had wanted Letitia Scargill dead. It was for the same reason he wanted me dead. We'd both become problems for him. And while I knew that the story I'd woven might create issues for me at some point, if I could get out of here relatively quickly, it would then give me a minor period of grace. The initial police response was much more likely to focus on who the intruder was and why he was waiting for Scargill, and I seriously doubted that road was going to lead them very far. Not that they'd know that for a few days. I hadn't given them the name 'Gary Holt', didn't tell them anything Scargill had told me, so if Holt was half as meticulous, organized and clever as Scargill believed him to be, the Met weren't finding him any time soon.

For now, that gave me some breathing room.

After the interview was over, Phillips didn't hang around. He said goodbye and then disappeared along a half-lit corridor towards an office door. It was almost 3 a.m.

Parkes led me out to the front of the station and I headed straight for the main doors.

'Raker.'

I turned, looked back at her.

'Hold on a sec.'

Pausing there, the door partly open, the bone-chilling cold drifting from out to in, I waited as Parkes came towards me, passed me and headed out to the pavement.

Confused, I followed her out.

'What's going on?'

'I don't know, I just . . .' She stopped.

'You just what?'

Her eyes flicked to the station, then back to me.

'Just be careful.'

I frowned. 'What are you talking about?'

'You know what I'm talking about.'

Again, her gaze went to the station.

'Do you mean Phillips?'

She didn't reply, didn't move.

'What about him?'

'Just watch your back,' she said.

And then she was gone again.

Pieces

Tom | *Last Night*

They arrived at Seven Peaks just as the gates opened.

As they passed through the turnstiles at the main entrance, Tom tried to forget the phone call he'd made in King's Cross, tried to forget everything about Room 634 and concentrate on this time with Leo. But even as the two of them entered a long, enclosed tunnel – used to funnel visitors from the gates to the fun fair itself without revealing all the behind-the-scenes machinery powering the rides, the lights and the music – Tom couldn't quite drown out the panic. The howl of a mountain wind was being piped in, interspersed with the far-off roar of a Yeti, and a series of vents were spewing fake snow, and none of it was working. He kept thinking about the meeting he had tomorrow morning with the woman he'd been talking to, about the footage she'd asked him to bring with him, and about whether this hell – this constant, unceasing anxiety that had started in that dentist's waiting room when he'd picked up a copy of *East/West* – would finally stop for good.

Forty-eight hours earlier, after taking Leo to the dentist, Tom got home to find the house was empty. It took him a minute to figure out why. His head was full of noise, the image of Kian Bauer that had run in the magazine article fixed like a beacon in his mind, and when he wasn't seeing the journalist, he was seeing the man who'd answered the door to Bauer's room that night at the Regala. He was seeing handcuffs and duct tape.

Sadie wasn't home because she'd left for a three-night spa break in Bath with a couple of old school friends. That meant that he wasn't going to get the chance to talk to her about what was going on, to tell her about what he'd seen in the magazine, to ask her what she thought he should do. It was going to have to wait until she got back. All he could do tonight was wait for the babysitter to arrive and then head into work.

'Daddy?'

He looked down at Leo. 'Yes, mate?'

'Can I watch some TV?'

'Yeah, that's fine.'

Leo ran off into the living room, leaving Tom alone in the kitchen. Out of his pocket, he took two torn pages: he'd ripped them out of the copy of *East/West* from the dentist's. Laying them on the countertop, side by side, he studied the pictures of Kian Bauer. When Tom had gone up to Room 634, he'd not seen the face of the man he now believed to be Bauer – only his legs, only a hand bound to the bedpost by those handcuffs – but Tom was certain, even without being in work and using the booking system to search, that he'd personally checked Bauer in.

He read the first paragraph again.

Last month, **East/West** special correspondent Kian Bauer vanished into thin air. A gifted journalist, whose work on institutionalized racism in the Met Police, and on the opioid crisis in Rust Belt America, won him multiple awards on both sides of the Atlantic, was last seen on 30 August leaving the **East/West** offices in Farringdon, London at 5.45 p.m. A resident of Toronto, Canada, where he lived with his wife Jessica, Kian was in London working on a story about the 37-year-old murder of his mother. He told colleagues he was going back to the hotel he was staying in to transcribe some interviews, and data from his phone showed that he did, indeed, return to the Regala on York Way in King's Cross.

What happened after that is less clear.

Tom swallowed. *What if I'm the only one?*

What if I'm the only one who knows about the man in Bauer's room?

He kept asking himself that as he got ready for the night shift, and once the babysitter arrived and he headed into the Regala, he tried to drown himself in work. But that night had been quieter than normal.

Soon he was thinking about Kian Bauer again.

He told his staff he was going into the back office to take care of some admin, and then slid in at a desk and logged into the system. He found the booking quickly.

Bauer's first night had been 27th August and he'd paid for four nights – or, rather, *East/West* had, as it was their credit card against the room. Tom scrolled past Bauer's room requests – a higher floor, no feather pillows – and stopped at his check-out information. He was meant to have checked out on the 31st, the day after Tom had been up to the room, and it said that was exactly what Bauer had done: the room card had been left in a deposit box at reception.

Tom stared at the screen, realising now why the police had hit a dead end. If Bauer had used the deposit box, there was no way of telling what time he'd left the hotel, even if it was possible to take a guess: the deposit boxes were mostly used when the front desk was at its busiest, which tended to be between nine and check-out time at eleven. Tom guessed that's what the day manager would have told the cops too.

He looked across the office. In a cabinet in the corner was all the hardware for the CCTV system; in the alcove next to it were a series of screens, each showing different parts of the hotel. Getting up, he headed across to one of the PCs, woke it from its slumber, and then searched the hard drive for the 31st August. The hotel had to retain a certain number of months for insurance purposes, so he knew the film from the 31st wouldn't have been deleted yet. He found the date quickly and then saw it had been divided into another long list of sub-folders, each for a different camera in a different part of the hotel, and each with twenty-four hours' worth of recordings. He started with the video from the front desk, and then opened a second file for the camera mounted on the sixth floor, next to the elevators.

He hit Play on the front desk video.

It began at 00:01 on the 31st and finished at 23:59, but Tom knew the first twelve hours of the video were likely to be where the answers were, because that would have been when Kian Bauer had checked out of the hotel. He kept the video going at 2x speed, fast enough to get through it quicker.

But Bauer didn't appear.

Had he dumped the card without Tom noticing?

He stopped the footage and rewound it, all the way back to 4.30 a.m., when the very first guest dropped their keycard into the deposit box. He focused on the box as the foyer became busier, the weather outside not helping. On 31st August, the weather had been dreadful, rain lashing in against the windows, puddles everywhere at the doors, and even with the lights on full blast, there was a duller, grainier feel to the footage. But at 9.33, Tom spotted something.

He hit Pause.

It's him.

Tom had missed him the first time because he'd moved so quickly, and had kept – presumably deliberately – close to the edge of the camera's range. He was only in shot for a matter of seconds, stepping in towards the deposit box, dropping the card into the slot, and then stepping back out again. There was also something else Tom hadn't noticed the first time: the man had a backpack on and two long holdalls. When he dropped off the key, he put the holdalls down; when he stepped back to the edges, he picked them up again. But it was him. It was definitely him.

The man who'd been in Kian Bauer's room.

Tom watched him leave and then closed the footage from the 31st and brought up the front desk footage from the day before – the 30th. He scrubbed the video on. The *East/West* article had said that Bauer had left the magazine's offices in Farringdon at 5.45 p.m. on the 30th, and – at 6.09 p.m. – he came through the front of the Regala. He looked exactly like the picture of him in the magazine – early forties, six foot, medium build, honey-coloured skin. He quickly vanished from view, heading to the elevators.

Tom kept watching, leaning closer to the screen. Three hours later – just after 9.30 p.m. – Tom spotted the man who'd been in Bauer's room again, except this time he was entering the hotel. He came into the foyer, sticking to the very periphery of the frame, just as he did the next morning. It was as if he instinctively knew how to stay out of the shot. As Tom shifted the video on, he noticed something else: the man had *just* the backpack on. No holdalls. Did that mean the holdalls were *inside* his backpack? Or did the holdalls belong to Kian Bauer?

And then the man was gone too, out of shot in the direction of the elevators. You needed a room key to access the floors, which he almost certainly didn't have – but it wouldn't have been difficult to tailgate another guest.

Palms sweating, head thumping, Tom switched videos, from the front desk to the sixth floor. There were no security cameras as far down as Room 634, so all Tom had to go on was a camera on the ceiling above the elevators. It didn't take him long to find the man on both videos from both days: the evening of the 30th and the morning of the 31st. As the lift opened, he had his head down, just the dome of his skull visible; on the 31st, when he returned the next morning, with both holdalls at his side and the backpack on, his head was down again. There wasn't a single moment where Tom was able to see the man's face clearly.

This was why the police had missed him.

Tom could barely see the man and Tom actually knew who he was looking for. The police had no idea.

And then two things happened.

The first was that Tom looked down at the torn-out *East/West* article and noticed that there was a contact number and email address in a panel on the left. Both the number and the email – under a header saying, *Do you have information that could help find Kian?* – were for another journalist.

The second thing was that he started to rewatch the footage of the man from the 31st, wondering what he could have stolen from Bauer, and he realized that – whatever the explanation – there was still one, big unanswered question.

How did Kian Bauer disappear from his room?

And that was when Tom rewound the footage again, and he started to see the way the man was carrying the holdalls, how – based on the angle he was at, and the slightly stunted rhythm of his walk – they were obviously both extremely heavy.

And slowly, a terrible idea dragged itself out from the darkest part of his thoughts, and he wondered if he'd just found out how Kian Bauer disappeared.

The pieces of his body were in the holdalls.

Tom and Leo emerged into the main grounds of Seven Peaks.

'Daddy, look – it's so cool!'

A vast, sprawling fun fair lay ahead of them. It was impressive: fake mountains, fake snow, everything echoing a Himalayan mountaintop and not a patch of brownfield off the M25. All the staff were dressed like mountaineers or sherpas, and all the rides fit the same theme: a big wheel to their left had huge banks of replica snow atop its swinging gondolas; a mirror maze had a fake warning sign about altitude sickness and confusion; somewhere ahead of them, backed by a cacophony of screams, Tom could see part of the rollercoaster that Leo had found on YouTube videos, one of its massive inversions visible above the roofs of the food huts, which were done up like a Tibetan village; and then there was a ghost house, its impressive façade like an abandoned Himalayan temple.

He felt Leo squeezing his hand, and when he looked down at his son, his nine-year-old eyes absolutely alight with awe, Tom had a moment where he very briefly forgot about Kian Bauer, the man in his room, and what might have been in those holdalls. He forgot about the footage he'd taken from the hard drive at the hotel and had hidden at home, ready to hand over tomorrow. All he could see was Leo – the joy in his face, the overwhelming love Tom felt for him.

'Where do you want to go first?' Tom asked him.

'Can we do the Snow Leopard?'

The Snow Leopard was the rollercoaster.

'I paid extra for a fast pass, mate,' Tom said, 'so we can jump the queue – but we can't use it until seven o'clock.' He looked around. 'Shall we do other rides first?'

'How about that one?' Leo replied, pointing.

Tom smiled. 'Okay.'

They headed towards the ghost house.

43

I took an Uber from Bethnal Green back to Wembley. By the time I arrived, it was three forty-five in the morning and the scene had mostly been cleared. Crime-scene tape still flittered at Scargill's driveway, a uniformed officer was standing guard, and the living-room light remained on. Otherwise, the street had returned to hibernation.

I got into my car, fired up the engine and turned the heaters all the way up, trying to clear the windows. It was freezing, every pane of glass sparkling with a thick blanket of frost. I dug around in the boot, searching for a scraper, and once the ice was cleared, slid back behind the wheel: now it was the condensation I had to deal with.

As I let the heaters do their work, I tried to second-guess what Holt would do next. He was injured, although not badly, and the last part of his mission – to drug us, to move us, to kill us – had gone south. But I'd got lucky. I'd seen enough in the few, solitary minutes outside Scargill's house to know that, and I could feel it and see it too as I examined my neck in the rear-view mirror, the echo of his fingerprints on my throat, a bruise flourishing darkly on my cheekbone.

The truth was, I had no idea what he would do next. I had no idea what his real name was, where he came from, who he even was – so how could I predict his next move? The only thing I knew for certain was that he was a predator – and a predator kept hunting until it finally got its prey. So would he do something bold like go to my home and lie in wait there? Or would he retreat, regroup, come up with another way to take me down? Where would he go to do that?

I reached into my pocket and took out the membership card I'd stolen from Ian Kirby's office. Could The Castle be his home? Was that how he'd stayed invisible for so long: by not owning property, by just living within the club walls somewhere, hidden from anyone except members he'd already vetted and had managed to compromise, like Scargill? If they were compromised, they weren't going to risk discussing him, or what they knew about him – which I imagined wasn't much.

The big question, though, was where Holt and Fiona Murphy intersected. As I watched the windscreen continue to clear, my thoughts landed back on the condolence cards. Reaching over, I took them out of the glovebox again. I wondered for a moment if Holt could have been the sender, but I instantly dismissed the idea. I couldn't see his reasoning for doing so. But *someone* had sent these to Rebekah and it was starting to frustrate me that I was no closer to finding out who. The cards were a detail that mattered, a lead that might open up this whole case, whether it was Fiona who'd mailed them or someone else.

And then, outside the car, something registered with me.

It had been a blink of light from further down the road. I put the cards away again and saw it a second time. Leaning forward, I tried to figure out what it was.

Another blink.

Another.

What *was* that?

A moment later, something shifted in the gloom. *A person.* I could make out a face – although it was grey, featureless – and the subtle glint of eyes. It seemed as if they were looking in my direction but I doubted if they could see me: it was dark inside the car and I was partially hidden behind the vehicles in front of mine. The engine was running, though – so whoever it was would know I was here.

I waited, didn't move, just watched.

Another blink of light.

And then, finally, there was a slight shift, the person turning – and a pale glow washed across the dark.

A phone screen.

The blink of light was a camera flash.

I leaned forward even further, trying to figure out if the person was one of the neighbours. If they were, why would they be out at this time of the morning taking pictures? Any activity at Scargill's house – anything exciting, anything that may have been worth gossiping about – was gone now. Apart from some crime-scene tape, the lone officer, and the last of the forensic teams inside, the place was deserted.

Another blink of light.

Maybe that's the whole point.

Maybe they don't want anyone else to be here.

I turned the engine off. The instant the street became silent again, I saw movement in the shadows. Whoever was hiding there had taken a step forward, a little more of them exposed, and for the first time I could see clearly that it was a woman. She was wrapped in a winter coat, a beanie pulled down, a scarf spiralling out from her collar, almost entwined with the dark cords of her long hair.

She was looking in my direction.

She was trying to figure out why someone would start up a car, scrape the frost from it, and then not go anywhere. She was alert, suspicious – and on edge.

I kept watching.

It was hard to tell how old she was – maybe thirties – but a second after she'd stepped forward, she stepped back, letting herself be swallowed by the murk again.

I couldn't see her now.

No phone. No more blinks of light.

She knows I'm watching her.

There was a long, pregnant pause, both of us staring into the night, trying to figure out who the other one was.

And then, suddenly, she tore out of the shadows.

She was running.

44

The woman sprinted towards the end of the road.

As I leapt out of the car and hurried after her, I saw the uniformed officer at Scargill's house glance across in our direction, reacting to the sound of footsteps. I instantly slowed to a walk, trying not to arouse his suspicions. After a couple of seconds, I stole another look at him. His attention had already switched to a forensic tech who had appeared on the driveway.

As I soon as I hit the next street, I broke into a run, trying to zero in on the woman. The entire area was residential, the roads lined with identical terraced houses, cars parked in matching lines on carbon-copy streets.

But then, briefly, I saw movement.

She was eighty feet ahead of me already, there and gone as she vanished into an alley in the middle of the terraced houses on the opposite side of the street to me. I accelerated and headed into the alleyway. It was a straight line into the next, parallel road and, as I got through, I could see she was halfway down another alleyway, glancing back at me.

'Wait,' I said to her.

She didn't.

If anything, she picked up her pace. She was fit, fast, wearing what looked like running leggings, and had white trainers on too, presumably for exactly this emergency.

'Wait a second,' I shouted after her.

Again, she ignored me, veering left at the next street. I got to the end of another alleyway and looked to see where she'd gone. More houses, same design, except, to my left, at the very end, were a pair of nine-foot gates, chained, padlocked, with a WARNING – KEEP OUT! sign hanging off them.

The woman was climbing them.

I hurried towards her, trying to bridge the distance between us as fast as I could. She could hear me coming, her feet slipping on the wire mesh, worried now that she wasn't going to get over the top before I reached her. I shouted at her again – 'Wait, I just want to talk' – but she didn't pause as she finally got to the apex of the gates. She swung her leg over, steadied herself for a second, then jumped.

She landed hard.

I could see the leap had hurt her: she tried to scramble to her feet right away but, hidden in the tangle of long hair cascading past her face, I glimpsed a grimace, her teeth pressed together, her hand automatically going to her left ankle.

Gingerly, she started running off towards a huge building made of corrugated iron, and as a security light came to life on the front, I saw it was a scrapyard. Immense towers of twisted metal, a warehouse, a crane paused amongst it all, its claw open and teeth exposed. An untarmacked path led right into the heart of the metal and out the other side to another rusting fence.

But then, for some reason, the woman stopped.

I got to the fence, unsure why she'd paused, still unsure as she turned and came back towards me, pulling up her hood again – readjusting, trying to disguise herself.

What is she doing?

I looked down, to the other side of the gate.

On the ground lay my answer: at the edge of a puddle, face up, was an iPhone. It must have fallen out of her coat as she landed. I stepped right in to the fence: it was close enough for me to see her screen – a photograph of what must have been her children – and then a notification for three missed calls, all from the same number.

I grabbed my own iPhone from my pocket, went to Camera, zoomed in on the woman's screen and took a photograph. I had no idea if the number might help me, but it was worth a shot. More useful was what I did next: as the woman got closer still – only ten feet from me now, her head down – I went to Wi-Fi and watched as, onscreen, my phone started looking for the nearest available network.

The scrapyard.

Wi-Fi networks at the houses behind me.

And then the only other phone nearby.

Hers.

She grabbed the iPhone off the floor, a foot from me now – the two of us only separated by the mesh of the fence – but she deliberately turned her head so that I wouldn't be able to get a clear view inside the hood.

As she walked away again, I said, 'I just want to talk, Catherine.'

She stopped.

I looked down at my phone, at the networks it had found here. At the bottom was the one I'd been searching for: *Catherine Vance's iPhone.* And then I switched my attention back to her, keeping my eyes on her – her back, her hood – the shapelessness of the raincoat making it hard to get a sense for her build, her weight, even her height. She was still breathing hard, though – I could see that much – clouds of cold air forming at her hood, and she was weighted slightly to the right, avoiding pressure on her left ankle. I imagined her head was spinning too.

She was trying to work out how I knew her name.

She turned slightly, the tip of her nose visible outside the hood now. Her septum was pierced, a thin silver ring sitting against the skin below her nose. And then she looked down at the mobile she was holding. Her breath kept coming, slowing now. She was trying to work out what to do, what to say.

'I'm trying to find Fiona Murphy,' I said.

Nothing.

'Jennifer Johnson?'

Nothing again.

'Do you know anything about The Castle?'

This time, there was a different reaction. Her head turned a fraction, a little of her forehead on show, more of her nose, the pink of her lips.

'Was that why you were at Letitia Scargill's house just now?'

But I didn't get an answer.

A second later, she took off again, her ankle clearly still sore, but good enough to carry her towards the mountains of scrap at pace. I immediately started climbing the fence. She looked back, a flash of a face inside the hood. Kicking a leg over the top, I made sure to get far enough down the other side that I wouldn't have to drop the same distance as her. As soon as I landed, I hit the accelerator.

But now I couldn't see her.

I stared into the scrap, its countless hiding places, and then off to the back fence – and that was when I noticed something. The fence was vibrating, its subtle movement catching and recatching what little light there was.

Something had disturbed it.

Or someone.

By the time I got to the fence, I knew it was already too late. Beyond the mesh, the ground instantly dropped away into a railway embankment. She was crossing the line, carefully tip-toeing her way over the live rails to a housing estate on the other side, and she didn't look back in my direction until she was almost at the top.

Soon after that, she was gone from view entirely.

I stood there for a moment, annoyed, frustrated, then – as I began making my way back to the front gate – got out my phone and put *Catherine Vance* into Google.

The surname was unusual.

That helped me.

It didn't help her.

Inside a second I had a page of search results, including repeated images of the same woman. I stared at her, positive it was the person I'd just pursued.

And every link and every image told me the same thing.

Catherine Vance was a journalist.

45

By the time I got back to the car, I was pretty certain Catherine Vance was just a pen name. Aside from her journalism, I could barely find anything out about her at all.

I'd seen other journalists do the same thing in the past, especially when they were digging around in murky water. A pen name added in a layer of protection, although ultimately any shield you put up was likely only temporary. If most of my contacts weren't still in bed, I could probably connect the dots from her pen name to her real name pretty quickly – but, for now, I'd just have to continue using Google.

I slid in at the wheel of the car and pulled the door shut. The windows had all iced up again. I fired up the engine and, as the car slowly began to warm, returned to what I could find out about Vance online: she was thirty-four, Welsh, and based in London. In Google Images, there were a few pictures of her, including what looked like a portrait taken when she'd been on staff at the *Guardian*, but from what I could tell she was now freelance.

When I went to the *Videos* tab, I found a recording of her talking on a panel at a festival in Budapest about the importance of a free press. She had the same long brown hair I'd glimpsed inside the hood, and the same nose piercing. She spoke quietly, confidently, her Valleys accent soft but there.

I went from *Images* to *Tools* and then narrowed down the time-frame for features she'd written to the last month. There was one. Otherwise, she'd barely published anything in the last four weeks. When I clicked through to the article, I saw it was a feature on how sections of the NHS were quietly being sold off to big US corporations and, even then, she'd only provided 'additional reporting'. Her recent publishing schedule appeared to be completely out of sync with what had come before: up until the middle of November, she was writing all the time, for big publications like the *New York Times* and *Rolling Stone*. So what had changed?

I switched the timeframe again to Past Year and started scrolling, the results all laid out chronologically, with her most recent one first. That was the article she'd contributed additional reporting to. Once I got into October, her schedule picked up and became much more like the one she'd been keeping until the November hiatus: two long-form investigations for the BBC and *Sunday Times*, a few shorter pieces elsewhere, and then the same again in the months preceding that.

In late September, she published an article in *East/West*.

I knew it well: it was the biggest weekly news magazine on the planet, huge in the States, but big in Europe as well, and although its HQ was in New York, it had offices all over the world, including in London. During Derryn's last year, after I'd decided to go freelance in order to stay closer to her, I'd been in to meet the Features Editor, who I'd worked with for years when we were both on the same newspaper, and had written pieces on South Africa, Las Vegas and Baghdad's Green Zone for them.

Except it wasn't the fact that – like me – Vance had written for *East/West* that stopped me. What had got my attention was the description beneath one of the Google search results.

https://www.eastwestmagazine.com > kian-bauer-disappearance

What happened to Kian Bauer?

By Catherine Vance | Last month, *East/West* special correspondent Kian Bauer vanished into thin air . . . Kian was in London working on a story about the 37-year-old murder of his mother . . .

A 37-year-old murder.
That would have made it 1985.
I clicked on the article and briefly skimmed it. There was no mention of who Kian Bauer's mother was and what had happened to

her, although the fact that her death occurred in the same year as Fiona and Jennifer went missing was too much of a coincidence to ignore. What was more obvious was that the police had no leads on Bauer's disappearance, and that he and Catherine Vance were old friends and – with the support of Bauer's employers at *East/West* – Vance had started digging into Bauer's life and had been trying to find out why he'd gone missing. It made me wonder if this might have been the reason why Vance had been so quiet in the last month. Could she finally have started to get answers about Kian Bauer in November?

I went to Google again, trying to find out who Kian Bauer's mother was, and whether there might be some connection to The Castle, to Letitia Scargill, to Fiona Murphy and Jennifer Johnson. But there was nothing. Mentions of Bauer seemed to be limited to him disappearing, not the story he'd been trying to write.

Next, I tapped on Photos, and the picture I'd taken of Catherine Vance's phone screen, with the three missed calls. They'd all been from the same number – an 01634 area code. It didn't take me long to find out where that was.

It was the code for Medway, a district out in Kent, stretching from the coast in the north, to the towns of Gillingham and Rochester in the south. I didn't really know that part of the world, only that it was right at the termination of the Thames as it carved between Essex and Kent and flowed out into the North Sea and the Strait of Dover.

I googled the number. No results.

So I called it instead.

It started ringing, and kept ringing, but I didn't hang up, hoping it might hit a voicemail message or an answer machine. It didn't. It just kept going, over and over.

I reached forward to end the call.

But then, just as I did, I heard a *click*. 'Hello?'

A woman.

'Uh, hi,' I said, quickly trying to think on my feet. 'I'm not sure if I've got the right number – but I was told this was where I could find Bruce.'

'Bruce?'

She was confused, and I didn't blame her. I'd just plucked a name out of the air.

'I don't think anyone called Bruce works here,' she said.

She had an accent, eastern European, her English excellent.

'Oh, really?'

'No. You could try calling back later, when we're open. If you speak to someone on reception, they might know. I'm a cleaner. There's no one else in this early.'

'That sounds like a good idea,' I said.

'But I wouldn't call on this number.'

'Why's that?'

'Well, it's just the public phone in reception.'

'Oh, of course,' I said, as if it were obvious.

'No one calls this number,' the woman added.

'They only use it to call out?'

'Yes. Like I say, it's for the public. I don't know why you're using it.'

I'm using it because someone phoned Catherine Vance from it.

And they did it three times.

'Actually, you know what,' I said, 'I might just pop in once you're open as I'm just down the road. Can you remind me of the street address there?'

She recited it back to me.

I thanked her and hung up, went to Google Maps, and put in the address the cleaner had provided. Instantly, a pin dropped into a property on the Kent coast.

A reception. A cleaner. A public phone.

Now it made sense.

The number was for a caravan park.

Safe

Unknown | *February 1985*

A few weeks after he landed in London, Holt was sitting alone at the kitchen table in Larsen's flat – where he'd been staying – when Larsen arrived home, excited about something. 'It's done,' he beamed, swaying into the kitchen.

'What is, sir?'

'The Castle. It's now officially mine.'

Holt didn't know whether he was serious to start with.

'Aren't you going to congratulate me?'

Holt stood and held out his hand.

'Of course, sir. I'm sorry. Congratulations.'

The two men shook, but then Larsen pulled him into an embrace. Holt was taken aback to start with – Larsen had never embraced him, ever; had never shown any emotion around his men.

'This is the start of something really good,' Larsen said, and then stumbled out of the embrace, reaching to one of the kitchen chairs for support.

He was pissed.

Holt had never seen Larsen drunk either.

'Best thing I ever did,' he said, his words slurred. He absolutely stank of booze. He pulled out the kitchen chair and slumped into it. Holt sat as well, watching his former CO, his comrade, his friend. Larsen looked at him. 'What did that fucker need all that money for, anyway?'

Holt had no idea who he was talking about.

'He was a *prick*,' Larsen spat, 'a sympathizer.' He started to tilt in the chair, his eyes getting heavy. Seeming to feel his weight going, Larsen righted himself, placing a hand on the table. 'Everyone thinks it was an accident – but we know different, don't we?'

Holt frowned. 'Who are we talking about, sir?'

'Kleindorf, of course.'

It took Holt a moment to catch up.

'*David* Kleindorf?'

'The very same,' Larsen said, the *s* of *same* drawn out on his lips.

Kleindorf had been a millionaire property developer. They'd suspected for a while that he'd been secretly funding the enemy but he had powerful friends at home and abroad and that had always made it difficult for them to yank him off the streets. Kleindorf was rich, and rich men didn't get forgotten easily. In the end, the matter resolved itself: Kleindorf had drowned in a storm after taking his boat out, and had washed up on a beach miles away a few days later – or so Holt had always thought.

'Are you saying Kleindorf didn't drown?'

'Oh, he drowned.' Larsen winked at him. 'I held his head under the water and then sailed that big boat of his down the coast.' Larsen smiled. 'Man overboard!'

Larsen started laughing.

'You killed Kleindorf?'

'And stopped the enemy in their tracks.'

Holt eyed his former CO.

There was something else.

'You took his money too, sir?'

Larsen smiled again. 'Three point four million. That's the whole reason I'm here. He had it hidden under the floorboards in that big old mansion of his. I watched him for months and no one but him even knew it was there. So I planned it all out, and I took it, and I made my escape to London.' Larsen opened his hands out, as if he'd just performed a magic trick. '*Ta-da.*'

He erupted into laughter again.

Holt smiled out of respect, but – inside – he felt the first murmur of disquiet. He didn't give a shit about Kleindorf. Drowning was too good for him.

But he gave a shit about the trail Larsen might have left.

And, as Larsen's eyes started to get heavy again, as his body began to tilt once more, for the first time Holt looked at his former CO and felt disconcerted by what he saw. In all the years they'd served together, Larsen had never let his standards slip like this. Not once. Even worse, a few weeks ago Holt had left home with nothing, left everything he'd ever known, and put his entire life in the hands of Larsen, and he'd been willing to make that leap because Larsen was the best man he'd ever known – ruthlessly disciplined, completely trustworthy, smart, discreet.

Except this version of Larsen wasn't any of those things.

And, for the first time, Holt wondered if his secrets were safe.

46

I headed straight from Letitia Scargill's house and arrived at the caravan park at 7 a.m.

The site was in the middle of the North Kent Marshes, a sweep of wetlands, of intricate tributaries and inlets, that stretched all the way from the narrowing of the Thames in the west to the Isle of Grain in the east. It wasn't exactly hidden, but once I parked outside the reception area, I started to see the appeal of the Coombe Marsh Holiday Park as a place to lie low in the dead of winter.

The main building not only housed the reception – and the payphone I'd called – but a clubhouse, a shop, and a laundrette. I could see glimpses of all three through the windows at the front, and everything was locked. Maybe over Christmas and New Year, things would open up, especially if the weather was half-decent. But, right now, the whole park was dead.

I looked off to the maze of caravans.

Most traced the gentle cant of the coastline down towards the water and as I started to head in that direction, more came into view. There were no vehicles outside any of them and no signs of life as I followed a thin concrete pathway out to the far edges of the park; another one then took me back through the middle. I detoured left and right, looking into windows, double-checking none were being used.

It was freezing, the wind tearing in off the estuary, the tide out, the beach – such as it was; really just a thin, half-mile slash of sand, strewn with black seaweed and blue-grey rocks – as deserted as everywhere else. There were definitely members of staff here somewhere, but I imagined it was a skeleton crew: there was only one other vehicle – a van, with Coombe Marsh Holiday Park emblazoned on the side – in one of the parking bays, and then a quadbike outside the back of the reception.

So who could have been calling Catherine Vance from here? One of the staff?

A bitter wind gathered as I made my way through the last of the caravans, a small L-shaped cul-de-sac at the north-east corner of the park. From here, you could see across the marshes, the snaking inlets grey against the blackness of the land. It was still another hour until sunrise, but the sky had begun to change just a little, the dark giving way to a murky sepia twilight. When I got beyond the last of the caravans, I paused, trying to think, trying to counter the feeling of frustration I had about driving all the way out here for nothing.

Except it won't have been for nothing, I thought.

There have to be answers here.

The call to Vance had come from this place, a holiday park two hours out of London where literally no one was staying. Not only that, the three calls had come from a public phone, and it was unlikely anyone would choose to do that unless they were deliberately steering clear of mobiles. You only avoided mobiles if you didn't want to make it easy for someone to find you.

A mobile phone gave you the exact location of a person.

A payphone only gave you a geographical area.

I turned, looking back through the labyrinth of caravans in the direction of the main building, wondering about the staff here, about whether any of them could have made the calls to Catherine Vance – and why. And then I thought about Vance herself. I needed to track her down. I needed to find out why she was at Letitia Scargill's house at 3.45 a.m. taking pictures.

Suddenly, a light came on in one of the caravans.

I stopped, sidestepping into cover behind the edge of a van to my left. The van with the light on was about fifty feet away, facing me so that I could see all the way along its flank – its windows, its door, a veranda area with a gas canister.

I waited.

Slowly, at one of the windows, a shadow formed – a person – and, as I edged further into cover, I watched the net curtains at the window twitch, parting in a V-shape. A set of fingers were now visible, half a face, an eye shifting from left to right.

It took me a second to realize it was a man.

And a second longer to realize I knew him.

47

The curtain dropped back into place.

As soon as it did, I tried to make sense of what I'd seen – and what it meant – and, a few moments later, the door to the caravan opened. He stepped out on to the veranda, looked around – cautious – and then Ian Kirby started to lock up.

What the hell?

What was the manager of The Castle doing here?

I inched back into cover, entirely hidden from view now, and then listened as he descended the steps, as his feet softly crunched on the loose gravel of the pathway.

He started walking off.

I shuffled the other way, back along the rear of the caravan, and watched him. He was heading in the direction of the reception.

I moved quickly – heart beating fast, chilled air coalescing in front of me. I wasn't going to have much time: it was a two-minute walk to reception, and about five seconds after Kirby got there, he'd see my car. I had to assume he knew what vehicle I drove, maybe even my registration number, because he worked with Holt, and Holt knew all about me. Once he saw the car, he'd probably hurry back here.

That gave me five minutes max.

I got out my picks. It didn't take long. Yanking the door open, I headed inside. It was a standard layout: an L-shaped run of seats to my left, with a table and a TV; a kitchen ahead of me; two bedrooms and a bathroom on my right.

There was nothing in the living room.

No phone, no laptop, no iPad.

Because technology gets him found.

A book was open, face down, on the table, and the TV had been left on, one of the breakfast shows playing. I checked some of the drawers but didn't find anything, and then moved to the kitchen: basic provisions, nothing lavish. There was a stack of 50p pieces at the window, probably for the laundry – or the payphone.

Two minutes had just passed in a heartbeat.

Hurrying through to the first bedroom, I opened the door and looked inside. It was untouched, beds made, the wardrobes empty.

I moved from one bedroom to the other.

The second I opened the door, I could see things were different in here. Not only had he slept in this part of the caravan, the sheets a mess, what few clothes he'd brought hanging up in the wardrobes, he'd also set up a desk.

On the desk was a notepad.

He'd filled every line on the first page. I went to the page after that, the next, the next: the first thirty pages were full. I quickly realized it was his memories of his time at The Castle – written chronologically – starting in 1994.

On the wall above the desk he'd stuck up some photographs.

One was a guy in his late thirties, wearing a uniform. I leaned in, trying to make out the name badge on his lapel. *Tom Brenner.* Under that was the name of a hotel.

The Regala.

Where Kian Bauer had disappeared from in August.

Next to Brenner were two much older photographs, fuzzy, a little indistinct. They'd been taken on film, the images soft. In the first, the weather was hot, the sky blue, and a group of men I didn't recognize were around a barbecue, beers in hand.

But then I realized I *did* recognize one of them.

Right on the edge of the photograph, slightly away from the group, seated in a triangle of shadow at the side of a whitewashed brick wall was Gary Holt. He didn't even look thirty. He was dressed like the others – in shorts and shirt sleeves – but he looked different, more serious, eyes darker.

The second picture felt more incongruous.

It was just a photograph of a window.

I leaned in closer.

It was taken from inside a house. Through the window, I could see the sky was blue again, cloudless, the land beyond the glass vast and sun-drenched. Inside, all I could see of the room was the window itself and some of the wall that surrounded it. As I studied it, a spark went off at the back of my head, as if something in the picture had stirred a distant memory I couldn't quite reach.

Had I seen a version of this picture before?

Where would I have seen it?

It was somewhere hot, the land outside the window dry, the mud cracked and red on a track leading away from wherever this building was. Either side of the track was grassland – swathes of it, the grass straw-coloured, bleached by the sun – and, in the distance, I could see a row of telephone poles and a strip of road.

There was something else too: both photographs had something printed in the corners – some sort of reference number – and were stamped with the letters *TRC*.

Outside, I heard a noise.

The thump of footsteps on the path.

I quickly took in the pictures below that. These faces I definitely knew, and not only because one of them was mine. Next to me was Kian Bauer, his picture cut out of the physical edition of the article which ran in *East/West* about his disappearance.

Under that were two other faces.

One was Fiona Murphy.

The other was Jennifer Johnson.

48

I'd barely had time to process the fact that Fiona and Jennifer were up on this wall – alongside Kian Bauer, and then the manager of the hotel in which he'd vanished, and then Holt, and then me – when I heard the telltale creak of the steps out front.

I hurried out of the bedroom, along the short hallway, moving as quietly as I could. Halfway up, the front door of the caravan had a small, frosted glass panel.

Kirby was trying to look through it.

I stayed out of sight, using the shadows of the hallway – but I knew he would already be on high alert. His fingers were on the handle, trying the door. He'd locked it on his way out but now it was open. As he pressed down, the door inched forward.

He knew I was inside.

Or, at least, he knew someone was.

I had a split second to think about what I was going to do next. Then I moved: as the door inched in further, I shoulder-charged it, hitting it with everything I had.

It whipped back, smashing him square in the face.

I heard him stagger, hit the railing around the veranda – and then I pulled the door open, grabbed hold of him and threw him back into the caravan. He stumbled, temporarily stunned, one hand holding his face where the door had struck him, one trying desperately to grip the edge of the kitchen counter. Before he had a chance to get his bearings, I grabbed his coat collar and yanked him away from the counter, dumping him on the floor. He landed like a dead weight.

Now he was winded, wheezing, his expression pained.

I dropped to my knees next to him, put my whole weight on him and forced a forearm against his throat.

He blinked; tried to swallow.

'Talk,' I said, 'or I break your neck.'

I wasn't a killer, but he didn't know that. I pressed my forearm harder into his throat, kept my gaze on his. He was terrified – his breathing ragged, his body frozen.

'You're supposed to be dead,' he whispered. 'You and Scargill.'

'No shit.'

'He didn't come for you?'

'He came for me – but he missed.'

'And Scargill?'

'Scargill's in the morgue.'

Kirby moaned. It sounded like he was on the verge of tears now, confused, almost delirious. 'I talked to him on the phone yesterday afternoon and he said the plan was to lure you both to Scargill's place, listen to you –'

I cut him off, forced my elbow into his windpipe, because I knew all of this already: Holt had lost faith in Scargill; he needed me to stop digging.

'What the hell are you doing here, Kirby?'

I released some of the pressure.

His hand went to my arm, trying to loosen my grip even more.

'Are you hiding from Holt?' I asked.

'Yes.'

'As of yesterday?'

'As of the moment you came in to The Castle.'

'Why?'

He looked at the bruise on my face, spreading like a pool of oil along the ridge of my cheekbone, blood flooding the corner of one eye. 'You coming into the club like that . . .' Again, he tried to force my arm away from his throat. 'The second you turned up asking questions,' he gasped, '*he* was going to ask questions: what you knew, what you didn't. He was going to start looking around, trying to make sure there weren't any leaks, anything that could compromise him. And somewhere in all of it, if he dug down deep enough – and he would – he'd find me.' Kirby swallowed. 'He would find out what I've done.'

'And what have you done?'

'I've turned on him.'

I glanced along the hallway, in the direction of the bedroom, to the wall full of photographs, to the notebook Kirby had filled. 'You and Catherine Vance are working together?'

I saw his expression change as he tried to figure out how I knew Vance, how I'd made the leap to her. It was obvious she hadn't been in touch with him yet this morning.

'*Are* you?'

'Yes,' he rasped.

'You've been telling Vance all about The Castle?'

'Yes.'

'Since when?'

'Since the start of November.'

Four weeks.

That was why Vance hadn't written anything in a month.

'What are you telling her?'

He blinked. 'Everything.'

'What do you mean, "everything"?'

'I mean, everything I know.'

'So – what? – you and Holt were a team?'

'No,' he said, shaking his head as best he could under my weight. 'No, nothing like that. He moves me around just like every other pawn he's got his claws into at the club; just like he did with Letitia Scargill and a hundred others. But I've been there so long now, I'm so trapped by that place, that he's told me things. He's not as careful around me as he is with other people. I'm scared of him and he knows it, and that means he's dropped his guard around me.' Kirby paused, his belly rising and falling.

'You've heard things.'

'I've heard them – and I've seen them.'

'What can you tell me about Fiona Murphy?'

'I don't know about her.'

I pressed harder with my forearm.

'I don't, honestly.'

'Her photo is on the *wall* in there.'

'I'm not lying to you,' he said, teeth pressed together, eyes creased up in pain. 'I don't know, I swear. Her photo is on the wall because Catherine put it up there yesterday, not me.'

'Did Vance tell you why?'

'No.'

'So what *do* you know about Fiona?'

'Nothing. *Honestly*. I'd completely forgotten those two women existed until yesterday. It was only after you mentioned them when you came in – and then Catherine asked me if I'd heard of them – that this vague memory came back to me of the men mentioning Fiona and Jennifer –'

'"The men"?'

He nodded.

'You mean Holt? And who else? The owner – Samuel Apphis?'

He nodded again.

'You heard them talking about the women?'

'This was a long time ago, I swear. This was before . . .' He paused. I pressed again with my forearm: *Before what?* 'It was just a long time ago. Decades back.' But there was something else in his face now that I couldn't interpret.

'You better not be lying to me, Ian.'

'I'm not. I swear I'm not.'

'What were Holt and Apphis saying about the women?'

'I don't remember much, I just know . . .' He trailed off.

'You just know what?'

'I just know they were taken care of.'

Taken care of.

My body immediately caved in. A part of me had known that, after so long, their deaths were coming – but knowing it and hearing it were two different things.

'Holt and Apphis killed them?'

'Yes.'

'Why would they want Fiona and Jennifer dead?'

'I don't know. Honestly, I don't.'

'Does Catherine Vance?'

'I don't know. Maybe. If she does, she hasn't told me.'

'So where do I find Apphis?'

Something flickered in his face. 'You don't. He's gone.'

'He died?'

'He died in 2001.'

'So – what? – Holt just maintains the lie that Apphis is still alive?'

'Yes.'

'Why?'

'It gives him an extra layer of security to hide behind; a place to bury secrets. People don't know anything about Apphis, don't know who he is, what he looks like, where he came from. They couldn't tell you one useful thing about him. That means it's a place he can use, an identity he can disguise himself in. It's all just a mask.'

'So there *was* an Apphis once?'

'Yes. He was the one that bought The Castle back in 1985.'

That flicker again.

'What aren't you telling me, Ian?'

'Nothing, I swear.'

'If I find out you're lying, I'm –'

'I'm not lying. I'm not.'

I hauled him to his feet. Physically, he wasn't a match for me, and that made it easier to play the part of a killer. Grabbing him, I shoved hard, forcing him on to the bench closest to us. Before he'd gathered himself, I clamped a hand to his throat, fingers at his windpipe, and squeezed. I hated having to pretend I was this person – someone violent and cruel – but I had a million questions, and if he was frightened, he'd talk.

'What about the other guy up there on the bedroom wall?'

'Other guy?'

'Tom Brenner.'

'He's the manager at the Regala.'

'I know where he works, but what's he got to do with all of this?'

'That's where Catherine is this morning.'

I stopped. 'She's with Brenner?'

'Yes. She's meeting him in an hour.'

The Shrine: Part 1

Tom | *Last Night*

Tom and Leo joined the queue for the ghost house.

As they waited, Tom looked down at his son, at his bright yellow backpack, his favourite Darth Vader T-shirt, and his white Nikes, which Tom and Sadie had got him for his birthday, and which he treated with absolute reverence, only ever dusting them off for special occasions.

Again, he felt overwhelmed by how much he loved his son.

'Look, Daddy!' Leo said, pointing at the Snow Leopard, which was much closer to them now. People were screaming as it completed one of its inversions – and then it immediately surged into a banked turn. 'It's going so fast. Are you feeling scared?'

Tom smiled. 'Are you?'

Leo blinked, looked at the rollercoaster again.

'It's okay if you are,' Tom added.

'A little bit. But I still want to go on.'

Tom put his arm around Leo's shoulders. 'Well, if that's what you want, that's what we're going to do.' Up ahead, a digital readout above the entrance to the ghost house said the wait time was twenty-five minutes. 'You sure you want to do this one?'

'Definitely. Ethan says it's awesome.'

Ethan was one of Leo's best friends.

The closer they got to the front of the line, the more Tom could see and hear: above the main edifice – the old, abandoned Himalayan temple – a huge sign said, *Dare you enter . . . The Shrine*, while eerie music and the sound of a wailing wind played constantly. The actual entrance to the ride was at the far end, past the temple front, through a huge, crooked door, and that was manned by a guy in themed gear:

dark trousers, a fleece, woollen gloves, a rope tucked into his belt, and a headtorch. He looked like an explorer from the 1920s.

It took them twenty-six minutes to get there.

'How you guys doing tonight?' the man at the door asked once they'd reached him.

Leo beamed and Tom said, 'We're doing well.'

'Are you ready to walk the hallways of –' his eyes widened, the pause deliberately long; both Leo and Tom smiled, '– the Shrine?'

'Yeah!' Leo said.

'All right, my man,' the guy said, and high-fived Leo. 'You're one brave explorer – *and* you've got the backpack.' He leaned in closer to Leo, and – winking at Tom – said, 'Make sure you look after your dad, okay? He looks like he scares easily.'

Leo grabbed Tom's hand and, absolutely sincerely, said, 'Okay, I will.'

The guy winked at Tom again, and then beckoned them forward, to a step just outside the door. Inside, Tom could see a small panel with a red and green light on it.

Red became green.

'Okay,' the guy said, his voice exaggerated. 'The Shrine awaits.'

Tom and Leo entered the ghost house.

49

'Where are Vance and this Tom Brenner guy meeting?'

'In a café,' Kirby said, 'close to where he lives.'

'Why?'

'Because he has something Catherine needs.'

'Which is?'

'A hard drive with a video on it.'

I eyed him. 'A video of what?'

'Tom figured something out a couple of days ago. He connected it back to this night at the hotel in August, this thing he shouldn't have seen, and he realized –'

I squeezed again, shutting him off.

'Stop talking in riddles.' He struggled, gasped for air, his throat pulsing against my hand. It was horrible to watch, worse to feel. It was all I could do to keep my hand where it was. With every flash of pain in his face, every contraction of his lungs, I just wanted this to be over.

'Kian Bauer,' Kirby croaked.

'The missing journalist? What about him?'

'Years ago, Catherine and Kian Bauer worked together at the *Guardian*. They were friends. After Kian went missing, Catherine started trying to find out where he went.'

'And?'

'Kian had spent years looking for the man that killed his mother.'

'*And?*'

'And he finally found him.'

I eyed Kirby. 'You're saying Holt killed Kian Bauer's mother?'

'Yes.'

I remembered in Catherine Vance's *East/West* article that Bauer's mother had been murdered in 1985. 'What month in eighty-five did Bauer's mother die?'

'January.'

Eleven months before Fiona and Jennifer disappeared. It felt impossible now that these events – these three women – weren't connected. And there was something else too: in January 1985, someone killed Kian Bauer's mother; a month later, Gary Holt first appeared on the radar in London. I'd speculated about whether the reason Holt might have fled Germany – *if* that was where he'd come from – was because he'd done something heinous.

Maybe I hadn't been so far off.

'So – what? – Bauer was going to publish a story about Holt being the man who killed his mother?'

Kirby nodded.

'But Holt killed Bauer before he could publish?'

'Yes. He murdered Kian in his room at the Regala. And the reason . . .' He trailed off.

'The reason what?'

'The reason no one can find Kian is because . . .' He stopped again. 'It's because Holt chopped up Kian's body and walked it out of the hotel in two holdalls.'

I stared at Kirby – stunned, repulsed.

'He just walked it out of there in full view of everyone,' Kirby muttered, his voice breaking. 'He got rid of the body parts – and then he went through Kian's life and got rid of every trace of the story Kian was going to publish.'

And every trace of himself in it.

'But he made a mistake. He had the TV up too loud in the room. He hasn't got many weaknesses but his hearing . . . it's just not as good as it was . . .' He faded out, a shimmer in his face. It said, *Holt might be getting older, his hearing might not be as good as it was – but he's still the most frightening human being I've ever met.* 'He turned up the volume on the TV so it would cover up the sound of . . . of him . . .'

He just stared at me. *Of him killing Kian Bauer.*

'Someone complained about the noise,' Kirby said.

Quietly, his voice rough now, abrasive, he told me about a night at the Regala back in August when Tom Brenner responded to a noise complaint in Room 634.

'So the other man Tom Brenner saw in that room was Kian?'

'Yes.'

'Was he already dead when Tom knocked on the door?'

'Dead, or close to dying.'

'And Holt made it look like – what? A sex game?'

'Yes.'

'But Tom Brenner knows the truth?'

'He told Catherine on the phone that he came across an article in *East/West* that Catherine had written. It was about the disappearance of –'

'Kian Bauer. I saw it. What about it?'

'Tom saw the article, he realized that Kian was the same man who'd been on that bed in that hotel room and he went searching in the hotel's CCTV.'

'And then he called Catherine Vance?'

'Yes. Her contact details were on the magazine article. That's what's on the video he's giving to Catherine today: Holt captured on film at the Regala.'

I paused for a moment, trying to think. 'Why now?' I said.

'What do you mean?'

'You've been at that club for twenty-eight years. You could have confessed any time you wanted – so why pick up the phone to Vance and tell her everything now?'

'I just . . .' I felt his Adam's apple shift. 'I just can't take any more.'

Six words that said everything.

The guilt. The lies. The secrets.

The death.

'You should have *said* something.'

'I just didn't . . . I just . . .' He stopped.

'You could have gone to the police and –'

'You don't get it, do you? He has people *everywhere*. They're feeding back information to him the whole time. That place, it's not just a club, it's an intelligence network. He actively seeks people out that he knows he can use. It's why Catherine and Tom haven't gone to the cops about Kian Bauer.' Tears welled in his eyes. 'We've got a ton of serving police officers on our membership roll. I *know* he's turned six of them for sure, just like he turned Scargill – but there could be more. They could *all* be rogue. Catherine knows that, so that's why she and Tom haven't been to the Met. It's why *I* can't go to the police. Plus, Holt doesn't think I'll have the guts to turn on him.'

'He's going to find out pretty soon that you have.'

'I know. But it won't matter.'

'Why not?'

'Once Catherine gets the video, she's going to publish.'

'Have you seen what she's written?'

'No. But I don't need to. After Holt killed Kian, he got rid of his laptop, his phone, erased everything Kian had ever put into the Cloud or saved on to a hard drive. But Kian had some physical documents too . . .' Something tremored through him, an act he was still unsure of. 'While Holt was down in the Mendips, dumping Kian's body parts in a quarry there, he told me to take care of the documents. He told me to shred everything.' Kirby looked at me. 'I didn't. I kept them. I hid them and when I finally decided to pick up the phone to Catherine, I gave everything I had to her. So that's what she's going to publish – the story of The Castle, of him, and who Holt really is.'

'Who he really is? You mean, before 1985?'

'Yes.'

'What he did in Germany?'

Kirby frowned. 'What?'

'Holt. He spoke German, right?'

'No. But he did enter the UK on a fake German passport.'

'So he *isn't* German?'

'No.'

'He never lived in Germany?'

'No, never. He just stopped over in Berlin for a few days to organize the passport.'

'Scargill said she heard him speaking German.'
'Then she was confused,' Kirby said.
'So what language did she hear him speaking?'
I freed some of the tension from his neck.
He swallowed, cleared his throat.
'She heard him speaking Afrikàans.'

50

He was South African.

In my head, I pictured the photos next door: the blue skies in both of them, the sunbaked land; men in shirt sleeves and shorts gathered around a barbecue – a *braai* – cooking meat and drinking beer. Then I thought of the photo of the window, of the view beyond it: the red dirt on a winding track, the bleached grassland sweeping out over the hills. Something in the image had lodged with me and now I wondered if it was that a part of me had instantly recognized it as South Africa: I'd spent months living there before and after the first free elections in 1994, and had gone back twice for extended periods over the next ten years to report on how things were changing, including once for *East/West*. I knew the country. I recognized the highveld captured in the picture, its elevated plains, rocky ridges and slopes. So was that all it was? Or was there something else in the picture that had connected with me, something I still couldn't get at? I couldn't grasp at the answer – and then my thoughts fell away. Beneath me, Kirby was squirming, trying to break free.

I dug my fingers into his neck. 'Why did he leave South Africa?'

He hesitated.

'*Kirby.*'

'Have you ever heard of Jacobus Cronje?'

He pronounced it *Yahcorbus Cronyeah.*

I frowned. 'No. Who's that?'

'That's Holt. That's the name he used as an adult.'

I paused, letting the information sink in. *Jacobus Cronje.* No wonder the first thing he did when he landed here was change it. His original Afrikaans name would make him stick out a mile. He needed a name that people would struggle to remember; a name that would help him instantly fade into the background.

'You said his "adult name". So – what? – Cronje's not his birth name?'

'Catherine spent two weeks in South Africa at the National Archives last month. "Gary Holt" was born in October 1959, according to his British passport, but she doesn't think that's when Cronje was *actually* born: she found Cronje's name in South African military records. He joined the army in 1972, aged eighteen, which means he was born in 1954 and is now sixty-eight, not sixty-three. But, before that, before he joined the army at eighteen, Jacobus Cronje doesn't exist. No birth certificate. No information at all.'

His entire childhood had been lived under another name – just another blank, like Gary Holt had been before February 1985. The same pattern, repeating. The military records that Catherine Vance found did seem to confirm one thing, though: Letitia Scargill had been right. Holt – *Jacobus Cronje* – had been a soldier.

'And Samuel Apphis?' I said. 'Was he South African too?'

'Yes. He was Cronje's Commanding Officer.'

'What was Apphis's real name?'

'Martin Larsen.'

But there was something else there now, the same thing I'd seen earlier when Kirby had been talking about Apphis, about his death.

I tightened my fingers.

'What's going on, Ian?'

'What do you mean?'

'You're not telling me something.'

'Google "Die Suidplaas",' Kirby said, quietly.

'What?'

He blinked, the fear on his face like a dye, a colour he could never wash out. 'If you want to find out about them – what they did together – google "Die Suidplaas".'

Except I'd heard him the first time.

My Afrikaans was less than basic – but I didn't have to be fluent to know what *Die Suidplaas* was. I loosened my grip on him automatically, drawing back, wanting to make sure I'd heard correctly. 'Die Suidplaas? The South Farm?'

Kirby nodded. 'Yes.'

And now I knew what the photo was of in the other room – the one taken out of a window on to the sunlit plains of the highveld – and why it was so familiar to me: when I'd been in South Africa, I'd seen versions of the same image; the same types of shots taken from the same room out of the same window, with exactly the same view. Those shots had been all over the newspapers. All over the TV.

They'd been photographs of a crime scene.

'Die Suidplaas is where they worked,' Kirby said.

'Holt and Apphis?'

'Yes. And it's where Holt – *Cronje* – murdered Kian Bauer's mother. But that was only part of the story Kian was writing, and part of the one that Catherine is going to publish as well. Kian Bauer came here to expose Jacobus Cronje, his hiding place, the lie that his name was Gary Holt and he was British. But he was also going to show the whole world who Cronje *really* was and what else he did. Kian came here to reveal Cronje's whole history.'

I let go of him. 'His "whole history"?'

'Kian Bauer's mother,' Kirby said, 'that was just the end of it all.' He massaged his neck, shuffled away from me. 'That was just the final act.'

I stared at him, already knowing how bad this was about to get.

'Google "Die Suidplaas",' he said again.

And then his eyes went past me.

To the bedroom.

To the photos, out of sight, pinned to the wall in there.

'And after you've done that, google "the Red Wolf".'

The Red Wolf: Part 1

Unknown | *January 1985*

They pull her car over on a dusty track in Kalbasfontein. They're driving a bakkie – a pick-up – and there are markings on the side. There are no street lights out here, just open skies, so the light is low and, in her mirrors – when she looks back – the markings along the flanks of the vehicle are going to make her think they're police.

In a way, they are.

But they won't be taking her back to a station.

And there's not going to be any trial.

Jacobus Cronje is in the passenger seat of the bakkie. He doesn't usually come out for the capture but this woman – Mienkie Bauer – has been on their list for a while, and he wants to make sure it goes smoothly. No fuck-ups. No witnesses. They've got the 'no witnesses' part right already because, out here, there's nothing, which makes it the perfect spot on the highveld – no houses, lots of trees, no lights.

It's the middle of the night in the middle of summer, and even though it's unseasonably cold, both he and the driver, Bosman, are in shirt sleeves. They're big men, built that way by genes, and by war. Bosman gets out of the bakkie first and already has a torch in his hand. He shines it along the flank of Mienkie Bauer's car and announces himself: 'Ma'am, switch off your engine, please,' he says in Afrikaans, knowing she'll understand because – like him, like Cronje – that's her first language, the language she's spent most of her life speaking. That's what makes her betrayal even worse: a beautiful, smart white girl from Pretoria, Stellenbosch educated, who could have given so much to her country, but instead turned against her people, her race.

Bauer switches off her engine.

The highveld quietens, but it isn't silent. As Cronje watches Bosman moving closer to the car, he hears a scops owl; somewhere closer in there's a nightjar.

Cronje knows every bird call out here, knows every sound – can hear the intricacy of the ecosystem beyond the ceaseless chorus of the crickets – not only because he's been out here so long, but because he's purposely learnt.

'How are you tonight, ma'am?' Bosman asks as he gets to the window of the car. He shines his torch into the front and, from where he is, Cronje can see the back of her head. Bosman, his beard thick, his arms like thighs, puts a hand on the frame of the window and leans in to her: 'What is it that you're doing out here?'

Cronje knows what she's doing out here.

All three of them know what she's doing out here.

She's using back roads because she thinks there's less chance of her being stopped. And somewhere in the car – or in her head – there'll be a message. It's what they do: they travel the dirt tracks, far from the glare of the highways, one terrorist cell to another, carrying instructions, supplies, weapons, taking all of it from cities to the black homelands, or even further afield to Lesotho, Swaziland, shitholes where they think the white man can't go. Bauer is a traitor, a member of MK – uMkhonto we Sizwe, or 'Spear of the Nation', the armed wing of the African National Congress – and tonight she's been caught. Whatever MK has tasked her with doing, it's failed.

The ANC are never going to see Mienkie Bauer again.

'I was just on my way home,' she says, finally, responding to Bosman, to his question. 'Can I ask what this is about?' She looks in her rear-view mirror, making eye contact with Cronje. She's never seen him before, he knows that, but he's done so much recon on her, has been watching her for so long, he feels like they've met.

'Identity book,' Bosman responds.

His tone is changing.

'What's this about?' Bauer says again.

Cronje comes around the front of their vehicle and leans against the bonnet, arms crossed. Bauer glances at him again in the mirror, expression changing.

She's scared now.

Bosman looks at Cronje.

Cronje nods.

And then, like a lightning strike, Bosman moves, yanking open the door and hauling Bauer out; one slick movement. She's on the floor, winded, before she even *realizes it, dust billowing up around her, her face starched white in the headlights.*

Bosman punches her once.

He breaks her nose instantly.

She's silent.

51

Kirby scuttled away from me, his hands instantly going to his neck, massaging it, red handprints tattooed on to his throat where I'd choked the answers out of him. As he cowered in the corner, I took out my phone and did exactly what he told me to.

I googled 'Red Wolf' and looked at the results.

https://www.sahistorynow.co.za > suidplaas-apartheid-death-squad . . .

Die Suidplaas – Den of the Red Wolf

Die Suidplaas was established in 1977 by commander of the Security Police Martin Larsen . . . C9 was essentially a 15-man death squad . . . ex-soldiers, including Jacobus Cronje, the notorious **'Red Wolf'** . . .

https://en.wikipedia.org > wiki > DieSuidplaas

Die Suidplaas – Wikipedia

Die Suidplaas (trans. 'The South Farm') is a farm 20km south-west of Johannesburg . . . headquarters of the apartheid-era counterinsurgency unit C9 . . . including Jacobus Cronje, the so-called **'Red Wolf'** . . .

https://www.southafricaremembers.com > trc-redwolf-absentia . . .

Die Suidplaas 'psychopath' Cronje charged 'in absentia'

Die Suidplaas killer Jacobus Cronje, who disappeared in 1985 . . . Truth and Reconciliation Commission denied him amnesty . . . **'Red Wolf'**, including 12 counts of murder, although he's believed to have killed . . .

https://www.horrorsofapartheid.co.za > die-suidplaas-c9-redwolf

The 'Red Wolf' apartheid killer, charged with 12 murders

The Truth and Reconciliation Commission today refused to grant amnesty
to apartheid killer Jacobus Cronje . . . largely symbolic as the so-called
'**Red Wolf**' vanished in 1985 . . . horrors of **Die Suidplaas** . . .

https://www.apartheidandme.co.za > government-sponsored-killers

Where is the so-called 'Red Wolf' hiding?

Murderer, racist, psychopath, monster: the apartheid government's most
notorious killer, Jacobus Cronje . . . never found her body, but the '**Red
Wolf**' is suspected of killing Mienkie Bauer at **Die Suidplaas** . . .

I clicked on the first link.

It immediately started talking about Die Suidplaas, about what it
was, what went on there, about the men who staffed it and where
their experiences were forged.

Ten of the fifteen members of the C9 unit that lived and worked out
of 'Die Suidplaas' had fought in the so-called 'border war' in
Namibia, a brutal armed conflict between South Africa, who had laid
claim to the country after the First World War, and Namibian pro-
independence rebels who wanted the racist policies of the white
minority government out of their homeland. The border war was
vicious: by 1986, about 2,500 South African soldiers had died,
which – per capita – was a higher death toll than the US suffered in
Vietnam, and – as is often the case – the more ferocious the war, the
more barbarous the acts that define it. Never was that better illus-
trated than in the highly skilled but utterly merciless activities of
'Koevoet', meaning 'Crowbar' in Afrikaans, a paramilitary group
sent into Namibia by the South African government. Search and destroy missions were supposed to be their aim. Instead, they were
accused of a number of high-profile atrocities, including assassina-
tions, torture, electric shock treatment, sleep and food deprivation
and, perhaps worst of all, tying the corpses of their victims to the

backs of their Casspir armoured patrol vehicles and parading the bodies around like trophies. Against this backdrop, and in the heat of the bush, monsters were formed. And there was no monster worse than Jacobus Cronje.

I already knew snatches of this story. After its existence was finally exposed in 1989, pictures of Die Suidplaas had run in the South African newspapers for years, including a few that echoed the photograph that had been stuck to the wall in the main bedroom of the caravan. During my time in the country, I remembered hearing of a farm out in the middle of nowhere that a brutal counterinsurgency unit called C9 had operated from. A small unit of only fifteen men, all cops and former soldiers, it was effectively a hit squad, a tool of the white minority government that was built to silence political opponents of apartheid, although the government always denied its existence, and it was often thought of as a myth, a story used to scare and contain. But it wasn't a myth and it wasn't a story.

It was real.

The unit killed people for the state for over a decade, vanishing them in the aftermath so their families would never know what happened to them. Many of the bodies were buried in graves in the dust-blown hinterlands near the border with Botswana. Others were burnt on open fires while the men of C9 sat around barbecuing steaks and drinking beers.

But then, in 1990, apartheid started to crumble.

And the full truth came to the surface.

By 1996, by the time the ANC had won the first free elections and were two years into their governance of the new, multi-cultural South Africa, everyone knew everything. It had all come out in the Truth and Reconciliation Commission, a court-like public hearing authorized by Nelson Mandela that heard the stories of apartheid from all sides. That was what the TRC stamp on the photographs in Kirby's bedroom had stood for. Those photographs were copies of official government documents used in court, where in return for answers, for their absolute honesty and openness, people – even members of C9 – were granted amnesty. I'd left South Africa by then and wouldn't return for another eight years, so some of what happened during the TRC hearings passed me by. It was why I didn't know much about Jacobus Cronje.

I didn't know about the Red Wolf.

But as I clicked on the Wikipedia page for Die Suidplaas, I started to see why the TRC had refused to grant Cronje amnesty, why, because he vanished in 1985, he was charged in absentia with twelve murders, but suspected of many more: amnesty was only granted if the crimes were politically motivated – and the TRC weren't convinced that was the case with Cronje.

The inference was obvious.

He didn't just kill because he was told to.

He killed because he wanted to.

The Red Wolf: Part 2

Unknown | *January 1985*

'What do you tell your children you do?'

Mienkie Bauer looks at him, her nose pulped, blood in a band around the middle of her face, strings of saliva running from her lips. He's on the other side of the desk from her, quietly watching her, her chair seven feet from where he is, bolted to the floor in the middle of the room like a drifting boat. He just checks his watch.

It's been twenty-four hours.

She's got some fight in her but she's finally starting to flag.

'Huh?' she says. 'What do you tell your—'

'I don't have children.'

She stops.

It's the first thing he's said for what seems like hours.

'I don't have children because, when you have children, you have an anchor. You have something people can use.' He goes to the top drawer of his desk. His gun is in there. But he doesn't go for the gun; he goes for the photographs that are on top and the Polaroid camera next to that. He puts the camera down on the desk. 'That's what the people you've hitched your wagon to don't understand.' He gets up from the desk and comes around, sitting on the edge of it, photographs in hand. She stares at him, eyes wet. 'The only person I've got left in my life is my father, and he's a piece of shit. Why do you think I left him at eighteen to go and fight in the fucking bush?'

She eyes him for a second.

'You fought in the border wars?' she says softly.

He nods.

'My uncle fought in Angola. Were you there?'

He says nothing.

'Namibia?'

'*Namibia,*' *he repeats back to her witheringly. Its proper name will always be South West Africa – and she knows it. Only the rebels fighting for independence up there want to call it Namibia. She thinks they're all one – blacks there, blacks here; the token whites like her, who've had their minds corrupted; she thinks they're all one force for good, fighting against the so-called oppressors. But she's deluded. She's not a freedom fighter, she's not some guerrilla, she's just an accountant running messages for the ANC. And he can see what else she's trying to do now: strike up a conversation with him; trying to get him to drop his guard.*

She thinks it might be a way out of here.

'*How long were you up there?*' *she says.*

Her nose is busted so her words are compressed. He stares at her, doesn't reply, just lets the sound of the farm fade in – the crickets, the birds, the highveld.

*Eventually, he says, '*A year in Angola, three in your so-called "Namibia".*'*

'*Those were brutal wars.*'

He looks at her and thinks, How the fuck would you know?

But, instead, he says, 'I was four when my father first took me hunting. I was so small, he had to tie me to his waist so I didn't get lost in the bush. Basically, that was one of two good things he did for me in my life. He was a skilled hunter. He was in the army; knew how to shoot. I got so good, I could shoot better than him by the time I was ten. He was a prick so he hated that, but when I was young, I absolutely worshipped the ground he walked on, so I never noticed. Afterwards, it turned out that that was the second good thing he did in my life: he didn't give a shit about me. He taught me that, once you disconnect the binds of the family, there's nothing left for people to hurt you with.'*

Mienkie Bauer sniffs. There's a thread of blood running from her flattened nostrils, but she can't get rid of it because her wrists are tied to the chair she's on.

'*I'm sorry you feel that way,*' *she says, sniffing again.*

'*Why are you sorry?*'

'*Everyone deserves a good childhood.*'

He looks down at the photographs in his hands. He hasn't shown her any of them yet, but he can see her staring, wondering what the pictures are of. When he looks up again, he says, 'This place is as close to a family as I've got now.' He waves a hand at the room, at the farm, at the people beyond the walls. 'We don't talk about normal things here, and we don't share the same sort of stories you might share with a regular family.' He smiles at her. It looks real to her. 'We talk about "police coffee". You know what that is? It's this shit we drink here, any time of the day. It's not actually coffee, it's Coke and liquor. Rum, bourbon, anything we can get our hands on.' He smiles again; a flicker in her face. 'We talk about always adhering to the Eleventh Commandment in our work too.'

'The Eleventh Commandment?'

'Thou Shalt Not Get Found Out.'

Again, he smiles at her. She smiles in return. He can see her watching him more closely now, wondering if she's actually managing to turn the tide here. If she can build some sort of bond with him, any sort of relationship, she stands a chance.

If she does that, she thinks she can walk out of here.

You stupid bitch, *he thinks.*

'What else do we talk about?' he says to himself, really playing the part now. 'Oh, I know. We talk about when your ANC friends detonated a bomb outside an office where the sister of one of my men worked.' Her face starts to drop, the smile vanishing. 'We talk about how a bomb like that — seven thousand degrees of heat — is so destructive, it rips the fillings from your teeth. We talk about how all he had left of his sister to bury was a jaw. It was the lightest coffin the undertaker had ever seen.' Cronje smiles at her again, like they're still bonding, but there is nothing on her face now. 'And then, after we're done talking about that, we talk about how we found that comrade of yours who put that bomb outside that office. We talk about how we brought him here, shot him in the back of the head like the dog he was, and put his body on an open fire while we braaied boerewors.'

Cronje pictured that night, remembered the smell of boerewors crackling on the coals of their braai, the smell of it mixing with the stench of human flesh.

'He took about seven hours to cook.'

'You're an animal,' she says softly.

'The fleshier bits — the ass, the thighs — they take longer. That's why you have to keep turning the body. One of my men raked over the ashes the next morning and he found a few remaining pieces of bone, so we gave them to the dogs to chew on.'

'One day, you'll have to pay for your crimes.'

That makes him smile.

'I'm defending our country,' he says.

'You're a racist piece of shit.'

He pushes off the desk, puts the photographs down on top, and turns his back on her. She's sniffing again, starting to whimper, but he tunes it all out and begins unbuttoning his shirt. When it becomes clear to her he's undressing, he hears her whimpering quieten. 'What are you doing?' she says. He turns to face her, popping more buttons on his shirt, and then he shuffles the whole thing off and lays it down.

She looks from his naked chest to his face.

'What, you think I'm going to rape you?' He bursts out laughing. 'You're spoiled goods, you arrogant bitch. Why the fuck would I ever want to touch you?'

He grabs a photograph from the desk, then holds it out for her to see what he means. The photo is of Mienkie Bauer, her husband, and their five-year-old son.

Her husband is black.

'Please, they've got noth—'

'Kian,' he says, cutting her off. 'That's your son, right?'

Her face blanches.

The room is almost silent now.

'Your husband is Austrian-Canadian, correct? Born in Vienna but brought up in Toronto? How does a black guy end up with a strong Germanic surname like Bauer?' He tilts his head, lets her sweat on what the right answer is, and then he smiles to himself. 'Don't worry, I don't give a shit. I don't give a shit about him and I don't give a shit about your mongrel son.'

He can see it takes everything she has not to bite back at him, to defend her son, to swear at Cronje, spit at him, to tell him in a fair society it's her right to fall in love with whoever she wants, whatever the colour of their skin, start a family with them, live freely. But she keeps it all back.

Softly, she just says, 'I love my husband and I love my son.'

He can see that she's trying a different tactic now: quiet, restraint.

'I understand your husband's back home in Canada at the moment,' Cronje says. 'Along with young Kian, of course. But you two met in Jo'burg, right? That makes me wonder what your man was even doing here in the first place. What, there's nothing over there in Canada to occupy his time, so he has to come

here?' He smiles, because he knows exactly what Mienkie Bauer's husband was doing in South Africa: his mother was Zulu, an academic who moved to Vienna in the seventies to teach southern African politics, so he feels an affinity for this country, feels like this is a fight he has to be a part of, or it will stain his soul forever. 'Toronto. That's where you and he got married, isn't it? I mean, obviously. You weren't going to be able to walk down the aisle here, were you?' He holds up the photograph again and taps a finger to the image of Kian. 'You weren't going to be able to show him off in polite society.' He waits for a comeback. Again, she doesn't reply. 'Why is a black Austrian-Canadian so interested in our little corner of the world? It's not his fight.'

'It's every decent person's fight.'

Cronje laughs, the sound destructive, a putdown, a way to tell Bauer she's misguided and pathetic. 'I hear he's in Toronto right now campaigning on behalf of your friends at the ANC; trying to get the world interested in "the cause", trying to get those all-important dollars. And you were due to fly out there in two days' time, is that right?'

She eyes him for a moment. Nods.

'Just had to get a few things done first, huh?'

She doesn't move, doesn't reply.

'So what message were you delivering for the ANC?'

'I wasn't delivering a message.'

'You were,' he says. 'It's the one in your head.'

'I don't know what you're talking about.'

'Sure you do. It's the message you've memorized.'

'I haven't memor—'

'What's the message?'

She sniffs. 'I was on my way home.'

'You're staying in Potchefstroom. That's the opposite direction.'

She doesn't say anything.

He watches her, waits.

Then, finally, he says, 'Okay.'

He looks at the photographs in his hands again.

'Then, let me ask you this: have you ever heard of the Red Wolf?'

A shimmer in her face this time. She has. All of them have heard the rumours about the Red Wolf: a faceless killer, working for the apartheid government, who *makes people vanish — ruthless, cruel, invisible. And then he puts the photographs down on to the desk again, and turns around, and he lets her see the truth.*

The Red Wolf is right here in this room.

He's real.

And, as she stares at his naked back, Mienkie Bauer starts to beg for her life.

52

I locked the caravan door and took the keys with me so Kirby couldn't go anywhere, and then went through to the back bedroom. There, I photographed everything: the shots pinned to the wall, the account Kirby had written about his time as manager of The Castle, the caravan itself, documenting it all in case I needed it at some point. After that, I did a second sweep of the place and, hidden under Kirby's mattress, found a six-page printed list with four hundred and thirty-two names on it.

It was every member of The Castle.

I started to look at it more closely – and then stopped. It sounded like the door to the caravan was being turned. Hurrying back through, I saw Kirby fiddling with the window next to the door. He had no hope of getting through. But he was desperate.

He startled as he saw me waiting behind him, and stepped back from the door, the window slapping into place again.

'You going somewhere?' I said.

He was about to speak when his eyes went to what was in my hand. As soon as they did, he began to cower.

'Relax,' I said.

'Relax? Why the hell do you think I'm trying to get out of here? You just tried to *kill* me.'

'I never got close to killing you.'

That stopped him. He was clever, switched on – you didn't survive around a man like Cronje as long as he had if you weren't – so it quickly started to dawn on him: 'All of that just now was an *act*?'

'I needed the truth.'

'Then why not just ask rather than break my bloody neck?'

'Would you have told me anything if I did?'

He didn't reply.

He was so tethered to what Catherine Vance was writing, to the story she was going to publish, that I suspected, if he'd had a choice, he'd have tried not to give me anything at all in case it jeopardized what he believed was his escape route.

I didn't like doing it, but threatening him had worked.

I handed him the membership list. 'Do you know how many cops on here are compromised?'

'No.'

'Holt – I mean, Cronje – didn't tell you?'

'No. Like I say, I know a lot, but not everything.'

I grabbed a pen.

'Mark on there who you know's with the Met.' He took the pen and started doing as I asked. While he did, I said, 'Have you ever heard of Mark Levin?'

He looked up at me, shook his head. 'No.'

'I think he might have been having an affair with Jennifer Johnson.'

He shook his head a second time and then went back to the names. 'No,' he repeated. 'I haven't heard of him.' He handed me back the list. 'I can't remember exactly how many cops we have on our books because we've got four hundred and thirty-two members. But I've marked forty-one I know about and put an asterisk next to the ones I know he's definitely turned, because those are the cops he's told me about. But, like I say, there could be more.'

I looked at the list properly for the first time. It was full of people who existed in the public eye – celebrities, politicians, high-profile sportsmen and -women – and for a moment it made me wonder if any of them had also been targeted by Cronje. But I quickly refocused and zeroed in on the seven asterisks. It gave me some insight into who I could trust and who I couldn't inside the Met, but – given that Kirby didn't remember every cop on their books – it was still way too dangerous to take all of this to the police. It was probably also impossible to figure out who'd placed the flag against Rebekah's name – if that even mattered now.

I saw the asterisk next to Letitia Scargill's name and asked Kirby about her. He thought that Catherine Vance must have heard about Scargill's murder from a source at the Met and, knowing that Scargill was on the membership list, gone to her house at 3.45 a.m. to take a closer look. Whatever the truth, though, I felt genuinely sorry for Scargill, that she'd become cornered and caught up like she had. And as I looked at her name, at the names of the six other compromised cops on the list, and then at all the others, I also felt a weird, perhaps inappropriate sense of relief that there were no other serving officers whose names I recognized. No Martine Parkes – but then I knew that would be the case already. More importantly, there was no Aiden Phillips. That meant, for now, I could forget about them. Whatever was going on with Healy, whatever trap Parkes and Phillips were trying to set for me and him, it was separate to all of this.

'Why did Cronje leave South Africa?' I asked.

'I don't know the full story.'

'Then what *do* you know?'

'I just know it was something to do with the murder of Kian Bauer's mother, Mienkie.' He opened his hands out. *That's it. Honestly.* 'When Cronje killed Mienkie Bauer, something changed. Suddenly, he had to flee the country. I don't know any more than that. Before he died, that was all that Martin told –'

'Martin? You mean Martin Larsen?'

'Yes. Before he died, he told me –'

'You said he died in 2001?'

'Yes.'

'How did he die?'

'His heart gave in.'

'"His heart gave in"? What does that mean?'

'What it sounds like.'

'What it sounds like is you're deliberately being vague with me.'

'No. I'm not, I –'

I studied him. 'If you lie to me, Ian, I will snap your neck and this time it won't be an act.'

'I'm not lying, I swear. I've told you everything.'

I took a step closer, but nothing shifted in his expression.

'Okay, so where do I find him?'

Kirby frowned. 'Who?'

'Who do you think? Holt, Cronje, or whatever name he's chosen today.'

'"Find him"?'

'Yeah. Where does he live?'

'What, you're going to try and take him *on*?'

He looked at me like it was the most insane thing he'd ever heard.

'Does he live at The Castle?'

'You're going to mess everything up if you –'

'*Does he live at The Castle?*'

Kirby blinked, rubbed at his brow. 'Yes.'

I got out my phone and opened the PDF of the floorplan that I'd downloaded from The Castle's intranet.

'Show me where.'

The Envelope

Rebekah | *This Morning*

Rebekah stirred and rolled over in bed. The sounds of the hotel room filled in around her: the soft hum of the air conditioning, the noise of the city beyond the windows. She opened her eyes, reached over and checked her phone for the time.

It was 8.31.

She flipped back the duvet and padded through to the toilet. As she sat there, her mind started going, her thoughts returning to her daughters – as they had done over and over during the past couple of days. She pictured Kyra and Chloe in their beds, both of them fast asleep, could almost hear the gentle sound of their breathing.

She washed her hands and looked at herself in the mirror, the exhaustion lying heavy on her. She still hadn't quite kicked the jet lag – but it wasn't just that. It was being so far away from her girls; it was everything to do with her mother. She dried her hands, thinking about her dad, about what he might say to her now to reassure her, to make her feel better, stronger, and then returned to bed.

As she did, she noticed something.

An envelope had been pushed under her door.

Rebekah bent down and scooped it up. Turning it over, she saw that the back hadn't been stuck down – just tucked inside – and there were no stamps. On the front, all that was written was her first name.

No surname. No room number.

She opened the flap and looked inside.

53

Just as I was driving out of the caravan park, my phone started ringing.

I looked at the centre console, at the number flashing up.

'Rebekah,' I said, after pushing Answer.

'David.'

She sounded different; panicked.

'Is everything okay?'

'I'm sorry to call you like this, I just . . .'

Her voice fell away.

'What's the matter?' I asked. 'Are you all right?'

'No,' she said softly. 'No, not really.'

'What's wrong? Are you safe?'

'Yes,' she responded. 'Yes, I'm safe.'

'Then what's going on?'

'I just got up and I found . . .' She paused. Sniffed. 'Someone put something under my door. An envelope. I opened it, and inside there was . . .'

Again, she juddered to a halt.

'There was what?'

'There was another card from my mother.'

PART SIX
The Tokoloshe

54

I called Catherine Vance using a mobile phone number that she'd given to Kirby.

She picked up after two rings.

'It's David Raker,' I said.

There was silence on the line, the only sound the soft *thump thump thump* of the tarmac under my wheels as I powered down the motorway.

'How did you get this number?' she said eventually.

'I've just visited Ian Kirby.'

She knew now that it was pointless running away for a second time, that if I'd been to see Kirby, I'd made the connection between them, knew what she and he had got planned, and that there was a good chance he'd given me everything.

'I suggest we meet,' I said.

'With a view to doing what?'

'We want the same thing.'

'And what's that?'

'To stop Jacobus Cronje.'

Another prolonged silence. I pictured her, using the photographs I'd seen of her online: blue eyes, a long cord of brown hair to one shoulder, the nose ring that had helped me ID her, and then a braid of other piercings tracing the fringes of each ear.

'Fine,' she said.

'You're meeting Tom Brenner in fifteen minutes.'

'Am I?'

'I know you are.'

'For fuck's sake. Is there anything Ian *hasn't* told you?'

'He didn't tell me what you knew about Fiona Murphy and Jennifer Johnson.'

'I'm not talking about all of this over the phone.'

'Okay, so where do you want to meet?'

She took another moment.

'Let me go and get this CCTV video from Tom and I'll call you back.'

She called back thirty minutes later. I was stuck in a traffic jam, two lanes of solid congestion snaking out of a turn-off that fed into the M25.

'There's a Starbucks half a mile from Seven Peaks,' she said.

'Seven Peaks?' I frowned. 'The fun fair?'

'Yeah. I'll see you there at eleven.'

'Why do you want to meet there?'

'Because I do.'

'Is Tom Brenner coming?'

'Just be at the Starbucks at eleven,' Vance said, and hung up.

The sound of a dead line filled the car.

I looked at Vance's number on the console.

Something didn't feel right.

55

The Starbucks was the middle unit in a bland, L-shaped retail park full of high-street stores and chain restaurants, and, apart from one table at the front, was completely empty. I dumped my bag in a booth at the back and ordered a black coffee and as I waited for it, I looked across to Seven Peaks in the distance. Its colossal crests rose up on the other side of a sweep of brown-grey farmland, its gigantic front blazing with light against the grey of a freezing cold winter morning. It had been built to resemble a seven-summit mountain range, all of them ragged and snowcapped, and the largest was like an enormous sail. It was so impressive, so lifelike, that if you looked at it quickly, you might genuinely think you were in the Alps or the Himalayas, not at the edge of the M25.

As soon as my coffee landed, I took a long, deep gulp. It was half-ten and I hadn't slept at all for almost thirty hours, so I felt exhausted, my whole body like a weight I was carrying. My face hurt as well, the bruise darkening on the drive back to London, changing like a sunset, from mauve to inky black.

Sliding in at the booth, I refuelled, finishing the coffee quickly, then ordered a second round and thought about Ian Kirby. I didn't entirely trust him, but I'd heard enough to know that he wasn't going anywhere and he wasn't about to pick up the phone to Cronje at The Castle and tell him I was coming. Kirby had betrayed Cronje by talking to Catherine Vance so he knew, whatever else happened from here, he needed to stay hidden, or Cronje would do to him what he had done to Letitia Scargill and so many others before her. I suspected, just by virtue of the fact Kirby wasn't going to be turning up to work today, that Cronje might soon become suspicious – but if he couldn't find Kirby, he couldn't get answers.

As I waited for Catherine Vance, I started going through the

pages I'd bookmarked on Die Suidplaas and Cronje. Even now –
even with the benefit of sworn court testimony via the Truth and
Reconciliation Commission hearings, and the hundreds of thousands of words that had been penned in the South African media
about the C9 unit ever since its existence had been revealed in 1989 –
Cronje's alter-ego, the Red Wolf, was still written about as if he were
a kind of mythical figure. At the start, I really didn't understand why.
But then, the more I read, the more it pulled into focus: so few
people had come face-to-face with Cronje, and the ones who did –
like Kian Bauer's mother, Mienkie – never lived to tell the tale. And
even the people that knew him didn't know him. There were no
records under the name Jacobus Cronje before the age of eighteen.
In the nine years he was in the army – including the two he spent
fighting in the notorious paramilitary group Koevoet – he hardly
appeared in any photographs, and could only be found on a few official documents. And when he arrived at Die Suidplaas – initially
under the tutelage of the only man he ever seemed to trust, his former CO Martin Larsen, before Larsen made a break for the UK – it
turned out Cronje and the rules of the C9 unit were perfectly aligned.
Orders were only given out orally. There were never any written
reports and nothing was ever committed to paper. The members of
the unit developed their own body language, where a nod of the
head, a wink, or even just a look, could mean someone getting a bullet in the head. And all of it played out miles from centres of
government, under a regime that was happy not to ask questions
and deny C9's existence completely, even as it carried out their dirty
work. That allowed Cronje to exist as the ghost he'd always wanted
to be.

It created the perfect conditions for rumour.

And from rumour, you forged myth.

I grabbed two notebooks from my jacket: the first was the one I'd
started this case with, one half of it now ruined by the tranquillizer
dart; the second was new, only the first ten pages filled with notes I'd
made off the back of my visit to Ian Kirby.

I had a better idea of who Cronje was now, but, in truth, the more

I found out about him, the more he frightened me. Every description of him I heard, every word in every article, made it clear that he was a ruthless killer and a chameleon, a hard-to-remember face that no one was ever quite certain they'd met before. That allowed him to move about unnoticed, and it had helped him survive here, anonymously, since 1985.

He was also smart, meticulous, and organized: he'd used the same techniques with Ian Kirby that he'd used with everyone else in his life, giving out disparate information and tasks, making it impossible for anyone to piece together a complete picture of what his intentions were. He'd trusted Kirby much more than he'd trusted Letitia Scargill, but his approach to both was essentially the same: enough, but never too much. Huge parts of Cronje's life were still a secret to Kirby and to everyone else.

As I'd driven here, I'd kept thinking about two things. The first were the moments, brief as they were, when something had flickered in Kirby's face. I'd pressed him on it two or three times, accused him of holding back on me, and he'd sworn that he wasn't. Even after he told me about who Cronje was, about the farm, about the Red Wolf and the twelve murders he'd been charged with, I got the sense that there was more. But I couldn't see the join, a seam where a truth and a lie convened.

So, for the time being, I had to let it go.

The other thing I kept thinking about was how lucky I'd been. But for a notebook in the right place, I would have blacked out and maybe not ever woken up. It scared me how fine that line was, how close to snuffing out my threat Cronje had come. But in a way, it scared me more that he'd failed. Because he wasn't going to fail again.

This is the only way to stop him.

That was what Kirby kept saying to me before I left him, before I headed back into London and made the calls I needed to: the only way to stop him was by letting Catherine Vance use the footage she'd got from Tom Brenner and publish her story.

Maybe he was right.

Maybe he wasn't.

I checked my watch. It was ten-fifty. I looked out, hoping Vance might be early, but there was no sign of her, so I went back to my notes.

Five minutes later, my phone burst into life.

It was Vance.

'Where are you?' I said.

'I haven't left home yet.'

'*What?* I'm already here.'

'I know.' A pause. 'I think something's happened to Tom.'

56

'What do you mean, you think something's happened to him?'

'He didn't turn up to our meeting earlier,' Vance said.

'What? Why didn't you say something when we spoke two *hours* ago?'

'I don't even *know* you, Raker.'

'You just sent me all the way up here to this bloody theme park.'

'*Listen* to me. I've been working on this thing with Kirby for weeks. I've been searching for Kian for *months*. I needed to give myself time to think, to try and work out what it all means and whether talking to you compromised it. I didn't know if I could trust you.'

'And now?'

'I've read up about you. I'm willing to trust you.'

'You just wasted two hours.'

She didn't say anything.

'I'm guessing you've tried calling Tom?'

'We don't speak on mobiles, only via a payphone in King's Cross.' She stopped; took a long, almost painful-sounding breath. 'I managed to get a number for his wife and called her instead, pretending to be from the Regala; a colleague of his. She's down in Bath on some spa break.'

'What did she say?'

'She said she hasn't heard from Tom since last night.'

'And that's out of character?'

'It sounds like it. I spoke to him yesterday afternoon about four p.m. He told me he was taking his son to Seven Peaks. He texted Sadie at 6 p.m. to tell her they were in the queue for the ghost house. He hasn't texted her since. I tried to play it down, told her I'd get him to call her when I got hold of him.' Vance stopped. 'I didn't want her to panic.'

It was hard to know if that was the right call, but it meant we were ahead of the cops for now. They clearly didn't realize Brenner and his son were missing because, if they did, they would already have been in touch with Tom's wife.

'So Seven Peaks is the last place you know Tom and his son were?'

'Yes,' Vance said.

'How old's his son?'

'Nine.'

I felt a knot in my stomach. This was Cronje. We both knew it. And he could have been keeping an eye on Tom Brenner for months, watching, waiting – ever since Brenner had been up to that hotel room and glimpsed Kian Bauer on the bed. This was what Cronje did, what he'd done on repeat: zero in on a threat, patiently wait for the right time, move in for the kill. But would he really hurt a nine-year-old kid? Part of me didn't want to think about it.

Because I knew the answer was *yes*.

'This is a disaster,' Vance muttered. '*Shit*. Have you got even the first idea who this guy is? Do you know what this means for Tom and his boy?'

'It means we have to find them.'

'They could be anywhere.'

'Or they could be at The Castle.'

A pause. 'You think he's taken them there?'

'He lives there. That's where he's most comfortable.' I took a moment, trying to think. 'You need to come here. We need a plan and it needs to be solid.'

'It's probably too late already.'

'It might not be.'

'Cronje's a fucking *psychopath*, Raker. Do you know the things that they used to say about him?'

Suddenly, Vance's reluctance to talk to me had gone.

It was panic.

It was fear.

'I've read some of it,' I said.

'They used to say the Red Wolf kept a Polaroid camera hidden in his desk. They weren't supposed to do shit like that in C9 because nothing they did was recorded or documented. But Cronje didn't give a damn. The rules didn't apply to him. And do you know what the men he worked with there said? They said he'd take pictures of the people he killed, like he was creating some work of art.'

'That sounds more like a serial killer than a soldier.'

'Exactly. Not that anyone got to see those pictures,' Vance said, talking fast. 'When the farm was closed down, they only found the camera, not the photos taken on it. The men at the farm said Cronje destroyed all the pictures. You know why?'

'Because they were evidence.'

'Because he probably killed more than the twelve he was charged with. One of the other men told the Truth and Reconciliation Commission it could have been as many as twenty. He said once Larsen left, Cronje ran the show. He'd get these "enemies" to the farm and he wouldn't let anyone else in. He didn't want to share the kill with anyone. They said they'd just hear the sounds of screaming, and then the next thing they knew, Cronje was disappearing away from the farm with a body in the bed of his pick-up.' Vance paused, her silence speaking volumes. 'Like I said, this guy's a psychopath.'

'You need to come here. If you really want to stop him, we need to do this right.'

'Okay,' she said.

'How long will it take you to get here?'

'Forty-five minutes maybe. An hour tops.'

'Hurry.'

But she didn't hang up.

'Have you ever heard of the "tokoloshe"?' she asked quietly.

'No.'

'Some of the black people who fought against the apartheid government, they still practised traditional beliefs. It was through them I heard it. They used to say the Red Wolf was part tokoloshe. In Zulu and Xhosa mythology, it's a malevolent spirit.'

I didn't know what to say to that.

'I know,' she said. 'It sounds like bullshit.'

Except I understood where it had come from.

I'd seen something of it myself: a man in a balaclava hiding silently in Letitia Scargill's house for hours without either of us knowing he was there; a man who simply walked out of a hotel with two holdalls full of body parts; a man who went to a crowded fun fair and abducted a father and son without anyone noticing; and a man who'd made two women disappear into thin air thirty-seven years ago and buried the truth where no one could find it.

'Do you know what the tokoloshe does, Raker?'

'I imagine it kills people.'

'Yeah, but it can do something else too.' She stopped. I heard her swallow. 'It can become invisible.'

57

At 11.15, an Uber finally arrived.

But it wasn't Catherine Vance.

Instead, Rebekah and Frank Travis got out.

As Rebekah came towards the front of the Starbucks, I watched Travis pause at the edge of the pavement, looking out at the retail park, taking it in – the faces, the cars. The cop in him was alive and well, doing exactly the same thing as I'd done when I'd arrived.

Checking.

Making sure we weren't being watched.

I greeted them both, got them some drinks, and as we sat down, Travis asked, 'Where's the journalist?'

'She's running late.'

On my call with Vance – after she'd told me about the tokoloshe – I'd told her that I was going to invite Rebekah to our meeting. I wanted the two of them to talk. I needed to know what Vance had found out about Fiona – and Jennifer – and I figured having Rebekah here, even if her memories of Fiona were scant, might be useful. I'd used the card Rebekah had found pushed under her hotel room door this morning as an incentive for Vance to accept the idea, and Vance had sounded keen to see it, to see all the other cards Rebekah had been sent, apparently from her mother. Rebekah didn't know yet that it couldn't possibly be Fiona who'd mailed the cards. Her mother's death – confirmed to me by Ian Kirby – was something I was going to have to find the right time to tell her about.

I was dreading it.

The other thing on my mind when I'd given her and Travis the address for the Starbucks was that, if it wasn't Fiona who'd sent those cards, someone else had been communicating with Rebekah – and while I didn't know what his endgame would be in doing so, I was still worried that someone was Cronje. I trusted Frank Travis, and knew he was strong and capable, but I preferred to keep Rebekah close, inside my sightlines. She was strong and capable too, but this was a different kind of enemy.

'Do you think she's going to bail on us?' Travis asked.

'Vance? No, she'll be here.'

I turned to Rebekah. 'How are you doing?'

'I'm confused.'

'Did you bring it with you?'

She nodded, reached into her jacket and took out the envelope, then placed it on to the table between us. I looked at her name, hand-written on the front. Opening the flap, I slid the card out. It was exactly the same sort of design as the others. No information about where it had come from, who had made it or where it had been printed, just an intricate rose design on the front.

Inside, the handwriting was exactly the same as in the other cards. But, this time, the message was different.

Welcome home.

'Do you think it's from her?' Rebekah asked.

No, it's not her. Your mother's dead.

But, in that moment, I couldn't quite bring myself to tell her the truth. I would have to eventually, hard as it would be, but my bigger concern right now was who the card had *actually* come from – and what, if anything, the message meant. *It means they know she's in London. It means they got close enough to her to post it under her door.*

'Who else could it be from?' Rebekah said.

'That's what we need to find out.'

I glanced at Travis and, although I barely knew him, I felt something pass between us. Instantly, he seemed to understand why I was holding back, an intuition built on conducting a thousand inter-views, across hundreds of cases, of knowing that – even when you'd done it countless times before – your heart still cracked a little when you had to give people terrible news. He reached over to Rebekah and touched a hand to her arm: 'I think we wait for the journalist to get here, then we can figure it out together.'

I nodded my appreciation – Rebekah's attention on the card – and then said to her, 'I haven't had a chance to fill you in on the case so far. There's a lot going on with it, a lot of moving parts, but I think Catherine being here will help fill in some of those gaps. This card . . .' I stopped, looking at it. 'It's kind of come out of left field.'

I checked the time.

Vance would be here in fifteen minutes.

'I know this is frustrating.'

'No.' She held up a hand. 'It's not. I'm just impatient.'

I silently tried to reassure her that I knew what I was doing, tried to exude the confidence she needed in order to keep faith in me, even if I was questioning myself. And as I did, she studied me, holding my gaze for a moment. In another place, at another time, I might have let myself wonder if there was more to the look, something deeper and more surprising – a temporary charge between us.

But then the look was gone again.

I shifted my attention back to the card, moving it further into the light from the windows, flipping between the cover and the handwriting inside.

And then I noticed something.

It was so faint I could only see it when it was right next to the window, the card fully flooded in light: in the top right-hand corner of the interior, above where the message had been written, was the merest hint of another word.

An impression of it.

It had clearly been a word written on to a separate piece of paper, but the pen had been pressed hard enough to leave a minor indentation on the card underneath.

I used a finger, tracing the depression in the card, trying to figure out what the word said, and then got up and went to the counter and asked the barista if they had a pencil I could borrow. After she'd found one for me, I took it back to the table.

'David?' Rebekah asked. 'What's going on?'

'Just give me a sec,' I said, and started to softly use the pencil, shading over the impression of the word until it began to appear in white amongst the grey. Pretty soon, I realized I was wrong. It wasn't a word.

It was some sort of code.

VC4732-a.

The *a* had the same tail on it as the *a*'s in the other condolence cards.

'VC4732-a,' Travis echoed. 'What's that?'

I shook my head. 'I've got no idea. Neither of you know?'

They both shook their heads.

I grabbed my phone, went to Google and did a search for *VC4732-a*. One hundred and ninety-one results came back and most of them were for the same thing: what looked like some sort of respirator mask. I clicked on the first link and followed it through to the manufacturer's website.

Except it wasn't a respirator mask.

It was designed like one, with straps that went over the head and around the ears, and a facepiece at the front that fitted over the chin, mouth and jaw, but the facepiece was oddly shaped with a circular grille at the front and a small box on one side. In the description below, the front was referred to as a 'speaking diaphragm'.

'Is that some sort of respirator?' Travis asked.

'No,' I said. 'It's a voice changer.'

They both just stared at me. Finally, Rebekah shifted, looking at my screen. 'A voice changer? I don't understand.'

I tilted the card again, trying to see if there were any other indentations on it, but otherwise the inside of the card was completely clean. Running a finger over the pencil and the white *VC4732-a* in the middle, I said to Rebekah, 'You haven't received any calls from anyone over the last few days?'

'No,' she said.

I stared at the code again.

'Wait a second, wait a second.' Rebekah again.

'Have you remembered something?'

'There was someone in the hotel bar yesterday.'

Travis frowned. 'What are you talking about?'

'In the afternoon. It was when you were resting upstairs.' She looked from Travis back to me. 'It was just the two of us in there.'

'Who were they?' I asked.

'I don't know. But I think . . .' She stopped, frowning. Her mind was going. 'I think they might have been recording me.'

'*What?*' Travis said. 'Why didn't you mention it?'

'I don't know. Afterwards, I just thought I was being paranoid.'

'What do you mean when you say, "recording you"?'

'They had a laptop with a video window open on it. I could see myself.'

'Man? Woman?'

'I'm not sure. Their back was to me. They were wearing a hoodie.'

But then the moment was shattered.

My phone was ringing.

I grabbed it out of my pocket, looking at the display. It was Liz. In everything that had happened overnight, I'd almost forgotten about Healy, about her, about that whole part of my life. 'Sorry,' I said to Rebekah and Travis, 'I'm going to have to take this,' and I got up from the table, and found a quiet corner.

Behind me, I heard Travis say, 'You should have told me, Bek.'

'I know,' Rebekah replied. 'I just . . . I don't know. Like I say, afterwards, it just felt like I'd over-thought it.'

I pushed Answer on my phone. 'Liz?'

'Raker.'

'Is everything okay?'

'No,' she said. 'No, not really.'

'Is it Healy?'

'Yeah.' A beat. 'Something's wrong.'

Healy

This Morning

Healy lay on his bunk, wide awake, listening to Jordan snoring above him. His mind was racing, had been all night, unable to shift the memory of what had happened in the showers. The man who'd threatened him – Rossiter, the thug with the buzz cut – had hovered at the door to his cell again prior to lockdown the previous evening, rocking on his feet like he was waiting for the right time to come in. And he probably would have if it hadn't been for the fact that one of the guards had been in conversation with a few of the prisoners out on Ones.

It had been a lucky escape.

But Healy couldn't keep getting lucky.

He rolled over, glancing across the darkness of the cell to the door. As soon as that thing unlocked in a couple of hours, Healy knew it was going to be open season. Nowhere in the prison was safe because everyone was going to know he was a former cop by now. And Rossiter wasn't the only psycho in this place.

There were going to be men even worse than him.

Healy thought about Raker, about Liz, about the phone call he'd had with her and the one she was in the process of setting up. And then he thought about Parkes, about what she'd said when she came in to see him.

I could be out of here in days.

He started trying to think about what he could give Parkes, whether he could steer clear of the biggest of Raker's infractions and hand her smaller stuff; things that might hurt Raker a little but not mortally wound him. But even that felt like a complete betrayal. Even if all he gave the Met was the smallest transgression Raker had ever committed, it would still feel like Healy was plunging a knife into the back of the only man in his life he could trust. And, anyway, he doubted a litany of minor law-breaking would be enough to sate Parkes, and it certainly wouldn't be enough for Aiden Phillips: if they were going to give Healy a pass, if they really *were* going to ensure he walked out of here a free man – see his boys again, and be out in time for the birth of his first grandchild – there was no way they were settling for scraps.

It was everything.

Or it was nothing.

Healy woke suddenly to the rattle of the cell opening.

Jordan was already up, checking himself in the mirror, halfway through his usual routine of dampening down his bed hair. He registered Healy moving, watched him kick off a blanket, and their eyes met in the scarred, misted mirror over the sink.

'Morning, boss,' he said.

Healy sat up, head ducked under the top bunk.

Jordan went back to fiddling with his hair, and as Healy rubbed at his eyes, as he looked outside the cell to where prisoners were already starting to line up for roll call, he thought back to the conversation that he and Jordan had had the previous night, after lights out. Healy had quizzed him about what he knew, about who else in here was saying he was a cop, and Jordan just repeated the same phrase over and over: *I don't know, boss.* It was just a rumour he'd wanted to ask Healy about.

Jordan headed out, leaving Healy to get changed. He pulled on his trousers, a T-shirt, his trainers, and then he exited the cell, immediately looking up at Twos. On the grilled walkway above, Rossiter and his flunky Patrick were staring down at him. Healy tried to maintain eye contact with Rossiter in an effort to show him he wasn't scared. But he was. Inside, Healy's belly was squirming, his head thumping. He felt nauseous, felt like his airflow was restricted, so he tugged at the collar on his shirt. The T-shirt was loose. There was nothing restricting his breathing.

Nothing except what he knew in his gut.

They were coming for him.

58

'I've been in court so I've only just got back to the office.'

I didn't like the way Liz sounded.

She was normally calm, composed, her voice even.

'He left a message for me.'

'Healy?' I frowned. 'What did he say?'

'He phoned through on our mainline.' I heard her moving things, the telltale squeak of a chair. 'I can play it for you. I'll hold my phone against the machine.'

An electronic clunk.

'*Liz, it's Colm Healy.*' He paused, his voice odd. '*I, uh . . .*' He stopped for a second time. '*I, uh . . . I just wanted to call you.*' And then, once more, he ground to a halt. I knew Healy's voice as well as anyone, knew the cadence of it, but you didn't even need to know him well to know that he wasn't right.

In the background, I thought I could hear voices on the call. But then I realized it wasn't the normal soundtrack of a men's prison – not the laughter or the shouting; not the rattle of metal doors, or the impatience of the men in the queue behind Healy for the phone. It was something more confusing.

A soft, continual, electronic noise.

'*I just wanted to thank you for offering to take my case,*' Healy said, and as soon as those twelve words were out of his mouth, I knew where this was going. '*But while I know you're a really good lawyer, and I know you work with really good people who I completely trust . . .*' He faltered again. People he trusted. That felt like it was a coded message; a reference to me. '*This time, I think I'm going to . . . I'm . . .*'

He couldn't get the words out.

'*I don't need you to represent me,*' he said finally.

He hung up, and then a second later, Liz was back on the line:

'Any idea what the hell is going on with him?' she said. 'Why wouldn't he want me to take his case?'

My mind was racing.

'Raker?'

'I don't know,' I said.

'He was all in on the idea yesterday.'

I closed my eyes, replaying Healy's message.

Come on. Think.

'Did you hear that noise in the background of the call?' I asked.

'Noise?'

'The electronic sound.'

'Yeah,' Liz said. 'What do you think it . . .'

But then she trailed off.

'Oh shit,' she muttered softly.

We'd both just realized what it was.

Healy

This Morning

After roll call, Healy went to get his blood pressure meds and then asked one of the guards if there was anything they needed doing. He didn't want to go back to Ones.

The guard eyed him. 'Is everything okay?'

No. Please help me.

But he knew, if he spoke to one of the guards about it, his life would become a million times worse than it was right now. He wouldn't just be a cop, he'd be a grass.

'Everything's fine, boss,' Healy said.

'Then we're all set,' the guard said, and watched Healy go, back towards Ones. When Healy got to the floor, he could see a group of men gathered outside the cells further down, some others talking, a couple more sharing a cup of tea at a table and playing cards.

But no Rossiter.

Healy looked up to Twos, to Rossiter's cell door: it was most of the way closed. And then his eyes went up again, to Threes, and he could see two men – both in their fifties – staring at him. One slowly and deliberately mouthed something.

Fucking pig.

Healy felt himself wobble. Suddenly, as he glanced ahead of himself, towards his cell, it felt like every pair of eyes was on him.

He put his head down.

Walked fast.

But then, as he did, he noticed something: one of the surveillance cameras just ahead of him had a thick slab of wet tissue paper stuck to the lens; another at the far end had someone's vest draped over it; when he looked back, in the direction he'd come from, he saw a guy standing on a chair, hand reaching up, fingers obscuring the eye of the CCTV unit. All three cameras were covered.

Fuck.

Rossiter was hiding in a cell to his right.

Healy didn't even see him coming.

Healy slowly turned his head on the pillow and checked to see where the nurse was. She was on the other side of a glass panel, waiting. She thought he was still on a call.

But he'd already finished with Liz.

She'd said the previous day that she was going to be in court in the morning, and he knew his message would go straight to her answerphone. It was easier that way. He still struggled to get his words out – not just because, even with the morphine, even feeling drugged and half-conscious, he was in so much pain; but also because he knew every word out of his mouth was treacherous.

His arm and his hand, currently holding the phone, was about the only thing that worked, that wasn't broken or fractured, bruised or torn. He laid the handset down on to the sheets, glanced at the nurse again and saw she was now talking to the doctor who'd just been in to see him, and then he punched in another number. He knew neither the doctor nor the nurse could come in while he talked to his solicitor.

Except this next call wasn't to his solicitor.

He lay there, squeezing his eyes shut, pushing out all the images of Raker, of everything the two of them had done together, and just listened to the phone ringing.

And then, finally, someone answered.

'Parkes.'

'It's Colm Healy.' He cleared his throat. 'I want to take the deal.'

59

'It was an ECG we heard on the call,' Liz said.

'Can you find out what happened?'

'I can call in a favour.'

'Thank you.'

She was quiet for a moment. 'Be careful, Raker.'

I rung off. As I paused there for a moment, I felt like the ground beneath my feet was shifting. I was struggling to think clearly about everything that was going on in my life right now, what direction the threats were coming from and from whom. I just decided to shut it all out and concentrate on what was immediately in front of me. That was Rebekah. That was Tom Brenner. And it was Catherine Vance.

I looked at my watch.

Where *was* she?

I headed back to the table.

'Are you okay?' Rebekah asked.

I must have looked frantic. I smiled, tried to settle any doubts she might be having about me. 'I'm fine,' I said, keeping the smile fixed to my face. But in my head I was already doing the maths, trying to work out what the next best move was.

I texted Vance.

Where are you?

She was almost twenty minutes late.

I watched the screen, saw that – pretty much as soon as the text landed – the three dots appeared, showing me that she was reading my text, and maybe replying. Relieved, I waited for her response.

Except the reply never came.

The three dots disappeared.

I stared at the phone, wondering if she was driving, and then turned back to Rebekah and Travis. 'Let's give her ten more minutes and then we can decide what to do after that. In the meantime, I need to tell you about a man called Jacobus Cronje.'

My mobile burst into life.

It was Vance.

Finally.

I pushed Answer. 'Catherine, where are you?'

Silence.

'Catherine?'

Nothing for a second time.

'Catherine, are you . . .'

But then I stopped.

I could tell the phone was being moved, could hear the slight change in sound, could hear muted footsteps – and then, very slowly, I started to hear another noise.

It was a woman sobbing.

Catherine.

'One little piggy,' a voice said.

I felt a prickle in my scalp.

Cronje.

The sound of more movement, more footsteps. I glanced at Rebekah, at Travis – both of them knew something was up.

On the line, more sobbing – stilted, deeper.

Different.

It was a man.

'Two little piggies.'

Tom Brenner.

And then he moved again, and as he did, as I listened to his footsteps, I felt my whole body shrink, as if I was trying to shield myself from what I knew was coming next.

'Three little piggies.'

The sound of a child crying.

Brenner's son.

The line went dead.

The Favour: Part 1

Rebekah | *This Morning*

Rebekah watched as David finished his call.

'I'm so sorry,' he said. 'I've got to go.'

Rebekah could tell he was flustered – or maybe *flustered* wasn't the right word. *Unsettled* might have been closer.

'Was that the journalist?' Travis asked.

David didn't appear to have heard.

'David? Are you okay?' Rebekah asked him.

It took him a second to return his gaze to her. 'Sorry,' he said for a second time. 'I didn't mean to get you all the way out here for . . .'

He stopped. *For nothing.*

'It's okay,' Frank said, recognising, like Rebekah, that something was up. 'Was that Catherine Vance?'

'No,' David said.

He looked between Rebekah and Travis. She could see his mind going, his brain firing up. She hadn't spent much time with him, but she'd seen more than enough in the hours that she had to know that he was agitated.

David looked beyond them both, out of the windows of the coffeeshop in the direction of Seven Peaks.

'I need to tell you about this guy, Cronje,' he said. 'But it's going to have to wait for now.' He stopped again and then looked at Frank. 'Do you have any ID on you?'

'You mean, a driver's licence?'

'I was thinking something more official.'

Frank frowned. 'Like a badge?'

'Like anything that suggests you're a cop.'

Frank levered his wallet from his back pocket, flipping it open in front of them. 'I had to hand my badge in when I retired. But I do still have this.'

He laid a business card down on the table. It was old, slightly dis-coloured, the edges a little wrinkled – but otherwise it was intact. At the top was the NYPD badge. Under that was Frank's name and the word *Detective*. Below that, *Missing Persons Squad* and his former work address at One Police Plaza.

'It's just a business card,' Frank said.

'That might be enough,' David replied, looking across at Seven Peaks again, at the ragged apex of the mountains. 'I need to ask you two to do me a huge favour . . .'

PART SEVEN

The Cellar

60

The Castle emerged from the shadows.

It was two in the afternoon and it felt like the sun had already gone down. On the drive over, the weather had turned bad, a veil pulled over the city: it wasn't just cold any more; it was wet, wind buffeting buildings and chasing along back streets. As I came up Bedford Row, I watched the back of the club form, a leviathan gradually taking shape, every window an eye. At the front, there was a Christmas tree behind a pane of glass and, on the first floor, light was coming from what must have been the bar or the restaurant. But there remained something ominous about The Castle.

It was a building with a black heart.

I stepped up to the door and placed the membership card I'd stolen against the reader. *He knows you're going to come here. He knows you can't leave it alone.*

This is a trap.

The door buzzed.

After a second of hesitation, I headed inside. On my left, at the reception desk, there was someone different to the day before. She glanced up and smiled. I greeted her, tried to look confident, and then quickly turned to my right, where a CCTV camera was fixed and focused on me. I didn't know if Cronje was watching, didn't really know much more than – according to Ian Kirby – he was in the basement area, in the furthest corner of the building. He'd been living out of it for almost the entire thirty-seven years he'd been in the UK. *He's under the restaurant*, Kirby had said. *It used to be a wine cellar.*

Have you ever been down there? I'd asked.

No. No one has. He always keeps it padlocked.

So how do I get to it?

Go through the restaurant. Look for the door with 'Private' on it.

'Is everything okay, sir?'

I glanced at the receptionist. 'Fine.' I didn't know who Cronje had working for him, who he'd compromised, so I started moving towards the door through to the bar and restaurant. On the other side, I found myself in a walnut-panelled corridor, further doors all the way down. These must have been the meeting rooms. I could hear the low hum of conversation from some of them.

At the end was the bar.

I stopped outside, looked through. There were two large windows, both with wooden shutters, but the slats on the shutters had been twisted most of the way closed, so the bar was low lit and murky. I could see some men at a table towards the back, and a group off to my right as well.

I pulled one of the doors back.

It squeaked slightly, almost everyone in the bar glancing in my direction. No one's attention appeared to linger – but that didn't mean anything.

Any of them could have been in on it.

Any of them could have been Cronje's foot soldiers.

This whole place could be a bomb waiting to go off.

I moved quickly, passing a long counter on my right with a glass back, and shelves full of liquor. Ahead of me, between a fireplace and a huge bookcase, was a set of oak stairs, and a wheelchair ramp next to that, both of them slanting up to a second set of glass doors.

The restaurant.

As I got to the doors, I saw that the design echoed that of the bar – shutters at the windows, a mix of tables, chairs and booths on the left, a kitchen on the right.

The subtle hint of cooked food hit me as I entered, mixing with the smoky smell of the fireplace. It was busier in here, noisier, so the sound of the door, my footsteps, my movements, seemed to go unnoticed. Once again, ahead of me, a staircase and a wheelchair ramp ascended to a set of glass doors. On the other side, though, there was what looked like some sort of small anteroom.

I moved again, swiping a steak knife from one of the tables on the way past. A second later, I was in the anteroom. My heart rate started to increase as I saw there were two further doors in here. One led through to male and female bathrooms.

The other said STAFF ONLY.

I entered.

There was a cleaner's closet on the right. I opened it and looked inside, found cleaning equipment – a mop, bucket, polish, cloths – and closed it again.

A second door was marked PRIVATE.

This was the one Kirby had told me about.

Except Kirby had said it would be padlocked. It wasn't. A hinge bracket was fixed to the door and there was a loop where the padlock fed through once the hinge plate was secure. But there was no padlock.

Something curdled in my stomach.

I took out the knife I'd swiped from the restaurant but didn't move any closer. This definitely felt like a trap. And I was walking right into it.

Doubt, and fear, and panic swamped me.

Go.

Just turn around and go.

Hidden somewhere beyond this door was a man who – in every part of me – I knew wanted me to do exactly this, a wolf drawing me deeper into a den whose layout he knew intimately. But what was the alternative?

Leaving him to kill three innocent people?

They might already be dead.

What's the point in dying too?

I took a step back, automatic, fearful, but then I forced myself forward again, placed my hand on the door handle, and slowly inched it back. As it came towards me, it made a soft moan. I wondered if it was an early-warning system, letting him know I was here.

But, unlike the other door, there was no cleaner's closet in here.

In fact, there was no room at all.

There was just a staircase leading down into darkness.

The Favour: Part 2

Rebekah | *This Afternoon*

Frank presented the business card to a woman at the front gate.

'I think you've been expecting us,' he said.

'Really?' the woman responded. Rebekah watched as she took hold of the old business card that Frank handed her. 'As far as I know, no one has called about the police dropping in, let alone from New York.'

'We definitely called ahead,' Frank lied. 'Is your manager around?'

'No, he's away until next week.'

Frank looked suitably disappointed but Rebekah knew it was a stroke of luck and he was about to make use of it: 'It was your manager we spoke to.' He looked beyond the woman, past the front gates of Seven Peaks, the fun fair not open yet, its lights not strobing, its tannoys not pumping out any music. The rides, the vendors, the dry ice, the wall of noise: all of it was drifting in and out behind a skein of drizzle. 'We called from the US twice,' Frank pressed.

'And you spoke to my boss?'

'Yes. Malcolm Dursley.'

They'd looked up the name of the Seven Peaks manager on the corporate website before coming down here. The woman glanced at the business card again, at Frank, at Rebekah. Rebekah shifted uncomfortably but maintained the stoic expression that she imagined an NYPD detective would have.

'And you two came all the way over from New York for this?'

'We did,' Frank responded. 'It's a long way but – as we said to Malcolm – this is important.'

The woman nodded.

Rebekah could see that she was wavering now.

'So what is it you need from us?' she asked.

'We need to take a look at some surveillance footage.'

61

I stood at the top of the staircase and looked down.

The steps were bare concrete and vanished into the black at the halfway point. Even as I got out my phone and switched on the torch, I only fractionally improved my view, revealing electrical wires on the wall to my left. Did that mean there was a light switch further down? Or were the wires powering something else?

I moved to the top of the steps, my body tense. As I did, my phone chimed once in my hand. It was Rebekah:

We've got video.

I switched to Silent and tapped out a quick reply:

Great. Keep me up to date.

Edging further in, I took the next step down, and then readjusted the knife in my hand. There was definitely no light switch this high up, so I had no choice.

I started the descent.

All I could hear in my ears was the hard thud of my pulse as I shone the torch ahead of me, trying to see to the bottom. The further I got, the more I could feel the temperature changing. The warmth of the club vanished and in the light from the torch, I could see condensation on the walls, the polished concrete steps slick with it too. I slowed my descent, trying to avoid slipping – and then, ahead, the staircase dog-legged to the left.

I stopped, peered around the corner.

Four more steps.

A second door.

It had no handle, only a keyhole. When I tried pushing at it, it didn't shift. I looked for a light switch, swung the torch around, but there was nothing.

I glanced up the staircase, to the rectangle of light at the top that felt so far away it was like an exit on the other side of the world, and then grabbed my lockpicks and went to work. My hands were cold, the picks hard to grip, the lock complex, its mechanism intricate. I kept hitting a buffer and having to start over.

Eventually, though, I felt it give.

I stood, grabbing the knife, the phone, pressed my fingers to the door and gently pushed. It fanned out into darkness.

Under the light of the torch it looked like the wine cellar Ian Kirby had talked about, a compact maze of rounded, low-ceiling roofs and brick archways. But it was hard to tell for sure. I should have been able to see stone walls, perhaps the spaces where bottles had once been stored.

I couldn't see any of those things.

I couldn't hear anything either.

There was literally no sound down here at all.

As I shifted the torch around, lighting up the corners closest to me and the spaces inside the archway immediately to my right, as I looked directly up at the ceiling, I suddenly realized why I couldn't see the walls or bottles, and why I couldn't hear anything.

There was black acoustic foam everywhere.

The whole cellar had been soundproofed.

62

I felt my body contract.

He didn't want anything escaping from this place.

Even noise.

I glanced either side of me. On my left, at shoulder height, was a switch buried within the soundproofing. I hesitated, wondering whether or not to flick it on, to alert him to my presence. But he already knew I was here – or at the very least on my way – and I needed any advantage I could get.

With the light on, I could see him coming.

I pushed the switch.

Ahead, through an archway to the right, a bulb came on. It was dull, offering little more than a sickly yellow wash. But it allowed me to see more of the layout. There were actually two archways: the one on the right and then one straight ahead which remained unlit.

I moved towards the lighted arch.

The space beyond it was small, only about twenty feet long by fifteen wide, although it looked even smaller – more oppressive – because of the soundproofing. There were no windows and no doors, just a hardwood desk in the centre with three drawers, two of them removed. Tucked in under the desk was a stool; on the other side was a chair. It had been set down, maybe seven feet from the desk, its metal frame dull in the half-light, one of its arms splintered.

The legs of the chair had been bolted to the floor.

I drew closer to the desk, the edges marked with chips and fissures, and pulled out the remaining drawer. It rattled on its runner.

Inside were several rolls of duct tape.

One had been used recently, the ends untidily stuck down.

I looked at the desk again, the dents and breaks along one side of it, as if the desk had been hit repeatedly. When I leaned in closer, I saw clumps of hair snagged in it. Skin. Dried blood.

A bubble of nausea formed in my throat.

I tried to imagine how many bones he'd snapped against this desk, how many wounds he'd inflicted, how many teeth had been broken. And then I grabbed the standing lamp – the source of the light in the room – and brought the whole thing with me. Its long lead unfurled as its glow skittered off, lighting my path towards the back wall. It remained shadowed, the weakness of the bulb not reaching all the way down.

As I got closer, I thought of a story I'd read online only a few hours ago about the room at Die Suidplaas where Cronje would interrogate enemies of the state; I'd read about a desk he sat behind as his victims begged for their life, and about a chair he put them on that had been bolted to the floor so it wouldn't move an inch.

He'd recreated all of that here.

And he'd recreated something else too.

I'd gone as far as I could with the lamp, so I set it down.

The back wall was built into a slight recess. There was no foam soundproofing on it. Instead, the entire wall had been covered in plasterboard.

On the plasterboard was a painted mural.

It filled everything, top to bottom, right to left: a large, hyper-realistic painting of one of the walls in Cronje's office at the farm. The window he'd had in there. The view out of it, on to the South African highveld. The row of telephone poles in the far distance and the grey ribbon of the main road. It was a replica of the picture that Ian Kirby had in the caravan: same blue skies, same scorched trails, same vast, sun-drenched grassland. Cronje had recreated everything he used to see at the farm almost four decades ago and six thousand miles away on a cellar wall ten feet under the earth.

Die Suidplaas was shut down in 1989.

But, here, a part of it lived on.

I'd barely taken that in when something else caught my eye. It was at the left-hand edge of the recess: a handle. I looked at that and then down to the ground. I'd missed the tracks embedded in the floor, like the sort you would find on fitted wardrobes. I reached across, grabbed the handle and pulled, and the whole mural slid sideways on the runners, disappearing into a gap in the recess.

The mural – the plasterboard – had been a false wall.

Behind it was the real one.

Except I still couldn't see the original stonework because the actual back wall was covered in the same acoustic foam as everywhere else. Mounted to the foam, five feet high by the same distance wide, was a large corkboard.

The corkboard was full of photographs.

My blood froze.

He used to keep a Polaroid camera hidden in his desk.

I stepped in closer, Catherine Vance's voice in my head.

He would take pictures of the people that he killed.

Rows of faces looked back at me.

When the farm was closed down, they only found the camera, not the photos that were taken on it. The men he worked with at the farm said he destroyed them.

But Cronje didn't destroy the photos.

He kept every last one.

He killed more than the twelve he was charged with. One of the men who was at the farm with him said it could have been as many as twenty.

Yet as I counted every picture on the corkboard – every Polaroid, every face in every shot, every pair of stark, haunted eyes – it was obvious that no one at the farm, not even the killers that Cronje had shared a roof with, knew the whole truth.

It wasn't twelve people he'd murdered in that place.

It wasn't even twenty.

The Red Wolf had killed thirty-six.

63

For a second, I couldn't look away.

Some had had their teeth broken, some their hair torn clean from their scalp; all of them were bloodied, bruised, beaten into submission. And all of them – thirty-two of them black, two of them South Asian, two of them white – shared exactly the same expression: it was the realisation this moment was their last.

The flash of the camera.

The whirr of the photo being developed.

The pull of a trigger.

I stood there, transfixed, wishing I could right this wrong, wishing – at the very least – that I knew these people's names, so that their families could find out what had happened to them. The families must have suspected long ago that their loved ones were dead. One or two of them might even have got lucky, the bodies of their sons, daughters, fathers, mothers finally brought home to them after testimony at the TRC hearings pointed them to an unmarked grave in the African bush. But most of the victims here would still be lost, just memories to the ones they'd left behind – not a headstone, not a proper goodbye – and I hated knowing their fate but not knowing something as basic as their name.

I knew just one of them.

She was in the middle. Her eyes were sheened with tears, her chin spattered in blood, and her nose was broken. But in her face remained the echoes of her son.

Mienkie Bauer.

I took as many photos of the wall as I could, knowing every shot I took would automatically upload to the Cloud, whatever happened to me from here on in. And then I ripped my eyes away from the faces, forced myself to turn my back on them, and headed out to the corridor.

On my right was the second archway, the space beyond filled with nothing but dark. I turned the torch on again.

As I inched forward, at the back of my head I kept hearing the same warning, the same words on repeat: *He baited you by making that call. He knew you were going to come here. So if he did all of that, if this was part of a plan, where is he?*

Why's he letting you see all of this first?

His crimes, his secrets.

Why hasn't he stopped you yet?

I edged into the dark of the second archway. I'd gone about seven or eight feet when a door appeared on my right. I spotted another light switch and flicked it on.

Beyond the door was a bed, bookshelves. I inched closer, paused, dropping my phone to my side.

It was a bedroom.

This is where he lives.

The bookshelves were full, the spines facing out at me, showing literature in both English and Afrikaans. There was a desk with a laptop on, a wardrobe, side table and electric heater. The floor had been carpeted and the walls had been finished in plasterboard. Another mural had been painted: a 360-degree view from the top of a peak, the sun pouring through breaks in a ragged white ceiling of cloud – almost biblically – to reveal a small town on a valley floor. The town was on the bedroom's back wall, Cronje's bed facing that way so he could look directly at it; to one side of the bed, as the mural wrapped around, I saw a dam in the valley, a grey-blue smudge against the vastness of the landscape; on my other side, above the desk, there were more peaks. Could this have been where he was from?

I went to the laptop and lifted the lid.

A password box appeared.

Pressing the lid back down, I moved out of the bedroom and looked right. The rest of the passage was dark. I held up my phone, trying to improve my view of what awaited me, and I saw that – ten feet ahead – the layout kicked left, into a sharp turn.

I still had the knife in my hand.

Now I gripped it even harder.

In my chest, my heart was pounding, its sound thumping in my ears. Why was he letting me see all of this? Why hadn't he stopped me? I glanced behind me, frightened, paranoid, unable to explain any of it, and then veered left at the turn. Ahead were two final doors, facing each other at a dead end.

I kept going, knife out.

Where are you, Cronje?

Halfway down, I heard something.

A bump.

A soft scrape of a chair leg.

It was coming from the left-hand door.

The lights from Cronje's bedroom, from the room full of photographs, were both gone now, replaced by the short-distance, single-beam white light of my phone. As I got closer to the left-hand door, I could see that it was ajar.

You're going to die down here.

I reached the door, stopped, listened. No sound. No bumps. No scraping. Whoever was in here would have seen the light from my phone.

Readying the knife, I pushed at the door.

The light flowed into the room, revealing a small closet – no more than ten feet wide by six deep. There was soundproofing on the walls and three chairs side by side.

On one was Catherine Vance.

On the others were Tom Brenner and his son.

They'd all been bound and gagged. Brenner's son was crying, tears streaming down his face. Brenner had been beaten, his cheekbone a balloon, his eye closed up. It was hard to even tell what Vance's injuries were because there was so much blood.

I stepped closer.

Vance's head was bowed, but Brenner and his son stiffened, both their eyes widening, their voices – their pleas for mercy – muffled and suppressed by the duct tape over their mouths. Brenner tried desperately to come forward, to lean in front of his son, to protect him, and that was when I realized that – because of the light from my phone – all they could see was a silhouette with a knife.

I dropped the light, held up a hand.

'It's okay,' I whispered. 'It's okay.'

They were still frantic.

'It's okay, I'm not going to hurt you.'

They started to calm a little, could see and hear that I wasn't Cronje. As they did, I looked at Vance. She'd managed to raise her head and turn to me, a deep gash exposed on the side of her face.

Are you okay? I mouthed.

She nodded.

Where is he?

A noise from behind me.

I swivelled, lifting the phone and shining it across at the opposite door, at the only other room I hadn't been in. The noise had come from there.

I looked back at Vance. *Is that where he is?*

She nodded again. *Yes.*

But then something else formed in her face.

Another message.

And, as I saw it, my blood ran cold.

None of us are getting out of this alive.

The Shrine: Part 2

Rebekah | *This Afternoon*

'There they are,' Frank said.

Rebekah shuffled in a little closer, the noise of the Starbucks – which they'd returned to – fading into the background. On her laptop, in the surveillance footage that they'd managed to get from Seven Peaks, Tom Brenner and his son were at the front of the queue for the ghost house.

'I felt bad lying to that woman about who we were,' Rebekah said.

Neither of them took their eyes off the video.

'I know,' Frank replied. He used the cursor to push the footage on a little further. 'But Raker said this was important, and I trust him. These two are missing. The man responsible – this Cronje guy – is highly dangerous and may also be the man who knows what happened to your mom.' Rebekah briefly glanced at Frank, Frank back at her. 'That's why we're going to do what Raker asked us to do: find evidence that Cronje took the Brenners.'

Tom | *Last Night*

They entered the ghost house.

Ahead of them, the corridor was black and then – like a pulse – a strobe light flashed, revealing a second doorway. The whole thing had been designed to look like it was a tunnel carved out of the mountain. 'Whoa!' Leo said, squeezing Tom's hand.

Tom smiled.

Leo was fully immersed, fully taken in by the way the corridor seemed to slant left and right, even though the truth was that the corridor was straight up and down; it was just the doorways that had been built at angles, giving the impression that the tunnel was about to collapse. As they edged further along it, the light strobed again and – in a cavity just around the next bend – Tom could see a man with a mask on.

'Are you ready?' Tom said to Leo.

'Why, what's happening?'

'There's a man around the next corner.'

Leo beamed. 'Is he going to make us jump?'

Tom glanced at the man, at the mask he had on: it was bone-white, skeletal, but with a big fur-lined bottom half that mimicked a Yeti's jaw.

'Yes, he's going to try and make us jump.'

'Okay, Daddy, I'm ready.'

Sure enough, just as they got to the bend, the man leapt out at them, growling theatrically. Leo jumped and then started laughing, and – after making sure he was definitely still all right – Tom led him through to the next part, which was a long, snaking corridor with doors on either side. The corridor had been made to look like a sub-terranean lair, and the doors were ragged shapes cut into the sides, mimicking a maze-like cave system. It was cleverly done, giving the impression that they were in some massive, elaborate honeycomb of caverns and hollows, whereas the reality was they were in a straight corridor and the cave spaces were no larger than wardrobes.

'You definitely okay?' Tom shouted at Leo, talking over the ear-splitting wind sound effects, which had been backed by the *drip drip drip* of water and warbling horror music to build the suspense. Leo nodded, and as Tom looked ahead, he glimpsed the telltale sign of a Yeti mask in one of the caves on the right. 'Get ready.'

Someone else jumped out on them.

Leo startled, drawing in closer to Tom, and then – from a cave on the opposite side – another member of staff appeared, this one crawling on all fours like an insect.

Tom knew the staff weren't allowed to touch them so he stood his ground as the insect-man stopped short of them, sniffing around them. Leo clearly didn't like it this time as he shifted in even closer to Tom.

'You okay, mate?'

'Yes,' Leo replied uncertainly.

Tom put a hand to the back of his son's head and they moved forward again, edging closer to the centre of the ride which, from what he'd read online the previous night, Tom knew to be the Shrine itself. But as they were getting there, as they moved level with the last of the caves, Tom felt something twinge in his throat.

Pain flared along his jaw.

He stopped, reached a hand up.

Something was sticking out of his neck.

Leo had wandered on a few steps from him, seemingly braver now that they were past the caves, but as Tom tried to call him back, his voice wouldn't form.

Leo, he tried to say. *Leo, wait*.

He couldn't get the words out.

As Tom reached up, pulling out whatever was sticking out of his neck, he saw brief movement to his right, a figure forming in the last of the caves. He looked down at the dart in his hand, the point painted red with blood from his neck, and then back to the pale face inside the darkness of the cave. Tom's head was starting to swim, his vision blurring, but – as he looked at the man's face, a mask pulled up and on top of his head – he thought, *I know this guy*. And, a second after that, he realized why.

Fuck.

He tried to call out to Leo.

But it was too late.

Cronje pulled him into the cave.

Rebekah | *This Afternoon*

The Brenners never came out of the ghost house.

It didn't matter how many times they watched it.

Frank kept pausing and rewinding, pausing and rewinding, but every repeat of the footage showed exactly the same thing: Tom and his son entered but never exited.

'They can't have just disappeared,' Rebekah said.

But then they rewound it, sat through it again, and the same thing happened.

'I'm going to get us some more coffee,' Frank said, and Rebekah watched him head to the counter, his shoulders a little slumped. She knew what he was thinking. Was he losing his edge? His instincts? His ability to solve complex cases?

Rebekah didn't have the same intuition as Frank did, or as David Raker did, but she was a doctor, she was smart and she dealt in facts. And, while it looked like the Brenners went up in a puff of smoke, she knew that was impossible.

The answers were here.

She pulled her laptop towards her, dragged the cursor along the slider, and hit the spacebar again. The footage began as Tom and his son moved inside the ghost house.

She knew from watching and rewatching the same video that, on average, the ride took around four minutes to complete. Four guys were ahead of the Brenners in the queue. A mother and her twins were behind them. Three minutes and twenty-six seconds after the Brenners entered the Shrine, the four men who'd been in front of them emerged. It should only have been another thirty seconds before Tom and his son exited. Instead a minute went by – and then the mother and her twins appeared.

Rebekah hit pause.

Using the cursor key, she edged the footage on frame by frame, knowing these moments were probably the crucial ones. She kept her eye on the exit door, trying to identify faces in the queue, faces standing around waiting for others, staff members.

And then she saw something.

But not at the front of the ride.

At the back.

It happened so fast she instantly had to play it again just to be sure, her view of it not helped by the fact that the whole thing took place in the top left-hand corner of the screen – in fact, almost completely *off* screen – in a walled area cordoned off from the public. On the laptop, it was no more than a square centimetre of space. The only reason she could see behind the ride was because of the angle of the camera; from ground level – where the public and all the staff were – you'd never see a thing.

'Frank,' she said, calling him back from the counter.

He hurried across. 'Have you found something?'

Rebekah returned her gaze to the video and then pointed to the area in the top left: 'This section must be what staff use, because it's directly behind the ride and the whole area looks like it's completely hidden from public view. It must also be where the people who work inside the ride come and go.'

Frank dragged his chair back in and sat down.

'You can barely see it,' he said.

'Exactly. This Cronje guy must have known that.'

'Is there any way to zoom in on that part of the screen?'

'No.'

Their area of focus was so tiny. Which had to have been the point: with almost nothing to see, and all the excitement of the ride, your eyes were never drawn there.

'He must have done a sweep of the cameras beforehand,' Frank said, 'seen where they were and what they were focused on, and realized this was the way to . . .'

But then Frank trailed off.

At the back of the ride, through a door Rebekah could only see a fraction of in the furthest corner of the screen, a masked man appeared, a second slumped against him.

'That's Brenner,' Rebekah said, pointing to the second man.

'It looks like he's been drugged.'

Neither of them had ever seen Cronje, but – if Raker was right – the masked man had to have been him. He was in costume, the mask pulled down over his face – and, as he paused in the staff area for a second, he took something from his pockets.

A beer can?

He opened it, tilted Brenner's head, and started emptying it down his throat.

'He's making it look like Brenner's drunk,' Rebekah said.

'Being drunk would give staff a reason to eject someone from the park.'

'And pretending Brenner's drunk means Cronje can walk him straight out.'

Beyond that point there was nothing more Rebekah or Travis would be able to do: cameras outside the boundaries of the theme park belonged to someone else – the council, other businesses, homeowners. That would take days – maybe weeks – to organize, not hours.

Onscreen, the two men shifted position and, as soon as they did, they were gone, off the edge of the laptop. Rebekah stared at the screen, waiting for the next part, because – from what David had told them – she knew Cronje had taken Brenner's nine-year-old son too.

'He must come back in a second,' Rebekah said.

And then, almost on cue, Cronje returned.

But, this time, something was different.

'Holy shit,' Frank muttered from behind her.

64

I dragged myself forward, the same voice in my head, over and over.

You're going to die down here.

I readied the knife and prodded the door with the toe of my boot. As it swung soundlessly back, the light from my phone flowed into the dark.

This room was much bigger.

Without a proper torch, it looked like it went on forever.

Immediately to the left of me, built into a large alcove – perhaps a former site for storing wine bottles – were a series of long shelves. Every last space on them had been filled up – and all with the same thing.

Files.

Thousands of them.

My flesh crawled as I realized what they were, as I saw surnames printed on the spines, saw the reams of paper spilling out of them. It was the members of The Castle. But not just the current ones. There were far too many for that.

This was anyone who'd ever joined, going back decades.

A noise, somewhere in the dark.

I swung the phone around, directing it out ahead of me, parking everything I'd just seen: the certainty that these files would go all the way back to 1985, to when Martin Larsen first bought the club; and that on one of those shelves I'd find Jennifer Johnson and Mark Levin, and maybe answers about Fiona too. I lengthened my arm, the knife out in front of me.

Where are you?

Where the hell are –

And then I stopped.

I'd reached the centre of the room and, even as I stared at what was ahead of me, even as I saw it with my own eyes – the image painted in the white bloom from my phone – it still took me a second to process what I was seeing.

I took another step.

Another.

I'm not seeing things.

This is real.

A pulley system had been fixed to the ceiling, chains hanging down from it; at the ends of the chains was a dense cord of rope and a pair of heavy-duty handcuffs.

Someone was attached to it all.

Their arms were above their head, wrists tied and handcuffed. Their toes and the balls of their feet were still touching the ground, but they'd been bound so tightly and hoisted so hard that the pulleys had completely lifted their heels away from the floor. Between their upstretched arms, their head was slumped forward, but they were half-turned in my direction – had come to rest at that angle – so I could see the dome of their skull.

There was blood all over it.

They'd been hit on the back of the head.

For a second, I could hardly move, my mind trying to work out exactly what I was looking at, but then I shifted and it all came in a flood: this was why Cronje had let me walk all the way down here unharmed, why he hadn't tried stopping me.

Because he couldn't.

Because he was unconscious.

Because he was chained and tied to the ceiling.

65

I moved closer, thrown, almost disbelieving what I was seeing.

His stomach was moving slowly but his head was slumped forward. I washed the torchlight over him, looking for other wounds, but apart from the one on the dome of his skull, I couldn't see any. Blood from that had crawled its way on to his face, the thinning, greying tresses of his hair clumped, matted.

What the hell was going on?

In my hand, my phone started buzzing.

I turned it so I could keep the light on Cronje but read who was flashing up on the display, and saw it was Rebekah.

It was so quiet, I didn't even need to put her on Speaker.

'David?'

'Are you okay?'

'There's a second person.'

I looked at the man chained up in front of me.

'*Cronje*,' Rebekah emphasized. 'He had help.'

'Someone else was with him at Seven Peaks.'

A pause on the line.

She could hear it wasn't a question.

'You already knew that?'

I forced myself forward, my blood throbbing in my ears, the harsh white light of the torch revealing more of the Red Wolf. I tilted my phone, following the pulley system all the way up to the ceiling. There was no way out of this for him.

I'd been worried about walking into a trap.

Cronje had already been in one.

'David?' Rebekah said. 'Are you there?'

'Did you see who the second person was?'

'No. They both had masks on. But one of them — we think

Cronje – took Tom Brenner, and then a second person came out of the ride with his son.'

Again, I looked at Cronje. *A second person.* Was that who'd strung him up here? Why would they do that?

'I'm going to have to call you back,' I said to Rebekah and hung up.

I moved in even closer to Cronje.

He was a dangerous predator, brutal and ruthless, a killer who had got away with the most heinous crimes imaginable, yet – under the light – he seemed old now. Still fit, still strong, still smart – but the evidence of his age was all over him.

Ian Kirby had talked about how Cronje's hearing was starting to go, and now I spotted – tucked in, almost out of sight inside his ear canal – a hearing aid; I could see the crags all over his face, the sag of the skin, the wrinkles, the crow's feet; I could see how delicate his hair was, how fine it had become; and I could see nicks, minor cuts and bruises, his skin thinner, his cells and tissue ageing and unable to heal as rapidly. As frightening as he was – scared as he made me, even tied up – Cronje still had one enemy that he would never be able to silence.

Time.

And then something else caught my eye.

I didn't take my gaze off it, just sidestepped to my right, looking past Cronje's body, my attention fixed on the corner of the room, on an area my light couldn't quite reach. There, it looked like the shadows were moving.

I raised the knife, coming around Cronje.

Another step.

A second.

'Stop.'

One word, spoken from the darkness.

There was someone else in here with us.

The Red Wolf: Part 3

Unknown | *January 1985*

Behind him, Mienkie Bauer is sobbing.

'Can you see why they call me the "Red Wolf"?' he says.

He stands there, his naked back to her, folding his shirt now, placing it neatly on to the arm of the chair. He fans out the photographs he took from the top drawer. There are four of them. One he's already shown her – the one of her, her husband and their son Kian – but he has others here that he needs to get answers about. He has his camera too.

He adjusts the Polaroid.

Brushes some dust from it.

He won't use the camera until the end.

'Can you, Mienkie? Can you see why they call me the "Red Wolf" now?' He shows her his back again but is able to watch her in the reflection from a blacked-out window on his left. He pulls down the blinds in here and blacks it out for a couple of reasons: because no one can see in; and because he can use it as a mirror.

It allows him to see these final moments.

Their faces as they realize the Red Wolf is real.

He picks up the photographs and moves across to her. She lurches back in her seat, the binds jamming, her eyes soaked with tears. She can't go anywhere – the chair has been bolted to the floor – but he feels a second of electricity as he senses how close he is now. A few more questions, and then he'll pick up the Polaroid, and he'll take a picture of her that will hang on the wall next to the others in his quarters. The men here think he's taking a risk with the pictures. They think – since Larsen left, since Cronje took over – that some of the founding principles of C9 – no paper trails, no evidence, nothing written down – have been forgotten. They don't actually say that to him, just with their eyes – but Cronje doesn't give a shit. He has two advantages here: the first is that he's in charge, so he gives out the orders; the other is that the men are terrified of him.

'Who are these people?' he asks, holding up the first photograph. It's a long-lens shot of Mienkie Bauer talking to two black men in overalls outside the City Hall building in central Johannesburg. 'Tell me the truth and we let you go.'

She says nothing.

'I mean it.'

'I don't believe you.'

'I swear to you, Mienkie. It's not you we're interested in.'

'You're a liar,' she says.

He just stares at her.

'You're all fucking liar—'

He grabs her by the neck, fingers snapping shut on her throat, and squeezes. It takes only seconds before she's struggling to breathe – gasping, choking, her chest expanding and expanding until it's like a balloon. He lets go of her.

She starts coughing.

'Who are the men?' he says.

She gives him the men's names. He writes them down, and then takes out the second photograph and shows it to her. It's another long-lens shot, this time taken in the rickety stand at a tiny sports ground just off the M2. Mienkie is seated way back in the shadows with a black guy in a suit. Again, Cronje asks her who the man is, and again she holds out, and again he grabs her throat. This time he chokes her for longer and, when he's done, she's coughing up blood. She leans forward – as far as the binds allow – and wheezes the man's name.

Cronje writes it down.

He puts the other photographs aside.

There's only one left now.

66

Vaguely, I could see the shape of someone at the edges of my torchlight.

They were little more than a faint grey outline deep in the shadows. It looked like they were dressed head to toe in black and had some sort of mask on.

In the gloom, it looked terrifying.

'Don't come any closer.'

The second they spoke, I froze.

It wasn't a mask they were wearing.

It's a voice changer.

I thought of the code I'd discovered echoed on the condolence card, the mask I'd found when I'd gone searching for what it meant.

I took a step forward. 'Were you the one that sent those cards?'

'If you come any closer, I'll put a bullet in your leg.'

The shadow-person raised their arm from their side: a gun. I could see the shape of it, the straight line of the barrel.

'Lower your torch,' the voice said.

I did as I was asked, the light falling away to the floor, the entire back wall of the room descending into absolute darkness.

'Who are you?' I asked.

I knew the question was futile, but there must have been a reason why this person was using a voice changer, why they were dressed entirely in black, why they were hidden in a corner ordering me not to come any closer.

They didn't want to chance being identified.

But could it have been more than that?

Do they think I might recognize them?

'Do I know you?' I asked.

'No, we've never met.'

'But you did this to Cronje?'

'Yes.' A pause. 'You see all those files over there?'

I didn't look, just kept staring into the darkness.

'Go and search them.'

I stood my ground, unsure if it was a trick.

'There's not one on Fiona Murphy,' the voice said. 'But there are others.'

I glanced across the room, to the alcove with the files in it. They were right on the edge of my light now, greyed-out. When I turned back towards the voice, I lifted the torch a little, trying to illuminate more of the space between the two of us.

Something clicked.

A gun being cocked.

'Go and take a look,' the voice said.

I did as they asked, moving past the suspended figure of Cronje. When I got to the files, I pulled one randomly out of the nearest shelf to me. It had ten pages inside and was made up entirely of information that the club should never have had access to: the member's bank statements, his phone bills, his internet use.

I put the file back and took another, then another. One after the other, they were all the same, the truth crashing against me. This wasn't only every person who'd ever joined The Castle, going all the way back to 1985; it was a huge collection of personal data. It was leverage. An affair, some decision or mistake that – in the wrong hands – could be used against the person in question. I thought of Letitia Scargill, of the trap that Cronje had set. When I found her file, I found a USB stick taped to the inside cover. It must have been the recording of the call she'd had with her sister.

Below the *S*'s were the *L*'s and the *M*'s, and I quickly went looking for Mark Levin, found his file and pulled it out. There was hardly anything inside. No evidence of the affair he'd had with Jennifer Johnson, no reconnaissance on him, no blackmail material. Levin should have been ripe for turning – he was a detective in the Met, he'd been having an extramarital relationship with a member of the club; the two of them were playing into Cronje's hands, making it simple for him. But there was nothing.

Why was Levin still such a ghost?

I double-checked M, just in case, but the person watching me from the shadows had been right: Fiona wasn't here. There was no file, because she'd never been a member.

I went up a row.

Jennifer Johnson's was fronted with not only her membership application but her employment record. Again, I was surprised to find nothing about the affair that Jennifer had had with Mark Levin.

It was like Levin had been erased from history.

But in Jennifer's file, I did find someone else.

Fiona.

Not Levin's search for her, not the reasons she and Jennifer were targeted by the two South Africans, but I finally had confirmation of what I'd suspected all along: the two women knew each other; were friends. Photos confirmed it: a long-lens shot, taken from the other side of the street of the women in a café; Fiona following Jennifer into her flat; Fiona and Jennifer in front of a car under a tree.

What were you two saying to each other?

There were two timesheets at the back of the file – one for Jennifer and one for Fiona. It was full of mundane details, the two women shadowed, the minutiae of their routines documented, what looked like daily activities noted in Afrikaans – none of which I could understand – until entries for Jennifer stopped on the night she vanished. Fiona's ceased only a week later, on Boxing Day.

The entry that day read, *Taak voltooi.*

Mission complete.

'He doesn't leave anyone alive,' the voice said.

I felt a sudden surge of emotion – fury, sorrow, failure. 'You say we don't know each other, so how do you know I'm looking for Fiona Murphy?'

'Because I make it my business to know.'

I glanced at Cronje. 'Why have you done this to him?'

'He needed to be stopped.'

'So you're a good Samaritan?'

'No.'

'Then what?'

Quiet. I hated how they could see me but I couldn't see them.

'I helped him take the Brenners last night,' the voice said. 'He needed someone capable at Seven Peaks, someone who'd follow his instructions. That's the thing with Cronje, the thing I've figured out: if you don't fight him, if you stick to the plan he's laid out – if he thinks you can follow commands to the letter – his guard drops. Just a fraction.'

I looked again at the man strung up in front of me.

'And – what? – he let his guard drop today?'

'The two of us brought the Brenners in. There's a second, hidden entrance right next to me here.' I tried to spot it, but still couldn't see a thing. 'And then I left – or so he thought. Really I just hid. No one's ever seen this cellar, as far as I know. I didn't even realize it existed until last night. And I knew, if I left, he'd never let me back in. He'd change the locks, barricade it. I had one chance.'

'So you've been here since last night?'

'Yes. In the shadows, just waiting for the right moment.'

The silence was as absolute as the dark.

'When he got back here earlier after taking Vance, he never saw me coming. He doesn't know it was me that did this. The blow to the back of the head put him out, and since then I've been keeping him sedated. He likes to do it to other people, now he's having it done to him.'

'And now?'

'He's going to be awake in about three minutes.'

'At which point he'll know it was you that put him here.'

'No,' the voice said. 'I told you, he never saw me coming. He's going to think it was you.'

'Even if he does, what's the endgame?'

'Well, you want answers, don't you?'

I frowned. 'So you're helping me now?'

No response. I looked between Cronje and the shadows.

'He's not just going to spill everything,' I said.

'Then you'll have to persuade him.'

I heard a brief, metallic clatter and then – a second later – something slid out of the dark across the floor towards me. It rattled to a stop at my feet.

Another gun.

'It's unloaded,' the voice said. 'But Cronje doesn't know that. If there's one thing he values above his anonymity, it's his life.'

I picked it up, pushed the thumb lever and released the magazine. There were no bullets inside.

'He won't believe I'm going to kill him.'

But then I stopped, thought of what had happened at the caravan park this morning, and realized I might be lying to myself. Maybe I *could* make him believe I was a killer. Maybe I could easily become the type of man I hated.

'What do you get out of this?' I asked.

For the first time, Cronje moved.

'He's waking up,' the voice responded. 'If you tell him it's not just you and him in here, I will kill you where you stand.'

Cronje's eyelids fluttered.

His wrists twitched inside the handcuffs.

'You have twenty minutes.'

'What?'

'You have twenty minutes to ask your questions.'

'And then what?'

But, this time, the voice didn't reply.

Next to me, Cronje opened his eyes.

67

He blinked and raised his head.

His bones clicked, his body stiff, as he looked up the chains to the pulley system. When his gaze returned to me, his expression was something close to admiration.

The plan had worked.

He thinks I've done this to him.

'I read that your father taught you how to shoot.' His voice crackled with age and pain, with the disorientation of waking from a sedative. And his accent was clear, even forty years on. Gone was the one he'd put on for people, the one he'd used as a disguise, the soft English dialect that he must have practised and practised until he'd got it off pat. This was the Afrikaner who had shown nothing of himself for four decades, except perhaps in private when he was alone with Martin Larsen. He glanced at the gun I was holding. 'That was one of the few things I could find out about you in the media. Your work life, that was easier. Your personal life, not so much. You've done a good job of hiding it.'

'What did you do with Fiona and Jennifer's bodies?'

He rolled his shoulders. 'You know, it might not seem like it at first, but you and I actually have a lot in common.'

'Why did you kill them?'

'Fathers,' he said softly, ignoring me. 'That's where we're definitely different, even if they both taught us to shoot. Yours sounded like a proper dad. Mine was a prick. Did you know, in strict Afrikaner families, we don't call our fathers *Pa*, we call them *Vader*?' He pronounced the *V* as an *F*. 'You know why that's significant?'

'*Vader* is a term usually reserved for God.'

A flash of surprise in his face. 'I forgot you spent time in South Africa,' he said, eyeing me in the same way he had when he'd come to my house pretending to be an estate agent; like he was trying to see inside my head – my life, my history, anything personal to me. 'You're right. A term usually reserved for God. What a fucking joke.' He turned his body, shifting on the chains again. It was obvious he was starting to hurt. 'But, like I said, the two of us, we actually have quite a lot of other things in common.'

'No, we don't.'

'We both grew up on farms. Do you know where Graaff-Reinet is?'

I did. 'Is that what's on your wall in there?'

'I like to remember where I'm from.'

It was a town in the Eastern Cape, the sixth oldest in South Africa, and a site of historical significance to the Afrikaans community because it was one of the starting points for the Great Trek, where Dutch-speaking settlers had migrated north from the British-run Cape Colony. Now the mural in his sleeping quarters made sense: the view of the town was from the Valley of Desolation, a sweep of vertical cliffs and dolerite columns stretching out across the semi-deserts of the Karoo.

'So why did you change your name to Cronje?'

'Because of *Vader*. When I joined the army, I wanted a fresh start. My name – my actual *family* name – it was a weight. I wanted to become someone else.'

'A fresh start where you killed thirty-six people.'

'Oh, I killed more than that.' He looked at me like I was simple, ignorant. 'Don't forget, I spent a year fighting in Angola, another three in Namibia . . .' His eyes flickered. 'Namibia taught me a lot about life. It taught me a lot about death too.'

'So how many have you killed?'

He shrugged. 'I don't know.'

'Do you even care?'

'I killed before those people at the farm, and I killed after them, and every person I killed, I killed *because* I cared.'

'Those people on the wall were innocent.'

'They weren't innocent in the eyes of the state.'

'Your state was run by racists.'

'We were patriots.'

'You were murderers.'

Instantly, he thrust his face towards me, as if he were a rabid animal going on the attack. I staggered away, almost stumbled, but he never even got close, the chains tightening and dragging him back.

I gathered myself, flush with anger.

'Don't ever speak about my country,' he said. 'You have no idea what we –'

I jabbed the gun into his neck, forcing his head away from me. 'You're right, my father *did* teach me how to shoot guns. But that's where you and I are different, because I hate them. I hate what they do. I hate everything about them.' I moved in to his ear. 'But if you think for one second I don't have the guts to pull this trigger, then you're mistaken. I do. I've done it before, and I'll do it again. You're not leaving this place a free man. It's over for you. You know it, I know it.' I paused, thinking of what the voice in the shadows had said to me only moments ago: *If there's one thing Cronje values above his anonymity, it's his life.* 'You can leave this place alive if you tell me what happened to Fiona and Jennifer. You can walk out of here in handcuffs. Or you don't tell me anything, and I pull this trigger, and I carry on looking while they're burying you in a potter's field. It makes no difference to me. I genuinely mean that.'

I slowly released the pressure, letting his head come back. He swallowed, tried to clear his throat. I kept my gaze fixed on his, hard as it was, trying to maintain the fiction that I was some kind of reflection of him; not the sort of killer he was, but someone who might be capable of taking a life. And as I saw him relent, another part of me crumbled away. I was becoming too good at this.

'Do you know why they called me the "Red Wolf"?'

'No,' I said, 'and I don't care.'

He turned on the chains, his binds jangling and adjusting, pivoting himself so that his back was facing me. His black top had escaped from his beltline and I could see a sliver of pale skin. The base of his spine was pronounced, like pebbles in a line, and as he glanced across his shoulder at me, he said, 'It's on my back.'

'What?'

'If you want to know where the name came from.'

I stood there, unsure if it was some kind of game.

But he didn't move; he just waited.

I lifted up his top.

68

It was hard to even comprehend to start with.

His entire back was covered, patterned, the image of a wolf – faded by time, by the age of his skin – tattooed on to him, the portrait of the animal starting in the groove between his shoulder blades and then fanning out across the middle of his back. The portrait had paled from what must once have been a blood-red to an anaemic pink – but despite that, despite his wrinkles and liver spots, his freckles and moles, it remained undeniably beautiful, a mini work of art: detailed, intricate.

But the tattoo was only a part of what I was seeing.

There was something else.

Something hidden inside the image of the animal.

Across the middle of the wolf, where the fur on the snout was, where the thick hair around its jaw and its head should have been, there was no tattooing at all. There were lines in those spaces, many of them, all of which mimicked the pattern of the wolf's coat – and at a glance, seemed to be a part of the tattoo – but all the detail at the jaw, head and ears hadn't been inked on.

Those parts had been there before the tattoo ever was.

They were scars.

Hundreds of them.

'I'd like to tell you I got them in the bush,' Cronje said, 'in war.' I let his top drop down and he turned to face me again. 'But the truth is, he gave them to me.'

His father.

'Most of the boys I worked with in C9 were from poor families like mine. A lot of our fathers were bastards but you had to go a long way to find one as bad as mine. And you know what the worst bit is?' He stared at me. For the first time, there was an odd kind of vulnerability to him. 'I still came back for more. I kept an eye on him from a distance when I got to England. Never spoke to him; never wanted to. But then I heard he was finally dying. Ninety-six years of age. Can you believe that *kak*? Doesn't seem fair that a man like that got to live as long as he did, but there he was, dying in his retirement home in Pretoria. So I picked up the phone and I called him.'

'You broke cover?'

'He had dementia. He didn't even know who I was. But I just needed to speak to him. I had these grand ideas about what I was going to tell him. In the end I still couldn't get the words out.' He took a long breath. 'When Scargill was telling you she heard me speaking German, that was the call she heard. I was phoning my father for one last time before he died.'

I looked at him. *Every killer was a child once.*

'We really are alike,' he said.

I shook my head. 'No.'

'We are.'

'*No.*' I took a small step back from him, as if I instinctively didn't want to be close to this monster, let alone compared to him. *I'm not the same as him.* But then I looked down at the gun I was holding. I thought about what I'd just said to him about pulling the trigger. And about what I'd done to Ian Kirby earlier.

'We are, David.' He adjusted himself, winced. 'You need to listen to me. It's not just because you and I grew up on farms. It's certainly not something as trivial as our fathers teaching us both to shoot. It's not even that, in our own ways, you and I have fought for causes we believe in: my cause was my country, yours is missing people.' He stopped. His expression had completely altered – it was serious, sincere. 'No, what you and I have in common is far more profound.'

I shook my head again.

'Yes,' he said. 'What we have in common is we've lost.'

'What are you talking about?'

'You lost your wife.'

'You don't know anyth—'

'You lost the love of your life,' he said, cutting me off, talking over me. 'And, like you, David, I lost mine.'

The Red Wolf: Part 4

Unknown | *January 1985*

Cronje holds up the final photograph.

It's of Mienkie Bauer with a group of other women at some kind of social gathering. Five of the women are black, the other three – Mienkie being one of them – are white. Her eyes widen. 'No,' she says, 'no, those girls are nothing to do with this. I swear. They're just friends. That was just a birthday pa—'

' "Nothing do with this"?'

She stops, looks at him, realizes her mistake.

'Nothing to do with what?' he says.

Her nose has started bleeding again.

'Nothing to do with your terrorist organisation?'

'They're innocent.'

'Names,' he says.

'They're just friends of mine –'

'Then you've got nothing to worry about.'

She stares at him, holding out. In a way, he admires her courage, but it takes about ten seconds to punch it out of her. By the time he's done, her eye has already started to close up and she's breathing hard. She's leaning forward again, because his last punch was to her kidneys. When she finally raises herself to look at him, he has the photograph up in front of her, and she starts to go through the names of her friends, one by one.

'She's completely irrelevant,' Mienkie says.

Cronje looks at the photograph.

She's talking about a white girl on the far left of the picture.

' "Irrelevant"?'

'She's not even South African. She was just here on holiday with her family.'
Mienkie swallows, winces. It looks like everything hurts. 'She's my second cousin.'

'Where is she now?'

'Back home.'

'Back home where?'

'In England.'

'What's her name?'

'Aren't you listening? This was the first time she'd even been to South Africa and she's probably not ever coming back again, because she knows what a racist —'

He punches her once in the chest.

All the air leaves her.

He can see the pain is excruciating.

'What's her name, Mienkie?'

It takes her a long time to recover.

'What's her name?' he says again.

'Jennifer,' she replies quietly. 'Jennifer Johnson.'

69

'Jennifer,' Cronje said.

I looked at him, remembering what he'd said only moments ago: *You lost the love of your life. And, like you, David, I lost mine.*

'What, you're saying you *loved* Jennifer Johnson?'

'It started with her,' he responded.

'What does that mean?'

But this time he just studied me. I could see something ticking behind his eyes, and I didn't like it. There was an insidiousness about it now, lingering like a scent.

'You seem surprised, David.'

'Yeah, because Jennifer was in a relationship with someone else.'

He angled his head. '*Was* she?'

'She was seeing Mark Levin.'

A blank expression.

'He was a cop,' I said. 'He worked at the Met.'

Nothing again.

'You've never heard of Levin?'

He frowned, and then his eyes glazed for a fraction of a second, as if he were pulling some distant memory back towards him. 'Mark Levin,' he echoed. 'He was a member here, wasn't he?' And in that moment, I could see this wasn't an act: he barely recalled Levin.

'Jennifer was having an affair with him.'

'She wasn't. I watched her for weeks on end. I followed her everywhere, as you would have seen over there.' He gestured to the files. 'If they were having an affair, I would have known. Levin was just a guy who got her a job here. He was clean. If I'd found any dirt on him, I'd have used it.'

Again, I could see he was serious.

And, again, I felt thrown.

One of the key pillars – one of the only things I really knew about Levin – had just collapsed. *There was no affair between him and Jennifer.* Did Levin's friend Len Graves lie to me about it? Or had he just read it all wrong? I cast my mind back to that night in the retirement home when I'd spoken to Graves: I'd asked him if he'd actually ever heard Levin *confirm* he was having an affair with Jennifer. And Graves had said, *He didn't need to. It was obvious.* Graves had just assumed it was an affair based on how Levin was, how he spoke about Jennifer. And I'd allowed myself to go along with it.

Stop. Focus.

You've got nine minutes left.

'You said it started with Jennifer?'

'Actually,' he said, 'technically, I suppose it started with Mienkie Bauer.'

'Meaning what?'

'Meaning, December 1984, Jennifer went out to South Africa because her and Mienkie's mothers were cousins and hadn't seen each other in years. Mienkie and Jennifer were related and basically strangers – but they were the same age and they had things in common, so I guess they clicked. Jennifer was always . . .' He shook his head disparagingly. 'She was always so *liberal*, just like Mienkie.'

He adjusted himself on the chains. The skin at his wrists was bone-white, the circulation cutting off. 'So Mienkie starts getting in Jennifer's ear and she begins to tell her all about the "struggle" –' above his head, he tried to make quotation marks with his fingers, tried to show how – even forty years on – the idea of the anti-apartheid movement was anathema to him, '– and Jennifer comes back to London afterwards with all this shit in her head, including the story – the *myth* – of the so-called Red Wolf. And none of that would have mattered a jot, except a month later I had to flee the motherland and ended up in London myself.'

'Why did you leave South Africa?'

A flicker of pain. Yet this wasn't physical, this was emotional, psychological, a raw ache inside him, even after four decades. 'Mienkie Bauer was told her father died when she was young,' he said. 'The reality was, her father was still very much alive when Mienkie left the farm.'

Left the farm.

As if she'd walked out the front door instead of being tortured, murdered and buried in the bush.

'Have you ever heard of Hamsie Malan?' he asked.

'No.'

'He was the Vice President of South Africa at the time.'

I eyed him. 'What, Mienkie Bauer's father was the Vice President?'

'Yes,' Cronje said. 'Ironic, eh?'

Her real father had worked right at the top of a government Mienkie had been trying to bring down, a government who saw her marriage to a black man, and her son Kian, as illegal acts.

And Mienkie never knew the truth.

'So Mienkie was – what? – the Vice President's illegitimate child?'

'Yes. Malan was married; had kids. A *fine* Christian man. So fine that he was secretly sending money to Mienkie's mother to pay for their house, Mienkie's medical aid, her schooling.'

And Hamsie Malan had kept it secret because, not only was South Africa at the time an extremely conservative, deeply religious country, he also knew it would be politically damaging – perhaps career-ending – for the public to have found out he'd fathered a child outside of marriage. Even worse, that his child was vehemently opposed to everything he believed in.

I looked at Cronje: 'So Malan would have known about Die Suidplaas.'

'Of course. He was the Vice President.'

And the rest – the reason that Cronje's reign at the farm had ended – fell into place: Malan found out that Cronje was the one that killed his daughter, so the Vice President sent in the dogs. Blood, it seemed, was stronger than a political system.

And so the hunter became the hunted.

'A guy I fought with in Namibia worked in the VP's office, in security. He called me and told me Malan had put me on a hit list. No one knew why, but the order had been signed off by the President. Malan was as bad as the people we were trying to stop. He always talked about being willing to die for his country, but he cared more about some daughter he never saw and didn't have the balls to tell the truth to, than he did about defending our homeland. He was soft. He wasn't a patriot, he was a traitor. But he had power and he had influence and that was enough. So, that was when I picked up the phone to Larsen and came to London.'

I took a breath, stilling my thoughts.

You've got seven minutes.

'Why did you kill Fiona and Jennifer? You said it started with Jennifer?'

He just stared at me; said nothing.

'You must have met Jennifer initially through The Castle, right? She worked there. You did too once you got to the UK.'

Again nothing.

'You met Jennifer there, you started a relationship with her, and that was when she saw your tattoo.' I paused, waiting for him to correct me. But he didn't. Instead, at the corner of his lips, I could see the faintest hint of amusement.

'Please,' he said. 'Continue.'

I pushed again: 'You started a relationship with Jennifer, she saw your tattoo. She puts two and two together and remembers what Mienkie told her about the Red Wolf.'

'No.'

'No what?'

'Even though we were both at The Castle at the same time, I barely saw Jennifer. I stayed hidden during the day, she did most of her shifts then. She was never on my radar, even after Larsen bought the club. She was just some waitress. I never had a relationship with Jennifer.'

I stopped. 'What? But you said –'

'I *said*, Jennifer was where it started.'

'You said you loved her.'

'No, I didn't. You interpreted it that way.'

'What the hell does that mean?'

'It means you've got all of this the wrong way around, David. Jennifer got back to the UK from South Africa in January 1985. A few weeks later, her cousin Mienkie leaves the farm in my truck.' He eyed me, waiting for a response, trying to goad me with the banality of his language, as if Mienkie's murder – and her body's final journey, deep into the bush – was as mundane as a trip to the shops. 'No one in the family knew what had happened to her, but it kept all of that shit that Mienkie had told Jennifer before she died at the very forefront of Jennifer's thoughts. And that became a problem when Jennifer and Fiona met up in London at the start of December 1985.'

December.

By the end of that same month, both women were dead.

'Why did it become a problem when Fiona and Jennifer met?' I said.

'Because Fiona decided to confess something.'

I paused. '*Fiona* confessed something? You mean Jennifer?'

'No, I mean Fiona.'

'What are you talking –'

But then, a second later, it hit me like a train.

I stepped back from him.

No.

'Ah, now you understand,' he said.

It felt like the whole room was spinning, and suddenly all I could see was Rebekah, an image of her, tearful, bereft, the devastation carved into her face as I told her the truth about her mother – about what Fiona had been doing in the months before she'd died, and who she'd been doing it with.

You've got all of this the wrong way around, David.

It was never Jennifer who'd had an affair.

It was Fiona.

70

'Fiona and you were . . .' I trailed off.

I couldn't even say it.

'She was the only person I ever let get that close to me.'

His face softened. It had been so hard to get a handle on him, on what was real and what wasn't, whether he was playing me, leading me, or being truthful. But these brief moments – these subtle glimpses of the human being entombed inside the devil – felt completely authentic.

'You lost your wife,' he said quietly. 'I lost Fiona.'

'How . . .' I gathered myself, trying to reset. 'How did it begin?'

'August 1985,' Cronje said, his expression more inscrutable now. His skin had rubbed raw at the wrists, a thin trail of blood worming under his sleeve. 'I was in Cambridge, doing some work for Larsen, and I called into a café and she was in there, in the queue. We started talking. I don't know what it was about her . . .' He paused. 'No one had instantly disarmed me like that. We only talked for ten minutes, but it was the most I'd said to anyone other than Larsen in months. I couldn't even tell you what we talked about, but it just felt . . .' He winced. 'It felt so simple.'

'And – what? – she just handed over her number to you?'

'No.'

He watched me, as if waiting for me to catch up. And then I glanced at the files on the shelves. 'Oh, I see. You did the same shit to her you did to everyone else.'

'No,' he replied quickly.

'You stalked her.'

'No, it wasn't like that. I wanted to find out more about her.'

'You found out where she lived and you stalk—'

'*Don't fucking corrupt it,*' he screamed, rage in his eyes. The switch was instant, terrifying. He tried to come towards me but the chains pinged and yanked him back. 'Don't corrupt it,' he said again, and then retreated, head down. 'You don't get it. I never forced her. Yes, I instigated that second meeting. I returned to Cambridge so I could bump into her – but that was the only dishonest thing I ever did with her.'

'That and murdering her.'

'She was unhappy at home,' he said, as if he hadn't even heard me. 'I could tell she was looking for something; something more. She was restless. We were alike in that way. Her childhood had been hard, like mine, and we bonded over that as well. I allowed her in. I didn't tell her the whole truth about my past, about why I came to England – how could I? – but I told her I was in the army, then the police. She said her husband had been in the army and had just joined the police in Cambridge – that he worked long hours, was never home, that a lot of the time it was just her and the kids. She and I, we were both needing to escape.'

I glanced at the time on my phone. *Four minutes.*

'So you met Fiona in August, and she and Jennifer met in December. That was when Fiona confessed to Jennifer about the affair she was having with you?'

'It wasn't an affair,' Cronje said.

Before he could tell me again that what they had was special, different, I said, 'And then at some point during Fiona's confession, she mentions the wolf tattoo?'

'Yes.'

'And that's when Jennifer realizes Fiona is sleeping with the Red Wolf.'

'Yes,' he said again.

The same ghost, the same myth, that Mienkie Bauer had told Jennifer about when she'd visited South Africa a year earlier.

He was looking down now, his face difficult to see. 'I could tell something was playing on Fiona's mind. To start with, I thought it might be the guilt. We didn't talk much about her husband, or her family. But then we were in the hotel we always went to, near the station in Cambridge, and she said, "Are you originally from South Africa?"'

He lifted his head, looked at me.

'It completely levelled me. The question, it just . . . it just came totally out of nowhere. I'd been in the country less than a year, I'd got the English accent off. I'd trained myself never to use my real accent unless I was alone with Larsen, so the question of where I came from . . . no one had ever asked it.' A sudden flash of anger. 'That stupid fucking *bitch* ruined everything.' It was hard to know if he was talking about Jennifer or Mienkie Bauer, because both, incrementally, led him to that moment.

'Fiona had no idea where I worked, or what I did. I didn't lie to her, she just never asked. We talked about everything *but* our lives. That was why I let her get so close.' A grimace on his face. 'When she asked me that question about South Africa, I said, "What would make you say that?" and she said, "I told one of my friends about us; I told her I knew it was wrong, I'm married, but for the first time in a long time, I'm happy." Fiona said that Jennifer never judged people, which was part of the reason she told her, and only her. And Jennifer didn't care that Fiona was having an affair. For Jennifer, it wasn't about the affair, it was about *who* the affair was with.'

'So Jennifer told Fiona who you were?'

'She must have done for Fiona to act the way she did after that. All of a sudden, Fiona was different.' He trailed off. 'I knew, in that second, it was over.'

I glanced at my phone. *Two minutes.*

'And then?'

'And then I confessed everything to Larsen.'

'And he told you to get rid of them both?'

'Yes. He was right. We were compromised. I stepped back from Fiona, made excuses – she stepped back from me too – and I started watching them both.' His face was neutral now: no emotion in it, eyes fixed on mine like he was reciting a passage from memory. 'I watched the two of them meeting up more often. Between August and the first week of December 1985, they'd only met up once.

Between the first week of December and the nineteenth, they met five times.'

The nineteenth: the day Jennifer disappeared.

'The big advantage I had was that Jennifer had no idea I worked at The Castle. That meant I could watch her up close. I could listen to her calls. She was lining everything up, this meticulous collecting of evidence; she was planning to fly out to South Africa again at Christmas and meet with Mienkie's mother, with anti-government supporters. I even heard her on the phone to Fiona one night, telling her she needed to try and see me. They were going to try and use Fiona as bait, try to get her to coax information out of me.' He ground to a halt, and it took him a long time to say anything else. 'We had to act.'

Stillness.

Nothing in the room moved.

'Larsen took care of Fiona, I took care of Jennifer. I couldn't face doing what I had to do to Fiona. I didn't know if I could go through with it.'

I remembered how Rebekah had described her last memories of her mother, how her father had talked about it, what was written on the missing person's report they filed: she left the house without a word, no keys, no money, no explanation.

'You and Larsen lured Fiona out of her house?'

'We didn't need to. I took Jennifer on the nineteenth of December; pulled her off the street when she was walking home alone after a night out. She was drunk. No one saw anything. It was simple back then. CCTV was barely a thing. We kept her alive for a while, questioned her, did what we were trained to do. And we kept watching Fiona at the same time: she was getting jumpy, obviously knew that her friend's disappearance was connected to me, the Red Wolf, to the things she and Jennifer had talked about. What played into our hands was that Fiona couldn't tell her husband, even though he was a cop, because then she'd have to lie about the reasons why Jennifer might have vanished, about the background to it all, about she and I being together. So, on Boxing Day, before I killed Jennifer, I forced her to call Fiona. Jennifer gave her a meeting place, and told her not to mention it to anybody. She said she'd explain everything once Fiona got there.'

'And Fiona walked right out the front door.'

One minute.

'Where did you put their bodies?'

Something about the question seemed to aggravate him, his cheeks flushing – perhaps because it brought home to him how trapped he was, how he was chained to the ceiling in a device of his own making, unable to escape, unable to retreat into the gloom and hide there, like he'd done so often over the decades.

'Same place I put all the bodies,' he said.

I thought of Kian Bauer, of what Ian Kirby had told me about where Cronje had taken his body parts. 'The quarry on the Mendips?'

Cronje nodded again. 'Yes.'

'Which quarry?'

He gave me the name.

And then, from the dark, something wheeled out towards me. Cronje heard it too and pivoted on the chains, looking down at the floor – confused, curious – both of us following it with our eyes. It hit my boot.

A roll of duct tape.

Cronje looked at me, then into the dark.

'You'll want to tie yourself up, David,' the voice said.

'What the fuck?' Cronje muttered.

He looked between us.

I didn't respond, just stared at the shadows. 'Tie myself up?'

'Ankles. A strip on your mouth. I'll do your wrists.'

'Why would I do that?'

Cronje turned on the chains again, rattling them, trying to loosen them, as he stared into the abyss at the back of the room. And then, almost instantly, something altered in his face.

He knows who it is.

He knows it's the second person at Seven Peaks.

He knows now that it was them that put him here, not me.

377

'Cronje, look at me,' I said.

I wanted to ask him who the second person was.

'*Cronje.*'

But he wasn't listening. '*You're* the one that did this?' he said, almost spitting the words into the black. His face flooded – fury, violence. He turned back to face me. 'You're putting your trust in this –'

He never finished.

The sound of a gunshot tore the room in two.

The Days After

PART EIGHT
The Wake

71

The sun was coming up as I pulled on to the driveway.

I could barely keep my eyes open, my body exhausted, my mind overwhelmed by everything I'd learned and seen over the past week; by the process of having to go through all of it for hours, bit by bit, inside a cramped, overheated interview room.

It had been fourteen hours since the police had turned up at The Castle. After binding my wrists and putting me on my belly, the killer with the voice changer had told me they'd call the cops once they were clear of the club. The Met arrived thirty minutes later and immediately released Catherine Vance and the Brenners, giving them blankets and shepherding them out. I glimpsed them all briefly, Leo Brenner in tears, Tom bruised and walking crookedly, Catherine's face still streaked in blood. When officers came back for me, they cut me from my binds and then strong-armed me all the way out to the back of an ambulance, where paramedics were waiting. I felt like a suspect being frog-marched to a police car, every step more draining than the last as I realized, even now, the officers attending the scene were eyeing me with suspicion, as if I'd played some part in my own capture.

Once I'd been patched up, I was driven to the nearest station and questioned, then eventually allowed to go home. After walking back to my car, I slid in at the wheel and stared at myself in the rear-view mirror. It was now closing in on two days since I'd had any sleep, and every minute I'd been awake over the past forty-eight hours was written into my face. I looked old, beaten and haunted. I wasn't helped by the bruise that had now fully flourished on my cheek and closed the corner of my right eye; and I wasn't helped by the dots of blood that had dried all the way across my mouth, a red, angry reminder of where the duct tape had been ripped off by the cops. I felt the throb at my ankles too, the ache where I'd been hogtied, my wrists tethered to my feet, my body bent out of shape.

I got out of the car, locked up and headed into the house. Keying in the alarm code, I paused in the hallway, my home cold, dark, and looked into the living room. I stared at the wall of notes and pictures that were still pinned up, and my gaze settled on a photograph of Rebekah. I'd texted her earlier to say I'd call her as soon as I was released from custody.

But, right now, I couldn't face it.

I took everything down off the wall and then headed through to my bedroom, undressed, my body hurting, and got into the shower. Turning the temperature all the way up, I let the water pelt me, let the heat scour my skin, and then afterwards I lit the fire and lay on the sofa with the TV on mute. A Sky News reporter was talking soundlessly from a crime scene at a prestigious members' club in London.

I closed my eyes.

I woke suddenly to the sound of someone knocking at the door.

Throwing off the blanket, I looked at the time. It was after 3 p.m., the fire just a bed of glowing ash, the TV still on mute. The news had moved on for now, to another reporter on another story – but before long they'd be back outside The Castle.

Thirty-six Polaroids would demand it.

I sat up, groggy, my head swimming for a moment, and then hauled myself up and headed through to the front door. In the square of frosted glass midway up, I saw two silhouettes. I knew straightaway who they were and felt irritated by them being here. I'd spent the whole night in a police station answering questions and now I was going to have to answer more. But these weren't going to be about Cronje or Fiona.

I opened the door.

'Hello, David,' Martine Parkes said. Next to her, Aiden Phillips simply nodded. Both their eyes went to the injury on my face.

The Castle was outside of Parkes and Phillips's jurisdiction but it didn't mean they'd be out of the loop about what had happened. As soon as my name popped up on the radar in connection with what had gone on there, someone would have called them, if only to gather background on me. But because Phillips was senior, and connected, I imagined he'd probably got a full, unofficial briefing.

'Can we come in?' Parkes asked.

'Do you have to?'

She just smiled.

I'd barely had the chance to think about Healy, about the message he'd left for Liz, or about the telltale sound of an ECG in the background of the call. I didn't feel ready for a sparring match minutes after I'd woken up, and only hours after I'd watched a man – terrible as that man was – have the back of his head blown out.

Reluctantly, I stepped back and they went through to the living room. As I put some coffee on, I tried to listen in to what they were saying, but all I could hear was silence. That could have meant any number of things – or nothing at all – but it was hard not to return to the last thing Parkes had said to me when they'd hauled me into the station after Letitia Scargill's murder.

Watch your back.

As I carried their coffees through, I could feel it like a charge in the air. There was something going on between them, something unspoken, and because I'd got to know Parkes a little, her mannerisms, because I saw her stiffen as I entered, glance at Phillips, cede control to him even though she was uncomfortable with it, I knew what was coming: they'd finally found it.

Something they can use.

They'd either caught Healy in a lie.

Or they'd turned him against me.

72

Phillips leaned forward on the sofa and took a sip of the coffee I'd made for him. He forced a smile out, as if we were just old friends catching up.

'We've come to your house, David,' he said, that same soft Scottish brogue, the quiet, controlled tone, 'because I want to give you the opportunity to tell us, completely off-the-record, anything that you think might be pertinent to our investigation.'

I looked between them.

He opened his hands out, waiting.

'You came all the way out here for this?' I said, sounding confident, affronted. But inside I was squirming. What did they have? What had Healy given them?

He wriggled out a notebook from his coat. I glanced at Parkes while Phillips's attention was diverted, but she didn't look at me. 'There's nothing?' Phillips asked.

'No,' I said simply.

'There's nothing in the last five months that we might go on to find is inaccurate, or – worse – a deliberate and calculated concealment of the facts?'

What the hell did they have?

'No,' I repeated.

Phillips's eyes returned to his notebook. Without moving my head, I glanced at Parkes again.

Now her eyes were on me.

Was she trying to tell me something?

Phillips flicked through some pages – moving back and forth between two in particular – and then looked up.

'You barely know Colm Healy,' he said.

But it wasn't a question, more like a mantra, a line he'd gone over and over during the past five months and relentlessly tried to unpick.

'You're sticking to that, are you?'

I had no idea what the safest answer was now, but I couldn't change my story without knowing what Healy had given them, so I said, 'Just get to the point.'

'My point? I'm not sure I have one, other than the certainty that nothing you say can be trusted.' He pushed his lips together; a grimace. 'I'm just going back over this story that you told my colleagues at Central North about what happened at The Castle this morning . . .' He studied his notes. 'There was a second person in there with you. They used a voice changer. They made you tie together your *own* ankles, put that gag over your *own* mouth, and then when they came to do your wrists, to hogtie you, they put you on your front so you wouldn't be able to see them. *So*, you have zero idea who they are, zero idea about their physical description because the room was so dark, and none of the other witnesses –' he checked his notes, '– not this journalist, Vance, who he drugged and abducted from her home, and not the father or the son he sedated and kidnapped at Seven Peaks, recall seeing anyone else except Cronje once they woke up at the club.'

'That's not true.'

'It *is* true, David. The father and son say they remember seeing a second person at the fun fair before the tranquillizer kicked in – but not once they got to The Castle.'

I felt thrown. What was he doing?

'And even if this mysterious second person, with no physical description and a voice changer, *is* the person who was helping Cronje at the fun fair, why the hell would they work with Cronje and *then* shoot him in the head? Why would they leave you alive, or the witnesses? This whole thing . . .' He trailed off, shook his head. 'It feels like every other piece of fiction you've spun the Met down the years; it feels like this crap with Colm Healy. And, frankly, David, I'm sick of it. You're dangerous.'

'Why are you here, Phillips?'

'I just had to look you in the eye. Because I *know* you're lying.'

'What, you think I was the secret mastermind? You think I took that duct tape and hogtied *myself*? Or maybe that I shot Cronje in the head and made the murder weapon magically disappear into thin air? I hate to break it to you, but there was no gunshot residue on my hands –'

'Well, we'll see for sure when the forensics come back –'

'There won't be. I didn't fire a weapon. It happened *exactly* how I said it did, and the only arrogant and dangerous person in this room is you, because all you care about is this petty revenge shit. You don't give a damn about anyone that man murdered or put on the walls of that place. I doubt you've even given a second's thought to the families who still have no idea what happened to the people they love. So don't ever come into my home and talk to me like this. In fact, don't come to my home again, *ever*, unless you actually plan to put me in handcuffs.'

We stared at each other.

He was seething. I could see it in the colour of his face, even if his expression remained neutral.

He snapped his notebook closed.

'You know,' he said, 'he's given you up.'

I eyed him.

'Healy. We've been in there for weeks now talking to him. And I hate to tell you this, David, but it really didn't take much. All the hard work you've been doing out here with your denials and your lies, all that effort you expended trying to deflect attention away from him and from yourself, and he was in there talking to DI Parkes the whole time. But then I guess you and he barely know each other, so what could he possibly tell us that would be a problem for you, right?'

My stomach was churning.

'Before we can finally put an end to this charade of yours, we just need to dot a few i's and cross a few t's.'

And then Phillips stood. I looked at him, surprised. I'd been waiting for him to go for the jugular; instead, he looked like he was about to leave.

'You'll be in those handcuffs soon enough,' he muttered.

He headed to the front door.

For a second, Parkes held back, making a show of taking a sip from her coffee, and as her gaze met mine across the top of her mug, her eyes flicked towards the sofa she'd been sitting on. She put the mug down, thanked me, and headed out.

I waited for the front door to click.

As soon as it did, I moved across to her sofa, and tucked into the seat, hidden from view by one of the arms, was a scrap of paper.

I picked it up, unfolded it.

In the middle was a message:

he's bluffing

73

I stared at the note that Parkes had left for me.

Why would she do this? Why would she go against her boss? Why would she risk incurring the wrath of her senior officer – and neuter her career in the process – to help me?

Maybe because she believes it's the right thing to do.

I tried to get everything into some sort of order but kept coming up short, and then my thoughts returned to Rebekah. I knew I couldn't delay it any longer. I'd asked the police for a short period of grace in order to deliver the news about Fiona myself, but now the clock was running down. If I waited much longer, Rebekah would be hearing the truth from a complete stranger.

I dialled her number. She picked up before the call had even got to its second ring. I asked her to come to the house and told her that I'd already organized an Uber to bring her and Travis out to Ealing.

When it arrived, she looked nervous, and as she passed me and headed into the house, Travis seemed to instinctively sense what was coming.

It was something that was going to floor her.

Quietly, he said, 'Don't hold anything back. Just tell her.' And then the rest was there in his face: *She's been lied to before in her life, been served half-truths and platitudes, and, if you've found out the truth, she deserves to hear it from someone she trusts.*

So after I'd made them both some tea, I sat down in the living room, I looked her in the eye, and I said, 'I'm going to tell you absolutely everything, Rebekah. But some of it will be very hard to hear.'

Over the next two days, the fallout from what had happened at The Castle continued.

Forensic teams from Avon and Somerset Police dredged the water in a disused quarry in the Mendips, searching for the bodies of Fiona Murphy and Jennifer Johnson – and for Kian Bauer. Eventually three bodies were discovered, spread out in the deepest part of the lake.

A fourth was recovered as well.

It was identified as male.

Decomposition suggested it had been there for a long time – in the media, 'sources familiar with the investigation' posited as much as twenty years – and, although the victim couldn't yet be linked to the other bodies or definitively identified as having been killed by Cronje, I had a gut feeling from early on that it was only a matter of time before it was. Small, incremental moments had stuck with me throughout the case, but a slowly developing theory I'd been working on had started to solidify after talking to Ian Kirby at the caravan park and to Cronje in the minutes before he'd been killed. With Kirby, I kept getting the sense that he was holding back on me. With Cronje, it was the way he'd only ever referred to his former CO as 'Larsen'. There was a coldness to it, an indifference, that shouldn't have been there based on everything I'd read about their near-brotherly relationship.

That was why I believed the fourth body belonged to Martin Larsen.

And I believed Cronje had killed him.

Larsen had been gone for twenty years, which was another reason it tied up. And then there was the way Kirby had told me that Larsen's 'heart gave in' when I asked how Larsen had died. Not a heart attack. Not heart issues.

His heart gave in.

It felt deliberately vague.

In the end, it was playing on my mind so much, and I was so convinced that I was right, that I picked up the phone and called Rob Hawlings – the SIO on the Cronje case – and told him what I thought. A long time ago, in my former life as a journalist, Hawlings had been an anonymous source on one of my stories, otherwise I wouldn't have chanced it. I trusted him, he trusted me, and as I expected, he heard me out.

'I'll let you know what we find,' he said.

74

On the third day, Hawlings and his team asked Rebekah to stay in London for a little longer in order to answer questions about Fiona.

'What are they expecting?' Rebekah said to me on the phone. 'Everything I know about my mother, I learned from you.' But she agreed to do it, even though Travis, reluctantly, had to fly home without her: he needed to be back in New York for a conference on police investigative techniques, in which he was delivering a keynote speech.

The only issue was that the hotel she was in was at full capacity in the lead-up to Christmas and couldn't extend her stay, and we struggled to find her anywhere else that wasn't a two-star pit, or miles out of the centre. So, in the end, I told her she could take the spare room at my house. Ealing was *also* miles out of the city centre but I did at least have a bed, a hot shower and a glamorous breakfast.

'What's glamorous about it?' Rebekah said, smiling.

'I've got very posh granola.'

She settled in while I made some calls, including one to Liz about Healy, trying to see if she could take a second run at trying to speak to him for me, and at the very least, attempt to find out what was going on. She told me she'd do her best but it was likely he wasn't going to want to talk. A few hours later, she called back.

'Did you speak to him?' I asked.

'No. I spoke to someone I know there, who knows someone else, who told me Healy is in a bad way. And there's something else too – he's also been meeting with a solicitor.'

'His original one?'

'Yes.'

'Do we know why?'

'It could be anything. Maybe he's got a court date. Maybe the Met have actually charged him with something.'

Or maybe he's drawing up some agreement.

A deal.

Me in exchange for his freedom.

I thanked Liz and hung up – confused, panicked. I didn't know if Parkes's *he's bluffing* message was a trick or the truth, didn't know whether the threat was coming from her, or from Phillips, or from whatever Healy was planning. As I wrestled with it all, Rebekah came through. She'd been in her bedroom, the door closed.

She'd been crying.

'Sorry,' she said as she wiped her eyes.

'Don't worry. Down the years, this house has seen plenty of tears.'

She pushed out a smile and glanced at my pictures of Derryn. 'Your wife was beautiful.'

'I always thought so.'

'How long were you two together?'

'Sixteen years.' As I said it, I realized – for the first time – that it was almost as long since she'd been gone.

'I don't know what's worse any more,' Rebekah said, her gaze moving from photograph to photograph. 'Mum walking out on us, or her cheating on my dad with that . . .'

Monster.

'If it's any consolation, I don't think she knew what he was.'

'But she still cheated.'

'Yes,' I said. 'She did.'

We stood like that for a moment, our thoughts on people we'd lost, on people we'd never know, and then – realising it had just turned 6 p.m. – I asked if she was hungry.

'You don't have to make me dinner, David.'

'I'm making for me, so I'm happy to make for you.'

A flicker of a smile. 'Okay. Thank you.'

I headed into the kitchen and started preparing some vegetables, and, shortly after, heard the sound of a FaceTime call coming from the living room, and then the tinny, excited squeal of Rebekah's daughters echoing through her iPad's speaker. In that moment, it was possible to forget everything else – the hurt; the unanswered questions; the confusion and betrayal – and just enjoy the sound of innocence.

But the moment didn't last long.

A few minutes later, Rob Hawlings called.

75

'You were right about Martin Larsen,' he said after I'd answered.

'He's the fourth body in that quarry?'

'Looks like it. We managed to recover some DNA from some items of his that Cronje still had and got a rush on it. Preliminary results say it's a match.'

'Did you ask Ian Kirby about it?'

'We've asked him about a lot of things since he was arrested. He's looking at an accessory charge so his solicitor's trying to make a deal: more information, less time inside. Even if he gives us absolutely everything he has, though, he's still going to prison – and he's going to be in there a while.'

I'd been wondering ever since the events in the cellar whether Kirby might have been the second person, so I asked Hawlings what he thought. He immediately threw it back at me: 'I don't know. Do *you*?'

'My instinct says no but . . .' I paused, my exhaustion weighing on me. 'I'm not operating at maximum right now so I could be missing something.'

'For what it's worth, one of the employees at the caravan park said they spoke to him around the time you were in that cellar. I mean, maybe the employee is mistaken about the time, maybe Kirby's lying – but, like you, I don't get the sense he is. We turned that caravan upside down, and his home, and we haven't found anything that puts him in that cellar with you. No clothing like our suspect. No voice changer.'

'Does *he* know what happened with Larsen?'

'Yeah.' A pause. '"His heart gave in" doesn't really cover it.'

I waited, but Hawlings didn't continue.

'Anything you share will go no further,' I said.

I heard the gentle click of a door. 'Kirby told us that Cronje and

Larsen had begun to drift apart, even before Kirby started working at The Castle in 1994. Cronje was still buttoned-up tight, still thought he was a soldier fighting a war. But Larsen . . . he'd become more relaxed in London, was enjoying the lifestyle, maybe a bit too much – the club, the people, the booze – none of which went down well with Cronje because Cronje believed it was all distraction. If you're distracted, you become careless, and Cronje, what he did at the farm, his crimes, those were all there inside Larsen's head, and if Larsen was getting careless – sloppy, loose-lipped – if he was drinking all the time . . .'

'He was a danger to Cronje.'

'Correct.'

'So he killed Larsen before Larsen could become too much of a risk to him. And the only person who knew about the murder was Ian Kirby?'

'Yes. Larsen and Kirby worked closely together – one was the owner, the other was the manager – so Kirby was immediately going to notice if Larsen suddenly wasn't around. Kirby was also shit-scared of Cronje, so I guess Cronje realized knowledge was another way to control him: burden him with the truth about what he – Cronje – had done to Larsen, tell him he'd be next if he ever talked. It worked, because it kept Kirby in line for the next twenty years, until he grew a pair of balls and talked to Catherine Vance.'

'So that was how Kirby found out about Larsen's murder? Cronje told him?'

'Not exactly.'

I heard the pages of a notebook being turned.

'You told me you always got the sense that Ian Kirby was holding back on you. Well, it turns out you were right. Even now, even all these years on, he has a strong sense of loyalty to Larsen, despite knowing what Larsen did in South Africa. And that's because Kirby kept – and was still keeping – Larsen's biggest secret.'

'His biggest secret?'

'The secret he hid from everyone in his life.'

'Which was what?'

'Martin Larsen fell in love with the wrong person.'

The Secret: Part 1

Unknown | *February 2001*

It was well after midnight and The Castle was quiet.

Cronje moved from the restaurant, through the kitchen, to the staff stairs, and started taking them all the way up to five.

The fifth floor was where Larsen was.

He'd sold his home – the home that Cronje had lived in for his first few weeks in London, once he'd moved out of the Rockingham – the second he finally bought The Castle, and moved into, and then converted, one of the top-floor office suites into his own personal flat. He'd been there ever since. It hadn't bothered Cronje to start with, because Cronje was living in the club too. But he was in the cellar, with no windows, and no one knew he was there.

Everyone knew where Larsen was.

He'd thrown parties in his flat.

That was the difference between them: Cronje knew what he'd done, and knew what he was running from; Larsen seemed to have forgotten. The booze, the parties, the women; it was like a fog for Larsen.

Cronje tried not to think about that, about any of the ways in which Larsen had pissed him off and was potentially putting them in danger, and concentrated on what he'd come up here to talk about: a new membership application that Larsen – as Samuel Apphis – had been trying to push through. Cronje didn't like the application. It was messy, incomplete, as if the guy just expected it to be signed off. What he liked least of all, though, was just how little he could find out about the applicant. The guy said he was a friend of Larsen. He was also a blank slate.

That part set Cronje on edge.

Even now, there were people – South African authorities, Interpol, the widows and widowers they'd left behind – who wanted Cronje and Larsen found.

Larsen needed to remember that.

Cronje knocked and waited. When he got no answer, he knocked again – and, once more, Larsen didn't come to the door. Cronje knew he was in there because he could hear him talking, so for a third time he knocked – and for a third time Larsen didn't respond.

The talking continued.

Cronje tried the door. Typically, Larsen had been careless and left it open. Cronje pushed it away from him and it swung back into a short hallway with a bathroom off to the left. Ahead of him, grey slate floors swept through to a living area with sofas, tables, a TV, a music system, and bottles of booze lined up on a shelf.

Cronje moved through, saw empty glasses and cigarette butts in ashtrays, and then headed past the mess that was Larsen's life towards the main bedroom, where the voices were coming from.

He stopped.

The double doors were ajar, a thin line between the edges allowing him to peer through to Larsen's room. To start with, Cronje thought he was seeing things, but he soon realized it was exactly as it looked – Larsen was in bed, entwined in the sheets.

But he wasn't alone.

There was another man under the sheets with him.

76

'Kirby told us that all the women Larsen used to party with were just a cover story,' Hawlings said. 'He was gay.'

Now I understood what Hawlings meant when he said Larsen had *fallen in love with the wrong person*. The reaction he'd have faced in apartheid-era South Africa would have been severe, where – even until as late as 1994 – male same-sex relationships were illegal. In an ultra-conservative society, where the boys who went on to serve in the army and in units like C9 were brought up in traditional, God-fearing families, Larsen – as a gay man – would have been a pariah. Men like Cronje would have seen homosexuality as a sin; they would have believed it was some kind of personality defect, a reason not to trust Larsen any more. They were killing people based on colour without a thought about where that fit into their religion – but being gay was base, a weakness.

It made zero sense to anyone but them.

'So Cronje killed Larsen because he was a danger to him, or because he was gay?' I asked Hawlings.

'Talking to Kirby, it's hard to gauge whether Cronje's main beef with Larsen was his decreasing lack of focus, him being gay, or him being gay and Cronje not getting as much as a whiff of it in all the time him and Larsen had known each other.'

Hawlings made a good point.

Cronje was a master manipulator, a psychopath who had ensured that he had eyes everywhere, on everything, always. Finding out about Larsen, discovering that something had been completely hidden from him – even more that it was a lifestyle choice that Cronje despised – would have made him rage.

The Red Wolf had finally missed something.

And it had been there right in front of his nose for years.

'So you said Ian Kirby told you exactly what happened?' I asked.

'Yeah, to the letter.'

'Because Cronje told *him* everything?'

'No,' Hawlings said. 'Because he was there when Larsen died.'

The Secret: Part 2

Unknown | *February 2001*

Cronje stared at the two men in Larsen's bed.

One was Larsen.

The other was Ian Kirby.

'What the fuck is this?' Cronje shouted, shoving the doors open.

The two men had been holding hands, talking, but now they both startled, Kirby grabbing a fistful of sheets and yanking them across to him, revealing Larsen's nakedness. Larsen's face flushed red. But he wasn't embarrassed.

He was livid.

He got off the bed and stormed across the room to Cronje, pointing a finger at him, saying 'What are you *doing*?'

'What am *I* doing? You're in bed with another ma—'

Larsen cut him off, grabbed him by the throat and smashed him back against the wall. It happened so fast Cronje was temporarily stunned. He couldn't remember the last time anyone had done that to him; was surprised by how strong Larsen still was, even in his late fifties. He kept the pressure up on Cronje's throat, squeezing. 'Never come in here, *ever*, without my permission,' he hissed in Cronje's ear.

'You're depraved.'

Larsen squeezed. 'Choose your words carefully.'

Cronje struggled to get anything out: '. . . nothing to me.'

'*What?*'

'I said you're nothing to me.'

That stopped Larsen. 'What the fuck did you say?'

'You heard me.'

Larsen squeezed again, his jaw jabbing in towards Cronje's,

Larsen's face so enraged his skin had rinsed scarlet. 'Don't you ever come in here and speak to me l—'

Cronje drove the knife up under Larsen's ribs.

Larsen hadn't even seen it.

He staggered away, clutching the wound, looking at it like he couldn't believe what he was seeing. Blood spilled out over his fingers and ran down his naked body.

Behind him, Kirby didn't move – stunned, terrified.

Larsen collapsed to the floor at the end of the bed.

Cronje stood there, peering down at a man he'd spent the early part of his life idolising. Now he was pathetic. Pale. Overweight.

Dying.

Larsen grunted, blood specking his face.

'You're a godless piece of shit,' Cronje said.

Larsen grunted again, and then a hint of a smile broke across his bloodied lips. He lifted his head. 'You've still got no idea,' he said, his words wet, slurred.

Cronje took a step closer. 'What?'

'You've *still* got no idea what I did.'

'*What?*

Larsen's smile became even bigger.

Cronje glanced at Kirby. 'What's he talking about?'

'I don't know,' Kirby sobbed, scuttling further back across the bed, frightened, confused, dragging the sheet with him. Cronje could see he was telling the truth.

Whatever Larsen was talking about, he'd never told anyone else.

'What do you mean, what you did?' Cronje said to Larsen.

'This isn't the only secret I kept from you.'

Cronje dropped to his haunches. 'What?'

Larsen smiled again.

'What do you *mean*?'

But by then it was too late.

Martin Larsen was dead.

77

Five days after the events at The Castle, the family of Jennifer Johnson organized a service of remembrance at a church in Peterborough.

Both her mother and her father had passed on – her father when she was still alive; her mother in 2014 – so it was left to one of Jennifer's cousins to arrange.

'Jennifer was a good person,' he said. 'She didn't deserve what happened.'

The service was a way to honour her memory, to remind the world what Jennifer brought into this life. I told him he was doing a good thing, but afterwards all I could think about was the fact that no one in the case, except perhaps for Jacobus Cronje, deserved what had happened to them: not Fiona, not Kian Bauer, and not his mother or the thirty-five other faces on the wall of the cellar whose families were only now finding out the truth about what had happened.

As I parked up outside the church, I wondered whether Rebekah would organize something similar for Fiona before she flew back to New York.

It seemed unlikely.

Originally, she'd planned to accompany me to Jennifer's service, but as we were about to leave, she told me she couldn't. She was still struggling to process everything, but I think a part of her felt like Jennifer's family would blame her for the things Fiona's affair had led to. I didn't try to persuade her, because to Rebekah it felt logical and painfully real. She was grieving. She was distressed. Most of all, she was angry. Even if she knew the reason her mother had walked out on them all, she had to deal with something else now: Fiona had been cheating on her father.

And she'd been doing it with a monster.

The service was well attended. I spotted Catherine Vance two rows ahead of me, and then bumped into Rob Hawlings as we were making our way out. Tom Brenner was there too. During the service, he sat with Vance, the two of them bonded by the experiences they'd shared in that cellar, and then – after I'd spoken to Jennifer's family and had made my way back to the car – I found them both waiting for me in the car park, standing next to Vance's battered Golf. If the circumstances hadn't been so tragic, the moment could have been comical: all of us looked like we'd just stumbled out of a boxing ring.

I shook hands with Tom and introduced myself properly.

He thanked me for rescuing them.

'I'm not sure I did much in the way of rescuing,' I said.

'You tried to stop him,' he replied. 'That was something.'

I asked him how his son was doing.

'He's doing okay. I think he likes all the attention he's getting, and he definitely likes the "get well soon" presents that keep arriving.' He smiled. 'He will be fine. Kids are so resilient. I think it's his dad who will probably struggle more.'

'It'll be hard for a while.'

He could see I was speaking from experience, reliving moments from previous cases where the fallout felt as frightening as anything that had preceded it.

'You did the right thing picking up the phone to Catherine,' I said. 'I know you probably don't think that's the case, but it is. If you hadn't made that call, Kian Bauer's family would still have no idea what happened to him; and we never would have found out the truth about what went on with his mother either.'

'He's right,' Vance said. 'Your call was important.'

'I just wish Leo hadn't had to . . .' He stopped, his voice tremoring.

Vance and I looked at each other. It was easy for us to say he'd done the right thing. We weren't there at night when he tucked his son in, when he held him so tight he never wanted to let him go. We weren't going to be there if Leo couldn't leave the horror of what had happened to him behind, if he was waking up screaming, or if the trauma manifested itself in slower, more subtle ways. We wouldn't be there inside the Brenner house at night when Leo finally went off to sleep after crying for hours and Tom looked at Sadie and – just for a second – he saw the blame in his wife's face.

I turned to Vance. 'When are you publishing?'

'I'm not sure.' She took out a pack of cigarettes. She offered them to us, and when we declined, lit one, took a long draw, and said, 'The piece is going to have to change now, given everything that's happened. The story's everywhere. The footage Tom got me to *prove* that Cronje was the killer . . .' She glanced at Tom and he seemed to shrink a little more: all that effort, all that time, the days filled with fear for himself and his family, and it was ultimately for nothing.

'You were there,' I said to her. 'I guess that's your story.'

She nodded. 'I just don't know if it's one I want to write.'

I understood.

Sometimes the stories were too personal.

'I heard Ian Kirby's co-operating.'

'Yeah. I've talked to a few people at the Met,' Vance replied. 'No one knows more than Kirby does. He'll cut a deal.'

A deal. I thought of Healy. Was that what he was busy doing right now? I didn't know, hadn't heard a thing from Parkes or from Phillips, who had threatened to come back and put me in handcuffs. I'd tried calling Parkes multiple times but she hadn't once picked up. The note she'd left for me was pinned to my fridge and, every time I looked at it, something fluttered at the back of my head. I didn't know if it was panic, or confusion, or just the overwhelming sense of drowning in a situation I had no control of. But it was there constantly, like a pulse.

'You haven't heard anything else from your end about who the second person might have been?' Vance asked.

'No. You probably know more than me.'

'Last I heard, the cops didn't have a clue.'

I glanced at Tom. 'You never got a look at the person at Seven Peaks?'

'No,' he said. 'They were wearing a mask.'

'You told the cops it was a man?'

'Yeah.'

'Based on what?'

'Just the way he moved, his strength. I was out of it. I barely even remember leaving the ride, but I have a brief memory of looking for Leo and seeing him being carried out by the other person.'

So who *was* he?

And how was I ever going to find him?

As I let my mind wander for a moment, I tried to think about the men in this case that I knew least about, and what their motivations might have been for being in that cellar. But all I really had was Ian Kirby. Cronje was dead. Larsen was dead.

And so was Mark Levin.

It still niggled at me that I knew so little about him, even now – the casework he'd done on Fiona and Jennifer was basically non-existent; he wasn't on anyone's radars, even Cronje's. I didn't know where he fit in, if he fit in at all.

I asked Vance if she'd ever heard of him.

'Levin?' She took a drag on her cigarette. 'No. Who's he?'

I explained but I could see that Levin meant nothing to her. His absence, his lack of a trail, was endemic, written into every single stage of this search, and I still had no answer for it.

But, slowly, I'd managed to build a theory about something else.

I'd wondered how Len Graves could have been so wrong about Levin and the affair he thought his friend was having with Jennifer, but now I was wondering if he might not have just misinterpreted it; that it wasn't an affair that Jennifer and Levin were engaged in, but a search for answers. I was starting to think that Jennifer might have approached Levin – a man she already knew, who she trusted and liked – and told him what she'd found out: that the Red Wolf, a killer who'd committed atrocities in South Africa, including the murder of her second cousin Mienkie Bauer, was right here in London. Levin started taking it seriously when Jennifer vanished – and even more seriously when he connected Jennifer's disappearance to Fiona's. Levin wasn't on Cronje's radar – by Cronje's own admission – so he could have got involved in searches for Fiona and Jennifer without Cronje or Larsen ever knowing, and that would have explained the blank look I got from Cronje when I mentioned Levin. But if that was the case, why was Levin such a ghost? Where was the proof he'd ever worked on Fiona's disappearance? Maybe I just had to start accepting that any work Levin did on Fiona's case was lost to time.

'I've got to go,' Vance said.

She ground her cigarette into the tarmac.

'Catherine.'

She stopped, looking across the roof of her Volkswagen at me. I thought of the pictures I'd seen at Kirby's caravan: I knew where the ones of Cronje and C9 had come from now – she'd pulled them from the national archives in South Africa – but Vance had never told Kirby why she went on to pin up photographs of Fiona and Jennifer.

'When did you first realize this started with the two women?'

'What do you mean?'

'You had Fiona and Jennifer's pictures in that caravan in Kent.'

'I had a lot of photos in there. I had yours.'

'I know. I'm guessing you had mine because Kirby came straight to you and said I'd been into The Castle asking questions.'

She nodded. 'Spot on.'

'So what about the two women? You didn't tell Kirby why they were up on that wall, or what their role in this was, but you clearly knew they were a part of it.'

'Actually, I didn't,' she said.

'I'm not sure I follow.'

'I had no idea those two women were in any way connected to Cronje until well after I started on the piece. Those photos just turned up in the post a few weeks ago.'

'Their photos were sent to you?'

'Yes.'

'Any idea who from?'

'No. But then a few days after that . . .' She trailed off and went to her mobile. She was searching for something. When she finally found it, she handed her phone to me.

Onscreen was a voice memo.

'Someone left a message for me.'

I touched Play.

The soft hiss of a silent line.

And then: '*Fiona Murphy and Jennifer Johnson. Look into them.*'

It was someone speaking through a voice changer.

78

Just as I was coming into London, my phone started ringing.

I answered, not recognising the number.

'Raker, it's Martine Parkes.'

I tried to think about the best way of playing this. I thought I could trust her, and maybe I still could; maybe she really *was* the person I hoped she was. But if I couldn't be one hundred per cent sure, I couldn't let my guard down, so I said, 'I've been leaving messages for you all week.'

'I can see that. We had a triple murder in Hackney. I basically haven't slept in four days. I have to be honest, Raker, your messages haven't been a big priority.'

'Well, luckily it's been really quiet at my end.'

'I know,' she said. 'You've been busy too. I get it.'

'I think we need to talk.'

'About?'

I frowned, thought of the note she'd left. Was she testing me? Was this the trap I'd been worried about? I had a sudden thought that the number she was calling from might be different because it was a line at the Met where they could record me; I had an image of Phillips and others in the background, poring over every word I said, searching for a slip-up, something to tie in to what Healy might have told them.

Say nothing, give nothing away.

'Raker?'

'I'm still here.'

'Where are you?' she asked.

'On my way back from Jennifer Johnson's memorial.'

'Ah yeah.' Another pause. 'Look, I'm not due back in the office until twelve, so if you want to talk, you can come here if you like. I live in Hendon.'

'You want me to come to your house?'

'It's on your way.'

I didn't know if Parkes was married or single, straight or gay, or if she had kids. I basically only knew her as a detective and I'd always assumed she'd wanted it that way.

'Okay,' I said.

Snow flurries scattered across the windscreen as she gave me the address. I cranked up the heaters. The part of me that trusted her figured Parkes must have been inviting me to her house because she wanted to talk to me away from the office – and away from Phillips – about the note she'd left for me. The part of me that didn't was worried this was a subtle attempt to get me to drop my guard in an environment that wasn't a police interview room.

Soon, though, my thoughts shifted again.

Another call was coming through.

'I'm going to have to go,' I said to her.

'Sure. I'll see you in a bit.'

I switched to the next call. It was Rob Hawlings. I'd only just seen him at the memorial service.

'Is everything okay?' I asked him.

'I'm back in the office.' There was a seriousness to his tone that instantly set me on edge. 'I didn't mention anything before because I wanted to get confirmation before I discussed it, but . . .' He trailed off. 'Do you know much about Georgie Levin?'

The question threw me. 'As in, Mark Levin's wife?'

'Yes.'

'Not really,' I said. 'I've only met her once. Why?'

'We set up a tip line for anyone who might have something they want to share on Cronje, and one of our guys has been going through the numbers that have called in. It appears that Georgie Levin has phoned us four times in the past two days and hung up every time without leaving a message.'

'I'm guessing you've tried calling her back?'

'The number she's been calling from isn't her own. The only reason we know it's her making those calls is because we phoned the number she's been dialling from and the person we talked to said it's a guest phone and she's the only guest they've got.'

'A guest? So she's staying at a hotel?'

'A B&B.' Hawlings paused. 'In Cheddar.'

'Somerset?'

'Yes.' Hawlings paused, the hush heavy, weighted with something. 'The B&B is three miles from the quarry that Cronje and Larsen dumped those bodies in.'

There was a deafening silence on the line now. What would Georgie be doing down there? And why had she tried to call the police so many times?

'There's something else,' Hawlings said. 'We got more DNA results back for the bodies in the quarry – not just for Larsen this time.'

'And?'

'It's Jennifer Johnson, Martin Larsen and Kian Bauer.'

I waited. Hawlings didn't say anything.

'But not Fiona?'

'No. We don't know who the fourth body belongs to. All we know is that it definitely isn't Fiona Murphy.'

79

The fourth body wasn't Fiona, Georgie Levin was only three miles from the quarry in Somerset, and she'd consistently tried to call the police over the last few days.

Something big was coming.

But first I had to deal with Parkes, Phillips and Healy.

The front door opened before I even got a chance to knock. Martine Parkes was dressed in a pair of running leggings and an oversized hoodie. She led me along the hallway to a kitchen at the back of the house. As I followed her, I glanced at some photos on the wall, running up the diagonal line of the stairs. It looked as if she was married – there were lots of photos of her and a guy in his forties – but there were no pictures of any kids. I didn't see any siblings either; just her with her parents.

'Do you want something to drink?' she asked.

'I'm fine. What's going on, Parkes?'

She filled a glass with water; made me wait.

'Healy's getting out this afternoon.'

I tried not to show any reaction, because I didn't know if she was watching for one, still didn't know for sure if the note she'd left for me was genuine or an attempt by her and Phillips to corner me. Instead, I casually pulled out a chair. My knees felt like they were going to buckle. I looked at her, as if the news was unimportant to me. But, inside, all I could feel was panic.

There was only one way Healy was getting out so fast.

'I went in to speak to him five days ago.' She took another drink, but her eyes stayed on me. 'He told me everything. I mean literally the whole thing: everything you and him have done since his "death" – the dodgy IDs you organized for him, the places you've hidden him, how he faked those DNA results – and how you lied to the police about it all.'

I tried to think what to say but my head was on fire. I didn't even know where to look, my eyes shifting from Parkes to the debris of the kitchen table: place mats, utensils, paperwork. On a gas bill addressed to her husband, one of them had written, *Sorry, didn't get a chance to call them about this.*

Suddenly, it all seemed so mundane compared to what Parkes was telling me.

'You're in the shit, Raker. The stuff you did . . .'

I tried again to clear my head. Where was my exit?

How the hell could I get out of this?

'If any of what Healy told me gets out, you're toast.'

She could see what had registered with me: *if* any of this got out. She put her glass down, turned it slowly on the countertop.

'You didn't think it was a little weird that I asked you to come to my house rather than hauling you into the station?'

I didn't say anything.

Was she being genuine?

Or was this the trap I'd feared?

I glanced across my shoulder, back along the hallway. She seemed to know what I was thinking and said, 'It's just you and me here.'

'What are you doing, Parkes?'

'What does it *look* like I'm doing?'

'That's the problem: I don't know.'

'Phillips can't see the bigger picture any more,' she said.

Phillips. I still couldn't shake the idea that it was a set-up by them both.

'And what's the bigger picture?'

'His police work . . .' She shook her head. 'It's been off. He's not leading like he should be, he's not making good decisions. Since Healy turned up, he's become so obsessed that he's getting sloppy. I'm spending my days trying to catch you two in a lie while people out there are actually, genuinely suffering. This triple murder I'm dealing with this week, I can't stay focused on it. I've got Phillips in my ear every five minutes. My SIO on these murders absolutely bollocked me yesterday for something I should never have missed and it's Phillips's fault. I *told* my SIO it's Phillips's fault – that Phillips is just using me because I managed to build a rapport with you and Healy after the Blackbird case – but Phillips is a DSU, so my boss just shrugs. All of this, it's pulling me away from the things that actually matter, like those murders.'

She pressed her lips together, frustrated, annoyed.

'So, yeah, I went in there and I spoke to Healy and he told me everything. And I imagine hearing that really pisses you off, especially given how you've gone out to bat for him, but he's between a rock and a hard place in there. If he didn't find an exit fast, he wasn't leaving prison alive.'

'So now you're Healy's cheerleader?'

'No. I'm just telling you the truth.'

'The truth?'

'Yeah.'

'And what's that?'

'The case against you two is dead.' She stopped, watched me. 'All of this, it's over.'

I didn't move, didn't speak.

'I mean it.'

'How can it be over if Healy told you everything?'

'Because Phillips has been backed into a corner.'

'Meaning what?'

'Meaning he's not going forward with the case against you.'

I stared at her in disbelief.

'It's true,' she said. 'But before I say anything else, we need to establish some ground rules.' Her expression altered; became harder to read. 'Everything I say to you from here on in – in fact, everything you've heard since you got here – stays inside these walls.' She held up a hand, cutting me off before I could even think about replying. 'You talk about *any* of what I'm going to tell you, and I promise you what Healy said to me ends up on a desk at the

Met, and some time after that, he goes back to prison and you go with him.'

'What are you –'

'I haven't finished yet. The reason Phillips has given up trying to bring you two down is because Phillips had a sudden . . .' She paused, searching for the right words.

'A sudden change of heart?'

She smiled. 'Exactly.'

'What did you do?'

'Phillips is a bit of a poster boy in the Met. All the higher-ups, they think he's God's gift to policing. He's clever, he's got an incredible track record of arrests, he's good with people – he inspires, he cares. It helps that he's nice to look at and has that beautiful accent too.'

'But?'

'*But* it's a façade. Behind the façade, he's a little less perfect.'

'Meaning what?'

'He split up from his wife a couple of years back.'

'So?'

'So have a guess as to why they split.'

'Did he cheat?'

'Worse.'

I eyed her. 'Did he hurt her?'

'Bingo. They hadn't been getting on – they *really* hadn't been getting on – and he got home late one night from work, pent-up, stressed, and he and his wife got into a shouting match. Like, apocalyptic. And Poster Boy, he lashes out. I don't think he has any real history of abuse, but once is once too much, especially when he then has to drive her to hospital to get her head stitched up. She did him a favour and didn't tell the doctors the truth, but she *did* tell her sister. And her sister sent Phillips an email to explain what a piece of shit he was.'

'And you got hold of the email.'

'Yes.'

'How?'

Her face hardened. 'Why do you look so pissed off with me,

David? I'm doing you and Healy a favour here. I put an anonymous note in the top drawer of Phillips's desk recounting what happened, what he did to his wife, and told him that, if he didn't want the world to see that email, he should drop the entire investigation into you and Healy. That's why he hasn't been back to your house to deliver on his promise of putting you in handcuffs.'

'He probably thinks I'm behind this.'

'He does. But would you rather go to jail?'

'You really didn't tell him *anything* Healy told you?'

'No.'

'And you've done this for me, why?'

This time, she didn't respond.

'Parkes?'

As I watched her, I tried to gather my thoughts, tried to forge a path into this mess and back out again. Yet nothing here made sense. I glanced at the table for a second time, at the detritus, at the gas bill, the scribbled note on it – *Sorry, didn't get a chance to call them about this* – just to try and buy myself a second to think.

And, this time, something stopped me.

I leaned in closer to the gas bill, to the words written at the top of it. *Sorry, didn't get a chance to call them about this.*

Sorry. About.

Everything in the room dropped away.

Sorry. About.

I was sorry to hear about Mike.

I was sorry to hear about your dad.

I was sorry to hear the news about John.

The same *sorry*.

The same *about*.

The same handwriting as in Rebekah's condolence cards.

80

I held up the gas bill, stunned. '*You* wrote those cards?'

'Shit,' Parkes said. 'Sometimes I forget how clever you are.'

'Wha— *Why?*'

Something played behind her eyes like a film – a memory, an answer, a plan. But all I could do was stare at the gas bill, at the *a*'s in *get a chance*, in *call*, in *about*, and remember what I'd uncovered – using the pencil – on the card that had been pushed under Rebekah's hotel room door: *VC4732-a*.

The code for the voice changer.

The *a*'s were the same; every one had the same flourish on the tail and was written by the same hand. And there was something else too, the thing that had been pulsing at the back of my head ever since Parkes left the note at my house, ever since I'd pinned it to my fridge: *he's bluffing*. I thought the thing that was bugging me had something to do with Healy, or with Phillips. But it wasn't that. It was the handwriting. It hadn't just been the *a*'s. It was also that the *he* in *he's* was exactly the same as the *he* in *Sorry to hear*.

'You're the second person,' I said.

She didn't react, just looked at me.

'You're a *killer*.'

Again, she said nothing.

And now the room was absolutely silent.

Time seemed to have stopped.

'*Parkes?* Say something.'

'I've been a killer for a while,' she said, quietly.

'You've killed before?'

'I killed for my country.'

I studied her. 'You were a soldier?'

'I joined the army at eighteen.'

Tom Brenner – sedated, almost unconscious – had been convinced that the second person at Seven Peaks had been a man – and I'd taken him at his word.

In his drugged state, Tom had watched Parkes perfectly echoing Cronje's skillset and physicality, his efficiency, strength and sense of purpose, and he'd made an assumption. It was unconscious bias – not helped by his confusion – where he'd defaulted to a stereotype buried somewhere deep at the back of his head about the military and men. But the second person hadn't been a man. It had been a woman every bit as good as Cronje. Maybe even better. After all, Parkes was alive. Cronje was in the morgue.

'I had a happy childhood – my parents gave me everything – but something was always missing from my life: a sibling, a best friend, *something*. It was this hole inside me and I thought the army – the camaraderie, the sense of belonging, those intense bonds soldiers forge in combat – would fill that hole. My parents were . . .' A hint of a smile. 'They were shocked. Mostly, they were frightened, especially when I got shipped out to Afghanistan. I worked as a Female Engagement Officer in Helmand; talking to the local population, trying to get the women in the villages to trust me. I learned the language, I went into their homes. But that place was just *relentlessly* hostile. It didn't matter where you were, you were constantly looking over your shoulder. It was inevitable I was going to have to fire a gun.' Her eyes went to the kitchen table, to the gas bill in my hand, and then back to me. 'You might not know this, but in July 2008, a soldier called Chantelle Taylor became the first woman in the British Army to kill an enemy in combat. Firsts are always big moments. After that, people stop counting. It's why no one ever talks about the fifth woman to kill an enemy combatant in Afghanistan.'

Parkes was the fifth.

'Killing seems to have become pretty easy for you,' I said.

She shook her head. 'No.'

'You didn't hesitate with Cronje.'

'Cronje was a fucking monster.'

'He should have –'

She held up a hand, stopping me dead. 'If it's all the same to you, I don't want to hear about your idealistic fairy-tale world where everyone – regardless of what they've done – deserves to face justice. No one will miss that man.'

It was hard to argue with the last part, but what Parkes didn't seem to realize was that – with Cronje dead – thirty-six families were still never going to get the whole truth about what had happened to their loved ones.

I glanced at the gas bill, at her handwriting.

I had so many questions, I didn't even know what to ask first. 'Why did you send those cards to Rebekah?'

'Because she'd lost people she loved.'

'Don't bullshit me, Parkes.'

'I'm not.'

'She lives on the other side of the *world* from you.'

'I know where she lives, David. I mailed those cards to her.'

We stared at each other.

'Enough,' I said. 'How do you know Rebekah?'

'I don't.'

But there was something else this time.

And a second later, it clicked.

I turned in my seat and looked back down the hallway, back to the walls full of photographs I'd passed on my way in. Closest to me was a shot of Parkes with what must have been her mum. I hadn't noticed it on the way in, hadn't really thought to look – but now I saw it lucidly.

And, as I did, a second, dizzying realisation struck me.

'Fiona Murphy is my mother,' Parkes said.

81

I stared at her, stunned into silence for a second time.

'I know,' she said. 'It's a lot to take in.'

She moved past me, into the hallway, and took one of the photo frames off the wall, then brought it back to the table. It was a picture of her and what I now recognized as a much older Fiona. It couldn't have been more than five years old. Fiona was in her early sixties.

Now I knew why her body wasn't in the Mendips with the others.

'She's still alive,' I said.

'She was until eighteen months ago.'

I glanced at Parkes.

'That was taken just before she got sick again.' She swallowed, her jaw tight, a flash in her eyes.

'What happened?' I asked.

'Cancer.'

It was definitely Fiona: an older, greyer version of the woman whose picture I'd studied on repeat over the course of the last week.

'I didn't know her as Fiona until a few years before she died.'

'What did you know her as?'

'Holly. In 1985, she organized a new identity, a new driver's licence, a new passport. She said she went through a wild stage in her late teens – drink, drugs, sex. She got to know some dodgy people, I guess, and those were the people that helped organize her fake documents. It was easier to fake a passport and driving licence back then – nothing was electronic. Passports were just paper with a plastic cover.'

'Who was your dad?'

'His name was Richard Parkes.'

'And they met when?'

'Nineteen eighty-seven.'

Two years after Fiona had walked out on the Murphys.

I tried to still the pace of my thoughts but all I could think about was Rebekah. She was at home dealing with the idea that her mother had been murdered, crushed by the knowledge that her father had been cheated on – and now the rug was being pulled out from under her again.

'So Fiona told you all about Rebekah?'

'Yes,' Parkes said. 'That case you had back in the summer – the Blackbird – it wasn't just coincidence that I ended up on it. I *asked* for it. Mum began opening up a bit when she first got sick and told me about the family she'd left; the more sick she got, the more came out. It continued like that until, about two years ago – after cancer round three – she *really* started to go downhill and she finally told me the complete truth: Henry, Johnny, Rebekah, Mike – and everything before it. I had two brothers and a sister I never knew – and now most of them I'll never *get* to know.'

Johnny was dead.

So were Henry and Mike.

All that was left was Rebekah.

'So I started looking into them, and – after Mum died last year – Rebekah was suddenly in the news.' Parkes was referring to the days and weeks after Rebekah had been left for dead in a place called Crow Island, an enclave off the coast of New York state. She'd been attacked, an attack that had given her the scar on her face. 'I started collecting all this stuff on her that appeared in the media about it – newspaper clippings; YouTube videos and news reports; the few interviews she did after. I didn't know what I was going to do with it all exactly, but it helped me know her better. And then I read about Frank Travis, about how him and Rebekah had grown close, and I saw that he was NYPD. And then I started to think to myself, "She's a survivor, she's smart and tough. Now she's got a friend that's a cop. Cops have resources. They can open doors."'

'You guessed she'd eventually come looking for Fiona.'

'Yes,' Parkes said. 'Looking for answers.'

She paused again, watching me. It seemed as if she was waiting for me to catch up. And then I did.

'You were the one that put a flag on the system,' I said.

'Yes.'

Letitia Scargill and I had assumed it was Cronje, using someone in the Met he'd compromised.

'I wanted to know when she arrived in the country. I wanted to know if she called ahead.' She glanced at the photograph of her and Fiona. 'And then it happened, just as I thought it might. Back in the summer, Frank Travis phoned the Met, asking about the Fiona Murphy disappearance. He was obviously doing Rebekah a favour, attempting to get her some answers. As soon as he called, the system alerted me. And so I called him back a few days later, trying to find out what he was planning, pretending I was following up on the conversation he'd had. I basically wanted to see if Rebekah was coming to England. I didn't know what I was going to do if she did, didn't know if I would even seek her out, let alone tell her the truth, I just . . .' She paused. 'A part of me didn't want to know her. Another part of me so *desperately* did. I admired Rebekah, the things I'd read about her. In some ways, I thought we were similar. Anyway, on the call Travis made to the Met, he mentioned your name.'

'Me?'

'He said you and Rebekah had met in New York.'

We had, back in May. A chance meeting, where the two of us had simply struck up a conversation in Bryant Park. That was where she'd first taken my business card.

'And that was why you made sure, a few months later, that you were on the Blackbird case,' I said.

'Yes,' she replied. 'I wanted to meet you. I wanted to be in your orbit if Rebekah ever came here and hired you. The part of me that was desperate to know her wanted to find out the truth about my mum, the other side of the story. I mean, I loved Mum, don't get me wrong. She was amazing. I get the feeling that she was everything to me that she couldn't be to Rebekah, Johnny and Mike. I think, in a way, I was her shot at redemption. She didn't get to do it right with them. She did with me.'

She took a moment, eyeing the kitchen table again.

'I bought the condolence cards from a cancer survivors' group that I took Mum to the first time she got sick,' she said. 'Mike was killed in that car crash a few months after she was diagnosed for a second time. I'd been keeping an eye on them all ever since she told me about the family she'd had, and when my Google alert pinged and I read about his death online, when I told Mum about it, she got very upset. I hadn't really seen her that emotional before. She was in chemo again, struggling to write, exhausted all the time, so I sent a card on her behalf. By the time Henry died, the cancer had come back a third time and she'd been told she was terminal. She sort of gave up in her last year. I told her about Henry and, on one of the few good days she had during those last months, we sent a card for him, with the same sort of message in it.' She shrugged. 'Those cards were made by a woman that volunteered in the survivors' group, so I knew no one would ever be able to trace them. Like I say, it was weird. I wanted Rebekah – and Johnny, when he was alive – to know me, but the idea scared me too. I guess that's why I made those cards so anonymous. And I guess it's why the very second Rebekah spotted me in her hotel the other day, watching her through my laptop camera, I bolted.'

'So who's in that quarry if it's not Fiona?' I asked.

'I don't know.'

'You don't know who that body belongs to?'

'No.'

I studied the picture of Fiona again. But when my gaze returned to Parkes, her expression had changed. Less distant, more focused.

She came to the table, eyes on it again.

'So now you know those condolence cards came from me,' she said, reaching down below the table. Underneath was a thin drawer, built into the underside. She placed a hand on the knob, held it there, looking at her fingers, at me. 'And so did everything else.'

She pulled open the drawer.

'I sent those photographs of Mum and Jennifer Johnson to

Catherine Vance. And I left that message on Vance's voicemail telling her their names.'

Inside the drawer was the voice changer.

Next to that was a gun.

I saw where this was going now.

'So this is the *actual* deal you want to make.'

'Yes,' she said. 'The Met never get to find out about what Healy and you have been up to for the last seven years – and you don't tell them that I was the second person in the cellar.'

'Why would you even want to make this deal? I wasn't close to figuring out you were in that cellar.' I lifted up the gas bill. 'Not until I saw this.'

'I think you're being modest, David. I realized after I left you that note about Phillips that I made a mistake. I only thought about it after – how the *he* on the note and on the cards would be the same – and by then it was too late. You had the cards. You had the note. I shouldn't have given Rebekah that last card either.'

'The *Welcome home* one?'

'Yes.'

'So why did you?'

'I don't know. Maybe because, for the first time, she was physically so close; all the times Mum had talked about her, it was like Rebekah was a story, not a reality, some ephemeral figure on the other side of the world. But then, suddenly, she was here, she was real. Plus, I wrote that card before it had clocked with me that the handwriting might get me found. At that stage, I'd sent three cards and no one had a clue where they'd come from. In my head, a fourth didn't matter. But then when I realized it *did* matter, the panic hit me because I knew details – *small* details – have always been your thing. It's written into every case you ever had. And then when I heard that the code for that voice changer was imprinted in the card, I knew it was giving you even more to work with. That *a* in the code was something *else* that matched. My *a*'s are so distinctive. I can see that now. And I knew, given time, you'd connect all the dots.' We looked at each other. 'I'm right, aren't I?'

'I wasn't there yet.'

'But it was coming.'

I nodded. I thought again of the pulsing at the back of my head every time I looked at the words *he's bluffing*. Parkes was right: I hadn't matched the writing on the note to the writing in the condolence cards – but I'd have got there eventually.

She pushed the drawer closed again, as if she didn't want to have to look at what was inside any longer. 'Like I say, Mum told me everything at the end.' Pain flickered across Parkes's face. 'Before that, she'd told me about the family she walked out on, but not why to start with, just that she was in a bad place psychologically, emotionally. When she was in remission, she kind of closed up again. I'd try to bring it up, but she'd always shut me down. But at the end, it just poured out of her like a flood.'

'Did your dad know?'

'About her life as Fiona Murphy?' Parkes shook her head. 'No.'

'So why did she tell you and not him?'

'Because I'm good at keeping secrets. I kept them in the army, saw things that I've never talked about, and never want to. And when I got back, and I joined the police, when I became a detective . . .' She faded out. 'Most of my work I never bring home. If you let that stuff fester, it kills you.'

That same flicker again, and then an overwhelming sadness. She didn't want to be a vessel for all this misery. But she was all the same.

'When she got told she was terminal, she started telling me about her childhood, her mum dying when she was only a kid, her dad being a drunk, going to live with Jonah Carling, the years when she was in the wilderness, rebelling, and then meeting Henry and starting a family.' She went to her pocket and removed something. It was another photograph. She handed it to me.

It was a shot of Fiona with Johnny, Rebekah and Mike. Mike was newborn, his tiny body swaddled, Fiona holding him in the crook of her arm. On one knee was Rebekah, barely two years of age; at her leg, holding her hand, was Johnny, four.

'First time she showed me this picture, she just burst into tears. It was the one and only photograph she had of them.'

'She took it with her?'

'No. She'd left it on her mother's grave a few weeks before that Boxing Day she walked out, but she went back and got it in the days after she disappeared.'

'What happened to Fiona?' I asked.

'What happened?' Parkes adjusted the photograph of her mother with her half-siblings, her eyes lingering on Rebekah. 'Something completely unexpected.'

82

'They lured Mum out using Jennifer,' Parkes said. 'You heard that part in the cellar. Mum went to a house a few streets away. That's why she didn't take anything with her. She thought she was just popping out for a couple of minutes. She said she got to the house and saw that it was boarded up. By the time alarm bells started going off, it was already too late.'

'Why?'

'Martin Larsen was waiting there for her.'

I remembered what Cronje had told me in the cellar: Larsen had taken care of Fiona because Cronje couldn't face doing it himself. He knew Fiona had to go. He accepted her fate. But he didn't know if he could pull the trigger himself.

'Larsen drove her out of London, into the countryside. When he got far enough out, he pulled over and said to her, "No one can know what I'm about to do, *especially* Cronje. He will kill me, and he will kill you, and he will kill your family. So if you ever go back to your husband and your kids, if you ever talk about this, if you ever mention Cronje, or me, if your name ever comes up on the radar anywhere, at any time, I will hunt you down and I will put a bullet in the back of your head myself. I will kill your family."' Parkes blinked; looked at me. This was what Ian Kirby had told Hawlings in his interviews; it was what Larsen had said to Cronje in the last moments of his life: *You've still got no idea what I did.* He was baiting Cronje, dangling another secret in front of him as revenge for the knife Cronje had just plunged into his stomach.

The secret had been Fiona Murphy.

'She saved Henry, Rebekah, Johnny and Mike,' Parkes said. A bleak, prolonged silence. 'If she'd gone back to them – and you have no idea how desperate she was to do that, how many times down the years she thought about it – they were dead. She saved their lives – and they never even knew it.'

'But why the hell would Larsen let her go?'

'He told her he was tired of all the death. Cronje was still at war in his head, with everyone, always. Larsen had moved on. He was living his next life.'

Free to be who he wanted to be.

He was a killer – and not only in war – and his decisions in that moment couldn't ever exonerate him of his crimes. But at the very least he'd drawn a line in the sand. In seven decades on this earth, Cronje had never drawn a line anywhere.

'Why did she even *start* the affair with Cronje?'

'I don't think she even really knew. She just said, back then, she had this part of her that would . . . it would just implode. I think when she felt too boxed in – too constrained by her circumstances – she'd push back and, more often than not, ruin everything good. And she ruined that part of her life: she left her kids behind, a husband who – from all she described – was a good man. It left scars. Then finding out the truth about Cronje, his history, what he was . . . I mean, if you don't regret that, you're not normal.'

'I don't understand what she saw in Cronje.'

'I know,' Parkes said. 'I asked her the same thing. She said he was quiet, but he was intelligent, intense, really listened to her when she talked. He was handsome too. Mostly, though, I think they saw a little of themselves in each other. They had some of the same damage from their childhoods. At the end, Mum couldn't really articulate very well, but I think, in those few, tiny moments in the cellar, when you were asking him about his father, and he was telling you about when he first met Mum, maybe *that* was the person that she felt drawn to.'

The person inside the monster.

'When I told you in that cellar that we'd never met before, it was a form of the truth. You've met Martine Parkes. You haven't met Hannah Martine Riley. Parkes is my maiden name. Martine is the name I've always been known by because there were tons of

Hannahs at my school and I wanted to be different. So most people in the Met have no idea that my real name isn't Martine Parkes. But if you look on that member list, Hannah Riley is there. She joined The Castle a year ago.'

'You joined The Castle? Why?'

'To get close to Cronje. Or as close as I could. He was a killer. He'd got away with it. I wanted to see this man that Mum had fallen for, ruined a marriage for, abandoned three kids for. He needed to be stopped and his crimes needed to be exposed. No one else was going to do it. But if I let him live after, the first thing he'd tell the cops was that I'd been working with him.'

Working with him, helping him – just like she had at Seven Peaks.

'Did he know Fiona was your mum?'

'No. I knew he would do a background on me but he never went deep enough into my family history to see photographs of Mum, so he never realized Fiona Murphy was now called Holly Parkes. Mum's new identity was solid. It had held up for years. And, anyway, like I say, Cronje wouldn't have gone that deep: by the time I joined The Castle, Mum was already dead. I don't imagine he looked twice in that direction.'

She leaned back in her chair, eyes distant.

'Was The Castle where you got to know Letitia Scargill?'

'No, I knew her from before. We were constables at the same time. She didn't even know I was a member at The Castle because *Martine Parkes* was never on any list and I was never really *at* the club. But, one night, we had a few glasses of wine and she started telling me about her sister, and about a guy who was blackmailing her at the club. She didn't name Cronje, but I knew it was him. I just knew it. So I told her I was interested in a man called Jacobus Cronje – who I believed was associated with the club – because I thought he'd killed a woman called Jennifer Johnson in 1985. And that was when she told me it was Cronje blackmailing her.'

'So you and she were working together?'

'In a loose sort of a way, yeah. I didn't know the full extent of what she was doing for him. I didn't know that he'd ordered her to follow you to Cambridge, or that it was his idea for her to call me from the train. I just figured she got in touch because I'd talked to her about my investigation into you and Healy. That was the thing with Letitia: she wanted out, she wanted to be free of him, but she was just too scared to cut the cord.'

'Did she know you were going to kill Cronje?'

'We didn't talk about it specifically but she was smart. She knew she wasn't going to be free unless Cronje was out of the picture. She was in a bind with her sister, and because of that she was doing a lot of work for Cronje – getting a close-up view of him. Without actually saying it aloud, we both realized we could use that. Letitia had always had a theory that Cronje was a soldier, and I knew if she could get me in a room with him that I could get him to trust me. He and I had both served. I was disciplined, I knew how to carry out a mission. And so that was what happened. She couldn't cut the cord herself, so she let me do it instead. She introduced us and once I told him my real name, as well as the name I used at work, he started to let me in, because he thought he had everything he needed on me. I built trust through that and by giving him things that were useful – ways in to the Met, things that he could use that weren't going to blow up big, or cost anyone their lives, but useful bits of intel; cops with pressure points. In return, he did some digging for me.'

It took me a second to understand – and then it clicked.

'Oh,' I said. 'He was the one that found the email Phillips's sister-in-law wrote; the one she sent to Phillips when he hit his wife. Cronje was how you got hold of it.'

'Yes,' Parkes said. 'I knew I could use that email to cut the investigation into you and Healy off at the knees. In return, Cronje asked me to go to Seven Peaks with him and help bring the Brenners in.'

'An exchange.'

'As much of an exchange as Cronje would ever agree to, yeah.'

That was why Parkes ended things that night in the wine cellar. She finally had Cronje cornered. She had him confessing. But there was no way she could let him out of that place alive afterwards, especially when – at the end – he put two and two together and realized it was her, watching from the shadows behind us. He knew too much about her, and *she* knew that one of the first things the Met would do after it was over was start digging into which cops at The Castle were compromised.

'Did you get rid of your file at The Castle?'

'Yes. I took it off the shelves in the cellar. I deleted my entry off the system. If the Met really go digging around in my financial records, they'll see direct debits for the club under my real name – but they won't go digging because I'm not a suspect.'

'So you're clean?'

A hint of irritation. 'No one comes out of this clean, David. *Life* isn't clean. *You're* not clean. In fact, you and Healy are the very definition of *un*clean.'

'Your plan got Letitia Scargill killed.'

'Your plan put Healy in the hospital.'

The two of us just looked at one another. Maybe she was right. Maybe I really was some kind of reflection of her – doing terrible things for what I thought were the right reasons. That was something that was only going to pull into focus further down the line when the dust had settled on this case.

But I still felt betrayed by Parkes, even though her actions were ultimately going to get Healy and me away from the mess we'd created. She wasn't the person I'd thought she was, so perhaps it was simply that my pride was hurt, a failure on my part to see the truth about who she was.

Or maybe it was something else.

Maybe it was that there was no happy ending here.

Parkes could simply accept that fact and move on, because her whole adult life was a series of beginnings and ends, of unhappy, unfiltered finales, of death and pain, of brief lulls filled with respectful observance, before she moved on to the next battle.

Mine wasn't.

It took me much longer to bury the things that hurt me.

'I think we're done,' she said finally.

I watched her return to the counter. She went to a drawer at the end of one of the kitchen cabinets, and removed something from it.

An envelope.

'I need you to do one last thing for me,' she said.

PART NINE

The Last Goodbye

83

It snowed the day Rebekah flew back to New York.

I got up early, my sleep still broken, the Fiona Murphy case – what I'd found out, how it had concluded – a permanent fixture in my head. I couldn't subdue it, the images, the sounds, built on the pain of families I knew were never going to get the answers they deserved. Rob Hawlings had told me they were co-ordinating with the South African authorities, but so many of the faces on that wall were tortured, killed and buried by Jacobus Cronje alone. He preferred working by himself once he got them back to the farm. He preferred dealing with the bodies afterwards, because he knew it would be done properly. The other cops who'd served in the C9 unit, and who'd given evidence at the TRC hearings, could, in theory, put search teams in the general area of where the bodies were buried; it's just that area was three times the size of Wales, and most of the bodies had been in the ground for over forty years. Memories dulled over time. Wind and heat, storms and droughts, changed the topography of the land.

If they found even one body, it would be a miracle.

Rebekah's flight wasn't until 5 p.m., so I left her at home to pack and took the Tube to Paddington. From there, I walked the rest of the way to Georgie Levin's house, snow coming down, rooftops and pavements covered, London like a different city.

The day before, Rob Hawlings had pulled Georgie in for an interview after she'd got back from Somerset. Hawlings had called me later and explained that Georgie had seen all the coverage about The Castle, had remembered that Mark had been a member there, and had then decided to call the police to find out if there was any information about Mark, about why he'd been so different in those last few weeks of his life, and why he'd started drinking again. She'd wanted to know whether any of it had anything to do with the man the media was talking about: Jacobus Cronje. But then, every time she'd called the tip line, she'd started to worry she was wasting the police's time, so kept losing her courage and hanging up.

I sensed there could be more, and it felt like Hawlings believed there might be too, and I wondered if half the reason he'd called me was because he wanted me to take a shot at trying to speak to Georgie myself.

'She mentioned that she thought you were "nice".'

I smiled. 'And you're not?'

'Oh, I'm the nicest person in the world,' Hawlings joked, 'but believe it or not, some people get a bit shy around the police.'

'All right. I'll pop round and see her.'

'I appreciate it.'

'Any more on the identity of the fourth body?'

'They're much older remains. Maybe as much as three or four decades older, which would put their death somewhere between the forties and sixties. There's no sign of trauma to the skeleton, and during the fifties and sixties that quarry was known as a suicide spot. Given that, we're pretty certain the fourth body is unrelated to this.'

'What about Cronje's real name?'

He'd only become Cronje at eighteen, trading his family name – his father's name – for something new. It was a small detail, but it was a detail that mattered.

'The South Africans got back to us this morning,' Hawlings said. 'We believe his birth name was Henrik Visser and, as he told you, he was born in the town of Graaff-Reinet. We think the month and year of his birth is August 1954.'

'Do we know if he's killed anyone else?'

'There's DNA all over that desk in the cellar,' Hawlings replied, and I recalled the dents and breaks in it, the evidence of violence. 'We think at least one set of DNA belongs to a former member of The Castle who's been missing since 2009. We suspect the same will be true of others. Cronje wasn't killing on an industrial scale like he was in South Africa, but it looks like he was still making people disappear when they became a problem for him and the club. It's just a question of where he put the bodies.'

'They're not in the quarry?'

'They might be. It's big. We're sending dive teams in again tomorrow.'

I wasn't sure what I'd been expecting to feel at the point that Cronje's real identity was finally dragged into the light – but it felt like it should have been more than this. All the death he'd inflicted, all the suffering, and in the end, Henrik Visser, like Jacobus Cronje, like Gary Holt, was just another shadow to hide in.

In the end, it was exactly as they said.

The devil had many names.

84

Georgie Levin opened the door, snow flittering into her hallway.

'Oh hello, David,' she said, and invited me in.

It was warm, the heating cranked up. She made us both a cup of tea and then brought it through to the living room, along with a couple of Danish pastries. 'I didn't know what you liked,' she said, waving a hand at the plate, her voice hoarse.

'Are you all right, Georgie?'

'Yes. Just a little cold, I think.' She dabbed a handkerchief to her nose, and then slid back into her chair. 'I've been reading about all that business at The Castle,' she said quietly. 'It sounds terrible. I'm glad to see you're okay.'

I smiled; pointed to my face. 'Mostly.'

'That looks nasty.'

'Nothing a Danish pastry won't sort.' I picked one up and popped it on to a side plate. 'Rob Hawlings said you'd been in to speak to him.'

'Yes.'

She went on to explain about the aborted calls she'd made, repeating the same story she'd given Hawlings.

'What were you doing down in Somerset?' I asked.

'I have a friend down there. She's in a retirement home now, which is why I was staying in that B&B, and when I saw everything on the news . . .' She moved her cup on its saucer. 'I don't know. I just thought that by going down there maybe I might find some closure.'

'Closure?'

'About Mark.' She eyed me. 'I remember him joining that club.'

'You didn't want to join with him?'

Her lips flattened. 'He never really asked.'

.There was something in her face now.

'I read in the newspaper about Fiona Murphy – you know, the one you were asking me about when you came to visit before. I read about that other girl too – Jennifer Johnson.'

'Yes, Jennifer he'd got to know through his work. She was a police informant. She had some difficulties, had got in with the wrong people, and Mark helped her out of that life, and arranged for her to get a job at The Castle. Your husband was good to her, I think.' I smiled at her, she smiled back. But then it was gone again. 'And then I believe that Jennifer may have asked Mark for his help before she died. She wanted him to look into Jacobus Cronje.'

She didn't say anything.

'Are you sure you're okay, Georgie?'

She was absolutely still now.

'You can tell me anything.'

Another long pause.

'Georgie?'

Finally, softly, she said, 'I think I've made a terrible mistake.'

I felt a flutter of unease. 'What do you mean?'

Her eyes went to the fireplace, to the photographs of her husband on the mantelpiece. 'I've known about Jennifer all along.'

'You have?'

'Yes. I thought Mark was having an affair with her.'

I stared at her.

'Why didn't you say anything when I came to visit you before?'

She swallowed. 'What you have to understand is, the Mark people saw out there –' a pale finger pointed towards the window at the front of the house, '– and the one who lived here, they were different. He never . . .' A wobble in her voice. 'He never stopped drinking. I mean, he did for a while, but what I told you, what *he* told everyone, wasn't the truth. For the last ten years of his life, he *was* drinking. He would never do it in front of me, in front of *anyone*, but I knew he was doing it. I could smell it sometimes. I found a bottle of vodka hidden in the bedroom once. And even if I couldn't smell it on him, or see him doing it, I knew when he was on the bottle: he'd get nasty – he was never physical, it was his words. They could hurt so much. They could make you feel so small . . .'

I came forward on my seat.

'I thought he was having an affair with Jennifer,' she said again. 'I heard him talking on the phone to her when he didn't realize I was there. I followed him a few times to The Castle and saw them go inside together. I believed he was having an affair because he'd done it before.' She looked up at me, eyes full of tears.

'He cheated on you?'

'All the time.'

'I'm so sorry, Georgie.'

'That picture I painted for you when you were here, it wasn't really the truth. When he retired, it wasn't nice having him around; we didn't have a good time on that trip we took to Italy. He was horrible to me. He would flirt with other women in front of me. I was naïve. I thought, after he retired, that things might change. I thought, without the pressure of his work, I might get the Mark back that I first married – this wonderful, kind, loving husband.' She shook her head. 'But he didn't come back to me. If it's true that he wasn't having an affair with Jennifer, that he was helping her, I believe you. But the only reason it wouldn't have happened is if Jennifer didn't *want* it to happen. Mark would have.' She touched the handkerchief to her nose. 'He was different with her. I could see it. It wasn't the same as all the others.'

'You think he loved her?'

'I know he did,' Georgie said. 'In those last weeks before he died, when he was trying to locate Fiona Murphy and found the connection from her to Jennifer, he was totally obsessed. Nothing else mattered. Fiona was his route back to Jennifer.'

I froze.

She's always known about the connection between the two women.

She's always known about the case.

'Georgie?'

'I got rid of everything after he died,' she said. 'All his paperwork on Jennifer, on Fiona, all the work he'd ever brought home, all the

440

other women he'd done favours for, just so they'd be grateful and let him into their bed. I forgot about the files that you found in the loft, that I'd put them up there after discovering them in the shed. I just remembered the box being full of junk, so I didn't really think it would matter when you went up and looked through it.' She blinked. 'Everything else of Mark's, though . . . Everything else he worked on I tossed in the fire.'

'You destroyed all his casework?'

'Every last page,' she muttered.

That was why Levin was such a ghost.

It was why I could never find anything he'd done.

'Oh, Georgie,' I said quietly.

'I know.' A tear broke free and traced the wrinkled contours of her face. 'But it was just this relentless barrage. Year after year, excuse after excuse, woman after woman, drink after drink. I couldn't take it any more.'

And then she looked at me.

And, in that second, I saw it.

Her final, devastating act.

'Mark didn't slip into the canal that night,' she said. 'I pushed him.'

85

When I got home, Rebekah was in the kitchen on her phone, her suitcase on the floor next to her. I didn't know what I was going to do about Georgie – I still felt like I was in a daze, the air knocked out of me – but I knew I had to clear my head before I made any decisions. I needed time. I needed to make the right choice.

'You ready to go?' I asked her, grabbing my keys.

'Oh, I was just ordering an Uber.'

'Well, he's arrived.'

She smiled. 'Are you sure?'

'Of course.'

I drove us out to Heathrow, snaking through slow-moving traffic all the way along the M4. At the turn-off, a lorry had jack-knifed on a patch of black ice, but we'd left early because I knew the roads would be a nightmare. As we waited for the scene to be cleared, Rebekah started checking herself in online using her phone.

'I bet you're looking forward to getting back,' I said.

'I'm looking forward to seeing my girls, that's for sure. The rest of it – you know, my mother and everything else . . .' She put her phone away and glanced at me. 'I'm trying not to think about it too much.'

'It must be hard not to.'

'It is. Trauma doesn't like to hide.'

That was a sentiment we both understood.

I glanced at the backpack she had at her feet. There was a zip pocket on the front of it. Inside was the envelope that Parkes had given me. I'd slipped it into Rebekah's bag as I'd carried her luggage to the car, just as Parkes had asked me to. I had no idea what Parkes had written inside and I hated the idea of Rebekah suddenly finding it, of having no idea how it came to be there, or *who* had put it there. No doubt, once she found it, she would give me a call and ask if it had been me. And, again, I'd have to lie to her and tell her it wasn't, because I was boxed in: I was keeping Parkes's secrets, she was keeping mine. Parkes had told me she didn't want to speak to Rebekah until everything that had happened in the last week had died down – and that meant, for the foreseeable future, I was playing by her rules.

'Are you okay?' Rebekah asked.

It was all I could do to maintain eye contact with her, my deceit an acid burn. I forced out a smile. 'I'm good.'

Her eyes went to the windscreen and stayed there for a while, the scene ahead of us still playing out.

'Is it normal to feel this scared?'

I looked at her. 'What are you scared about?'

'I didn't know my mother at all. And then, thanks to you, I knew her a little. I'm scared about what else might come out and how it might change my mind *again*. I can't . . .' She stopped. 'I just can't keep lurching from one side of the argument to the other. I can't hate her, feel sorry for her, hate her, feel sorry for her – it hurts too much. It's too exhausting. All I really want is the complete truth.'

The complete truth.

I felt another surge of guilt.

We began inching forward – the police on the scene now and directing traffic – and, soon after, we were heading along the Great South West Road in the direction of the airport. In front of us, the snow continued falling, the sky a bruise of mauve and grey, and as we reached the drop-off at Terminal 3, Rebekah said, 'Thank you, David.'

I pulled the car in.

'What you've done for me . . .' She studied the colour of my face, the reminder of that night at Scargill's house, the brand this case had put on me – at least for a while.

'I'm not sure I've made things better,' I said.

'You have. I can tell you feel like you've let me down because you don't have all the answers –' *except I do*, I thought, *I just can't tell you*, '– but I'm not disappointed.'

I glanced at her bag again, at the zip pocket.

'If you ever wanted to talk about any of this . . .' But then I paused. Why would she ever want to talk to me? She was going back to New York, back to her life over there, back to her kids, and her job, and her friends. All of this was just a bad dream.

Just another trauma to bury.

But then she said, 'I'd like that.'

She picked up her backpack, put it on her lap, opened the door. Cold air surged inside the car, followed by the noise of the airport. We got out and I took her case from the boot and then we stood there for a moment.

'We could talk over Zoom,' she said. 'Or, you know, if you ever happen to find yourself in New York again . . . you could look me up.'

I smiled; she did too.

Something passed between us.

She leaned in and kissed me on the cheek.

'I'll see you around, David.'

'See you around, Rebekah.'

86

I watched the snow fall across the back garden, thick sheets of it swirling in on the tail of a bitter winter wind, and by the time the sun had gone down, everything was covered – the lawn, the beds, the decking. The house had altered, its colours reduced to monochrome. I glanced back across the living room, to the sideboard, to the pictures on top of it. Even in the shadows, I could make Derryn out.

The garden had been hers, and in the years since she'd died, I'd tried to keep it going, tried to maintain it, show it the same care, the same love that she had. Now it was covered by snow, hidden from me – a blank canvas for someone else to paint on.

It's okay, David.

Somewhere against the deadened sounds of the evening, I listened to a crow squawk and then watched as it took flight across the grey of the sky.

It's okay, David.

Her voice again, as clear as if she were in the room with me.

You can go now.

You can move on.

This was just our house, not everything we were.

Just before nine o'clock, there was a knock at the door.

I'd barely moved from the sofa since dropping Rebekah off at the airport, and as the fire crackled I ate junk food and watched movies I'd seen before, so I didn't have to concentrate, and could instantly catch up when my thoughts started to drift.

And they would drift often. I'd start thinking about Rebekah, and Parkes, and Cronje, and the faces on the wall of that cellar. I'd think about Fiona, and Jennifer, and Kian Bauer. But mostly I thought about how quiet the house seemed now, how empty, and how much

I'd enjoyed having company over the last few days; someone to talk to, and to connect with, about something other than work. I lived and breathed missing people – it was the oxygen in my blood – but it took everything from me.

Sometimes I just needed something else.

I needed ordinary.

I needed conversation with people who were actually in the room with me, not just memories contained in old photos, always spoken about in the past tense.

I hauled myself up, put on the outside lights and, through the square of glass in the door, could see what looked like a man, half-turned.

I opened up.

'How you doing, Raker?'

He looked terrible, his body stiff, awkwardly angled, leaning to one side as he tried to offset the pain of his broken ribs. He had bandaging on his right hand and a cast on his wrist, and his entire face and shaved head was a mesh of cuts and bruises.

'I win,' Healy said, gesturing to the single bruise on my face.

'It's good to see you, Colm.'

He pressed his lips together; an apologetic grimace. 'I just wanted to say –'

'It's okay,' I said.

'I could barely look at myself in the mirror –'

'It's okay. Honestly. I understand why you had to do what you did. And it doesn't matter any more: we're both in the clear.'

'They're not going to charge you with anything?'

'No.'

'Why?'

'Let's talk about that another time.'

Snow settled against his shoulders.

'Are you all right?' he asked.

'I'm good. Why?'

'You look kind of . . .' He paused. 'You look tired, Raker.'

'I *feel* tired.'

446

'Is it the move?' He gestured to the SOLD sign out front, but we both knew he wasn't talking about the stress of moving home. He knew what this house meant. He knew whose memories were woven into every fibre of it.

'Maybe a little of everything,' I said, stepping back, inviting him in.

He shuffled past, wincing, and began unbuttoning his coat. It was as painful for me to watch as it must have been for him to do, so I finished the job for him and then told him to go and sit as I hung up his jacket. I made us both a coffee.

'Can I borrow your phone?' he asked. 'I need to call a hostel about –'

'Stay in the spare room for a while.'

'No, that isn't why I came tonight.'

'I know. But stay. It'll be good for me too.'

'Are you sure?'

'Positive.'

He nodded. 'Thanks, Raker.'

We were quiet.

'So what are you going to do now that you're officially free *and* alive?'

'I don't know,' he said. 'Get a job, I guess.'

'Somehow I can't see you on the tills at Tesco.'

'I can't really afford to be fussy.'

'No, I guess not,' I replied, and both our eyes went to the TV where a news reporter was camped outside The Castle. 'You know much about missing people?'

A grin formed on his face. 'I have some experience.'

'That's good.'

'Why, do you know someone who's hiring?'

'I might,' I said.

Mother

Rebekah | *This Evening*

The cabin lights dimmed.

In the seat next to her, a woman had fallen asleep, her headphones still on, the film she was watching still playing. They'd talked for a while at take-off, the woman telling Rebekah that she was flying to New York to see her daughter, who worked at the United Nations, and who she'd only seen once since the Covid lockdowns.

'What about you?' the woman said.

'I live in New York, so I'm heading home.'

'Oh, I see. Have you always lived there?'

'In New York? No. I'm originally from London.'

'Ah, that explains your accent.'

Rebekah smiled politely. 'I think they call it mid-Atlantic.'

'It's lovely, whatever they call it.'

'Thank you.'

'So were you in London visiting family?'

'No. I came to find out more about my mother.'

The woman looked at her, clearly intrigued.

'She died when I was young,' Rebekah said.

'Oh, I'm so sorry.'

'It's okay. It was a long time ago.'

The woman in the seat next to her, asleep now, turned, adjusting her position, and then one of the cabin crew passed. Rebekah asked him for a bottle of water, and when he came back he had the bottle and a muffin. 'I didn't know if you were hungry,' he said. Rebekah thanked him – she was – and then, after he was gone, reached down to her backpack and searched the front pocket for some antiseptic wipes to clean her hands with. She found the wipes quickly.

And then she found something else.

She took the envelope out and stared at it for a moment, at her name, written in the familiar handwriting she'd seen on the condolence cards.

What the hell is this?

She turned it over and broke the seal, tearing gently along the top. Inside was a letter.

Three sheets of A4, handwritten, words on both sides. She stared at it for a long time, so long that when she looked up again, the woman's film had finished on the TV screen next to hers and every reading light in their part of the cabin was off, except hers. And then she shuffled the letter out, opened it up and read the first line.

By the time she'd read the second, she'd started to cry.

My darling Rebekah,

How can I begin to find the words to express to you how sorry I am for everything I've done? I can't. I never can. I only hope you can hear me out. There are a lot of words here, I know that. I hope you will read them all, but I understand if you choose not to. On these pages, you will find the reason I walked out on you all. I will tell you, as difficult as it is to admit, the terrible thing I did to Henry, your wonderful father – an act of self-sabotage that I've regretted for so long now. You will realize pretty quickly that, while I disappeared in December 1985, I didn't die, I just went on to live a different life, under a different name, never once not thinking of you all. And in this letter I will tell you about what the future holds for me, about the reason I can't write this thing myself – only dictate it – as well as whose handwriting it is here and on the cards you received in New York. I will tell you about a sister you never knew you had.

I will tell you all of that, Rebekah, but not before I tell you something else: with all my heart, with everything I have left of this fading body, I swear to you, there has not been one day since I walked out that door that I haven't thought about you, Johnny and Mike. Not one. For five years, you three were my life. I know you remember nothing

449

of me, but I remember everything of you. I've committed it all to memory, and have kept it there ever since — all the tiny moments that brought me so much joy; all the times I would look at the three of you and feel overwhelmed by how I felt. As my body dies, my memories of you don't. Some days, it's like I can hear you, can smell you; some days, I close my eyes, and I'm back in that bedroom, just before I left. The last thing I ever said to you three was that I loved you. I swear to you, I turned to each of you, I took your tiny hands in mine, and I told you I loved you.

And I meant it, Rebekah.

I meant it then, I mean it now. Before I go on in the rest of this letter to tell you about what happened to me, about all the mistakes I made, about the reason I never came back to you kids in the years after I disappeared, I need you to hear this and hear it clearly: I love you, Rebekah. I've always loved you. You were — you are — my brilliant, brave and beautiful girl.

You are my daughter.

And, every day of my life, you've been my world.

Author's Note

For the purposes of the story, I have taken some minor liberties in terms of the way British policing works, especially with regard to their databases and what information is stored on them. Team structures, investigative approaches and interview techniques have also undergone a few alterations. Any decisions I've taken have been made purely to keep you turning those pages, and my hope is that the changes have been subtle enough for you not to have noticed until now.

In terms of the South African components of the novel, a number of things are fictional – mostly to give myself the leeway to take the story where I need it to go – but I've tried to include real people, places and organisations as much as possible. Where I've taken creative licence, I've nevertheless tried to echo actual, recorded history.

During the apartheid era, opponents targeted by the white minority government were taken to Vlakplaas (not Die Suidplaas), a farm 24 kilometres from Pretoria (not Johannesburg) and from where many of them never returned. C10 (not C9 as I've named it in the book) was a unit that hunted down and killed anti-government activists, and some of the men that worked there did indeed fight in the border wars in Angola and Namibia. Koevoet, or *Crowbar* in Afrikaans – the military unit that Jacobus Cronje was a part of in Namibia – was real, and *was* later accused of war crimes, but both Martin Larsen and, of course, Cronje himself are entirely fictional. There never was a Red Wolf, nor anyone similar. That said, in the apartheid South Africa that actually existed between 1948 and the early 1990s, five men ran C10, and the last of them, Eugene de Kock, was given two life sentences in 1996 – plus a further 212 years – for crimes against humanity. He faced eighty-nine charges overall, which included six murders that were found not to have been politically motivated.

For anyone interested in the stories of apartheid South Africa, and who may still be unaware of Antjie Krog's novel *Country of My Skull*, I highly recommend it. Covering two years of testimony from the Truth and Reconciliation Commission, its blend of prose and reporting – Krog was a journalist who covered the hearings – paints a lucid, often extremely upsetting picture from a terrible period in history, but has important messages about identity, forgiveness and renewal too.

And one final thing: my wife is South African, so I have visited the country countless times over the years, and while I realize this book paints a dark picture of a horrendous period in its past, it goes without saying that this isn't reflective of the South Africa you will encounter today. While it still has its fair share of problems – which country doesn't? – it is truly one of the most beautiful, inspirational and welcoming places you could ever hope to go.

Acknowledgements

Even after fourteen books, I sometimes have to pinch myself to make sure that this *is* actually happening and that I *do* get to make up stories for a living. Because of that, I'm continually grateful to the amazing team at Michael Joseph who have been with me every step of the way and whose brilliance, passion, creativity and friendship is never taken for granted, ever.

A huge thank you, as always, to Maxine Hitchcock, my editor and publisher, who places complete trust in me to go off for a year and write whatever I want. Thanks also to Clare Bowron, who worked so hard on the edits, and to Emma Plater, Sarah Bance, Jennie Roman, Beatrix McIntyre and Caroline Pretty who continually and tirelessly knocked the manuscript into shape. At Michael Joseph, and Penguin more widely, Jennifer Harlow, Mubarak Elmubarak, Jon Kennedy, Stella Newing, Helen Eka, Christina Ellicott, Laura Garrod, Hannah Padgham, Sophie Marston, Kelly Mason, Anna Curvis, Akua Akyamaa-Akowuah, Colin Brush and Charlea Harrison have all played crucial – and often unsung – parts in making this book happen, and I'm just so appreciative of all your hard work and dedication. Thank you!

None of my books would be possible without Camilla Bolton, my agent and my friend, who is, quite simply, one of the best people ever. Thank you also to the team at Darley Anderson, including Sheila David in Film & TV, Jade Kavanagh, Rosanna Bellingham, and Mary Darby, Georgia Fuller and Salma Zarugh in Rights.

A big thank you to Martine Parkes and Ian Kirby for being the winning bidders in Clic Sargent's 2021 and 2022 Young People vs Cancer auction and whose prize was to be turned into characters in *The Blackbird* and *The Last Goodbye*. A belated thank you as well to Louise Mason, whose winning bid in 2020 (aka The Covid Years) flew under the radar a bit, but is equally amazing and generous.

A sidenote: Louise's namesake played a big part in *Missing Pieces*, the novel that – for people who haven't read it – may fill in some questions you may have about Rebekah Murphy's past.

For helping me maintain my sanity, and for sharing the pain, thank you to my amazing writing pals Chris Ewan, Claire Douglas and Gilly Macmillan.

Thank you to my family, both here and in South Africa: my mum and dad, who are the best parents anyone could ever ask for – and who are one of the major reasons I'm a writer (thanks for the type-writer!) – my sister Lucy, as well as Rich, Hannah, Sam, Delme, Kim, Declan, Nathan, Josh, Boxie, Di, Jo, John and Barry. And, of course, an XXL-sized thank you to the two people who have to put up with me every day of their lives and are kind enough not to complain about it: my wife Sharlé, who never, ever rolls her eyes at my jokes (and also happens to be an amazing proofreader and timeline-unraveller), and my daughter Erin, who makes me so proud every day, except when she goes on her phone instead of watching the Arsenal game.

Finally, thank you to you, my wonderful readers. It's no exaggeration to say that, without you, there would no David Raker series. I owe you everything.

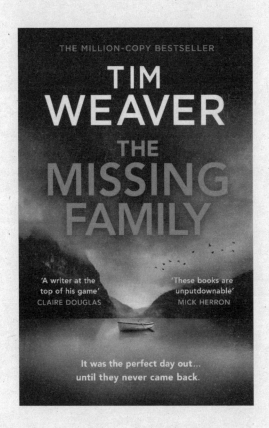

POLICE: Could you please state your full name?

RAKER: David Raker.

POLICE: David, I need to inform you that this interview is being both audio and visually recorded and may be given in evidence if a case is brought to trial. Do you understand that?

RAKER: I do.

POLICE: Thank you. As you know, my name is Detective Inspector Phillips and I'm with the Metropolitan Police. I work in the Major Crimes unit here. We've got a lot to get through but I'd like to start by asking you how – and where – all of this began.

RAKER: It began how it always does for me.

POLICE: And how's that?

RAKER: With a missing person.

One Year Ago

After they arrested him, they took the suspect down to the basement.

It was vast, a maze of nearly identical corridors and entranceways. Some of the doors had nameplates on but most didn't, and it would have been impossible for an outsider to memorize the layout. They could see that he was attempting to, could see that his eyes were going to the minimal signage that existed down here, trying to anchor himself to something – anything – as if he were hoping to lay a trail of breadcrumbs in his head that might help him find a way back out again.

The two men either side of him knew exactly where they were going. They were long-time employees of the Skyline Casino and Resort and knew the layout of the basement intimately. Linkers had just celebrated his fourth year in the job; Ramis had been here since the Skyline opened in 2008 and was the most senior member of security. Before this, he'd done twenty-five years in the Met.

Ramis glanced at the suspect.

He hadn't been on shift when the guy had actually been arrested. Instead, he'd arrived fifty-five minutes later, after a 2 a.m. call from Linkers saying the suspect had returned to the casino and was now seated at one of the blackjack tables. Ramis had immediately told Linkers to arrest the man, get him away from the public and into a side room. Linkers had done as Ramis had asked.

It had taken Ramis almost an hour to get into the casino, having struggled to find his sea legs at home. He'd had to pause at the edge of the bed, bones aching, head swimming, before hauling himself into the shower. It had been like this for a while. He was a week from retirement and knew, even if his mind was still fast, his body was calling time on the late nights, irregular hours and constant stress. As he'd dressed, his wife had told him gently that he didn't have to go in. But he said he had to be there.

'I need to be in when the cops arrive,' he explained. 'This is the guy.'

Lorna, his wife, didn't need to know more than that.

Ramis was still aching a little now, over an hour on, but he pushed it all down. They'd almost arrived at the holding cells, four consecutive rooms that looked exactly like cells in a police station: small spaces with a bench, and a reinforced glass panel in the door that slid up and down.

They were all empty.

There had been no other arrests so far tonight.

Linkers opened the cell closest to them. As he did, Ramis glanced at the suspect again. He estimated the guy to be in his mid-twenties, although Ramis had never been great at ages. People aged differently based on the comforts they'd gone with or without, the kind of lives they'd had. The suspect returned the look, and Ramis could see the man's eyes were a deep blue. The guy was handsome, he supposed.

'Can we get you a drink?' Ramis asked.

The man shook his head. 'No, thank you.' His voice was quiet. Ramis guided him into the windowless room, sitting him down on the padded bench. Everything smelt of disinfectant. Mostly, people ended up in here because they'd been caught trying to cheat the casino, or they were drunk. Sometimes they got pickpockets, or small-time con artists working gullible patrons; sex workers in the bars pretending they were hotel guests.

But they'd never had anyone like this guy.

Never a cold-blooded killer.

Linkers pushed the door shut. He then turned the handle ninety degrees to the left. Another clunk as a heavy-duty deadbolt embedded itself.

Ramis and the man stared at each other through the glass panel, and then Linkers slid down the reinforced steel plate. Ramis could no longer see the man but, softly, he thought he could hear him starting to cry. He glanced at Linkers, whose expression seemed to echo his own. Somehow this felt different to what they'd expected. The man seemed smaller and more vulnerable than they'd imagined – a frightened animal trapped inside a six-by-seven room, with no window, an unbreakable steel plate, and a door that could withstand two hundred and fifty pounds of pressure before it even shifted a centimetre.

This guy butchered a man and stole his money.

Now it was all over.

No exit.

No way out.

It seemed such a perfunctory ending.

There was a kitchen opposite and Ramis started the coffee machine. In the meantime, he told Linkers to get back up to the casino floor and meet the two detectives from Thames Valley Police. As Ramis waited, he went to an app on his phone his daughter had downloaded for him, which contained articles he'd saved from newspapers and websites. He loved current affairs, loved knowledge, and especially liked to be up to speed on the things young people were talking about, because that way he could seem more interesting to his children and grandkids. He was midway through an article on an actress he knew his daughter loved when he heard a voice from the cell.

'Sir?'

Ramis decided to ignore the man.

The police would be here soon.

They could deal with him.

Ten minutes later, Linkers and the cops entered the corridor.

Linkers did the introductions.

Detective Inspector Bakhash. Detective Sergeant Clarkson.

Bakhash's eyes went to the holding cell. 'We appreciate what you've done here. If you two hadn't have been on the ball, we might never have bagged him.'

'I was in bed,' Ramis said, 'so all the thanks should go to Neil.'

Linkers broke out into a smile. The younger man was chuffed with the praise from Ramis. He was a nice kid. Ramis nodded at him and gestured to the cell. Linkers grabbed the keys from his pocket, and began to unlock the door.

The mechanisms clicked and released.

Bakhash stepped into the doorway.

'What's going on?' he said, immediately.

To start with, Ramis thought he was talking to the suspect.

But then Bakhash glanced back across his shoulder at Ramis.

'I said, what's going on?'

The two security men moved closer; Ramis saw Linkers stiffen, heard him mutter, 'What the hell?'

Ramis stepped all the way inside the cell.

'I don't . . .' Ramis trailed off. 'I don't understand.'

The cell was empty.

The killer had vanished.

Now

I

I parked my car in the same spot the Fowlers had left theirs in eight months ago.

It was May and the sun was out but the temperature hadn't quite caught up: it still felt like early spring, a cold wind whipping in off the moors, a sea of yellow gorse close to the road shivering in the breeze.

The road I'd parked on ended twenty feet ahead of me at an old wooden gate. On the other side was the stone path that eventually led to the quarry. It was hard to see much of Dartmoor on my right because of a large, ragged tor, but on my left the moorland swept away from me in waves, a vast, undulating ocean of brown grass, grey crags and wind-battered trees.

I locked up the car and headed to the gate.

It happens the September before.

It's a Sunday and the five of them have left early and driven up from their home in Totnes. The drive takes just over an hour. There's no parking close to the water so they have to leave the car in a layby on the nearest road and walk the rest of the way, following a winding stone track half a mile up to the quarry. Marc and Kyle carry the boat between them, Clara the chairs, Sarah has the cooler box, and two-year-old Mabel totters along behind them all.

It's a warm day, more like summer than autumn, the skies a pristine blue, and even on the elevated peaks of Dartmoor, there isn't a breath of wind. When the five of them finally arrive at the quarry, the lake is still in shadow, the ragged wall of granite on its eastern flank high enough that the sun hasn't yet crested it. There's an almost identical sweep of speckled granite on the western edge, except this gently curves in an L-shape and creates a natural amphitheatre around the lake. The cliffs that encircle the former quarry are dramatic and beautiful, and that beauty is complimented by the tranquillity of the lake itself: once, Parson's

Quarry had been a vast tin mine, crumbling miner's huts still scattered at its edges; now it's one of the best wild swimming spots on the moors.

That's exactly why the Fowlers have always loved it here.

It's why they're here today.

But, by sunset, three of them will have disappeared.

It took me just over twenty minutes to walk from the car to the mouth of the quarry, so it would have taken the Fowlers longer as the two men had been carrying the boat, and Sarah would constantly have been waiting for Mabel – uninterested in her pushchair – to catch up.

After the initial dip into the ravine, the approach was almost all ascent, which would have added minutes too.

I looked around me on the way up, but there wasn't much to see: the climb had a hidden, secluded feel, views of the rest of Dartmoor obscured, and the hillside was littered with old, crumbling miners' huts.

At the top, the quarry almost seemed to appear out of nowhere, having been hidden by an amphitheatre of granite. The cloud-scudded sky was like a roof over it all, and as the trail faded under my feet and I passed onto the grass banks that fed down to the edge of the lake, it was as if I'd entered some secret chamber.

I understood straight away why the Fowlers had loved this place.

Other families begin arriving at the quarry an hour after the Fowlers have set up, but what Marc and Sarah have always loved about this place is how – even on the sunniest days – it's never packed. That's partly because a lot of people still have no idea it's a wild swimming spot. But it's mostly because there are only seven parking spaces in the layby, and the next nearest place to leave your car is over two miles away.

The sun crests the eastern flank of the quarry just after ten and, from there, Sarah spends most of the rest of the day running around applying lotion to Mabel, who in turn immediately tries to wipe it off, gets it in her eyes, and then starts to cry because it stings. Sarah perches a chair at the edge of the water and she and Mabel build mudcastles, throw a beachball around, and paddle together, while the others get out on the lake. Mabel has armbands on, even though she's not keen on the water. Sarah's not one for taking risks. At 19, she took a drunken risk with her then-boyfriend, and nine months later Kyle was born.

'Marc, give me a hand.'

Sarah looks up to see Kyle handing Marc an oar.

'I need to stay here with your mum, mate,' Marc says, glancing at Mabel, who is fully into the clingy stage and throws a tantrum if Sarah isn't nearby. Sarah has been on toddler duty for almost eight hours, and Marc has promised her that he's going to attempt to take the reins for a while to at least give her a few minutes to herself. 'Plus it's almost six,' Marc adds. 'We'll have to start packing up in a bit.'

'Ah, come on,' Kyle responds, and throws the oar to Marc.

Marc has no choice but to catch it.

He looks at Sarah.

The rest of the families that were here earlier have gone now, and much as Sarah likes it here, she's more than ready to go home.

'Please, Mum,' Kyle says, and gestures to Clara, at the sling she's sporting. 'My shipmate's injured, and the dinghy's so awkward without two of us rowing.'

Sarah wants to say no.

Instead, she says, 'Okay. But don't be long.'

'We'll just go to the middle and back,' Marc says.

'And make sure he doesn't drown,' Sarah tells Kyle, pointing to Marc.

Marc pretends to be offended but Kyle and Clara both laugh. 'Bloody cheek,' Marc replies good-naturedly, and sits down in the boat.

Kyle and Marc grab an oar each and start to row the three of them out. The dinghy is just under twenty feet long, but unlike many boats of that size, it doesn't have a motor, making it easier to transport. Instead, Marc paid to have a clip-on roof put onto the back, so – if either he or Sarah take Mabel out – they can sit her in the shade. The roof also has roll-down sides that can be untied and dropped to provide further protection from the sun, and as the men continue to row out, Sarah can just about make out Clara behind the yellow plastic of the sides. Her body is slightly weighted to the left, some of the bandaging on her shoulder visible beneath the green of her beach dress.

Sarah collapses into her chair.

She's so tired.

I went all the way down to the shore.

There was no one else here, just as there had been no one else here at 6 p.m. on that Sunday in the middle of September. I was right in the middle of the shoreline – perfectly centred between the east-west sides of the quarry, which were about two hundred metres apart – and I knew, from what Sarah had told me already, that this was roughly where she'd been seated with Mabel as Marc, Kyle and Clara had rowed out. North to south, the lake was slightly bigger than it was from east to west – about three hundred metres end to end – so when the dinghy finally came to a stop in the centre of the lake, it would have been a minimum of one hundred metres away from land. I also knew that – exhausted from a day of running around after a two-year-old who wouldn't leave her side – Sarah had been unable to keep her eyes open, and, although only very briefly, dozed off for less than a minute as Mabel played at the shore.

But less than a minute was it all took.

Sarah's eyes ping open.

Mabel is hitting her spade against the arm of Sarah's chair, trying to get her attention. Sarah sits bolt upright, squeezes her eyes shut and tries to wake herself.

She glances at her watch and feels a wave of relief. She's only been out for a minute. She thinks she's been aware of the sounds around her the whole time – the water lapping at the shore, the birdcalls – but it doesn't bring her any comfort. Because when she looks at Mabel – how small her daughter is – at her nappy, she realizes a minute, even semi-conscious, would have been enough. Mabel could have wandered off. She could have drowned, even with the armbands on. She could have injured herself.

She grabs Mabel and brings her in for a hug. Mabel tries to wriggle out of it, but Sarah holds on and it's as if the two-year-old realizes her mum may need this moment, because she settles, presses her head against Sarah's chest and goes quiet.

Sarah's gaze switches to the lake.

The dinghy is right in the middle now but no one is rowing anymore. It's come to a stop, the back of the boat facing her, Marc, Kyle and Clara obscured by the clip-on hood.

All around the boat, the lake is still, the surface like glass.

Sarah frowns, steps forward.

Something isn't right.

She moves down to the edge of the lake. One of the oars has become detached from the boat and is gently floating away. And as the oar drifts, as a throbbing at the back of Sarah's head instinctively tells her something about what she's seeing is definitely off, the dinghy starts to turn, the point of the bow edging around in her direction.

That's when she sees that there's no one under the roof.

In fact, there's no one on the boat at all.

Marc, Kyle and Clara are gone.

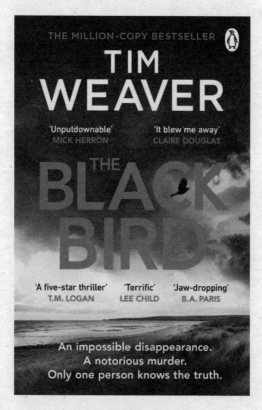

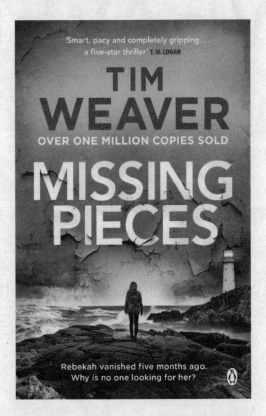

TIM
WEAVER

Stay in touch with Tim and get the
latest David Raker news
via Tim's newsletter at
timweaverbooks.com/newsletter

 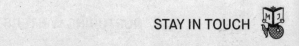